# EXTINCT

Ike Hamill

EXTINCT

ISBN: 0692283811
ISBN-13: 978-0692283813 (Misdirected Books)

Special Thanks:
Tom Bruns
Emilio Millán
Kathryn Deaner Holdt
Brian Holdt
Melissa Cole

# CHAPTER 1: ISLAND (FALL)

CHANNEL TWO SAID THE storm wouldn't hit until Sunday, but they were wrong, as usual. Winter hit like a hammer, right on Thanksgiving Day.

Nobody stuck around on the little island off the coast of Maine for the holiday. Thanksgiving had always been a quiet day with most of the residents traveling back to the mainland to visit family. Last Christmas, almost a thousand people inhabited the island. On the Fourth of July, with all the summer folks and people over for the day, you could have found more than thirty-five hundred. But on Thanksgiving, the island was like a ghost town.

For Robby Pierce, this would be his first Thanksgiving ever on the island. He usually went with his mom over to Grandma's house and stayed the weekend. Dad was always too busy with the ferry to take any time off to visit his mother-in-law's. This year, Robby sat in the front room by the window with his book and watched the snow fall while his mom crashed about in the kitchen. This was her first year cooking the turkey alone and having to cram it into a small oven. Robby smiled. He missed his grandmother, but he was thrilled he would finally eat Thanksgiving dinner with his mom and dad as a family.

"Robby?" his mom called.

He jumped up and set his book down. He guessed what she would ask and he wanted to answer her face to face so he could gauge her response.

"Yeah?" he asked as he crossed the threshold to the kitchen.

His mom knelt before the small oven. She had been praying to the gods of turkey.

"How long did Grandma cook this thing?" she asked.

Robby had his answer prepared. He paused to make sure she heard him properly.

"You should leave it in for four an' a quarter hours," he said. This was not an accurate answer to the question she posed. His grandma always cooked the bird for three and a half hours, but that had been a smaller, unstuffed turkey. His mom purchased a "biggun'," thawed it recklessly, and stuffed it tight with breadcrumbs. He would have padded his estimate up to five hours, but their oven always ran hot. At least the dark meat would cook, even if the breast would dry out. Mom's awesome gravy would fix that. She became an expert at cooking the sides and sauces while Grandma did the main dish.

"You sure? That seems like a long time," she said.

Robby nodded once.

"Okay," she said and nodded back. That's how he knew she would take his answer as gospel and Dad wouldn't have to yell about salmonella.

If his dad saw even a hint of pink in bird meat he'd say, "Sarah, I do believe you're trying to kill me," and even though it sounded like a joke, nobody ever smiled.

✪ ✪ ✪ ✪ ✪

The wind picked up just after lunch and Robby had to move away from his window perch. His dad hadn't installed the storm windows yet and the wood stove didn't throw its heat all the way to the front hall. Robby moved to the living room where the aroma of the turkey seemed to warm the air.

The book sat in his lap. His mind kept wandering back to the storm. It looked like a nor'easter, the way the wind swirled in the crook between the shed and the peak of the garage roof. The storm itself didn't bother him too much, but he didn't like how surprised the weatherman appeared. Robby could see it just below the man's subdued TV delivery. Panic fluttered beneath that demeanor; the same panic the island pharmacist showed when the pharmacist's wife came down with cancer. Robby didn't have much experience with panic—he was, after all, only thirteen years old—but he possessed a talent for recognizing patterns.

"Hey, how about you get off your butt and set the table?" his mom yelled.

Robby had been waiting for her to ask. She preferred to ask for help rather than accept volunteer assistance. He cleared the kitchen table and wiped down the plastic table cloth with a wet sponge before he folded it up. The felt backing caught on the peeling corners of Formica. The new tablecloth had orange and red stripes and fall-colored leaves woven into the pattern. His mom ironed it once, but the fold-lines from its time in the package still popped up. Robby smoothed them down the best he could before he set the table.

The back door thumped.

"See who that is, Robby," his mom said. He could tell her—it had to be Jim, from up the road—but then she would think he knew Jim was coming.

"Okay," he said. He went to the door and saw Jim peeking through the glass.

"Hey," he said to Jim as the door let in a gust of wind and snow. "It's Jim," he called to his mom.

"My mom wants to know if you still have power," Jim said.

Robby's mom, Sarah, approached, wiping her hands on a dish-towel. Jim stood on the rug just inside the door. Flakes of snow melted into his jeans as he stood there.

"What are you doing out in this mess, Jim?" she asked.

"My mom wants to know if you still have power," Jim repeated.

"All day, not a flicker," Sarah said.

"Oh," Jim said, "okay. Our phones don't work, neither."

"Tell your mom and brother to come over here. We'll make do if the power goes out here too," Sarah said.

"No, that's okay," Jim said. "She said she'd pack us up and go on the ferry. Dad's still shore-side anyways."

"All right then. You tell her the offer is open," Sarah said. She flipped the towel over her shoulder and returned to the kitchen.

Robby thought for a second—why would Jim's mother send him down to find out about their power if she already planned to pack up and head for the mainland?

Sarah reappeared in the kitchen doorway. "Do you need someone to look after your house while you're gone, Jim? Make sure the pipes don't freeze until the power comes back?" Sarah asked. Apparently she had also been puzzling about the reason for Jim's visit.

"Nope," Jim said. "Dad's coming back tomorrow. The house will be okay until then."

Robby joined the guessing-game, "Do you need to know how late the ferry is running?"

"Yeah," Jim said.

All the islanders knew the regular ferry schedule, but the holiday schedule seemed to mystify them.

"Two forty-five," Sarah said. "Don't be late. Earl Ray's running the last boat." Earl Ray had a reputation for closing the gates even if he saw his best friend coming down the hill. Everyone called him "Early Ray." Sarah left them with this information and returned to the stove.

"Do you want to ask your mom if you can stay with us?" Robby asked Jim. Robby liked Jim. In fact, Robby would have called Jim his best friend, if asked. But he wasn't inviting Jim to stay because he liked him, he was inviting him to stay because he thought Jim might need his help. Something—about the holiday, or the storm, or the way the island seemed so empty—bothered Robby. When things went wrong, Robby tried to help Jim. Even though he really looked forward to spending Thanksgiving alone with just his parents, Robby wanted to look after Jim.

"Nah," Jim said. "I want to go on the ferry and see the waves. My brother said they have twenty-foot swells. I bet it's like a roller coaster."

"I'll see you on Friday then," Robby said.

"Yup," Jim said. "Take it easy."

Jim let himself out and Robby closed the door tight behind

4

him. He stood there, watching through the glass, until Jim trudged down the path and out of sight. Robby smiled and tried to guess the first thing his dad would say when he got home. He pushed his hair behind his ears. He'd probably make a comment about his lovely daughter Roberta—a light-hearted jab at the length of Robby's hair. Lately, Robby's long hair drew a lot of attention from his dad, but Robby didn't want to wear it short anymore. He thought it made his forehead look too big.

An hour later, when Samuel Pierce burst through the door from the garage, his son's hair was the last thing on his mind.

"Jesus Fucking Christ," Sam said before the door could bang against the stop.

Robby, sitting at the table, looked up from his book. Sarah sat the pot of boiling onions back down on the burner instead of dumping them out in the colander.

"What's wrong?" Sarah asked.

Sam cursed under his breath, kicked his boots into the tray next to the door, and waved-in a smaller, clean-shaven man.

"Hey, Paulie," Sarah said. Paulie Carver waved and nodded. "What's wrong, honey?" she asked again.

"Nothing a permanent move a thousand miles south wouldn't fix," Sam said.

Sarah leaned back against the counter and waited for Sam to get around to explaining his frustration.

Sam turned to Paulie. "The landline is in the front room." Sam pointed Paulie down the hall.

"Cells are out," Sam said to Sarah. To demonstrate his disgust, he tossed his cell phone to the table. "Power's out to the port, and more than half the town is dark. Paulie's supposed to Mate over to shore, but Early disappeared."

"Disappeared?" Sarah asked.

"Poof," Sam said. "He came aboard with Paulie. I saw him. Then we couldn't find him."

"Overboard?"

Sam shrugged.

"Is Master Johnson taking her back across?" Sarah asked.

"We were going to ask him that very same question, but it

turns out we couldn't find him either. Can't even find the Harbor Master," Sam said.

"Jesus," Sarah said.

Sam looked down at his feet, shaking his head. When he tilted his head back up, his face softened. Robby admired the way his dad could always tuck away his worries and find his way back to his normal mellow state.

"Hey, smells delicious," he said. Sam cross the room and put his hands on Sarah's shoulders. He pulled her in for a quick kiss. Sam leaned down to reach her—he stood at least a foot taller than his wife. Sarah held on to fear much more tenaciously. After the kiss she chewed the inside of her cheek as she processed all the information Sam brought home with him.

Paulie appeared in the doorway. "Your phone is out too," he said. "I get a dial tone, but I can't connect to anything. I guess I'll head back to the docks and wait for Early or Johnson to show back up."

"I'll go with you," Sam said.

"You don't have to do that," Paulie said. "Smells like your supper is almost ready and all."

Sam glanced at Sarah before answering. "Plenty of time to eat later. We'll both go down," he explained to both Sarah and Paulie. "And if nobody shows up in an hour, then we'll shut her down and both come back here for turkey, and you can stay on the couch tonight."

"I appreciate that," Paulie said, "but I can hole up in the lounge. I've done it before."

"Nonsense," Sarah said. "It'll be as cold as a cave in there tonight."

Robby watched the conversation and noted that all the adults seemed resigned the ferry wouldn't be running back to shore that day. The boat wouldn't run without a captain, but Robby had never heard of the ferry staying overnight at the island. Sam caught a ride to the mainland  before each shift, so he could maintain his residence—the only thing his parents left to him—on the island. Any one of these things happening—the ferry staying overnight, the captain disappearing, the Harbor Master missing—

would have been extraordinary. Together, the events of the day seemed almost incomprehensible.

Sam pulled his boots on and Paulie fished his gloves out of his pockets. They exited back through the door to the garage and Robby stood up. He would have to shovel under the garage door as soon as they left. Otherwise the snow tracked in by the Jeep would stop the door from shutting all the way.

"Don't forget your hat," his mom said.

✪ ✪ ✪ ✪ ✪

The shoveling took forever. First, the snow drifted into the garage as fast as Robby could shovel it out. Then, Robby stayed outside and started shoveling down the driveway. It wouldn't really help. His dad would use the snowblower in the morning and the extra shoveling wouldn't give him much of an advantage, but it kept Robby out of the house and away from his mom, who would be trying to hum away all her worries. Robby could picture her in there, standing at the stove, nervously mashing potatoes, and humming a tuneless song.

His dad would be back in an hour. Robby wondered if he could stay outside that long. He had his good jacket on, but he wasn't dressed for the wind. A black shape up the street caught his eye. The falling snow made it hard to see past the end of the driveway, but that big black mass hadn't been there before, he was sure of that. Robby kept shoveling, but kept his eyes trained on the shape. When he flicked the shovel to throw the snow, his hood pulled to the right, blocking his vision. When his hood came back to center, the shape moved closer.

Robby backed towards the garage door. He had closed the big door, so more snow wouldn't drift into the garage. The path to the back porch sat under a foot of powder. The black shape shifted, right before his eyes. It moved to the end of the driveway. It stood tall in front and trailed off towards the back, like a centaur. Robby backed onto the path to the back porch, slogging through the drift. The black shape—the centaur-thing—approached faster, closing the gap to Robby.

Robby dropped the shovel he had been dragging. He turned to run for the door. His feet couldn't keep up with his momentum and he pitched forward into a drift. He flailed on hands and knees in the snow. When he stole a glance over his shoulder, the centaur-thing reached all the way to the shoveled part of the driveway. Robby flipped over on his butt, so at least he would be able to defend himself when the beast came for him.

Just before his eyes made sense of the shape before him, Robby's brain put together the clues. His centaur-thing had to be Ms. Norton, trailing her two sons—Brandon and Jim. On that deduction, Robby pushed himself to his knees and got back to his feet. He picked up the shovel just as Ms. Norton approached.

"You'll move a lot more snow with the shovel than with your hands, Robby," she said.

"Yes, Ms. Norton," Robby said.

She turned to her youngest son and said, "Jim, you help Robby clear this walk and then you both get inside." She held a big white bakery box from the island's grocer out in front of her, the cardboard nearly soaked through from the snow.

Ms. Norton waited for Robby to step off to the side and then she led Brandon towards the house. When Brandon passed Robby, he pushed Robby in the chest, sending him backwards into the snow. Jim grabbed the end of the shovel and hauled Robby back to his feet.

"My brother's a dick," Jim said.

"Yeah," Robby said.

Jim took the shovel and started clearing the path out to the driveway while Robby brushed himself off.

"So you guys aren't taking the ferry?" Robby asked.

"No," Jim said. The rest of his response was carried away by a gust of wind. He repeated himself, "Early's not there."

"Master Johnson?" Robby asked. Technically, Early was a Master too but everyone just called him Early.

"He's gone too," Jim said. "Not enough people to crew the ferry. Your dad said he's coming home presently."

The boys finished their shoveling and then headed back inside.

✪ ✪ ✪ ✪ ✪

The boys pushed the coffee table out of the way and sat on the floor in the front room. They had a deck of cards and three stacks of Monopoly money. The game was Texas Hold 'Em.

In the kitchen, the adults crowded around the little kitchen table. As soon as Robby's dad and Paulie came back, they shooed the kids away so they could talk. Even Ms. Norton, Haddie, kept her voice down as they talked. You could usually hear her three floors away. Unable to hear the conversation, Robby focused on the card game.

Robby gave away a couple of small pots to Brandon's aggressive play. He wanted to see how Brandon would bet when he had a good hand.

Jim showed no backbone; he could be chased out of almost any hand with one good raise, and his face instantly revealed the strength of his cards.

Jim dealt the next hand and Robby saw what he wanted. Brandon came in with the minimum raise. Robby called him. He gave up a quarter of his money to see Brandon's cards, but it was worth it. Now he knew what Brandon would do with a really good hand. On the next hand, Jim came away the winner. Robby frowned. It should have been his pot, but Jim misread the cards. Jim played as if he held a pair of jacks, but he unknowingly had a straight. That beat Robby's three kings.

He would have to adjust his approach to compensate for Jim's mistakes.

"This is stupid," Brandon said. "Let's watch TV."

"Cable's out," Robby said. "All you can get is channels Two and Five."

"You don't have satellite?" asked Brandon. He tossed the deck of cards into Jim's pile of money.

"With your power out, neither do you," Robby said.

"If my dad were home, he'd start up the generator, and then we would," Brandon said.

"Isn't the generator still broke?" asked Jim.

"Shut up," Brandon said. He turned back to Robby and said,

"If your dad was smart enough, he could start up the ferry and take us back to the mainland. Then we wouldn't even be stuck here. I'm turning on the TV."

Robby thought about stopping Brandon. His parents didn't like him to watch TV. They all tried to keep their viewing to a minimum; they usually read books or magazines. But stopping Brandon would be tough. The boy stood several inches taller than Robby and had a mean temper. Perhaps Robby and Jim could stop him together, but it would take a while to convince Jim to oppose his brother. From Robby's experiences in school, he always assumed family would stick together. Robby got lucky—his father came in before Brandon found the remote control.

Sam stepped over the coffee table and pressed the power button on the side of the TV.

"We're gonna fire up the boob tube and see what's shaking," he said.

Paulie, Sarah, and Haddie Norton followed him into the room. They all stood in the center of the front room, looking at the television. The boys gravitated to the couch to get out of the way. Sam punched another button on the TV to switch it over to the antenna and then tried to navigate down to channel Two.

"I got it, Dad," Robby said. He hit the button on the remote control to tune in the station.

A commercial for toilet paper filled the screen.

"There's no crawl or anything about the storm," Paulie said. "Usually they have text across the bottom of the picture when there's an emergency or a storm warning or whatever."

"Try channel Five, Robby," Sam said.

Robby hit the button for channel Five. They found a rerun of a daytime talk show.

"Nothing there either," Paulie said.

"Well, maybe this storm's not a big deal for the rest of the state," Sam said. "Wouldn't be the first time our island problems didn't make the local news. You boys keep your eyes glued to that TV and let us know if something happens."

"I'll stay here with the boys," Haddie said. She sat next to her son Jim on the couch.

Robby jumped up and caught his dad before he could go back to the kitchen.

"Hey, Dad," Robby said, "I think those stations are fed down from the network via satellite."

"Yeah?" Sam asked. "What are you trying to say?"

"Who knows for sure," Robby said, "but they might not even have anyone there. Maybe we're just seeing the network feed because everyone disappeared, like Early or Master Johnson."

"Do you have any reason for that speculation?" Sam asked.

"No," Robby said. "But I was just thinking—if we assume this is a local problem, we might decide to wait it out. If we assume it's a larger disaster, the worst-case scenario, then that might suggest another course of action."

"Sometimes you think too much, son," Sam said. He put his hand on Robby's shoulder. "And you talk like a textbook. Sometimes we just get a freak storm on Thanksgiving and the phones go out. But if you get any more information, you let me know."

"Okay," Robby said. He smiled and tried to imitate his dad's easy way of letting go. But he couldn't let go, and as he sat down in the big brown chair his mind kept spinning. His dad was right—he had no solid evidence. Robby liked to be cautious; he liked to prepare for the worst case. With no way to get information from the outside world, how could he set his mind at ease? Robby slipped from his chair and headed for the steps. In his room, he turned down the volume on his clock radio before turning it on. Static came from the speaker. Robby wasn't surprised—he never used the radio. Who knew when it had been last tuned in to an actual station? He rolled the dial all the way down and then slowly scanned through the frequencies. He didn't hear anything except the constant fuzzy white noise.

Robby stopped next at the hall closet. His mom kept a portable radio there, next to the sewing machine. He dragged it out and took it to the bathroom to plug it in. He found the same result on that radio—nothing but static. The radio went back into the closet. Robby flushed the toilet, so nobody would ask where he had been, and walked back downstairs. He had just taken his seat again when his mom entered.

"All right, everyone, let's eat before it turns to mush. We don't have enough room at the table, so you kids can take your plates to the coffee table," Sarah said.

Aside from a few mumbled compliments to the chef, the procession remained silent as each person made their plate. The turkey turned out great—just a tiny bit dry. They had plenty of food; Sarah cooked for maximum leftovers.

Sam waited for everyone else before fixing his plate. He had the old camping lantern at the head of the table. Sam wrapped the old lantern mantle in a sandwich bag before slipping his small scissors in to cut the string. The old mantle dissolved as he pulled it from the lantern. Robby watched him fit the new one on and knew the next step—his dad would burn the mantle to prepare it for lighting.

Sam stood up and said, "I'm going to the garage to burn this in."

"I'll go with you, Dad," Robby said. He set down his plate and followed his dad.

"No, you get your food," Sam said.

"But I want to get the box of candles and the spare flashlights, anyway," Robby said.

Sam nodded.

In the garage, Sam set the lantern on his bench and turned to Robby.

"Okay, let's hear it. What has your big brain cooked up now?" Sam asked.

"Can I ask a couple of questions?" Robby asked.

"Shoot," Sam said. He trusted his son, and respected his son's intellect, but he sometimes lost patience with Robby's tendency to analyze every situation.

"Were there less people on the ferry when you landed than when you set off?" Robby asked.

Sam had a great poker face. He didn't show the slightest reaction to the question. He just considered how to answer— should he try to gloss over the facts and comfort his son, or tell the truth? "Perhaps," Sam said.

"Did you see anyone downtown?" Robby asked.

"Yes," Sam said.

"Anyone aside from Paulie, Ms. Norton, Jim, and Brandon?" Robby asked.

"No," Sam said.

"Any lights on in any of the houses as you came home?" Robby asked.

"No, just ours," Sam said. "But the power is out to who knows how many houses."

"But it's pretty dark out with the storm, shouldn't you have seen flashlights, or candles, or firelight?" Robby asked.

"It's pretty much a whiteout," Sam said. "You couldn't see the hand in front of your face."

"Okay," Robby said. "Any tire tracks? Footprints? Signs of life?"

"With that blizzard? Any sign would be wiped out in minutes," Sam said. "Perhaps you're getting to a point?"

"Yeah. Just one more thing: did you see any wildlife?" Robby asked.

Sam managed to keep his face neutral again. "Some deer," he began, "maybe a couple of raccoon." In fact, he and Paulie had nearly been stampeded by a herd of deer as the men walked to the ferry parking lot. The island had a healthy deer population, but Sam never saw so many together at once.

Robby nodded.

"Okay," Sam said. He struck a match and lit the lantern mantle. "What's it all mean, Mr. Holmes?"

"Too early to know for sure," Robby said, "but it could be a local extinction."

"Of?" Sam asked.

"Of people," Robby said.

"Huh," Sam said. "Why would you assume it's just local?"

"I don't, but I think it's the only possibility that gives us clear direction. If it's a global extinction, then we either have to figure out the cause—which could be impossible—or we just got lucky. Nothing to do, either way. If it's a local extinction, then we have to try to get out of the affected area. It's the only scenario where we could take action that might save our lives."

"And what if it's just a bad storm which freaked out the animals, and everyone else is just holed up?" Sam asked.

"We could go door-to-door to people who should be home. That could be risky though, if it's a contagious thing," Robby said. His dad considered this option. Robby had never had such a long, frank conversation with his dad before. A few years earlier, when his parents planned to refinance the house with an interest-only mortgage, Robby drummed up the nerve to talk his dad out of it. That had been a quick exchange though. He presented his information—a couple of articles and some charts showing the financial impact—and then left his dad to make the decision. It must have been hard to hear from an eleven-year-old boy, but his parents took his advice in the end. Now, at thirteen, Robby felt like his dad was starting to take him seriously.

"If it's contagious, then I've already got it," Sam said. "I've been exposed to people all day. We'll check on the neighbors after supper, just to be sure. Then we'll make a decision."

"Okay," Robby said. "Thanks, Dad."

"Thanks, nuthin', I haven't done anything yet," Sam said.

He grabbed the lantern and Robby got the extra flashlights and candles.

# CHAPTER 2: INLAND (SUMMER)

SIX MONTHS EARLIER...

✪ ✪ ✪ ✪ ✪

Brad took a deep breath and tried to stay still. Intense pain washed through his lower leg. Blood wept from a dozen little pricks around the back of his right calf. He'd walked through this patch of vines before and knew they featured nearly invisible thorns up the stalk, but he'd always possessed the sense to wear jeans before today. These vines were strange—like something you'd see in the rainforest, he thought. The slightest touch made them curl up. He'd seen moving plants before, like the Venus Flytrap, but nothing on this scale. These vines looked like they could pull down a rabbit. Brad looked around, happy he'd only taken a step or two into the patch before being ensnared.

Clipped to the back of his belt he kept a utility knife. Brad grabbed it and folded it open. The almost-new blade looked fresh and sharp. He kept his legs straight and bent at the waist, thankful he could touch his toes from countless hours of yoga, and began to slice through the root of the vine. He pinched it against the side of his sandal and severed the vine curled around his calf. Brad clenched his jaw and started to slide his right leg back. The vine, though cut off, tightened around his leg.

He took one more deep breath and then leapt backwards. He

landed on his ass, just past the edge of the vine patch. One of the vines at the edge twitched and flopped towards his foot. Brad shuffled back.

"Damn!" he said, as the vine twisted even tighter around his calf. "What are you?"

He picked at the top of the vine, up near his knee. It looked almost like a baby fern—a fiddlehead. The thorns were barbed. As he pulled the vine away from his leg, bumps of skin rose too.

"Ow!" he said to the woods.

Brad liked to talk to himself while he worked outside. He spent a lot of time alone, and he sometimes missed the personal contact of working in an office or living with someone. When he spent time in his woods, almost a mile from his nearest neighbor, he talked out loud. He unwrapped about half the vine from his leg when he decided to pull from the other end. As soon as he let go of the tip, the vine curled around his leg again, but with a lot less strength.

"Oh, come on!" he said.

This time he used his utility knife to cut the vine in several places before he started to peel it away from his skin. He tossed the little segments back into the vine patch, except for the end with the tip. He held the segment up to the sky so he could see the sun glint off the clear thorns. With his other hand he waved at the cloud of black flies buzzing around.

"Yeah, they've got little hooks," he said. "Almost looks like a thistle burr." The vine twitched in his hand and he dropped it onto his shirt, laughing. "You scared me. So it's not just movement you react to. Is it breath?"

He picked up the vine by the tender, curled tip and blew across one of the baby leaves. The vine twisted itself up when his warm breath hit it.

"So you go after breathing things, too? Couldn't be the warmth... Maybe the carbon dioxide in my breath? That's the same thing that attracts these damn black flies, I think," he said.

He held the short segment of vine away from his body as he inspected his leg. Some of the punctures were weeping lines of blood, and others were swelling up slightly. His leg looked like it had been attacked by a spiral line of very hungry mosquitoes. Brad got to his feet and headed back for the path. He maintained a rough road between the back pasture and the house, but he almost always just walked back there. It was only a couple hundred yards —not too far to carry a chainsaw and some tools.

Today he carried nothing. He was just out for a walk, not intending to do any clearing or be attacked by killer vines. The bottom half of his right leg ached and itched. Brad picked up his pace.

"Where did you come from?" he asked the segment of vine he carried. "You weren't up there last year. And I walked right through that patch last week and I didn't notice anything trying to grab my jeans. Did you develop more, or is it just because I had bare skin today? That's an idea. I should bring gloves and see if one of those vines goes after a gloved hand. If you haven't poisoned me."

The vine wasn't trying to curl up anymore. It flopped as he walked, limp in his fingers. Brad slowed down and breathed on the vine. It didn't stir.

"Oh well," he said.

His stride felt normal most of the way back to the house. By the time he reached the mowed part of the yard, his right leg hitched a little. His calf and knee felt tight. It looked swollen, but not enough to alarm Brad. He entered his house through the back deck.

In the kitchen, Brad dropped the little segment of vine into a plastic bag and thought better of it.

"Let's see if you like this," he said. He drew some water into a small glass and then poured off all but a half inch. He hooked the top of the vine over the rim of the glass and let the severed base fall into the water.

In his bathroom, he slipped off his sandals and sat on the edge of the tub. The cool water felt good on his swollen calf, so Brad just let it flow for a couple of minutes. He touched a puncture on his ankle. A little invisible splinter from the thorn still stuck out of the wound. Brad reached the vanity drawer and got his tweezers. He couldn't see the thorn, but by brushing the tweezers over his ankle, he could feel it. When he pulled, the skin pulled up too. The thorn's barb tugged at his flesh.

"Why would you be so persistent?" he asked the thorn. "Usually with burrs there's a seed or something to transport," he said.

The other bloody spots were surrounded with leg hair. He couldn't tell if they still had thorns or not. He plucked out several hairs before giving up. After scrubbing the rest of the blood from his leg, he dabbed some antibiotic cream on the worst spots.

Back in the bedroom, next to his bed, Brad kept a little diary with a pen stuck in its spiral binding. He flipped it open to the ribbon he used as a bookmark and wrote, "Plants that move." This book served as his Internet reminder list. It used to be his ex-wife's dream journal. Aside from the smell of her hair conditioner, the journal was the only thing of hers left in the master bedroom. He sat down on the edge of the bed and scratched his leg. A few of the bumps really itched. He opened the diary again and wrote, "Venomous plants?" He put the book back on the nightstand.

The pillow sat right there at the head of the bed. With one quick move he could stretch out and kill the whole afternoon with a nice nap. This was the problem with working at home and vacationing at home, he decided. Every moment turned into a decision—should he stay busy, or just relax? Which would lead to a better quality of life? Brad usually chose activity over leisure. He gained a great deal of satisfaction from a job well done. This week would be tough. He had the whole week off to catch up on chores and home projects, but he couldn't finish everything on his list. No matter what he did, he would remain disappointed at the end of the week.

He pushed to his feet and then flopped back down. On second thought, he figured a slothful hour or two wouldn't hurt anything.

When he woke up, the sun had already set. The clock read nine something. He felt stiff all over as he rolled over to turn on the lights. He immediately looked to his leg. No real sign of the injury remained. He found a couple of slightly red spots on the back of his calf, but his leg looked so intact that he started to wonder if it had just been a dream. Brad jumped up and headed for the kitchen. His little glass still sat on the counter with a tiny amount of water in the bottom, but he didn't find the vine.

"That's odd," he said.

The phone started ringing. Brad just stood there, staring at the glass. He almost didn't get to the phone before the call disappeared into voicemail land.

"Hello?" he asked.

"Hi, Brad?" asked the voice. His client, Phil Anderson, didn't wait for a response before he continued, "I'm so sorry to bother you on your day off. Is this a bad time?"

"No, not at all, Phil," Brad said. He rubbed his temples with his free hand. "What's going on?"

"We've got a surprise slippage with some of our programmers. We're looking for a white knight here."

"Yeah?" Brad asked. Phil couldn't possibly be this dumb, Brad thought. He'd sent a memo to Phil almost a month before, predicting this exact circumstance. How could he describe it as a "surprise slippage?"

"Yeah," Phil said. "I thought we addressed this quite a while ago, but apparently not everyone got the message."

"You know I'm working for Cincinnati next week, right?" Brad asked. He tried to keep his voice upbeat and friendly. The most important part of contracting, more important than the work itself, was being perceived as a positive, friendly, team-player. Brad learned that lesson years before. But he also knew you must show up on time, and the Cincinnati project was twenty times more lucrative than Phil's unexpected emergency.

"I know, I know," Phil said. "We're just trying to get you for the next five days. I know you're supposed to be on vacation until Monday, but we'll pay you ten percent over your normal rate if you can lend a hand."

"Absolutely, Phil," Brad said. This was another technique he'd learned from previous jobs—you always agreed with the client. You agreed, and then you presented your caveats. "But since today is Wednesday, then I only have four days to give you. And the ten percent is unnecessary, because you know my contract states I get time-and-a-half for weekends. So, Thursday and Friday will be regular time, and Saturday and Sunday will be time-and-a-half."

Normally, Brad would leave the details of his rate to the accountants, but Phil managed his budget with tight fist. If he didn't have a solid agreement on the phone, Brad would never get his money out of Phil at the end of the month.

"That's right," Phil said. "Fifty percent over for weekends, I remember. But what about Wednesday? You can't work tomorrow, buddy?"

"I'm sorry?" Brad asked. He looked up at the calendar. It was Wednesday, right? The glass on the counter caught his eye. He stared at the little bit of water in the bottom of the glass and tried to remember the events of Tuesday.

"Brad?" asked Phil.

Brad looked at the phone. The display read Tuesday, June seventh, almost ten o'clock. Why was Phil calling him so late?

"Yeah," Brad said. "Yes. I can work five days. Wednesday through Sunday."

"Great," Phil said. "That's just great. Hey, maybe you'll finish early and you'll still have a weekend."

That would be perfect, Brad thought. He could work on his vacation week and then save Phil the time-and-a-half by finishing before the weekend. He thought he might somehow figure out how to stretch the work through the weekend. He would finish after exactly eight hours of work on Sunday, all for his buddy Phil. That was the reward he received for finishing his part of the contract on time—he got to clean up after the grunts they paid one quarter of his hourly wage. Could be worse, he thought. He could be in the opposite situation.

"I'll check in tomorrow morning then," Brad said.

"Great," Phil said. "Talk to you then."

Brad hung up and propped his arms on the counter, staring at the glass. He could imagine losing a day, but he couldn't begin to understand how he gained another Wednesday. One day was like the next though. He had very little to hang a calendar on. He remembered the letter. He always wrote a letter on Tuesday night. Since he'd just woken up he couldn't have written one yet, but he remembered what he'd written. He nearly ran for his office.

The legal pad sat in its normal spot, propped next to his printer. He grabbed it and flipped to the middle. The last entry was from June second—a week earlier. He wondered if it was possible to dream an entire day with such clarity that it seemed real. Brad flipped the page on his yellow legal pad. Each Tuesday night letter was to his ex-wife. He never sent them anywhere. After divorcing Brad, Karen put the final stamp on their relationship by dying. He sat down to rewrite the letter he thought he'd already written.

Dear Karen,

I should tell you straight-away—the Cartonio place burned down. I know you'll be heartbroken. Nobody was hurt, thankfully. I showed up just after Butch kicked in the kitchen door and pulled the dogs out of there. Butch smelled and heard the fire down at his place, so you can imagine it was pretty far gone by the time he got there. Luckily, the dogs were in the kitchen and the fire started over by the garage. All those propane tanks, old mower engines, and junked cars were exploding when I happened to drive by. It sounded like the Fourth of July. Now the nearest neighbor to this house is almost three quarters of a mile away. There goes your theory— this place is getting *more* rural every year. I'm certain Cartonio won't try to rebuild the place. He didn't have any insurance, and he owes the town a bunch of back-taxes anyway. If the town puts a lien on the property then he'll have to sell, and I'll try to pick up the land cheap. I'd rather pick up more property I don't need than have someone put up another shack.

This summer has really heated up. Hard to believe after the cold, wet spring. I heard it was the second wettest spring on record. I've got some really interesting plants out back. Your pasture is almost done. At least the clearing part is almost done. I know, I've said it before, but I finally broke down and bought one of those brush clearing machines, so it really does look like a pasture now. I'll get one of the Hucker brothers over here to level it out and then maybe hydro-seed it. I wish you were here. I can't remember exactly what seed mixture you wanted out in the back pasture.

Anyway, this one type of plant popped up this spring in a place I cleared last fall. It's over near the oak tree you said would straighten out once it got full sun (it never did straighten out, but at least it filled out). This plant is a short vine with two sets of leaves on it. The big leaves look almost like grape leaves, but it also has these tiny, oval leaves running up the stem. It moves! It's like a mimosa. When the plant is disturbed, the leaves fold up towards the stem. That's the one I'm thinking of, right? The stem also has these little barbed thorns. When the leaves fold up the whole vine kinda curls, and it sinks its thorns into your legs. Really odd—I've never seen anything quite like it. You'd probably know exactly what it is, I'm sure. I just thought it was a nuisance until I went back there with shorts on today. When that vine muckles ahold, it's really painful to get it unstuck.

Well, that's the bulk of what's going on. I miss you so much.

Much Love,

Brad

## CHAPTER 3: IN THE SNOW (FALL)

"WE'RE STICKING TOGETHER," SAM shouted. He addressed Paulie and Robby in the driveway.

The storm had erased Robby's shoveling while they ate. The wind drove the snow sideways. The two men huddled together at Robby's level so he could hear. Paulie tapped Sam's shoulder and the two men stood up to confer alone.

Robby couldn't hear Paulie's question, but he heard his Dad's response.

"Because he sees more than most people, and he can figure stuff out better than either of us can," Sam said. "No offense. He'll be fine—he'll stay on my right hip the whole time."

Sam turned to include Robby. "Wontcha, Robby?"

Robby nodded. He moved to his dad's right side to punctuate the point.

Paulie nodded, but glanced back to the house.

Only the kitchen windows glowed with light. The power went out halfway through supper and they started up the lantern just to see their plates. Sarah interrupted her supper to draw buckets of water as soon as the power went out. They would only have a limited quantity of pressure from the island water supply. It probably wouldn't be a problem with so few people on the island, but Sarah didn't like to be without fresh water. She and the Norton boys were using some of the water to rinse the dishes while Sam's expedition went to look for other islanders.

"Grab ahold of my jacket," Sam told Robby.

Robby fell in behind his father as they got out to the sidewalk. The snow was too deep to walk side by side. Paulie fell in behind Robby.

They headed south on Cottage Lane. Paulie suggested they go check up on Irwin Dyer, a sixty-ish bachelor who lived a few doors down. He never traveled for Thanksgiving or any other reason if there was a football game on. Sam trudged through the thigh-deep snow to cross the street so they could follow the Sampson's picket fence. The snow and wind made it difficult to even walk in a straight line.

Paulie closed ranks from behind until Robby felt sandwiched between the two men. They moved in lockstep, leaning into the wind. Despite the cold, Robby started to heat up with the effort. When the fence ended, Sam cut across Irwin's yard. They saw a faint light coming from his living room window as they approached.

They huddled on Irwin Dyer's porch. Sam pounded on the door. When he didn't get a response, Sam unzipped his hood and pressed his ear against the door. Paulie took down his hood as well.

"Anything?" asked Paulie.

"What?" Sam asked.

"Did you hear anything?" Paulie yelled.

"Nope," Sam said, shaking his head, "nothing."

He pounded again. This time the door knocker bounced with each blow.

"See if you can see anything," Sam said. He pointed Paulie to the living room window. Paulie leaned out over the porch railing and cupped his hands up to the glass to peer inside.

"Nothing," Paulie said.

"He won't mind if we let ourselves in," Sam said.

Sam cracked open the door a bit and yelled inside. "Irwin? Ya home? It's Sam Pierce here." He looked back to Paulie, shrugged, and then pushed the door open.

Robby had never visited Mr. Dyer's living room, and never entered the house through the front door. They usually came in through his mud room when they visited Irwin, because they were usually returning one of his wandering dogs. Mr. Dyer didn't let the dogs in the living room either.

They knocked the snow off their boots the best they could, but they dragged a lot in with them. The folds of their clothing held secret caches of powder that fell to the carpet as they entered.

"Irwin?" yelled Sam.

Paulie closed the door behind them. A single lantern, much like the one they'd left hanging in the kitchen with Sarah, lit the living room.

"Mr. Dyer?" yelled Paulie. "You here?"

"Why didn't I think to bring a flashlight?" Sam asked.

"Here you go, dad," Robby said. He fished a flashlight out of his jacket pocket.

"And you didn't want him to come," Sam said to Paulie.

"You know what I meant," Paulie said. He smiled at Robby.

Sam crossed through to the dining room and clicked on the flashlight. "Well, where's old Irwin? He's probably just in the kitchen, getting his supper ready," Sam said. He pushed through the swinging door into the kitchen. He paused in the doorway and turned back to address Paulie and Robby. "You coming? I thought we were going to stick together."

"Hey," Paulie said, "do you think we should just go through his house like this? Seems strange just letting ourselves in to poke around."

"If Irwin turns up, I'll apologize for all of us, don't you worry. He went back a ways with my dad, your dad too. I think we owe it to him to make sure he's okay, in light of the circumstances. At the very least, we've got a real bad storm that's popped up and the power's out."

Paulie nodded and followed.

The kitchen was dark, cold, and empty. The door to the mudroom stood half open and a few inches of snow had drifted in. Sam walked through the room slowly, pointing his flashlight left and right, not wanting to miss any details. Robby found a battery-powered lantern on the table. It gave off a thin blue glow and a low buzz.

"Back door's open," Sam said. The kitchen featured a little mudroom off the back. The door to the outside stood wide open and the mudroom floor was covered with a fresh drift of snow.

Sam closed the outer door as far as it would go against the windrow.

"Looks like someone left and didn't intend to come back," Paulie said.

"Maybe they were just raised in a barn," Sam said, smiling. "It has to happen sometimes. Everyone talks about it. Seriously though, he's got to be around here somewhere. He wouldn't just abandon his house and go out fucking around in a blizzard."

"And his dogs," Robby said. "They must be around too."

"So where would he go, Robby?" Sam asked his son.

"I'm sorry?" Robby asked. He stared at the little drift of snow, which now had a big clean arc drawn through it from the travel of the door.

"If you're right about this local extinction, where would the people go?" Sam asked.

"I couldn't really say," Robby said.

"Now c'mon, Robby, this is no time to be coy," his father said. "I'm not asking for rock solid, I'm asking for your best guess. Fire up your thinker and give me a guess."

"Well... It's the *why* more than the *where*," Robby said. He sensed his father's frustration at his answer and quickly amended —"Most extinctions are gradual, and based on resources, environment, habitat, or predators. If this is really a local extinction, then it's more likely some pathogen, since we can rule out volcano or meteor strike."

"If it's a disease, then why haven't we got it?" Sam asked.

"We may yet," Robby said. "Or we may have a natural immunity. Maybe we haven't been exposed to the wrong combination of things yet."

"Or maybe we're just overreacting," Paulie said.

"That's always a possibility, Paulie," Sam said. "But I vote we treat everything as the worst case, just so it doesn't surprise us if it is." He turned back to his son. "So where do you figure the sick people are then?"

"It could be like brodifacoum," Robby said. His dad raised his eyebrows. "You know, that stuff you use for rats."

"Oh, d-CON," Sam said. "The rat poison. Draws them to water?"

"Yeah," Robby said. "It's an anticoagulant that's used as a rat poison. It makes the rats so thirsty that they..."

Sam finished the sentence for him, "Leave the house just before they die. So whatever's making people sick could also be making them disappear before they die."

"If it's a water thing, that would explain why all those people disappeared off the ferry today," Paulie said.

"It would also explain why we were almost mowed down by that herd of deer trying to get to the shore," Sam said. "So that's what's going on you think?" he asked Robby.

"It's just a working theory," Robby said. "We don't have enough evidence to support or refute it, but it's something we can test against."

"Maybe we'll find some tracks outside then. Give us an idea of where he went. Let's go check upstairs first, just to be sure," Sam said. He led the way back into the dining room. First they looked in the little privy, off the back hall, and in the den. Upstairs, they found two bedrooms and a bathroom. They were all empty. After making a quick check of the rooms, Sam led them back into each one so they could poke around in the closets, just to be sure.

Sam stood at the top of the stairs, shining his light at the access panel to the attic.

"He couldn't be up there," Paulie said. "There'd have to be a ladder here somewhere. Irwin wasn't exactly a gymnast."

"I'm just thinking," Sam said. "There's a panel like this under the rug in the privy. I saw it when I helped Irwin snake out his shitter."

"Can't be much more than a crawlspace under here," Paulie said. "This place is right on the ledge."

"We might as well be thorough," Sam said. "No sense in turning out the whole house just to stop now."

They found the living room as they had left it, but the lantern started to sputter. Sam gave it a couple of pumps and adjusted the valve until it burned silently again. The two men and the boy collected in the back hallway and opened the door to the small bathroom. It contained only enough room for a toilet and a vanity.

Sam reached for the thick throw rug which sat between the toilet and the sink.

He paused just before his hand touched the rug. "Corner is turned under," Sam said. He grabbed the corner of the rug and pulled. The thick rug hid a panel set in flush with the floor. Sam pulled a metal ring and lifted the panel open. Cold air seeped up from the hole. Sam propped the panel against the vanity.

Sam shone his light down into a shallow cellar. It had a rough ladder built in to the left side, but the dirt floor was only four or five feet down. A light switch was mounted on the right side of the opening. Forgetting the power was out, Sam flipped the switch on and off, expecting lights to come on below.

Paulie leaned over Sam's shoulder, trying to see down into the cellar.

"Irwin?" Sam called down the hole. Sam swept his flashlight around, trying to see as much of the cellar as he could without committing to going down into the shaft.

He suddenly straightened up, kept his eyes locked on the access hole, but addressed his son. "Robby, I want you to go stand by the front door. You hear me give the word and you dash home, okay?"

"Yes sir," Robby said. He turned and walked back down the hallway to the living room. He didn't obey completely. He stayed near the door to the hall so he could listen to his dad talk to Paulie.

"You think that's blood?" asked Paulie. "Could just be motor oil or something. Hard to tell on a dirt floor."

His dad replied to Paulie, but Robby couldn't make out the words.

"Oh, no shit," Paulie whispered. Robby heard that part, loud and clear.

Sam yelled out to his son. "By the *door*, Robby."

Robby moved to the front door, wondering how his dad knew. Robby's eyes danced from the swinging door to the kitchen, then to the hallway, the staircase, and back again to the kitchen door.

The living room was bright enough, with the lantern throwing off sharp shadows, but the doorways were gaping black holes. Anything could come out of those doorways. Robby backed up until his elbows pressed back against the front door. He took off his glove and rested his hand on the door knob behind him.

It felt like forever, waiting for his dad and Paulie. As soon as he took his post at the front door, he decided he had to pee. With every second he stood with his back to the door, his need to urinate grew exponentially until he could think of nothing but peeing and monsters coming out of the kitchen doorway, or zombies lumbering down the gloomy staircase.

The lantern on the coffee table began to sputter again. With each pop it flared a little brighter, but then dimmed even more when it fizzed. Robby knew what to expect—they kept nearly the same lantern at home. It took liquid fuel, white gas, and required pumping it up to keep it going. But his dad pumped it earlier, so it would need a refill to stay lit. He knew he only had a few more minutes of light before it would sputter out.

At least the failing light gave him something other than his bladder to worry about. Robby almost welcomed the distraction. The shadows throbbed with each sputter of the lamp; they became deeper, like they were gaining strength. The ebb and flow of the shadows made the door to the kitchen look like it was swinging slightly.

Pop-hissssss-POP-hiss-pop-hisss, Robby felt himself swaying with the rhythm of the lantern. He couldn't pull his eyes away from the kitchen door. It looked like the swinging gained momentum. Robby imagined that soon it would swing open all the way, and Irwin would be standing there.

Robby shook his head and tried to look away from the door. It had to be an optical illusion making it look like the door was swinging; just a trick of the wavering shadows cast by the failing lantern. When he first heard the squeak, he almost ignored it. It made perfect sense—it sounded like the squeak of a rusted hinge, in perfect time with the apparent movement of the door. But that would mean the door was moving. Robby tried to remember if the door squeaked when they had entered the kitchen earlier. He couldn't recall.

The lantern would fail at any second, and he would be alone in the dark with the squeaking door and whatever was making the door swing in and out. Robby straightened up and stood tall. He didn't especially want to know what was behind the door, if anything was, but if he had to, he wanted to find out while there was still enough light to see. He took a step towards the kitchen door and then stopped.

"The wind," he whispered to himself. That was the answer—the wind must be blowing through the back door enough to swing the kitchen door. That would also explain the throbbing of the lantern. It would react to the breeze in the same way. Robby relaxed for a tiny fraction of a second before he remembered his dad closing the back door tight. There shouldn't be any wind.

"Robby?" his dad called from the hall.

He was afraid to respond. He was afraid that as soon as the thing on the other side of the door heard his voice, it would come for him.

"ROBBY?" his dad called.

He kept his eyes glued to the kitchen door and started to move sideways towards the hall. From his new angle it looked less like the door was moving. He shuffled a little faster.

The lantern went out.

Robby felt a hand clamp down on his shoulder. Robby gasped and struggled to not piss himself.

"Come on, Robby, your dad wants to talk to you," Paulie said, from the darkness.

"Okay," Robby said. It came out as a whisper.

Paulie led Robby down the dark hall. His eyes adjusted quickly, and Robby could see the outline of the doorway to the privy and his dad's feet sticking out into the hall. He expected his dad would yell at him for not answering. Instead, he found his dad sitting on the floor with his legs straddling the hole to the cellar. He pointed the light down into the hole.

"I want you to see something, Robby," his dad said. "I would just take a picture, but we didn't bring a camera. I figure your memory is just as good as any camera."

"Okay," Robby said.

"But there's some other stuff down there I don't want you to look at," Sam said. "I'll go down first, and then you're going to look in this direction," he waved towards the back of the house.

"Okay," Robby said. "Hey Dad, there might be something in the kitchen."

"Paulie, can you go check out the kitchen?" Sam asked. Paulie nodded and headed off.

Sam swung his legs through the hole and dropped down into the cellar. He held his arms up for Robby like when Robby was a little kid. Robby sat down on the edge of the hole and slid towards his dad's arms. Sam set Robby down on the dirt floor and turned him towards the back wall.

The little cellar was carved out of the rock ledge that ran up their street. They stood on a dirt floor and hunched beneath the low ceiling. Sam pointed the flashlight at the stone foundation. On top of the ledge, to even out the dips and sways of the rock, a stone wall held up the back wall of the house. Below the stacked rocks, on a big flat slab of ledge, dark red shapes had been painted on the stone. Robby studied language. Letters and numbers from different cultures fascinated him, but these were nothing he recognized. They looked like a cross between Chinese characters and hieroglyphics. The symbols weren't in lines, or divided up into words, they were just spread out across the bottom of the wall in random groupings and sizes.

"What do you make of that?" Sam asked.

"I don't know," Robby said.

"They go from here, all the way to over here," Sam said. He swept his flashlight across about twenty feet of rock. In places, the symbols were so densely packed, they almost looked like a picture.

"Is it words?" Sam asked.

"I don't know," Robby said. "Could be, I guess. But I don't recognize any of it. Except this one here. This one that looks like a guy with his knees up. There's an Egyptian symbol that either means a god or a young woman, depending on the context. It looks like that."

"Huh," Sam said. "Does it just look like it, or do you think that's what it is?"

"And these two here," Robby said. "These look like Japanese kanji. Slightly different than the Chinese versions of the characters that mean supernatural power."

"Is it a code? Or a message?" Sam asked.

"Could be," Robby said. "But I think it would take a while to figure out if it is."

"Can you remember it?" Sam asked.

"There's too much. I can memorize parts of it, but I don't think I could memorize the whole thing. At least not quickly."

"Well, get what you can and let's get out of here," Sam said.

"Dad? What was it you didn't want me to see? Is this blood?" Robby asked.

Sam put his hand on Robby's shoulder and squeezed gently. "Don't worry, Robby. Nothing important. Just see what you can figure from these pictures. Take a few minutes."

"Okay," Robby said. He closed his eyes, took a deep breath, and let his shoulders drop. He cleared his mind. It was easy to do with his dad right behind him—he felt safe. It would have been easier to do with an empty bladder, but he managed to relax. When he opened his eyes again he tried to take in the whole picture; he tried to see the whole foundation as one big image. He couldn't make out the far edges, they weren't well lit enough, but the center of the wall burned a picture on the backs of his eyes. He opened his eyes wider and let it all sink in.

Robby forgot about the storm, and the house, and the kitchen door, and Thanksgiving, and just saw the wall. His heartbeat slowed and his eyelids dropped slightly. The next thing he knew, his dad was shaking him gently by the shoulder.

"Robby? You got it?" asked his father.

"I think so," Robby said.

"Good. Let's go," Sam said.

Sam backed up and led Robby over to the ladder. He shone the flashlight at the bottom rung, so Robby could place his foot. When he lifted his head to look up, Robby caught something out of the corner of his eye. It looked like a big pile of rope and a bunch of sticks. He didn't see any colors. The dim light and his peripheral vision turned the objects black and white, but they looked shiny and wet. He climbed up into the dim bathroom and saw Paulie standing in the doorway. His dad followed right behind him up the ladder.

Sam brushed off his pants and then replaced the floor panel and the throw rug.

"Can I use the bathroom first?" Robby asked.

"Will it be quick?" asked his dad.

"Yes."

"Make sure it is," Sam said.

He set the light on the counter and stepped into the hall with Paulie. Sam left the door open and waited for Robby to start urinating before he conferred with Paulie. Robby couldn't hear a word they said.

"You done? Let's go," Sam said to Robby.

"Okay," Robby said. He didn't flush or wash his hands—standard operating procedure when the power was out. Sam went first down the hall, followed by Robby and Paulie. "So there was nothing in the kitchen, Mr. Carver?" Robby asked Paulie.

"Nothing but the wind," Paulie said. "I think it blew the back door open."

Sam stopped. "You didn't say that before," he whispered to Paulie.

"Yeah, I did," Paulie said.

"Was the outside door open, or just the one to the mudroom?" Sam asked.

"Both," Paulie said. "But the outside one was just open a crack, like you left it. And there were no tracks in the new snow that blew in."

"Good enough then," Sam said. "Let's get out of here."

Sam swept the flashlight around the living room one more time before turning it off. He opened the front door. Outside, the sky had grown darker but the snow wasn't falling as heavily so they could see a bit better. The wind worked at filling in their tracks from earlier; the trudging was difficult.

Robby grabbed the back of his father's jacket, and Paulie grabbed a handful of Robby's. They formed a train and slogged up the hill towards the house. Their feet fell in rhythm. Robby pushed back his hood and looked to the side as they marched. He could make out the outline of their neighbor's house.

They followed the picket fence of Mrs. Lane's yard. Only the tops of pickets still poked through the snow drifts. Robby watched this house closely when he passed. He hated this house. It had expanded through the years, long before Robby's time. It started out as a just a summer cottage, and you could still its humble roots in the structure. A big belt of a beam wrapped around the middle where the first floor roof had been raised to two stories, and then two-and-a-half. On each side of the roof, dormers poked out, looking like angry devil horns.

The cottage belonged to the Lanes and had since settlers moved to the island. In fact, Robby's road used to be called the "Lane Cottage Road," but constant postal errors shortened it to "Cottage Lane." The Lanes never appeared on the island after Labor Day, but Robby watched the house carefully anyway. Its big black front door, surrounded by windows, looked hungry.

The roofline of Lane Cottage cut a black shape out of the gray sky. As Robby watched, a giant black form rose from one of dormers and floated across the peak of the roof and settled on the other dormer. Robby stumbled and fell into his dad's legs. Paulie, still gripping Robby's coat, came down on top of the boy.

"Straighten up back there," Sam said. He turned and hauled on Robby's arm, pulling him to his feet. Paulie pushed himself up and brushed the snow from his jacket.

"Dad, look," Robby said. He pointed to the dormer of the cottage. He looked as he pointed and saw what his father saw—nothing but the dormer.

"What was it?" Sam asked. Paulie leaned in close to hear too.

"I saw a big black thing up there," Robby said. "But it's so dark, I guess it could have been nothing."

"Move fast," Sam said. He took Robby's right hand and moved with determination. Paulie grabbed onto Robby's hood and they trudged double-time. Robby's only choice was to keep up. He felt like if he lagged, his father would pull his arm out of its socket. Sam drove his legs up and down, pumping at a furious pace.

Paulie tugged on Robby's hood, pulling the zipper into the boy's throat. Robby reached up with his free hand and tried to pull the jacket forward to release the pressure, but Paulie was pulling too hard. He tried to look around to see what was wrong, but suddenly the zipper was being pulled up into the underside of his chin, making Robby gag.

He sucked in a ragged breath through his compressed windpipe. He squeezed his dad's hand, afraid to let go, and flailed with his free hand at his dad's back.

Robby's feet rose as Paulie's tug on his hood lifted him off the ground. He tried to yell, but he couldn't get enough breath to make a sound. Robby's eyes bugged out, and the world started to fade out as the pressure built up in his head. He was now pulling his dad's arm upward, but his dad still trudged forward, intent on getting home.

Robby's grip on his dad's hand started to fail. He felt his glove starting to pull from his hand. Robby now dangled almost a foot off the ground, pulled up by the zipper and under his armpits. With the last of his grip on his fathers hand, he yanked upward.

Sam turned and immediately leapt for Robby. He nearly climbed his son, pulling the boy's arm, and then pushing down on Robby's shoulder to get to Paulie's hand. He managed to grab Paulie's glove, but it came off in Sam's hand and he collapsed to the ground next to Robby.

Sam didn't waste any time to figure out Robby's condition. He looped his arm under Robby's shoulder and jumped to his feet. He drove his feet through the snow, sprinting across the street towards their house. At first Robby just flopped alongside his dad, still struggling for breath. He pawed at the zipper with the hand that still had a glove hanging half-off. When it gave way it tore a chunk of skin from Robby's neck. It burned, but the relief of a deep breath more than made up for cut. He got his feet to the ground and ran alongside his dad as they found the driveway. Sam ducked and ran the last twenty yards in a low crouch. Robby ducked too, but couldn't see what they were ducking from.

35

The only finished room in their basement was the laundry room. Haddie Norton put her boys down there on an inflatable bed. Robby stayed upstairs in the kitchen with the adults. Sam closed all the blinds and even moved the rocking chair so they could close the door to the living room. The lantern burned so low that a candle would have given off more light.

When Sam and Robby had burst through the back door, Sam immediately called out orders. Sarah and Haddie didn't raise any questions—they heard the urgency in his voice. After securing the house the best they could, they wanted to know the details. Sam insisted Robby join the conversation, even though Sarah pushed for him to go downstairs with the other boys.

They sat at the small kitchen table.

Sam took a deep breath and lowered his shoulders. "Paulie's gone," he said.

"Where?" Sarah asked.

Sam raised his eyebrows. A look of surprise dawned on her face, but Sam repeated anyway—"He's gone."

"Oh no," Haddie said. Everyone knew Haddie loved tragedies, and especially seemed to enjoy the misfortune of others, but she made a good show of looking shocked and saddened.

"What happened, Sam?" Sarah asked. She touched her husband's hand.

"I can't say for sure," Sam said. "It's beyond my understanding or experience. That's the best way I can put it."

Robby rubbed the cut on his throat. His mom had slapped a bandage on it before he had his coat all the way off.

"By the time I turned around," Sam said, "the only thing I could see of him was his hand holding on to Robby's hood. I tried to grab his hand, but I only got the glove."

"He didn't make a sound," Robby said.

"What about the rest of him?" Sarah asked.

"I couldn't see him," Sam said. "Just his hand. It wasn't even very dark, or snowing very hard, I can't explain it. It's beyond my understanding."

"I didn't hear anything either," Robby said. "Except the wind."

"That's true. It was completely silent," Sam said.

"Should we go look for him?" Sarah asked.

"It's not safe," Sam said. "I think something was stalking us. You could feel it on the back of your neck, and Robby saw something on top of the cottage."

"We can't go out there," Haddie said. "It's not safe."

Sarah didn't acknowledge Haddie's comment with even a glance. Instead, she addressed her husband again. "So what do you figure we do?"

"I think we pack up the Jeep, wait until morning, and then head for the docks," Sam said.

"Wouldn't it be safer to hole up here?" Sarah asked. She glanced around their kitchen, as if she'd misplaced something important.

"I don't think so," Sam said. "For one, if there's something here taking people, I don't think we could hole up good enough to stave it off. Second, if this is a local problem, our best chance is to try to get away from it. Irwin Dyer's place was empty—it's like he just decided to wander off. I don't know what got him, but I don't think being inside helped protect him at all."

"I'd just as soon get to my husband," Haddie said. "He'll know what to do."

"What boat will we take?" Sarah asked.

"We'll take Carl's old boat," Sam said. "He's always said I can use it any time, and I think he'll understand. It will take a few of us to handle that thing properly. She's a beast. Brandon's got some experience, doesn't he?" Sam asked Haddie. "He can help get us launched and landed?"

"Certainly," Haddie said.

Robby kept his face still, but inside he flinched because his father immediately thought of Brandon. Boating terrified Robby—not because he thought he would drown, but because he got so sick every time they went on the water. They'd tried every remedy, from drugs to ginseng root, but nothing could stop Robby from vomiting if he even set foot on a boat smaller than the ferry.

Sarah took charge. "You guys pack some rations and plenty of water. I'll get all the first aid stuff together. Who knows what we'll need once we're underway."

☼ ☼ ☼ ☼ ☼

Robby went downstairs to the laundry room after his parents gathered everything together for the trip. His only contribution was to suggest they take along a few household chemicals—bleach, baking soda, rubbing alcohol. He didn't have anything specific in mind, but he wanted to have some basic supplies along in case of a crisis. Robby also liked that he'd been consulted, and was happy to have an answer.

He found the Norton brothers—his friend Jim, and Jim's jerky brother Brandon—sitting on the air mattress with a flashlight between them. Brandon was playing a game on his phone, and Jim was playing with an iPod.

"Nice job letting go of Paulie Carver," Brandon said.

"I didn't let go," Robby said. He realized too late he should have just let the comment roll past him.

"Remind me not to trust my life to you," Brandon said. "Your friend is going to get us all killed," he said to his brother.

"Shut up," Jim said, under his breath.

Brandon hauled back and punched Jim in the shoulder. The action bounced a blanket on top of the flashlight and the room was lit only by the game screens.

"Move over," Robby said to Jim. "We gotta get up early." He slid past Jim to claim the edge of the air mattress closest to the dryer. He kept on all his clothes but kicked off his shoes. Brandon bunched all the pillows on his side of the mattress. Robby's mom had also put out a few blankets for the boys, so Robby bunched one up to use as a pillow. He couldn't sleep. He could barely keep his eyes shut. Upstairs, the adults were still talking. Robby knew there must be more to the story—stuff his dad didn't want to say with him around. It probably regarded Mr. Dyer's cellar.

Robby thought about the cellar. His father had insisted he not look behind him. Robby wondered what his father had been protecting him from. It must be something violent, he figured. That would be the only thing his dad would want to protect him from seeing—he wouldn't want Robby to be disturbed by seeing some gruesome result of violence. Robby had already seen a dead person. He'd seen his own dead grandmother at her wake. So this would have to be a gory death.

Robby closed his eyes and thought of the strange symbols on the foundation wall in Mr. Dyer's cellar. He remembered as many as he could and made sure to recall them in their exact sequence. He'd already written them down twice.

Behind Robby, Jim and Brandon fought over a pillow. They both seemed younger to Robby since the crisis started. Brandon was fourteen-almost-fifteen, and normally didn't even bother to talk to his little brother. But that day he was acting like a ten year old. Robby thought back to his own behavior. He recognized moments of immaturity. Being scared of the dark and not being able to control your bladder were certainly not appropriate for a teenager. Robby took a deep breath and let it out slowly, letting his body sink into the mattress as he exhaled.

The basement was cooler than the rest of the house, but Robby still wore his pants and sweatshirt, so he was comfortable enough. He tried to forget about everything from that day. His hand moved up to his throat and held the spot where his zipper had drawn blood. He drifted off to sleep while Jim and Brandon were still fighting about their sleeping arrangements.

In the night he heard someone climbing the stairs. He looked up to see Jim going upstairs, using his iPod as a flashlight. On the far side of the mattress, Brandon snored into his own armpit.

✪ ✪ ✪ ✪ ✪

"Robby, Brandon, wake up," Robby's dad said. He was holding the lantern above the mattress. Sam stomped on the edge to shake them awake. "Get up."

Robby pushed himself up and then climbed to his feet. Brandon moved slower, blinking hard against the lantern light.

"What time did Jim leave?" Sam asked.

"I don't know," Robby said. "Where is he?"

"Did he say anything? Did you see him?" Sam asked.

Brandon didn't respond. He slid to the end of the mattress and started pulling on his shoes.

"Dad, what's going on?" Robby asked.

"We don't know where Mrs. Norton and Jim are," Sam said. "The door to the garage is open."

"I don't know what time," Robby said. "I don't have a clock or anything down here. Did you notice?" he asked Brandon.

"I didn't even know he left," Brandon said. He got up and headed for the stairs. "Why didn't you wake me up?" he yelled back to Robby as he started up.

"I didn't..." Robby started. "I just thought he was going to use the bathroom or something. I didn't think anything of it."

"It's okay," Sam said. "Get your shoes on, we've got to figure out what we're doing."

"How long have they been gone?" Robby asked.

"We don't know," Sam said.

"Mom's still here, right?" Robby asked.

"Yeah, she's upstairs."

Robby grabbed his shoes and ran for the stairs without putting them on. When Robby got to the kitchen he found his mother trying to calm Brandon down. The two were lit only by a set of candles set on the microwave.

Brandon yelled into Sarah's face, "Where is she? Where did she go?"

Sam came into the room holding two jackets. He stepped between Brandon and his wife and shoved one of the jackets at the boy. "Put this on," Sam said. "You and me are gonna do some scouting."

"Sam?" Sarah asked.

"We'll stay right near the house," he said, "and we'll have this." Sam held up a length of rope. He knelt down and fed it through Brandon's belt loops and then tied a sturdy knot. He repeated the process, tying himself to the other end of the rope.

"We'll finish getting the Jeep ready," Sarah said. She moved back towards the sink, and leaned back against it, folding her arms.

Sam took a couple of steps and closed the distance to his wife.

He nearly pulled Brandon off his feet when the rope pulled him by the waist. Sam kissed Sarah on the cheek and said, "We'll be right back."

"You better," Sarah said. She smiled.

Sam led Brandon out through the back door, leaving Sarah and Robby in the kitchen.

"What time is it?" Robby asked.

"About five," his mom said.

"Can I get something to eat?" Robby asked.

"Oh, yeah, of course," she said. "I made you a turkey sandwich."

"For breakfast?" Robby asked.

"It won't kill you," Sarah said. "Jeez, you think I'd just offered you rat poison or something."

Robby smiled. He sat down at his place at the table and his mom got his sandwich out of the refrigerator. He took a big bite. "So we're going on Mr. Deemer's boat?" he asked through a mouthful of food.

"Well, depends on..." Sarah started.

"On whether we find the hands at the school? We're going to check the school first, right?" Robby asked. He was referring to the deckhands for the ferry. The ferry usually ran with a captain, mate, and three hands.

"Yes," Sarah said. Robby only finished her sentences when he was preoccupied or stressed. He knew she hated it when he did that. She'd only needed to tell him a couple of times—it made her feel transparent.

When Robby was smaller, Sarah thought he was psychic. He always knew what she and Sam were thinking. Eventually, they came to believe Robby was just good at deduction, and Robby learned when he finished too many sentences he made people uncomfortable.

This time, Robby guessed Sarah and Sam had discussed going to the school to see if they could find any other people. It would be a tough trip to get over the hill without a plow, and it was in the opposite direction from the docks, but it was a common gathering place during emergencies and power outages. The three deckhands might have made their way up to the school. Even though the main entrance would be locked, all the islanders knew you could get in through the attached Lion's Club banquet hall, as long as none of the Lions were there to question you.

"Do you think we'll find anyone there?" Sarah asked Robby.

Robby turned his sandwich around, so he could take a bite out of the side that was starting to bust apart. "No," he said.

"Why not?" she asked.

"We've lost half our people, and we were pretty sure something bad was going on, so we were pretty careful. They probably never guessed anything was happening, so I bet they're all gone," he said. "Some of the people would have panicked and tried to run, too."

Sarah wondered if Robby was right. When he didn't have enough information to form an opinion, Robby always kept his mouth shut. A thorough answer from him usually meant a correct answer.

"So you don't think we should bother going over there?" she asked.

"No, I understand why we have to," he said. "Like you said— some things you do just because they're the right thing to do."

Sarah couldn't remember when or why she'd said that, but she was pleased Robby remembered. Robby finished off his sandwich and Sarah gathered the last supplies. They switched on their flashlights and blew out the candles.

"Put your plate in the dishwasher," she said.

"Why?"

"Because I'm not coming back to find a house full of mice," she said.

"Oh," Robby said. He put his plate in the empty dishwasher and closed the door until it clicked.

"Do you want anything from upstairs before we go? Any of your things? If you do, I'll go with you," Sarah said.

Robby thought for a second. He knew his mom packed some of his clothes, and all his winter gear was in the mudroom. He could fill his pockets with his things, but that was almost like admitting he didn't think they'd ever come back to this house.

"No, I'm okay," Robby said. He wanted to be like his mom. He wanted to believe they would all return someday to their normal island life, with all their possessions intact. All they would need to do is run the dishwasher, and everything would be back to normal.

His mom took the driver's seat and Robby got in the back of the Jeep. She started it up to get it warm, but they sat in the dim garage, lit only by the running lights of the Jeep. Their house had been in Sam's family for three generations, and was one of few with an attached garage. Most of the islanders barely needed a vehicle, let alone a taxed addition to store it in. Sam was proud of his garage, and he kept it neat. Looking through his window, Robby studied the rows of orderly tools hung up on the wall. Sarah scanned through the dial—the radio wouldn't lock on any stations. When she manually tuned into some of the local stations, they only heard static.

When they saw lights dancing through the windows on the garage door, Sarah hit the button to make the door go up. Nothing moved.

"Shit," she said. "Power's out. We have to raise it up manually. You stay here."

Sarah left her door open and went around back. She stood on the bumper to reach the orange pull-cord. Robby pressed his face against the glass to watch her. The door wouldn't open—the snow pressing against it on the outside stuck it in its tracks.

"You need help?" Robby yelled.

"Nope," Sarah said. She climbed into the driver's seat and shut her door. "Your dad can open it when he gets back."

Robby slid over to the other side, the rear passenger's seat, and opened the door. He flipped the little switch to turn on the child safety lock. With that switch turned on and the doors locked, the door couldn't be opened from the inside.

"What are you doing?" Sarah asked.

"Nothing," Robby said, "just checking on something." He slid back to his own seat, behind his mother.

Sarah jumped when the door from the house swung open. They caught a glimpse of Brandon coming through the door and then he pointed his flashlight right at the Jeep and Sarah and

Robby couldn't see anything but the bright light. When the second flashlight appeared, Sarah let out her breath.

Sam and Brandon came around the front of the Jeep. Sam untied his knot by the time he reached the passenger's door. Brandon piled in the back with Robby.

"I couldn't get the door open," Sarah said.

Sam just nodded and turned around. He kicked the door first, delivering a good blow to the bottom panel, and then flung it upwards. When he closed his car door, he immediately hit the button to lock all the doors.

Robby wanted to ask about his friend Jim and Mrs. Norton, but he held his tongue. No news was bad news, he figured.

"To the school?" Sarah asked.

"Got to," Sam said.

Sarah gunned the engine to hit the snow bank with as much speed as possible. The Jeep wobbled a bit in the fresh powder, but Sarah backed it out with confidence. Her hands fluttered over the wheel to correct any loss of traction before it led them astray. She used the wide part of the driveway to whip the front end of the Jeep around and put in drive.

The Jeep's big wheels pointed up the hill, and Sarah counter-steered the slight skid. A light snow fell now. Sarah put the windshield wipers on low.

Robby looked over—Brandon was staring out the window into the dark. The snow looked blue in the soft pre-dawn light, almost like it gave off its own glow. Down at the library they displayed black and white photos of the island; that's what it looked like to Robby. Everything looked still and dead. None of the houses had any lights on, or their walks shoveled. No smoke rose from the chimneys.

Sarah took a right on Church Street.

"Easy now," Sam said.

A rusty old Toyota blocked the right side of the street.

"I see it," Sarah said.

"Not that," Sam pointed to the car, "that!"

To the left of the Toyota a snow-covered lump sat in the road. Sarah pulled the wheel to the left and skipped the left wheels onto the soft shoulder, but their right wheels still bounced over the lump. Robby and Sarah just bounced a couple of inches. Sam and Brandon, on the passenger's side, flew up out of their seats. Sam bounced the top of his head off the Jeep's roof. He reached around and pulled on his seat belt.

"Sorry," Sarah said.

"So's Tom, I bet," Sam mumbled.

Robby twisted in his seat. The Toyota belonged to Tom Willard, any islander would have recognized it. The tired old vehicle only had one seat, and could only be registered for island use. Tom used it to carry supplies from the dock up to his restaurant. There wasn't enough light out to be sure—Robby guessed the lump *might* have been Tom. Robby wondered if his father knew for sure the lump was Tom.

"Dad, do you think it was him?" Robby asked.

"Not now, Robby," Sam said. "We've got bigger fish to fry."

"It's just that... Wouldn't he be the first we've seen?" Robby asked.

Sarah took a left on Pepper Lane.

"No, Robby," his father said. "Hold tight."

Brandon put his palm against the window and pressed his forehead to the glass. Robby ducked and bobbed, trying to see what Brandon was looking at. Against the charcoal sky, black shapes moved across the rooflines, keeping time with the Jeep.

"Mom," Brandon whispered. He reached down and unhooked his seat belt.

"Brandon?" Robby asked. "Brandon?" He touched the older boy's arm.

Brandon spun and glared at Robby. "What?"

"Did you say something?" Robby asked. "You took your seat belt off."

Sam watched the exchange from between the front seats.

Robby glanced to his dad and then back to Brandon. "It sounded like you said something."

"I didn't," Brandon said.

"Put your seat belt back on, Brandon," Sam said.

"No need," Sarah said. She pulled the Jeep to a stop in the side parking lot of the schoolhouse. A few spaces down, two other cars sat covered in snow.

Sam leaned forward and looked over the building. There wasn't much to see on this side—just a long wall dotted with a few windows. Everyone dropped off their kids on this side.

"I'll go in. You guys stay here," Sam said. "Keep it running."

"In and out," Sarah said.

"In and out," Sam replied.

Sam's door swept a flat surface through the snow. He plunged his foot into the powder. After closing his door he pointed down and mouthed, "Lock it." The snow drifted deep here, against the southern edge of the building, and Sam waded through it to get to the door. He expected the school door to be closed, but the door to the Lion's club was around the other side, so he thought it worth checking.

The handle turned. He pushed his way inside. The hall to his left housed all the cubbyholes where the kids kept their gloves and boots. With all the boots at home, the cubbies currently held their Japanese house slippers. Sam pulled a flashlight from his pocket and pushed through the curtain to the main schoolroom. He didn't need the light. The skylights and windows provided enough ambient glow for Sam to navigate. He turned off his flashlight and crossed the room.

On the opposite side, the curtain that led to the other outside door was fluttering. He pulled it aside and found snow drifting in through the door to the playground. The door stood open about a foot. He looked through the window out to the playground. He didn't see any tracks or signs of life, just a snow-covered jungle gym, swing set, and benches. He pushed the outer door shut and headed back for the main room.

Past the wood stove, Sam used his light to see down the hall. He shined his light in the teacher's office, and then into Robby's study room. Robby had his own study room away from the rest of the kids. His teachers discovered years before that Robby needed several hours a day to study independently. Without his alone-time to read, research, write, and figure problems, Robby tended to zone out and not interact with anyone at all.

Sam found nothing out of the ordinary in either of the rooms, so he continued down the hall to the utility room. The far end of the schoolhouse shared a wall with the Lion's club, and the only door between them connected a dressing room with the school's utility room. Flashing lights lit up one corner of the utility room. An emergency power supply for the furnace flashed to announce it was out of juice. Sam read the LCD display. It read, "Batt. Fail - 2:37:12." The twelve counted to thirteen and fourteen as he watched.

"Yeah, how much battery does it take to tell me you're out of battery?" Sam whispered.

A clank made Sam whirl around. He circled his flashlight around the room to the two doors, and to the racks of janitorial supplies.

"Hello?" he called.

He crossed to the Lion's club door and swung it open. Sam made quick loop through the Lion's club. It didn't have many rooms—just a big auditorium, some backstage area, and the bathrooms. He stopped behind the bar at the back of the auditorium. The booze should have been all locked up, but on the floor behind the bar he found a spilled bottle of rum. He set it upright. He touched the floor around the puddle of rum. The floor felt sticky for about an inch surrounding the puddle.

Glass shattered at the other end of the room. Sam stood up and flicked off his flashlight in one motion. His eyes adjusted quickly, but he didn't see anything but the empty meeting hall. One of the curtains fluttered and snow blew in through a broken pane. Sam quickly moved towards the outside door to look for footprints. The door was shut, and he didn't see any footprints outside when he opened it.

"This is Sam Pierce," he shouted. "Come on out if you need help."

He heard no response. Sam turned his flashlight back on and moved fast backstage and then through the schoolhouse. He suddenly wished he hadn't left his wife and son in the car. He threw open the door, expecting to see the Jeep gone, or worse—the Jeep still there but empty.

The Jeep still sat there with just a dusting of snow accumulated on the roof. The wipers swished and he saw his wife, turned around and talking to the boys. Sam waded back through the snow. Sarah unlocked the doors as he came up to the side of the Jeep.

"Anyone?" she asked as he slammed his door.

"I couldn't find anyone," Sam said. "Let's head for the shore."

"I want to go back to my house," Brandon said.

"Brandon, I thought we agreed you should go to the mainland so we can look for your dad," Sam said.

"My mom is still here," he said.

"And she can take care of herself, right?" Sam asked. "Drive, honey," he said to Sarah.

Sarah backed up the Jeep, following their tracks.

"No!" screamed Brandon. "I have to go home." He grabbed for his door handle and yanked. Robby had set the door so it couldn't be opened from the inside.

"Brandon, calm down," Sam said. "Your mom knows we're leaving this morning. If she wants to come with us, she'll be at the dock. Otherwise we can just assume she's staying here with Jim."

"If she's staying then I am too," he said. Brandon pushed the button to lower his window. He started climbing out as soon as the window opened. The rear window in the Jeep couldn't descend all the way, so Brandon struggled against the top of the glass.

"Brandon," Sam yelled. "Sit down."

Brandon still had the length of rope tied around his waist. It dangled behind him. Robby grabbed it and held as Brandon's torso disappeared out the window.

"Stop for a sec," Sam said to Sarah. She had already started to slow down.

Sam jumped out of the Jeep and grabbed Brandon by the shoulders.

"You're my responsibility right now, Brandon, and I'm going to see that you stay safe. You're under eighteen, and until we find one of your parents, or you turn eighteen, you're going to do what I say. We're getting off this island, and then we're going to find your dad."

Robby removed his seat belt and slid closer across the seat to hear what his dad was saying.

"But my mom," Brandon protested.

Sam lowered his voice, "Your mom might already be gone, okay? We didn't see *any* footprints, remember? She's not in the house, and there were no footprints. There's no sense in us continuing to look—we have no clues where she or anyone else went."

Some of the tension seemed to slip from Brandon.

"Let's get back in the car and go find your dad, okay?" Sam asked.

Brandon didn't reply, but he started to shimmy back through the window. Robby moved back to get out of his way. The window caught Brandon's jacket and it bunched up around his shoulders. Sam got about halfway into his seat when Brandon stopped him.

"Mr. Pierce?" asked Brandon.

"Call me Sam," Sam said.

"I'm stuck," Brandon said.

"Well, come on, you'll have to go out to come in," Sam said. He jumped back to the snowy street and grabbed the teenager under his armpits. "Try not to break the window," Sam said.

Sam pulled and Brandon wriggled to get through the window. His kneecap banged against the window glass and Robby helped him turn his boot so he could get his feet through. Sam set him down in the snow. He pulled the boy in close and whispered in his ear.

"Thanks," Brandon said.

Sarah hit the unlock button so Robby could push open the rear door before sliding back to his own seat. Sam patted Brandon on the back twice. His third pat passed right through the space where Brandon had stood. Robby, even with a better view, didn't really see much of the disappearance. One second, Brandon turned and started to lift a foot so he could climb back in the Jeep. The next moment, Brandon jerked and flew upwards and out of sight.

Only a couple of details registered to Robby. He noticed that Brandon's head and limbs seemed to go slack just before he vanished, like a marionette with its strings cut. Next, he saw the space around Brandon darken, as if the light were being absorbed. Finally, he saw the rope, still tied to Brandon's waist, whisper upwards like a snake's tail.

Sam's mouth dropped open and he tilted his head back, looking up. His hand swiped at the air, as if he could grab the rope that flew by seconds before.

"Get in!" Sarah screamed.

Sam's face hardened instantly. He dove towards the open door.

Robby felt a low moan starting within his chest. He didn't mean to yell, but it started coming out anyway. His dad was still mid-leap when the space around his legs started to dim. Robby's moan built into a scream as his father's legs started to rise upwards faster than Sam moved forward.

Sam's legs flipped up and over his shoulders as he rose up and forward. His head flipped around and he tried to grab the doorframe of the Jeep as he rose. His forward momentum took his head into the pillar between the front and back doors. Robby saw his father's skull deform with the impact. Blood squirted from his dad's nose and spattered on the car seat. The Jeep rocked with the hit.

Sarah and Robby heard Sam's arms flail against the roof of the Jeep. Robby threw himself back against the door, trying to get away from the blood. Motion to his left drew his eye, and he saw more blood drip down the outside of his window.

Robby formed his rising scream into words. "Go! Go! Drive!" He pounded the back of his mom's seat.

"Sam?" Sarah called.

"Drive, mom, drive! Just go!" yelled Robby.

Sarah gunned the engine and looked forward. She shook her head several times. The engine raced, but the Jeep didn't move.

"The clutch," Robby said.

"Oh," Sarah said. The Jeep lurched and bucked when she let out the clutch too quickly. The passengers' doors flopped.

"Take a right," Robby said. He buckled his seat belt. The doors slammed shut as Sarah skidded to the right onto Kirker Street. They sped down the steep hill towards the harbor.

✪ ✪ ✪ ✪ ✪

Sarah pulled the Jeep as close as she could to the pier where Carl Deemer moored his boat. She turned in her seat and looked up the hill, back towards the schoolhouse.

"Mom?" Robby asked.

She didn't reply, she just looked up the hill—where they last saw Sam.

"Mom?" Robby asked again.

"What?" she finally responded.

"We have to assume he's gone," Robby said. "He'd want us to get to a safe place, and that's not here."

"I know, for Chrissakes, I know," she said. Sarah looked into Robby's eyes. She blinked hard and composed herself. "Carl's got his boat at the pier, so at least we don't have to punt all this shit out to it. Grab what you can, stay low, and run for the boat."

"Okay," Robby said.

"I'll go around and open up the back. You come over the seat. I want you inside as long as possible," Sarah said.

"Okay, mom," Robby said.

Sarah did what she said—she ducked out of the Jeep, stayed low, and ran to the back of the Jeep. The wind coming off the water swept most of the snow away from the pavement. Only an inch or two collected, crunching like cotton as she ran through it. They'd packed all their supplies into a backpack, a couple of bags, and two boxes. Sarah lifted the rear door of the Jeep and grabbed the bags. She slung the straps over her head to opposite shoulders, so the straps hung like bandoliers across her chest. She pulled one of the boxes out of the way and Robby climbed over the seat. He grabbed the backpack and the big box.

"It's this first one on the left?" Sarah asked.

"Yeah," Robby said. "You got the keys?"

"Yes," she said. "Not that we'll need them again."

"Yeah we will," Robby said. "We're coming back, remember? Besides, Carl's keys are on that ring."

"Thank goodness for your memory," Sarah said. "You start running, I'm right behind you."

Robby hunched as low as he could, carrying the heavy box, and shuffling towards the pier. Sarah closed up the Jeep and followed close. The bags banged into her hips and nearly knocked her off her feet as she and Robby ran.

Carl's boat bobbed and banged against its fenders. Robby started feeling nauseous just looking at the swaying motion. He skidded to a stop near the stern. The snow on the pier was slushy from the damp air and Robby almost lost his footing. He set his box down on the pier and jumped onto the deck of Carl's boat. Robby had only seen this boat from a distance—Carl usually kept it moored out in the harbor.

After the fishing tourism ended for the fall, Carl finagled a spot at the pier so he could replace the engine of his Cape Islander boat. Fortunately for Robby and Sarah, he'd just completed the job. He'd bought the boat for hauling lobster, but switched to hauling tourists instead. The boat looked huge and yet unsteady to Robby. His stomach flopped as the boat lurched from the swells pushed in by the storm.

Robby leaned back towards the dock and tried to grab his box. He stopped and steadied himself on the rail, not sure if he would be sick. Sarah set down her box and tossed the duffel bags into the boat.

"Get in the cabin," she said. "I'll get the boxes."

"You'll need help shoving off," Robby said.

"Get us untied then," she said. Sarah grew up around boats. Being raised on the island you almost had to become familiar with them. But she hated the nervous tasks associated with launching or landing a boat. In her experience, when the mobile, freewheeling boats came in contact with the immovable piers, trouble ensued.

Robby secured the bow line and looped the stern rope around the mooring while his mom moved the boxes and made her way to the cabin. Robby leaned over the edge, not knowing when his turkey sandwich would make a return visit. He fixed his gaze on the farthest thing he could see—the buildings up past the Jeep. He unlocked his knees and tried to float over the deck's surface to keep his head steady.

His mom was taking too long, he figured. She must be having trouble figuring out the...

The big diesel engine turned over and black smoke puffed from the exhaust pipe at the back of the cabin. Robby got ready. His job would be to release the bow line and then pull in the fenders as his mom backed the boat from the pier. Sarah guided the boat back, making sure to clear some space between the boat and the pier as quickly as possible. The wind battled her steering, trying to push the boat back towards the pier.

When he'd pulled in the last fender, Robby started collecting their supplies. He dragged them towards the small cabin. When he opened the door, his mom surprised him.

"Take the helm," she said.

"Pardon?" Robby asked.

"Take the helm. Head for just to the right of that marker. I'll stow everything below. Steering will help you deal with your seasickness," she said.

"What if I have to throw up?" Robby asked. He knew it would only be a matter of time before his nausea kicked into overdrive. The swells in the harbor were tiny compared to what they would find once they cleared some distance from the island.

"Here's a barf-bag," she said, rooting through the backpack, "and I packed you some soda crackers. Keep chewing on these."

Robby's stomach felt like a tight knot. Tart saliva started to water in the back of his mouth. A tiny headache formed at the top of his skull. These were all signs of imminent upchuck. He took the wheel and gripped his fingers at ten and two. He understood the logic immediately—he was focused on the horizon, steadied by the wheel, and concentrating. All these activities should settle his stomach.

The wind picked up. A sudden squall of snowflakes decreased visibility and the wind made Robby correct the wheel to get back on course. Robby squinted through the wall of snow.

Sarah stowed the last of their supplies in the space below the bow deck and then closed the cabin door.

"Is there heat in this thing?" she asked.

"Huh?" Robby asked. He turned to look at his mom and

instantly regretted it. The quick swing of his head disturbed the delicate truce he'd negotiated with the turkey sandwich. He doubled over with a big retch and coughed up the contents of his stomach into the barf-bag. Sarah reached over and held the wheel while he puked.

"Here," she said, handing Robby a towel.

"Thanks," he said. He put his hands back on the wheel and fixed his eyes back on the horizon.

"I'm going to figure out how to get the heat on," she said.

"Can you wait?" Robby asked. "The cold is actually helping a little."

"You're the Cap'n," she said. Sarah propped her feet up on the console and sat on a storage locker. She massaged her temples and sighed, looking out the back window towards the island. "We're going to be okay," she said.

"I know, mom," Robby said.

"At some point you're going to have to figure out this GPS," she said. "It's like the space shuttle in here."

"Okay," Robby said. "Maybe you can describe what you see and then I can keep my eyes forward?"

"Aye aye, Cap'n," Sarah said.

Sarah talked through the buttons and displays while Robby guided the boat. He pieced together a mental picture of the controls until she got lazy with the narrative and he stole glances down at the panel. His churning stomach reminded him not to look away from the horizon for too long. With her son's guidance, Sarah got the instruments powered up and gave Robby a heading to follow.

The crossing by ferry usually took between seventy-five and ninety minutes. Sarah expected their trip in Carl's boat to last a bit longer.

"Your dad insisted on bringing enough supplies for days," Sarah told Robby.

"Makes sense," Robby said.

"He wouldn't say why," Sarah said.

"I think he wanted to take us south, but didn't want to say anything in front of the Nortons," Robby said.

"How far south?" Sarah asked.

"Until we found people," Robby said. "From the TV and the radio, Dad would have guessed that the same thing that happened on the island was also happening on the mainland. The best bet would be to head south."

"Until we find people," Sarah said. She shook her head and bit her lip. "I wish we'd just stayed put."

"We weren't safe there," Robby said.

"What the hell is happening?" Sarah asked.

Robby didn't have an answer. "Do you want to head south?" Robby asked.

"On a boat? No. It would be easy for your dad, but not with just us," Sarah said.

"Good," Robby said. "I hate boats."

"I know you do, honey," Sarah said.

# CHAPTER 4: BRAD (SUMMER)

FIVE MONTHS EARLIER...

✪ ✪ ✪ ✪ ✪

"Fax? You mean like fax machine?" Brad asked the phone.

He sat in his special high-backed desk chair—the kind that cost more than a good used car.

"Yes," Phil said. His voice came from the speakers on either side of Brad's computer monitor. "You do have that capability, don't you?"

"Sure," Brad said. He pondered the idea. He could crawl through the attic, find his fax machine, print out his estimate, and then send it over, but why? He'd already emailed the document; why would anyone need a faxed copy? Brad suddenly realized he could probably find an online service to turn his email into a fax. He calmed down a bit, now that he could dismiss the chore of going up to the stifling-hot attic.

"We'll review your quote and get back to you by the end of the week," Phil said. "Then you'll start right away?"

"Absolutely," Brad said.

"Great," Phil said. "Talk to you soon."

Brad flicked his computer mouse to wake up his monitor. He disconnected from the call.

He pushed back and put his feet up on his desk. Phil would

probably stand by the fax machine, waiting for his transmission, but Phil could wait. Brad knew that Phil would never get approval by the end of the week. If Phil promised you a contract on Friday, he really meant you should expect it sometime in the next month.

The project had turned into a nightmare. Phil talked him into a five day engagement that turned into six weeks of work. Worse than that, Phil convinced the Cincinnati office to use another contractor so Phil could have Brad all to himself. Brad liked to make himself indispensable, but Phil was turning into a stalker.

Now, with the project nearly complete, Phil let the stakeholders change several major requirements. Two major sub-systems would have to be reworked, and one of the supporting applications overhauled. Brad produced an estimate for the change order, and now waited for Phil to get approval for the work.

"I'll be lucky if I hear from him by September," Brad said to the ceiling. "On the other hand, I don't have to work until September, if I don't want to."

Despite the lower hourly rate, Phil's insistence on overtime and weekend work netted Brad a huge windfall for June and July. He always kept a decent financial cushion to weather the lean times. Now he had enough money saved to coast for a year without another contract; not that he would ever indulge himself to such a degree.

Brad intertwined his fingers behind his head and leaned back farther.

"What if I just quit?" he asked nobody. "What if I just fax over a picture of my middle finger? Phil can get one of the Prague guys to finish up this mess. Sure, it will take him three times as long, but they only charge half as much. He'll be a hero until they figure out the Prague guys don't know jack shit about their data."

Brad closed his eyes and tried to imagine what his life would actually be like if he quit. He always pictured a perfect life—he would have time to work on the house, clean up the yard, or maybe meet some new people in town. But he knew better. Between jobs he always obsessed about money and trying to find a new job. He wouldn't be able to enjoy a stress-free life; it would make him anxious.

He shifted his weight and dropped his fingers to the keyboard. In a few minutes he figured out how to fax his estimate to Phil.

"Now I just have to wait," he said to the monitor. The clock on his computer read half-past ten. "Looks like a good day for a pre-lunch walk."

✪ ✪ ✪ ✪ ✪

Brad started down the path looking at his feet. This time he wanted to be careful where he stepped. Remembering his encounter with the mystery vines over a month before, he wore his hiking boots and jeans. A clicking sound ahead made him stop and look up. He stood, still a hundred yards from the place where the vine had wrapped around his leg, and listened to the clicking.

The clicking was loud, and sounded like it came from up on the hill. Whatever it was clicked about twice a second, then sped up to several times that rate, and then slowed again. Brad almost felt hypnotized by the rhythm. He started forward again, keeping his focus on the clicking. Nobody ever came back here except Brad. Even in hunting season, people didn't stray this far. Dragging a deer a mile through thick woods didn't appeal to the local hunters.

One year a neighbor he'd never met came to the door and asked Brad to unlock the gate so he could get his deer out to his truck. That was back when Karen had still been alive and married to Brad. She stood behind him as he talked to the hunter on the porch.

Wearing an orange hat and camo shirt and pants, the man had introduced himself and then explained his request, "I'm wondering if you can unlock your gate so I can haul out my deer." The man stood drenched in sweat despite the cool November day.

"Boy," Brad said, "you look like you've been dragging that deer for half a mile."

"No," the hunter laughed, "not quite that far, but it was quite a haul."

"So, less than half a mile?" Brad asked. He felt Karen's hand on his back. The hand might have meant "good job," or maybe just "back off." He didn't know.

"Maybe a few hundred yards, I guess," the hunter said. His smile faltered.

"So a quarter of a mile?" Brad asked.

"Look, if you could just open the gate, or maybe loan me the key?" asked the hunter.

"I'm just asking because our property extends at least a half mile in every direction from that gate, unless you took the deer across a road," Brad said. "And since we spent the better part of five hundred dollars putting up signs every fifty feet, I would assume you know—we don't allow hunting on our property."

"Look, I'm sorry," the hunter said. "I didn't see your signs, and I didn't mean to hunt without your permission."

"Understood," Brad said.

"But I've got a deer right on the other side of your gate. I certainly won't hunt your land again, but what do you want me to do? Should I just leave it there, or are you going to let me through the gate?"

"I tell you what," Brad said. "You can haul it back around our fence, or you can leave it there and I'll have the game warden come collect it."

The hunter left, furious. The confrontation didn't give Brad any satisfaction.

Brad recalled his anger as he stood listening to the clicking sound. He didn't even realize he'd stopped moving. The confrontation with the hunter had been years before, but he'd seen it play out right before his eyes, like a movie. He wanted to turn around and go back to the house. He forced his feet to move forward, up the hill, towards the clicking.

When Brad reached the edge of the clearing, the clicking noise stopped. It had been loud enough to echo off the trees to his left. After the clicking stopped the normal noises of summer began again. Birds sang, the occasional early cricket chirped, and squirrels rustled through the underbrush. Had it been his imagination that those sounds were absent during the clicking? Brad couldn't decide.

The vines had spread since he'd been there last. They now

covered the entire cleared area and stretched across the path where it picked up on the other side. On his left, he saw the vines curling up the trunks of the trees. Some trees were nearly choked with vines. The leaves looked brown on these trees—they wouldn't live to see another spring. Pink and purple flowers stood out on the vines, but none were close enough for Brad to inspect. These vines were too long to cross. If they acted like the one he'd seen back in June, they would wrap all the way up to his neck, he figured.

Brad thought about going to town, to the garden center with the big greenhouse. They would know what the vine was, and probably how to kill it. He pulled his gardening gloves from his back pocket and crouched, grabbing the smallest vine near his feet. When he tugged on the vine, it immediately constricted, like a boa, on his gloved hand. Brad slashed at it with his knife, cutting off about a foot. He put his gloved hand in a plastic bag and pulled off the glove and vine.

Brad was still crouched down on his haunches when he heard the click again. It sounded just once. He moved only his head and looked up. He couldn't see anything unusual. Trees, bushes, vines —tons of vines, a big rock, and clear blue sky.

Click—he heard it again.

Brad's brow furrowed as he scanned the clearing again. Something was out of place. The rock—what was that giant gray rock doing over near the far tree line? He and Karen had cleared every inch of the pasture themselves. He would have remembered a big stately boulder at the edge of it. There was another problem with the rock—it didn't have vines draped all over it. Everything else he could see was covered by the creeping menace. Only the rock sat unmolested.

He wanted to get a closer look, but didn't think it wise to try to cross the vine patch. From where he stood, it looked like a truly horrible idea. Just one of those vines had incapacitated his bare leg a month and a half before, and it only measured a few feet long. Now the vines were piled in a tangled mess, looking waist-deep in parts.

Brad backed down the path until he found a clear patch of

alders. He struck out on a course tangential to the edge of the clearing, hoping to circle around through the woods to the other side. A couple dozen yards later, he was stopped by the vines again. A swath of vines, about ten feet across, passed through the trees. Some curled up the trunks to choke out the low trees, but most just piled on themselves to form a little river of vegetation. Brad swung the bag containing the glove and piece of vine back and forth and considered his options.

He followed the vine river for a while, away from the clearing. It didn't show any signs of petering out.

The clicking started again: click, click, click, click-click-click-click, click, click, click. Brad turned and listened. It was almost soothing. He reached out to steady himself on a tree and nearly put his hand on a curling vine.

Brad thought about his grandfather, Grandpa Joe. Grandpa Joe was a logging man until he started working as a surveyor for the state. By the time Brad was old enough to spend his summers with Grandpa Joe, the old man retired, but still cut firewood as a hobby. He used to take Brad out in the woods with him when Brad would visit.

Grandpa Joe always cut with his four foot bow saw, and delimbed with a razor-sharp axe. Joe carried the saw over his left shoulder and the axe in his right hand, so Brad carried the small chainsaw. Grandpa Joe called the chainsaw "Justin."

"Why do you call the chainsaw Justin?" Brad asked one day.

"Same reason I keep it in a case," Grandpa Joe said.

"Why's that?" asked young Brad.

"I don't intend to use it, but I have you bring it along Justin Case," Joe said.

Grandpa Joe smiled at Brad when he saw that Brad finally got the joke. The old man could bring down a tree and have it bucked into perfect, four-foot segments before most people could even get their chainsaw started. And Grandpa Joe moved almost silently through the woods. The only noise you'd hear would be when he crashed the next tree to the ground.

Brad blinked several times and snapped himself from the memory. He shook his head and rubbed his eyes with his free hand. He felt like he'd been asleep on his feet. The clicking stopped again.

"Am I crazy, or did you get closer to me?" Brad asked the vine river. He pulled his phone from his back pocket to check the time.

"What?" he whispered. For some reason the clock on his phone read one in the afternoon. If it was right, somehow he'd spent over two hours on his twenty minute walk.

"Jesus," he whispered. Movement drew his eyes to the right. On the tree a few feet away, blossoms opened up on the curling vine. They started from the tip of the vine and opened one at a time down its length. To Brad it looked like the world's slowest fireworks display. They were a plush, throaty blossom, reminding Brad of Morning Glories. The flowers alternated in color: pink, purple, pink, purple. The ones down near the base of the tree were larger than the ones at the tip of the vine, which were almost at eye level.

Brad backed up two steps without taking his eyes off the strange flowers. He pulled out his utility knife, thinking he should get a sample with flowers on it, but then changed his mind. Those vines hadn't been there when he zonked out. What if he was just one more hypnosis away from being enveloped by the vines? He tore his gaze away from the pretty flowers and scanned for a good exit route.

He could feel his heart beating faster. It had been so long since Brad really felt fear, it was almost nice. The fear felt like a leftover emotion from childhood; something he wasn't sure he would ever experience again so completely. There'd been an adrenaline rush the time the woman at the gas station almost backed into his car, but no real fear. Brad fed into the emotion, wanting to keep it going. He started walking.

The vine river spread out—Brad walked almost directly downhill to get away from them. His direct route back to his road had been flanked. After a minute of picking his way through the woods, the vines around Brad started to peter out. His pace slowed until the clicking sound started again. It was still coming from up the hill, from his clearing, but it brought Brad's fear back with a rush. He started to run downhill through the woods, back towards his house.

✪ ✪ ✪ ✪ ✪

Brad dropped his latest vine sample back at the house and grabbed his binoculars from the laundry room. He hauled his biggest ladder from its hooks on the outside of the garage and headed for the big pine trees down near the pond. His property sloped down from the new pasture out back, and then up from a gully to the house. From the ladder, he thought he might be able to get a look at the pasture.

He propped the ladder just below a cluster of branches and started climbing. Way off in the distance, he could still hear the rhythmic clicking.

"Music," he said to himself. For a second, he tried to fish the earphones out of his pocket while he stood on the ladder, but then he changed his mind and climbed back down.

Brad talked to himself while he hooked the earphones up to his music player. "Just in case. Justin Case. Maybe if I can't hear you, I won't get hypnotized? Worth a shot." He found some classic rock to act as his soundtrack for his little spying mission.

Even at the top of the ladder, he was still a little lower than the clearing on the far hill, but he had a pretty good view. The branches he leaned on were covered in sap, but they felt more stable than trying to balance on the ladder. Brad propped his elbows on a branch so he could steady his hands for the binoculars.

He could see a portion of his overgrown road and the vine-covered clearing. The strange rock sat dead center in the clearing.

"I thought you were closer to the trees," Brad said to himself. He couldn't hear himself over the music. He glanced around, suddenly self-conscious and certain he'd see new vines climbing up the pine tree, or even the ladder itself. The drums on his music dropped into a low, steady beat. Brad thought he could hear the clicking beneath the beat.

With the binoculars at maximum magnification, his view jittered with each small movement of his hands. It almost looked like the rock was moving, but he couldn't tell for sure. Brad switched back and forth between looking through the binoculars and pulling them down to squint over the distance.

He took a deep breath and let it out slowly. The breath steadied his hands. That's when he figured it out—the rock wasn't *moving*; it was *spinning*. It spun very slowly, clockwise. One of the bumps on the right profile of the big boulder slowly melted as it moved to the left. It took several minutes, but eventually he saw the same bump appear on the left side.

Brad hung the binoculars around his neck and fished his cell phone out his pocket. He turned off the music and ran through the contact list until he found the name he wanted. He started to dial and then changed his mind. Brad put the phone away and climbed down the ladder.

Once he stood safely on the ground again he dialed his friend.

✪ ✪ ✪ ✪ ✪

"Thanks for coming over so fast," Brad said.

Brad walked his old friend Stavros back towards the pine tree where the ladder still stood against the tree.

"You sounded pretty panicked," Stavros said. "Besides, I was just watching the crew dig up the culverts down by the fire station."

Stavros Orestes acted as the Code Enforcement Officer for Kingston. Technically, Brad's property was in Kingston Depot, which had a completely separate town government and a different enforcement officer, so Stavros was only there unofficially.

"Honestly? I'm a little freaked out," Brad said. "Something strange is going on in my back forty."

"Yeah, I heard. Apparently something so strange you wouldn't even give me the slightest clue on the phone," Stavros said.

"Wait, stop," Brad said, "do you hear that?"

"Hear what?" asked Stavros.

"That clicking noise. Way off in the distance, do you hear it?" Brad asked. It was obvious to Brad, but he knew exactly what to listen for.

"I hear a thousand things clicking," Stavros said. "You're going to have to be more specific."

"Never mind, you'll hear it better from the ladder anyway," Brad said.

He walked his friend across the back yard, around the blackberry patch, and down to the big pine tree where his ladder stood.

"Here, take these," Brad said, handing the binoculars to Stavros. "Look straight across this way, over at the clearing at the top of the hill."

"What am I looking for?" asked Stavros.

"The whole thing is covered in a weird kind of weed, but you'll have to see it up close. Look for the rock in the middle of the clearing," Brad said.

"Okay," Stavros said.

Stavros Orestes wore his casual work clothes—cargo shorts, hiking boots, and a short-sleeve chambray shirt. He was accustomed to getting dirty during the course of the day and had no objection to climbing a ladder or a tree. He held the binoculars in one hand and quickly climbed the ladder with the other.

"I see the clearing, but no rock," Stavros said.

"It might not be in the middle anymore," Brad said.

Stavros lowered the binoculars and looked down at Brad, who stood on the ground looking up.

"Say that again?" Stavros asked.

"Just keep looking," Brad said.

Stavros scanned the clearing for a few minutes before descending and handing the binoculars back. Brad couldn't stand it—he climbed up and verified the rock had disappeared.

"I didn't think it would move that fast," Brad said. "I was looking at it right before you showed up."

"So it's not a rock?" asked Stavros.

"I would have sworn it was," Brad said, "except it was rotating."

Stavros spun his finger in the air.

"No," Brad said, "not rolling. On a vertical axis. Clockwise. Like this." Brad demonstrated, making a stirring motion with his own finger.

"That's definitely not normal," Stavros said, smiling. "You've got your rolling stones, and your stationary ones. Those are usually the only two types. Why don't we just walk up there and you can show me where it was?"

"I think it might be dangerous," Brad said. "I think vines try to hypnotize you so they can eat you."

"Not to be an ass or anything," Stavros said, "but you're feeling okay, right? Not too much stress with your job or anything lately? Any dizziness, change in medication?"

"Come inside," Brad said. "I'll tell you the whole story and show you a piece of vine."

Brad walked Stavros into the kitchen, relating all the details as they walked. The plastic bag with the vine lay on the counter. Brad's hands shook a little as he dumped the bag out on the counter. He expected it to be empty; for the hunk of vine to have disappeared just like the last one. The glove fell out, but nothing else came out of the bag. He turned it inside out and let out a relieved breath when he found the piece of vine clinging to the bag.

"This," he said. "And look, it has a flower."

"So it doesn't move once you cut it?" asked Stavros. He leaned in close to peer at the vine.

"Yeah, it only stayed alive for a little while once I clipped it off last time," Brad said. "But I was able to get a reaction when I..." Brad blew on the vine. One end flipped up off the counter and the vine spun itself into a tight coil. "See!" Brad said.

"Wow," Stavros said. "I've never seen anything like that."

"Yeah, like I said," Brad said.

Stavros reached out and touched the vine before Brad could stop him. The vine's action had weakened, but it still curled around his index finger, sinking its tiny thorns into his flesh.

"Shit!" Stavros said. He plucked at the end of the vine and pulled it away from his skin.

"They're barbed," Brad said. "I told you."

"Yeah," Stavros said, grimacing with the pain while he pulled the thorns from his finger, "I guess I like to see for myself."

"So what do you think it is?" Brad asked.

"How the hell should I know?" asked Stavros. "What do I look like, a botanist?"

"Not since about twenty pounds ago," Brad said, laughing. They had become friends and then roommates in college, when Stavros studied botany, and Brad studied engineering.

Stavros pulled out the last thorn and tossed the piece of vine back on the counter. He sucked on the side of his finger and both men watched as the vine flipped over one last time.

"So what's the connection to the rock? Anything?" asked Stavros.

"I don't know, but the vines didn't touch the rock-thing, and it was right in the middle of them," Brad said.

"Yeah, well even those thorns wouldn't do anything against a rock," Stavros said.

"If I had to guess," Brad said. "I think it might be just a really big animal camouflaged to look like a rock. A rhino kinda looks like a rock, or a big turtle."

"So you've got some new species of plant back there," Stavros said. "At least they're nothing indigenous, and nothing I've ever heard of before. How dangerous is this clicking you were talking about."

"As far as I can tell, it just kinda hypnotized me for a little while," Brad said. "But those vines got pretty close while I was out. It's like a psychic game of 'Red Light, Green Light.' I wouldn't want to find out what happens if they win."

"You said you heard the clicking when we were walking," Stavros said, "but you didn't pass out then."

"Maybe it wasn't loud enough?" Brad asked. "Who knows. I wore headphones when I was up on the ladder before and I was fine. I don't know—maybe I would have been fine without them. Hell, I don't even know if the effect was caused by the sound or what. Could have been a smell, or anything."

"We've got a whole lot of questions and not many answers," Stavros said. "I still know some working botanists; do you want me to have them check this thing out?" He pointed at the vine.

"Sure," Brad said. "I've got acres of the things."

"Okay," Stavros said. "In the meantime, I'd suggest you don't venture out back there again until we have an answer."

"Fine by me," Brad said.

"And if they really do grow as fast as you said, you'd better keep a good eye on the yard," Stavros said. "If you see any of those things creeping up on the house, just get in the car and drive," he said, smiling.

"Yeah, will do," Brad said, laughing. "Attack of the killer plants."

"Seriously," Stavros said, laughing too. "Those things hurt."

Dear Karen,

I saw Stavros today. He came over to look at those plants I was telling you about. He didn't know what they were either, but he said he would send my clipping off to a friend of his. I wish we got together more, like we used to. Those dinners on the porch, watching the sun set over the hill—I think that was the greatest time of my life. Half of the women Stavros brought were totally crazy, but I don't think he ever really felt comfortable hanging out with us as a couple when he was alone. Now that I'm alone, I think Stavros and Julianne feel bad for me.

It's been a long time.

I know I told you this before, but when Stavros tried to set me up, I wanted to kill him. It may have been Julianne's idea—in fact it probably was—since she worked for the same company as Julianne. You were always the outgoing one. I met more people through you than from all other aspects of my life. My only friends used to be your friends and my work friends. Now, since I'm doing contract work all the time, I don't meet anyone. Stavros is the last person from growing up I'm even still in contact with.

Sorry to sound so melancholy. You know what? I'm going to sign up for the yoga class you used to take down at the old mill. I never wanted to go with you because I was so bad at it, and I didn't know any of the moves. Now that I've had a few years of practicing with videos, I can probably fake my way through it.

Maybe I'll meet some new people there. I'll probably even meet some people you knew, once upon a time. I miss you.

Much Love,

Brad

Having handed the problem off to his friend, Brad found it easy to temporarily ignore the odd things going on in his back pasture. He did his usual Tuesday night routine—ate an early dinner, wrote his letter to his dead ex-wife, and didn't send it. The letter spoke mostly of the adventure out back, but also featured a section about Stavros. Karen always loved Stavros.

Brad went to bed early. He tossed and turned through a long night of tortured dreams he could barely remember when he woke up. Somehow, he'd slept right through his alarm.

He took his coffee out to the deck and sat on the stairs, looking up towards the hill out back. Random chores kept popping into his head. He needed to clear the brush around the fence line. He needed to paint the trim on the windows. He needed to weed the front flower beds. Brad decided the only way to get peace from his chores would be to write them all down and prioritize the list. At least then he'd have a chance of knocking a few of the big ticket items off before he got another call about a contract. Brad sighed and stood, ready to go inside and make his list.

As he turned, a pile of dirt caught his eye. He set his coffee down on the railing and descended the stairs. Right next to where the deck met the foundation of the garage, Brad saw the edge of a big pile of freshly-turned dirt. The top of the dirt on the pile had just started to dry out, but the bulk of the sandy pile looked fresh and moist.

Brad reached the lawn and saw the extent of the damage. His deck was big, and stood about five feet above the surrounding yard. Next to the foundation of the garage, a giant hole had been dug, easily seven feet across. Almost all of the excavated dirt was piled under the deck. The pile Brad saw initially was a tiny fraction of the amount under there. Brad backed up and gaped—the dirt pile under the deck ran the entire twenty-foot length.

"That's enough dirt to fill the living room," Brad said to himself.

He reached up and gripped the back of his head with his hands. Brad spun slowly, looking for any tracks on the lawn.

"It would have taken an excavator all night," he said under his breath. "I was just out here last night. Last night."

Brad approached the gaping hole slowly. The hole exposed the side of the concrete foundation, where it descended into the soil. The concrete was still dark under the soil-line, where it had recently been in contact with the dirt. His foundation went down about four feet below the grass, but the hole went lower. Brad leaned forward to see the smooth edge of the bottom of the concrete footing.

Eight or ten feet down, the bottom of the hole curved towards the garage, like a tunnel. Brad looked at the grass beneath his feet. The grass was completely undisturbed right up to the ragged edge of the hole. Aside from the mammoth pile of dirt under the deck and the small pile he'd seen first, the area was completely clean. Brad couldn't even imagine how one would dig such a perfect hole in any circumstance, let alone over the course of just one night. Instead of going back up the stairs to the deck, Brad left his coffee behind and walked around the garage and opened the big door. His biggest ladder still rested against the pine tree out back, but he had a smaller, more appropriate ladder for this job anyway. He retrieved his six-foot step ladder and carried it overhead to get it past his truck.

A tan sedan pulled down the driveway and parked alongside the fence as Brad set the ladder down.

Brad walked up to within ten feet of the car and waited for the man to get out.

The man looked tired, but extremely precise. He glanced through the car window at Brad, gave him a single, clipped nod and then opened the car door. His feet hit the gravel drive together, perpendicular to the car, and the man stood with one quick motion, not pushing against the doorframe or pulling on the door for assistance. Brad just watched, not making any movement to introduce himself or greet the man. The man wore a golf shirt and crisp khaki pants—no pleat.

When the man stood to his full height, Brad was surprised. Brad stood about six-foot two, and didn't expect to be dwarfed by the man in the tan sedan. The man was thin, too. Brad guessed they probably weighed the same, even though the man stood several inches taller. The man removed his sunglasses and perched them atop his crew cut before he closed the door and approached Brad.

The man put out his hand to Brad.

"Good morning, sir," the man said. "I'm Herm Gunther, I want to talk to you about your plants?"

"Plants?" Brad asked.

"Yes," Herm said. "Your name is Brad Jenkins, correct? You gave a sample to Stayev-ross Orestus last Tuesday?"

"Yesterday," Brad said, nodding.

"I'm sorry?" asked Herm.

"I gave a sample to STAVross OrestES *yesterday*. On Tuesday," Brad said. He crossed his arms and looked at Herm's shoes. They were casual boat shoes, which Herm wore with no socks. Brad could see a half inch of bright white ankle between the shoes and the khakis. He guessed Herm's ankles didn't get much sun. His hands and forearms did though, Brad saw tan lines about halfway down the man's biceps.

"Would you be more comfortable if we moved inside?" asked Herm.

"No, I'm fine here," Brad said.

"Do you have a cell phone on you by any chance?" asked Herm.

"Yes, I do," Brad said. He didn't move for a second, but then pulled the phone from his back pocket and waved it at Herm.

"Good," Herm said. "Would you like to check the date?"

"Okay?" Brad said, with a hint of uncertainty creeping into the edges of his voice. The phone informed him of the current date: Thursday, July twenty-first. Brad's eyes shifted from side to side as he tried to figure out where Wednesday had gone. He remembered Tuesday, then writing a letter, and then going to bed a little early. How was it Thursday?

Herm watched Brad's puzzlement and rubbed his eyes while Brad tried to piece together his calendar. "These plants are close to your house?" he asked.

"No," Brad said. "No, they're out back. Who are you again?"

"I'm Herm Gunther," the man said. "I work for USDA on the abatement of aquatic and arboreal invasives. Have you taken any trips to Georgia or South Carolina recently?"

"Nope," Brad said. "I've been right here. Are you saying that plant is from Georgia."

"More than likely," Herm said. "It's been on the Federal Noxious Weed list for years, but it's just starting to show up in other parts of the country. Would you mind showing me where you took the clipping?"

"Well, perhaps," Brad said. He put his hands on his hips and then thrust them into his pockets. "I'm, uh, I'm a little concerned though."

"Concerned?" asked Herm.

"Well, I'm not sure why, but the last time I was out back I kept going into a little of a dream state or something. I know this sounds weird, but maybe since you've heard of this plant, you've heard of this as well?"

"Dream state?" asked Herm.

"Yeah," Brad said. "It was... It was like I became unconscious for a few moments. I thought maybe it was a sound or a chemical the plant is giving off?"

"Did you see any out of place puddles, patches of fog, boulders, piles of sand, or lava flows?" asked Herm.

"Lava flows?" Brad asked. "Do you think I would be talking to you about plants if I'd seen any out of place lava flows?"

"Flows or pools—any molten or even iridescent metals?" asked Herm.

"No," Brad said. "But a boulder, yes. I did see an out of place boulder."

"And the boulder was with the plants?" asked Herm.

"Yes," Brad said.

"Did you hear a loud 'tock' sound, like a giant clock?" asked Herm.

"Yes. It was more like a click, but yes," Brad said.

"Thank you," Herm said. He walked back to his car and opened the door. Herm reached across the seat and his torso disappeared from Brad's view for a second. When he reappeared, he was holding a hand-held radio unit. "Can you show me the area now?"

"Like I said, I'm a little concerned," Brad said.

"Don't worry," Herm said. "I've read about this. We'll be fine. I'll call into the office, and if we don't check back in, one of my co-workers will come. But there's really nothing to be worried about."

"Okay," Brad said. He was still hesitant, but Herm knew about both the rock and the clicking sound, so he felt inclined to go along with him. Plus, Herm seemed very professional—not likely to take unwarranted risks, despite how tired the man looked.

"Let me just change my shoes first," Brad said. "You might want to consider socks, if you've got them."

"Thanks, I'm fine," Herm said.

Brad shrugged and walked over to his side door. He kept his boots on the tile floor of his entryway, so he sat down on the porch to change into them. While Brad laced up the boots, Herm just stood there, looking off into the distance.

"Hey, um, Mister ..." Brad said. He couldn't remember the man's name. It was something silly sounding—weird nickname— he remembered.

"Herm," the man said, "call me Herm."

"Thank you, Herm. You can call me Brad. May I ask, what was the rock thing I saw out back?" Brad asked.

"I have no idea," Herm said.

"But you mentioned rocks as part of your list, with the lava flows, and the iridescent metal, and the mist?" Brad asked.

"Patches of fog," Herm said. "Yes, it's one of the things I read about."

"Read about from?" Brad asked.

"We get bulletins from the Office of Communications. The rocks were mentioned with your plants in one of those," Herm said.

"Huh," Brad said. "But they didn't say what they were?"

"Probably not important," Herm said. "I just need to make an identification for the abatement group."

Brad finished with his boots and stood up. He walked past Herm and waved for the man to follow. "And the abatement group does what, exactly?" Brad asked.

"They just work to eradicate or control the invasive infestation. You can imagine—herbicides, bush hogs, maybe some burning," Herm said.

"Sounds like it's going to cost me," Brad said.

"Nope," Herm said. "Your tax dollars at work. It's for the common good, so the government foots the bill."

"Good to know," Brad said. He held open the gate between the driveway and the field and let Herm walk through first. He pointed ahead and said, "Straight back to the other gate."

"You've probably seen our guys before on the side of the highway with the orange jumpsuits. We get a lot of invasives along the highway, from tourists," Herm said.

"I can imagine," Brad said. Brad noted how talkative Herm had gotten once they were underway. But it seemed like just as quickly as the conversation began, it was over. Herm didn't offer any more information.

Herm walked at a fast pace. Brad unlatched the back gate and Herm was already dozens of paces away by the time Brad buttoned the gate back up. Brad dropped into a half-jog to catch up with the tall man.

"You might want to watch your step," Brad said. "Those things grow at a pretty fast pace, and I wouldn't envy you if one wrapped around your ankle."

"Thanks," Herm said.

They walked in silence for a while down Brad's path to the back clearing. Walking side by side, they brushed the trees and bushes which crowded in from the sides. Brad usually cleared the brush along the path once or twice a month during the summer when he wasn't too busy with work. This year he'd have to wait until fall, when the weeds were a bit more manageable.

Brad broke the silence when they had walked about halfway to the clearing, "So," he said, "how long have you worked for the USDA?"

"Ten years," Herm said. The answer came fast and didn't reveal anything to Brad. He usually got a sense of whether someone liked their job just by how they answered that question. A sigh, a smile, a head-tilt all meant something, but Herm snapped off his answer and kept his eyes moving, scanning the sides of the path.

"Good work?" Brad asked.

"The best," Herm said. His tone stayed flat.

"Wait," Brad said. He put out his hand to stop Herm, but Herm had already stopped. "Did you hear it?"

"No," Herm said.

"I thought I heard a click," Brad said. "Probably just a squirrel."

Herm started walking again. Brad fell in behind him and Herm picked up the pace, walking fast up the hill to the clearing. Herm stopped at the edge of the weeds.

"I should have brought a knife or something," Brad said. "Did you want a sample."

Herm didn't answer right away, he scanned the tree line at the far edge of the clearing. Brad knelt to look at the vines, but Herm stayed upright.

"You saw a rock over there?" Herm finally asked.

Brad looked up; Herm pointed to the spot where Brad last saw the mysterious spinning boulder.

"Yeah, that's the spot," Brad said. "How did you know?"

Herm bent down and reached for the end of a vine.

"Careful!" Brad said, shuffling back a half-step.

Herm's hand never slowed. He snatched the very tip of a vine between his fingers and pulled it back. The vine thrashed as Herm pulled it back. Brad moved out of the way and Herm stretched the vine several feet before it pulled taut. The vine stopped trying to flip and curl as Herm tugged. Brad stepped to Herm's side and leaned in to look at how Herm was holding the vine. The very tip curled around Herm's index finger, but it didn't look like it had sunk any thorns into the man's flesh.

"Is it what you thought it was?" Brad asked. "The thing from Georgia, or whatever?"

Herm didn't answer. He tugged at the vine several times, about once every two seconds. Flowers popped open near the base of the vine. He tugged four more times and flowers, orange and purple, started opening on the suspended portion of the vine.

They heard a loud "tock," from somewhere on the other side of the clearing, deep in the woods. Herm stopped tugging.

"Back up," Herm said.

Brad scrambled back down the path and Herm backed up until he held the vine at arm's length. He dropped the vine and stepped away. The vine floundered and twisted. Each flop brought it closer back to the vine patch until it regained the company of its fellow vines.

Herm reached to the radio clipped to his belt. He pressed a button on the side twice and then turned towards Brad.

"We should head back," Herm said.

Brad could barely make out what Herm said. A loud "TOCK!" interrupted the sentence, but Brad got the gist. Brad started down the hill first and Herm followed close behind. The heard a few more of the loud clicking noises while they walked, but the volume decreased as they moved away from the clearing.

"So that's what you expected?" Brad asked over his shoulder as they walked.

"Yes," Herm said.

"You're going to get people out here to remove those vines?" Brad asked. "I can't believe those things are commonplace. They seem pretty extraordinary. I've never seen plants move or spontaneously bloom."

"We'll get a crew out here as soon as we can," Herm said.

"When do you think that will be?" Brad asked. They reached the bottom of the hill and started back up the small slope to the yard.

"I don't have any insight into the schedule," Herm said.

Brad opened the gate and let Herm through. He thought twice about shutting it—instead, he swung the big gate open and pinned it to a pole sticking up from the ground. He did the same to the other side of the big gate, so a truck could drive through.

"I'll leave these open," Brad said. "For the crew."

"Thank you," Herm said.

Herm headed back up to his car while Brad walked over to the gate on the road. He repeated the procedure, opening the front gate to give access to vehicles pulling in from the road. When Brad got back up to the house, Herm was talking to someone on his radio. Brad arrived in time to hear Herm signing off.

"Will do," Herm said.

"So, just the vines, a rock, and the clicking sound? Nothing else strange?" Herm asked.

"Yes," Brad said. "Isn't that enough?"

Herm smiled and said, "Yes, I think so. Do you mind if I sit here in my car for a few minutes? I've got some paperwork to fill out."

"No problem," Brad said. "Do you want to come inside and use a table?"

"No, thanks, I've got everything I need in here," Herm said. He patted the roof of the tan sedan.

Brad crossed the driveway and sat down on his front steps to take off his boots. The ladder leaning against the front of the garage drew his eye. Brad thought about what Herm asked him —"Nothing else strange?" Did a giant hole next to the back foundation of his garage qualify as something strange? If he'd taken Herm out the back door instead of down through the side yard, the man would have already seen the hole and probably asked about it. But, as it stood, Herm didn't know about the hole. Brad made a snap decision—he wouldn't tell anyone about the hole until he investigated it further himself. He welcomed the idea of a team of workers in orange jumpsuits who would come and rip out all the killer vines from the back pasture, but as for the hole, he wanted a chance to evaluate his new discovery.

Tucking his laces into his boots instead of retying them, Brad walked over to his ladder. He glanced at Herm, but Herm was sitting in the sedan with his head bent over some papers. Brad picked up the ladder and carried it back into the garage. He walked it around his truck and to the door to the mudroom. From his mudroom, he carried the ladder out to the back deck. He backtracked to take one more look at Herm, to make sure he was still busy with his papers, and then Brad hauled his short ladder over to the side of the hole.

He lay down on the grass next to the hole to drop the ladder in just the right spot. The bottom of the hole curved away, but the soil was loose enough that Brad could wedge the legs down and lean the ladder right against the edge of the hole. The top of the stepladder stopped well below the edge of the hole. Brad considered the hole and studied where it curved under the knee wall of the garage foundation. The soil looked damp, and the hole was as black as midnight where it passed under the concrete.

Brad pushed up to his feet and headed back into the house. From the garage, he fetched a coil of rope and his long flashlight. Through the open garage door, Brad peeked at Herm, who still sat in the sedan with the door open. The tall man still looked down; Brad figured he was still doing paperwork.

Back at the hole, Brad tied one end of the rope around one of the deck's posts. He dropped the coil into the hole. If the base of the ladder wouldn't anchor in the dirt, he wanted a reliable tether to the above-ground world. With his flashlight tested and his boots retied, Brad lowered himself over the lip and descended the ladder. Gripping the rope in one hand and ready to scramble back up the ladder, Brad squatted down and pointed his flashlight under the garage.

The hole looked like the den of some huge animal, and a big part of Brad's brain suggested he might be disturbing something dangerous. He could barely see into the hole. It was such a bright day, his flashlight was almost no help at all. Brad removed his hand from the ladder to shield his eyes from the sun. He shuffled closer.

After passing under the concrete footing, the hole dropped off. Brad shuffled even closer. He stopped again about halfway to the garage. Brad peered into the darkness, imagining some giant creature sleeping under there. He reached down to his feet, grabbed a handful of dirt and pebbles, and tossed the dirt into the black. Barely any sound came back to him—just the odds and ends of dirt hitting dirt in the dark.

He looked around for something more substantial and his eyes settled on the rope. Most of the rope was still bunched in a loose coil at his feet. Brad straightened the loops out a bit and then flung them into the dark.

"Okay," he said to the hole. "If there's anything under there, I'm coming in."

Brad crept forward and crouched right next to the foundation, where the hole went under his garage. He had about four feet between the bottom of the footing and the bottom of the hole. Brad braced his hand against the concrete and stuck his head far enough under so his eyes could adjust.

The cave under his garage slowly came into focus. Directly ahead of him, the rope fell away into another deeper hole. Above him, in spots, he saw the underside of the concrete which formed the floor of his garage. Something had excavated almost all the dirt supporting the garage.

"I've got to move my truck," Brad whispered.

Across the pit in front of him, on the opposite side of the cave, a ledge of dirt looked compacted compared to all the loose soil which made up the walls.

A noise behind him startled Brad and he spun on the balls of his feet, aiming the flashlight into the sun.

"It's a breeding hole, as far as we know," Herm said. The tall man, Herm, had somehow climbed down the ladder and snuck up on Brad. "You best come out of there—you don't want to know how far down that hole in front of you goes."

"Breeding hole for what, and how do you know anything about it?" Brad asked.

Herm held out his hand to Brad and said, "I'll feel more comfortable when you come away from there."

"Fine," Brad said. He didn't take Herm's hand, but pushed away from the concrete and stood next to Herm, looking him in the eye. "How about you tell me what's going on here."

"I will," Herm said. "Can we go inside?"

Brad stooped and picked up his rope, gathering it into a coil. He waved for Herm to go up the ladder and the tall man obliged. He looked like he barely even touched the steps. Herm's legs moved, but it almost looked like he floated up out of the hole. Brad followed, carrying the coil of rope. When he got near the top, Herm leaned down and took the coil from him so Brad could use both his hands to get back up on the grass. Lifting the ladder out of the hole took Brad a few grunting tries until Herm helped him.

Brad waved his guest up onto the deck and in through the back door.

"Brad," Herm said, "I'm afraid you've got some hard changes coming your way."

"How's that?" Brad asked. He led Herm down the hallway to the living room.

"I'm going to come clean with you now. It's going to feel at times like you're a prisoner in your own house, but you have to believe, it's for the greater good," Herm said.

Brad stopped and turned in the middle of the living room. He didn't sit down, he just stood in the middle of the room and looked at Herm, who stood near the arch to the hall.

"Can you back up and tell me exactly what the hell you're talking about?" Brad asked.

Herm gestured towards the window. Brad's mouth fell open as he regarded the driveway. Men wearing golf shirts, cargo shorts, and boat shoes, milled about carrying equipment and having discussions in tight circles. Several sedans parked side by side in the driveway behind a white panel van. Brad counted about a dozen men before he saw the Humvee pulling through the lower part of the yard and out through the back gate.

Brad rushed to the window to get a better view.

"What the fuck?" he whispered to himself.

Towards the front of the house he saw a bucket truck from the cable company working on the wires at the telephone pole.

"We have to deal with the situation out back," Herm said, startling Brad. He had crept to within arm's length while Brad looked out the window. The tall man could sneak up on a chipmunk.

"What exactly is the situation out back? Are you really from the USDA?" Brad asked.

"No, not the USDA," Herm said. "I work for the government. Truth is, we're not exactly sure what's going on with the vines."

"I thought so," Brad said. "From Georgia? Not likely."

"You're right," Herm said. "Why don't you have a seat and I'll explain." He gestured towards the couch.

"I think I have some phone calls to make first, if you don't mind," Brad said. He pulled his phone from his back pocket. The phone read full-strength signal—unusual for his living room—and where the carrier normally displayed, instead of "AT&T," the display read "NOS."

Brad called Stavros.

"Hello?" asked a voice.

Brad looked at his phone—he dialed correctly, but it wasn't Stavros he was talking to.

"May I speak with Stavros please?" Brad asked.

"I'm sorry sir, I've been instructed to hold your calls until you speak with Mr. Guntner," the voice said.

"Gunther," Brad said. He looked at Herm. "He told me his name was Gunther."

"That's what I said, sir. Gunther," the voice said.

"Sure," Brad said. He ended the call. "Okay," Brad said, throwing up his hands and flopping down to the couch, "You've got my car blocked in, my phone redirected, and I'm guessing you won't let me just walk away, so you might as well talk."

"I know we're stepping on your liberties here, Brad," Herm said.

"You can call me Mr. Jenkins," Brad said.

"Yes, Mr. Jenkins," Herm said. Herm's shoulders sagged, and the corners of his eyes betrayed his exhaustion again. "We're stepping on your liberties because we need to get control of this situation before it causes a panic. Most people would be a little disconcerted to learn that you've got some unknown species in your little portion of the Maine woods."

"You can't just cover up something like this," Brad said. "Wait a minute, did you guys cause the fire at the Cartonio place? Was it part of your cover-up?"

"No, sir, no," Herm said. "This isn't some giant conspiracy going on here. If you could just stow the tinfoil hat for a minute, I'll explain. We've found these same plants and animals other places, but nowhere near any population until yours. And this isn't a cover-up, we're just keeping a lid on the publicity until we have a better understanding of what we're dealing with, and how to proceed."

After a very quick rap on the door, a man walked in. He looked older and even more tired than Herm. He wore khakis, a Hawaiian shirt, and a baseball cap. "Sorry about the intrusion here, Mr. Jenkins. You copacetic for cocktail hour, Herman?" the man asked.

"Blue skies, Ollie," Herm said.

"Take care, Mr. Jenkins," the man said. He ducked out through the door, closing it softly.

"Your superior?" Brad asked.

"I'm sorry?" asked Herm.

"I'm just working on this theory," Brad said. "Looking at those guys in the driveway, it seems like the more covered up you guys are, the higher the rank. You've got pants and a golf shirt. That guy is wearing a Hawaiian shirt and a cap—which makes him your boss, or at least higher rank. The guys with the cargo shorts must be pretty low on the totem pole, and the one hanging on the back of the Humvee was just wearing a tank top and soccer shorts, is that the lowest rank?"

"You're pretty observant, and you're correct," Herm said. "And I was just about to try to establish rapport by revealing something I shouldn't. Guess I don't need to now?"

"You'd have to go a long way to establish rapport at this point," Brad said.

"Let me try," Herm said. "I'll just be as straightforward as I can. We're intercepting your phone and we run a delay on everything you say. If you try to reveal anything, we drop your call or fuzz it out. We've got a similar system hooked up to your internet connection. My guys say you work from home, programming, right? You can keep doing that, but remember, all your communication will be gated through us. That means documents, code check-ins, emails, everything."

"I won't be able to work," Brad said. "All my communication with the office has to be through secured channels. You're either flying blind or you have to block it completely."

Herm smiled and nodded.

"The guys have tricks even I don't understand, Mr. Jenkins," Herm said. "Just continue to live your life as normal, don't try to alert anyone, and everything will go smoothly. Before you know it, we'll be out of your hair. We'll do your shopping, your errands, and you even get a stipend for the inconvenience."

"My friends and family are going to suspect something's up if I don't turn up," Brad said.

"Our research guys put together a plan before I showed up here, Brad. I don't think we have much to worry about," Herm said. "I'm going to leave you to mull things over for a bit. I'll be back later to answer any questions."

Herm stood and held out his hand for Brad to shake. Brad just stared at the tall man and kept his place on the couch. Herm shrugged and showed himself out.

## CHAPTER 5: ON THE WATER (FALL)

SARAH AND ROBBY STOOD side by side on the bridge of the borrowed boat, looking at the coast. The snow stopped falling, but the skies still looked heavy, like there was more snow to come. That wasn't what drew their eyes.

Robby killed the engine and they bobbed in the swells, about three quarters of a mile from the coast.

"South?" Robby asked.

His mom didn't take her eyes from the horizon as she answered, "I think we'd better."

They both stared at the little port town on the coast. Robby counted seven funnel-clouds darting and dancing over the town. They touched down one at a time, ripping apart buildings and tearing up leafless trees. All seven spun in a slow circle, as if connected by invisible spokes to some center point. Each tornado picked up a load of material and carried it around until it hovered over the ocean. When the cloud brought its load over the water it dispersed a bit and dropped the wreckage into the surf.

Sarah looked down and saw a red door float by. It had brass numbers—two-one-seven—mounted above a tarnished knocker.

Robby put the engine in reverse, not wanting to get any closer to the destruction. He kept his eyes locked on the church steeple. It gleamed whiter than the rest of the buildings, and the tornados seemed to move around it without ever touching it. Almost like it was responding to his thought, the next tornado to come around dropped directly on the church, lifting and crushing the steeple into meaningless debris.

"Robby," Sarah said. "Robby! You're headed for the breakwater, turn this thing around."

"Yeah," Robby said. He fumbled with the throttle and spun the wheel. He'd made it almost thirty minutes without vomiting, but the sudden change in direction and speed were too much. Sarah anticipated and handed him a fresh trash bag. For all his retching, only strings of yellow film came out. Robby spat into the bag and then pushed the engine a bit harder. They needed to backtrack to the west far enough to get around the point before they could head south.

Robby settled his gaze on the lighthouse and tried to adjust to the new swells they were hitting from their new course. Inside the breakwater, the waves calmed quite a bit, but now they were headed back out to the big stuff. Robby wiped his mouth on his jacket sleeve and handed the bag towards his mom, figuring he was done for a while. In fact, he figured, he might be done with food for a while too, since it looked like they had to stay on the boat.

Sarah didn't take the bag.

Robby shook it and said, "Mom? I think I'm done." He heard the door—the one that led to the stern of the boat—close behind him. Robby dropped the bag, forgot about nausea, and spun around. Sarah was looking off to the horizon, back towards the shore, like she couldn't tear her eyes from the destruction of the once pretty port town.

"MOM!" Robby screamed, throwing open the door.

She didn't look around. The boat chugged on, still heading roughly west. Robby sprinted towards his mom. She was only a few steps away, but with the bobbing motion of the deck he felt like he was running through molasses. She got to the stern before he reached her, and he saw his mother put a foot up on the taffrail and step up.

She didn't jump in, or even complete her climb. Robby's mom just got plucked from the back of the boat into nothing. She jerked upwards and then simply disappeared. Robby skidded to a stop and pumped his legs furiously backward, like he could kick away what he'd just seen. The boat bobbed and the deck came up to meet Robby's feet. He slammed himself backwards into the cabin door, which swung shut.

Robby pawed at the handle, threw open the door, and pulled it shut behind him. He stared through the window at the space where his mom had stepped up into nothing. He scanned the sky for any sign of her. The engine rumbled on while Robby tried to process what he'd seen. When Paulie and his dad were pulled up and away, he figured they must have gone somewhere, not just vanished. His mom had been mid-stride, then she'd been jerked upwards by an unseen force, then poof, gone. Robby pushed back from the window and backed into the wheel. He tore his eyes from the stern and looked around to the instruments.

The boat drifted off-course a bit. Robby corrected it, looked at the GPS, and then pegged the throttle. He swallowed hard, and willed himself to not throw up again. Every few seconds he took his eyes off the horizon and looked down to fiddle with the chart. He wanted to be sure he had a clear shot—the coast of Maine has so many islands and channels even a local could get turned around, and Robby barely ever traveled by boat, let alone navigated.

He only glanced back twice to check the progress of the tornados. Part of him wished he'd somehow see his mom back there, and another part feared she'd be there, hovering just over the transom, beckoning for him to join her. He tried to work the problem; tried to figure out what had motivated her to leave the cabin and step up to be taken.

✪ ✪ ✪ ✪ ✪

"Mom?" Robby called out into the whiteness. All he could see was white. He woke up on the deck of the boat, shivering in the cold, damp air and surrounded by dull, thick white on all sides. Robby hugged his arms around himself and his jacket crackled with ice.

"Mom?" he yelled again. "I'm here. Where are you?"

Robby stopped breathing and just listened. He couldn't hear

anything except the lapping of the ocean against the side of the boat. Logic started to return to his sleepy brain. When he woke up to the white fog, he thought he'd finally been taken. He thought he'd been plucked into the sky. Now, as he considered the rocking of the boat and the sound of the ocean, he realized he was still on Earth and his mom, dad, and all his friends were gone.

He dropped to his hands and knees and crawled until he found the side of the boat. From there, he guessed the direction and found himself back at the cabin of Carl Deemer's boat. He let himself in. All the instruments were dark; nothing on the boat worked at all. He couldn't get the engine started or even see anything out the windows except the white fog.

The motion of the boat finally overcame Robby and he started to retch again. His back arched and it felt like his esophagus was collapsing in on itself, trying to vomit up stomach contents that weren't there. Robby shook and gagged and collapsed to the floor of the cabin.

His gags turned to sobs. Robby balled up his gloved hands and cried into them. He cried for his mom and dad, and Jim, who always stuck by Robby. Jim even changed schools when Robby did, just so they could still eat lunch together everyday. Robby cried for Brandon, and Ms. Norton. He even cried for Paulie, who'd been plucked from the Earth while still holding on to Robby's jacket. If his dad hadn't held on so well, Robby would have sailed right off with Paulie and he never would have needed to deal with everything all by himself.

Robby hugged his knees to his chest and curled up into a ball.

Robby cried for the puppy he was supposed to get next summer when Bill Carver would finally breed his pretty black lab again. He was going to name the puppy Buster and teach him how to do all kinds of tricks. The tears and snot turned cold on his sleeves and Robby pulled his hood further down over his head.

The boat drifted, the waves lapped at the hull, and Robby cried.

Robby hitched in shallow breaths into his heavy lungs and eventually he dozed.

The second time Robby woke up on the boat it was from

hunger. He glanced up at the windows—everything was still white outside the cabin—and slid over to the backpack his mom packed with leftovers. He took off his gloves to peel apart a turkey sandwich. He thought he could handle the mayo-smeared bread, but the turkey seemed too daunting. His stomach clenched and twisted around the bread, so he chased it with water until it settled down. Both the bread and the water were ice-cold. They felt good going down—chilling, but pleasantly shocking.

He stood up slowly, slightly swaying on his feet, and steadied himself on the console. A garbage bag with spit and vomit sat on the floor a few feet away. Robby looked out the window and waited for his nausea to return. He knew it was just a matter of time—the boat still swayed and bobbed, and he couldn't lock his eyes on the horizon. He figured his meal of bread and water wouldn't stay down long.

The fog looked like it might be thinning. He wasn't sure until he looked out the back windows. He could now see the stern of the boat, whereas before he could barely make out the deck. Back at the console, all the instruments still sat dead. He flicked switches and turned dials, but nothing responded. The only thing moving was an old gimbaled compass. It rocked gently with the movement of the boat, and the needle spun like the second hand of a clock.

The fog brought a heavy cold—the moisture seemed to penetrate his clothes and go right to his bones. When Robby was a little kid, his parents took him down to Washington DC in January. The cold down there felt like this. Even though the temperatures in Maine dipped well below zero, it was a surface cold. All you needed to do was brush off your clothes and stand next to a fire for a minute, and you could warm back up. Cold with humidity felt much worse. Now, with the engine dead and the meager heater dead with it, the cabin felt like a cold, clammy tomb.

Robby let himself out onto the deck. It was even colder outside, but moving around felt good. Robby put his gloves back on and carefully made his way around the boat. He looked for any way to propel the boat—an oar, or even a long plank—but he realized he didn't even have a way to figure out which way was west.

At the side of the cabin, Robby found a handle and a bar mounted as a handhold. He grabbed it with both hands and stepped gingerly up onto the rail of the boat, where the lip was covered in a no-skid surface so you could climb to the bow. He worked his way, keeping his belly pressed tight to the outside of the cabin. The gentle swaying of the boat seemed amplified once he was clinging to the side. On the bow he found a gaff—a long hook with a stick—and a square hatch which led to the ship's hold.

He sat down on the hatch and looked out into the fog. He shoved up his sleeve. His watch stopped at twelve twenty-one. The date said it was still the twenty-fifth. Robby wasn't certain how long he'd spent asleep before he woke up in the fog. In fact, he didn't even know why he had fallen asleep in the first place.

Right after his mom had disappeared, Robby had moved to what he felt was a safe distance off the coast. He held the boat about two miles west of shore and navigated south and west. The last thing he remembered before the fog was deciding to swing the boat wide around a bunch of islands which showed up on the GPS. He didn't know if the disappearances of his friends and family were related to proximity to land, but he hadn't seen anyone disappear in the open water, so he figured he would test that theory.

Now, adrift in the fog, he didn't know if he was out to sea or a hundred yards from the rocky coast.

He took a mental inventory of his supplies. His mom packed enough food to last several people a couple of days. Now he was alone and he could probably ration it out to more than a week if he needed to. Of course, he'd be lucky to keep anything down, but at least his hasty meal of bread and water was still sitting pretty well.

On his way around the other side of the cabin, Robby's glove slipped on the bar and his foot skidded off the rail. He dangled for a precarious second before getting his footing back. He bit down on his glove and tore it from his hand. The bar was almost painfully cold to touch, but he figured it was warmer than the water below.

Back in the cabin, he sat on the bench and tried a piece of the turkey from the dismantled sandwich. It tasted good, and felt fine going down. It seemed like as long as he just let himself sway with the boat and didn't try to fight it, he felt okay.

A burst of static exploded from the radio and Robby spit a piece of turkey on the floor.

He jumped up and ran over to the controls. He turned down the volume and swept up and down through the radio frequencies. He found nothing but static.

"I must have left it on when I was screwing with stuff?" he mumbled. "Oh!" he said.

He tried the engine. It cranked slow at first, then the starter seemed to warm up and the engine sputtered and coughed to life. Robby flipped on the navigation system and the heat while the engine idle evened out.

The GPS display flashed a message reading "Acquiring Satellites," for several minutes and then settled down to a warning —"No Satellites Found. Check Antenna."

Robby sighed. He turned on the electronic compass and the depth finder. The instruments declared the depth of the ocean beneath him was thirty-one meters. The compass numbers seemed to change randomly, never settling down to one figure. On the gimbaled compass, the old manual standby, the needle swung back and forth between forty and two-eighty.

Robby cranked the wheel to the right and gave the throttle a little nudge. The compass continued to fluctuate, but the average heading it reported moved counter-clockwise around the dial. Robby kept spinning the boat until the compass needle pointed towards the stern of the boat most of the time and then he tried to straighten it out. It turned out to be difficult to find "straight." He adjusted the wheel for several minutes until he got the compass needle where he wanted it.

Now that he thought he was pointed roughly south, Robby turned his attention to the depth gauge. It climbed to the upper thirties. Robby steered the boat a little to the east and kept an eye on the depth, hoping to not get too close to shore unexpectedly.

Very slowly, the fog thinned. First, he could clearly see the bow, and then he caught a glimpse of the ocean in front of the boat. The compass began to even out as well. Robby dug through a pouch mounted behind him and found a chart. He didn't have any way of knowing where he was on the map. Even the depth didn't give him a clue—the depth soundings showed he could be twenty yards or two miles out to sea.

Robby smiled when the GPS flashed back to "Acquiring Satellites." He held his breath until the device found the signals it needed to show him a map. The arrow showed the boat moving roughly south, about a mile east of a little island, still off the coast of Maine. He increased the speed a little and steered a little to the right—starboard, he corrected himself—so he could head in closer to shore. Even though his nausea passed, Robby didn't want to get stuck out on the boat if the fog happened to come back. He figured his best bet was to head for shore.

He didn't reach the shore before he spotted more fog rolling in from the north. The fog spilled over the snow-covered trees that lined the coast and then rolled out over the water in his direction. Robby turned the boat south and pointed it to the left of a small peninsula. The map showed a small town on the far side of the peninsula. Robby made up his mind to land there.

When he rounded the peninsula, Robby jerked the wheel to the left. The same dancing tornados had landed on this town too—tearing up buildings and dropping debris into the ocean. Robby pressed his face to the glass to see the destruction while the boat carried him safely away. It looked like these tornados had just started their work. He watched as the windows exploded out from a house about halfway up the hill. The shingles peeled away in patches before the building was obscured by the dark funnel cloud.

At the shore, a couple of piers had slips for medium-sized boats. They bobbed in the turbulence created by the trash dropped in the water by the tornados. Robby squinted at a shape on the pier. He reached down and dug through the pocket mounted to the wall, coming up with binoculars. It was tough to get them focused, and his stomach did a low, sick flop, but he managed to train the binoculars on the shape on the pier.

He reached down and killed the throttle, dropping the engine back to idle. The shape on the pier was a person—an adult—

waving his or her arms. Robby turned the wheel and eased the throttle forward, bringing the boat around to face the town. The water between him and the pier was dotted with floating debris. Robby clenched his teeth and increased the throttle until the engine throbbed and the bow cut through the waves.

Swells rolled out from the shore. One of the tornados dropped a big load of bricks and rocks and the splash obscured Robby's view of the person on the pier. He stared, unblinking, until he could see the person again. They backed up a little, away from the end of pier, and Robby could see why—something dropped on the end of the dock and knocked away a giant section.

A flurry of papers rained down, blown out by the wind, and landed on the boat. One document stuck to the windshield and Robby ducked to the right to see. A police car dropped into the ocean. The nose sank first, and the trunk stuck up out of the water like a big blue tombstone before it slipped out of site. Off to the right, a red pickup truck landed with a giant splash.

Back at the shore, the person still waved both arms overhead. It looked like a man, Robby decided.

"Why don't you get out of there?" Robby whispered.

A giant log floated directly in Robby's path. He pulled back on the throttle and maneuvered around it. He was immediately blocked by a section of clapboarded wall. Robby put the boat in neutral and banged his way through the door to the deck. He climbed the ladder which ran up the back of the cabin. With a little elevation, he saw the extent of the problem. The ocean between him and the man on the shore was becoming a minefield of debris, and every second the tornados dropped off more pollution to block his course.

Robby climbed down and went back in the cabin. He couldn't even see the man anymore, the air was thick with dust, and everything on the shore was a fuzzy blur. He tried to use the binoculars, but couldn't find anything to focus on.

Robby stood there, trying to spot the man, while junk floated out to him and started to surround the boat. When another car splashed down a few dozen yards from the boat, he jumped and nearly screamed. He frowned and spun the wheel to the right. He brought the boat around so his back was to the pier before he gunned the throttle. The boat ground through the chop and the waves at its stern seemed to help push the boat along. Robby never looked back to try to spot the man again.

Down the coast he saw two more towns being dismantled; he gave them a wide berth. Robby lost track of time. He just steered the boat to the left of the next point or the next island and checked the charts to make sure he was staying out of shallow water. Eventually, the GPS told him he was entering Casco Bay, and then across the bay, the entrance to the city of Portland. Robby veered the boat to the left, dreading the destruction he would see to the small city.

Eventually, his curiosity won out and he let the wheel drift to the right a bit. He passed within a mile of the islands which protected the port, and saw glimpses of the city skyline. He expected destruction, but he couldn't spot any, even with the binoculars.

The fuel gauge showed a little less than half a tank. Robby decided to keep heading south.

✪ ✪ ✪ ✪ ✪

Even from out on the water, Robby could see the snow accumulations south of Portland didn't nearly measure up. Some places looked like they'd only received a dusting, although the grey sky seemed to promise more was on its way. Robby spotted a private dock that looked like it had deepwater access, and he headed to shore.

His landing was tentative, but reasonable. He was so afraid of bringing the boat in too quickly, it took him forever to sidle the boat up to the dock. He reversed several times to account for lateral drift, but eventually he got the boat alongside the floating dock and jumped out with the stern rope. He tied it up the best he could and looked to the shore.

There was no beach here—the land came down to the water's edge and then dropped off suddenly. A wooden staircase, built into the side of the hill, gave access to property above. Robby filled a backpack with some food, flashlight, and basic supplies and climbed up the stairs. He gripped the railing to make it up the stairs. They were fine—not slippery, and not too steep—but Robby's balance was tweaked from the long boat trip. He constantly felt like he was falling to the left, and his rubbery legs wanted to compensate.

At the top, he found a well-groomed lawn, still greenish, under about a half-inch of snow. A flagstone path led past a flagpole, between gardens, and up to the back of a big building. The side facing him was virtually all glass, affording excellent views of the ocean.

Robby walked up the path, crunching the snow and scanning back and forth for signs of life.

In the distance he could hear an engine, humming away at a steady pace. He approached the lower door of the building. The windows looked in on a big empty room. Stacks of chairs lined the far wall, a big fireplace and hearth took up most of the left wall, and on the right, overhead fixtures lit up a long bar. To Robby, it looked like a fancy version of the Lion's Club recreation hall. He reached towards the door and then stopped his hand.

The pulsing engine in the distance troubled him. He figured it was probably just a generator—that would account for the lights over the bar—but would it automatically come on? On the island the power had been out for a while; should this generator still be running? Robby turned from the door and circled the building in the direction of the engine sound. He found the unit about halfway up a steep slope. It didn't say "Generator," but it had big cables leading inside and was plumbed to two big propane tanks up near the corner of the building. Robby continued around the perimeter until he found himself at the front of the building.

A narrow driveway led to the door from a parking lot a little ways off, down in the woods. He counted fourteen cars parked down there. No tire tracks disturbed the thin layer of the snow and he could see dark patches beneath the vehicles—they had been parked there since before the snow.

A sign near the glass double-doors read "Towering Pines Conference & Renewal Center." Robby approached and looked through the glass to a small lobby. He knocked three times on the door. A green lamp lit up a desk, but nobody was sitting at the office chair. He tugged on the metal handle with his gloved hand. The door swung open and Robby stepped inside.

The air inside felt pleasantly warm, but it smelled wrong. It smelled like the cabinet where his mom kept her vitamins—a slight edge of old urine and sweat. Robby wrinkled his nose and let the door swing shut behind him. He was looking for keys, if he could get them. His dad already taught him to drive the island truck they shared with another family, so he would prefer to find truck keys, but he would take whatever he could get. He wanted to head south, to find out for sure if the disappearances were indeed local. The lack of snow this far south bolstered his confidence in the idea that he could find help somewhere farther south.

Robby crossed the oriental carpet of the lobby and pushed through the door on his right. He found himself in a hall leading to the back part of the building. Some light came through the glass doors behind him and the window in the door at the far end of the hall, but the emergency lights in the ceiling—presumably lit by the generator—drove the shadows from the middle of the hall. On his right, a door led to an empty conference room. On the left wall, he found doors to the bathrooms.

When he got to the men's room, his body responded as if on cue. Robby stayed in the hall and swung the door in. Compared to the hallway, the minimal emergency lighting barely lit up the bathroom. Robby debated; he stood in the hall and peered into the cave-like bathroom. It looked clean, had one urinal and three stalls, and he suddenly really needed to go. He stepped in and let the door swing shut behind him. The smell crept up on him as the darkness folded around him. The room smelled worse than the hall. Robby dropped his backpack to the floor and walked to the nearest stall.

He changed his mind and went back for the pack. He hung it from the hook on the back of the stall door and locked himself in. He kept his jacket on, but pulled off the gloves and stuffed them in his pockets.

Robby tried to go quick, but his bowels became shy in the

gloomy bathroom. He pulled paper from the roll and folded it around his hand. He would take a bunch for his backpack, in case he needed it later. Robby sighed—almost ready to give up—when things finally started moving. His eyes adjusted to the dark and he could make out more detail in the tiles on the floor. They made a pattern of grey and black rectangles. His eyes rearranged them into different shapes.

Robby's gaze drifted to the side, where a black line interrupted the pattern on the tiles. He kept his eyes locked on the line—he couldn't quite make it out in the shadows—while he reached up to his backpack. He pulled out the flashlight and turned it on against his palm, so it wouldn't blind him. In the red glow the light made through his hand, Robby could see the line was a shoelace in the next stall. He leaned forward and saw the edge of a shoe. His body pulled away, but he forced himself to lean forward. A little higher up the shoe he saw four curled fingers and thumb.

He shut off the flashlight and sucked in a shocked breath. The smell suddenly seemed more intense. Robby hastily cleaned himself up and reflexively flushed the toilet. He cringed from the sound and pressed himself against the opposite wall of the stall, sure the hand would shoot out and grab for his ankle. Robby unlocked the stall door and it swung gently inward with the weight of the backpack.

While the water still filled the bowl, Robby placed one foot and then the other up on the toilet seat. He leaned forward with the flashlight and put his hands against the stall with the shoe and hand. The hand didn't move at all when the light hit it. Based on the smell, and that he could hear his own breathing, but nothing from the neighboring stall, Robby figured he was sharing the bathroom with a corpse. He needed to be sure.

He turned on the flashlight again—full strength this time—and pointed it over the top of the stall. He waited a second and listened. When he didn't hear anything, he poked his head over the top of the stall.

The man on the toilet was slumped forward. His torso rested against his legs. His head turned to the side, like he was trying to listen closely to a secret his knee was telling him. The man's tongue stuck out and a splash of blood soaked into his tan pants. The man's chin was pulled back, like he had gagged on his last breath.

What shocked Robby most about this corpse—the only corpse he'd seen other than at his grandmother's wake—was the eyes. The man's eyes had burst, leaving dark red holes. Robby could see one clearly, and just the outline of the other. A splatter pattern on the stall wall suggested his eyes had exploded with some force.

Robby started to feel seasick again. He lowered himself to the floor, still careful to stay pressed to the opposite wall, and grabbed his backpack before shuffling sideways out of the stall. He backed to the door and let himself out of the bathroom. He turned off the flashlight and backed down the hall towards the rear of the building. Something inside him insisted the door would swing open at any second and the eyeless man would stagger down the hall after him. Robby jumped when he backed into the door.

He propped himself up against the door until he got his breathing under control. He flipped the flashlight around, so he could use it as a weapon if he needed to, and pushed his way to the back room of the building.

Light filled every corner of this room from the windows along the back wall. Easy chairs and couches divided up the room into five seating areas, each with a round coffee table in the center. Nearly every seat held a well-dressed corpse. Robby took a deep breath of fetid air and let it out slowly. He scanned back and forth, looking for any movement. They all shared the same symptoms—gagging mouth, lolling tongue, and exploded eyes. For some, eye juice and blood dripped down their cheeks. Others had turned to one side or the other, allowing their eyeballs to leave streaks down the back of a leather couch, or down the front of a button-down shirt.

A distant rumbling broke the silence. Warm air came from a vent to Robby's right.

He counted thirty-eight bodies. With the corpse in the toilet, that meant almost three times more people than cars in the parking lot. Either a lot of people came together, were dropped off, or he had missed a bunch more cars. He didn't think many of the people here had walked—they looked like they were dressed too well to have walked.

Robby wanted keys. He wanted keys to a truck, if he could get them. He repeated that to himself in his head, trying to get up the courage to frisk the corpses.

"I'm looking for keys to a truck. Who here would drive a truck?" he asked himself inside his head.

It doesn't have to be a truck, he reminded himself. Any car would do, it's just he was accustomed to a truck, and thought somehow the seats were up higher and would be more familiar. He tried to remember if he had even seen a truck outside, but couldn't recall. That wasn't like him. Usually anything he saw or heard was pretty much at his disposal. This was different—his mind was clouded by the stress of being in this room of thirty-eight exploded-eye corpses. Surely that was enough to break the concentration of anyone.

He moved his lips as he repeated the thought. "I'm looking for keys to a truck. Who here would drive a truck?"

Robby kept his back to the wall and side-stepped closer to the back of the couch in front of him, where a bald man's head rested on the back. From the shower of blood and slime on the man's lap, Robby figured he had been looking upward when his eyes exploded. Robby stood behind the couch and extended his hand to touch a finger to the dead man's head. He poked him again, a little harder. The man's neck was stiff and he barely moved at Robby's touch. Robby slapped at the head. He jumped back at the sound. Nothing else in the room moved.

Robby took a deep breath and let it out slowly. He reached forward with a shaky hand and pressed his fingers to the left side of the man's neck, where his jugular should be. Nothing—cold skin, no pulse. He braced himself to search the man and then stopped. He wondered—what if they used a valet? This looked like a fancy crowd; maybe someone parked the cars and the keys were hanging on a board somewhere in the lobby? He almost walked away to go search someplace that didn't contain a bunch of corpses, but then he saw the irregular lump in the man's slacks, just where his left pocket would be. Robby kept his eye's on the corpse's face as he reached down and touched the slacks. He felt angular metal under the fabric. Perhaps he would find keys elsewhere, perhaps not, but now he knew he would find keys here.

With one more glance around the room, Robby leaned over the back of the couch and drove his hand down into the pants pocket. He turned away from the face of the corpse—just inches away from his own face. He leaned farther than he expected, but he managed to hook his fingers through a key ring and pull them back. The keychain held car keys, house keys, and a clicker to unlock the doors from a distance. Robby nodded and stuffed the keys into his own pocket. Some of the eyeball-juice rubbed off on his sleeve.

Robby skipped the woman next to the bald guy and moved on to the next man. After groping for an eternity, Robby found the next man's keys in his jacket pocket. He wanted several sets in case he got the key ring of a carpooler. Robby worked the edges of the room, not wanting to be surrounded by the corpses. With seven sets of keys in his pockets, Robby circled around the perimeter of the room to get back to the door to the hall.

He almost made it around before he realized he was being watched. The man sitting in the easy chair at the corner sat perfectly still with his hands on the armrests and his legs casually crossed. One of his eyes was a gory mess, splattered on the inside of his glasses and stringing cord and gel down the man's cheek, but the other eye stared directly at Robby.

Robby could circle around the length of the room the other way, or go past the one-eyed man.

The man wore charcoal grey slacks and a tweed jacket, with patches at the elbows. Robby broke the stare and looked down at the man's chest. He couldn't detect any rise and fall, but it would be hard to tell at this distance. Robby took a step closer, now about three paces from one-eye.

Robby squinted at the man's glasses. Something looked weird. Something aside from the exploded eye on one side and piercing blue eye on the other. He took another half-step closer. When he realized the discrepancy, a little half-smile flashed across Robby's face and disappeared. The glasses looked funny because the lens on the exploded side was a bifocal, and the other one wasn't.

"Glass eye," Robby whispered. He immediately looked around to see if any of the corpses stirred at the sound of his voice. Glass eye or not, Robby pressed his back to the windows and inched along the wall as he passed the man. The eye didn't follow him.

Robby passed by a big open staircase on his way back to the hall. He'd already seen the lower floor through the windows downstairs, and he knew nobody was down there. He preferred that exit strategy as opposed to having to go down the dark hallway with the bathroom door. He still pictured a toilet-corpse crawling after him.

Robby took one last look at the room full of dead people and jogged down the stairs to the big meeting room. It was cooler down here. He rounded the bar and made his way quickly to the back door. The footprints in the snow leading up to, and away from, the door gave him pause until he realized they were his own. Robby put on his gloves and pushed his way outside, glad to be away from the smell of decay.

He scaled the hill quickly, passed the humming generator, and jogged down the driveway to the parking lot. The first set of keys, General Motors, had a remote control fob. He pressed it several times, spinning to look at each car as he hit the unlock button, but nothing responded. The next set he pulled—Toyota—didn't have a remote control, and he didn't see a Toyota parked there.

He got lucky on the third set. A big SUV parked several spaces away from the other cars chirped when he pressed the button. The lights flashed and then stayed on.

"Sweet," Robby said to himself.

He tried the other sets as well, and found he also held the keys to two sedans. The SUV was his first choice. He peeked through the tinted windows and found it empty. He opened the door and inserted the key to discover a nearly full gas tank. He might get more range out of one of the smaller cars, but then again the SUV probably contained a much bigger tank to compensate for the lower fuel economy. Robby weighed his options briefly and then settled on the SUV. He tossed his backpack inside, started it up, and locked the doors. A dusting of snow covered the windshield, but the wipers took care of it. Before he pulled the seat belt across, he took a moment to lean back between the seats just to verify he was alone in the SUV. Ever since old one-eye, Robby felt like he was being watched. He even pushed far enough back to see over the rear row into the back storage area.

The snow crunched under the SUV's tires as Robby backed it up slowly out of its spot. He hesitated at the thought of leaving Carl Deemer's boat tied up to the dock. The floating dock would rise and fall with the tide, but would the water be deep enough? He acknowledged the feeling and tried to let it go, as easily as his dad would have.

Robby moved the seat up until he felt comfortable behind the wheel. When he got out to the main road he realized he didn't really know where he should go. On the water heading south and west was easy; on the roads he needed a route to follow. He found a Maine atlas in the pocket behind the passenger's seat, but without a flashing "you are here" dot, like the one on the GPS in the boat, it was of no use to him. He studied the map briefly to try to guess where he was. He was anxious to get moving.

Depending on how far south of Portland he'd gone in the boat, he figured he should either hit Route 77 or Route 9 if he headed west. He adjusted the rearview mirror and saw the glowing green "N" in the corner. At least with a compass he would know which way to turn. Robby took a left.

The roads were mostly empty. When he did see another car, it was usually off to the side of the road in a ditch or crashed into a tree. He slowed down the first few times and then sped back up when he saw eyeball splatter on the inside of the windshield and a slumped-over form behind the wheel. He navigated down narrow streets, lined with big houses and big yards.

Robby felt better when he reached the road sign marking the next road as Route 77. He still wasn't exactly sure where he was, but if he followed that road he would be able to find his way to the highway. From there he could decide on his course.

A bead of sweat formed on Robby's forehead. He realized the heat was up all the way. He pulled over and took off his jacket, dropping it on the seat over his backpack. Robby relaxed his grip on the steering wheel a little and leaned back against the seat.

Some of the tension dropped from his shoulders. One of the displays on the dash told him he could drive another three-hundred miles before needing to fill up.

Robby slowed again when he saw the supermarket. On the island, their grocery store was small and old. Robby had only been in a real supermarket a few times, and this one was bigger than any he'd seen. The lot was empty save for a few cars. The same light dusting of snow showed no footprints or tire tracks, so he pulled in and stopped right near the door. Only dim lights were on inside.

Robby put the SUV in park and detached the remote for the door locks so he could take it with him, but still leave the vehicle running. He tested it—unlock, lock, unlock, lock—before shoving it in his pocket and grabbing his jacket and backpack.

He peered through every window and studied each mirror before jumping out of the SUV. It idled quietly as he locked the doors and walked towards the doors of the supermarket. The snow squeaked and crunched under his boots.

The automatic doors didn't open, and he couldn't push them open. The sign read, "Closed—Thanksgiving Day." He tried a number of things—his flashlight, his boot, the standing ashtray by the bench—before he found a brick behind the wheel of the last shopping cart. With the brick, he smashed the lower pane of the glass door. It made a terrible racket, and Robby looked around nervously for the better part of minute before convincing himself his vandalism hadn't summoned the authorities—whatever authorities might remain. He ducked through the door and found himself in the produce department. He grabbed a basket and nearly sprinted through the store.

He found one body, back near the meat section. The woman wore a blue short-sleeve shirt tucked into tan cargo shorts. She was face-down near a scattered pile of cereal boxes and a hand cart with more inventory. Her hair was pooled around her head, but Robby could see a little blood seeping out around the edges. He gave the corpse a wide berth and trotted down the next aisle to grab crackers and cookies. He tried to fill his basket with filling, non-perishable staples. His hunger drove him towards stuff his mom would call junk. He didn't want to get anything which required cooking.

The basket was too heavy for one arm by the time Robby made his way to the door. He set it down on the floor and jogged back to the second aisle for a can opener. Robby tucked the tool into his backpack and ran for the basket. A shadow passed by the front window of the store and Robby froze between the cash registers.

He panted as he squatted, waiting to see if something would pass by the windows again. The basket scraped on the tiles as he pushed it ahead of him so he could get a better view. When he heard a "click," from the back of the store, he whipped around, saw nothing, and then spun forward again.

"Small stores only, next time," he whispered to himself through clenched teeth.

With the basket clutched to his chest, Robby ran in a low crouch towards the broken door. The broken glass scattered on the mat made for terrible footing as Robby tried to pass the basket through the lower half of the door. When he'd negotiated the basket and his own body through the door, he stopped again. The SUV still sat there, idling. He leaned down and looked under the vehicle—he couldn't see anything on either side. Unless someone was standing directly on the other side of the tire, he was alone.

Robby clicked the remote twice. The lights flashed and he heard the clunk of the locks. He hauled the basket to the rear passenger's door and tossed it on the seat. After slamming the door shut and sprinting halfway around the back of the SUV, Robby's foot slipped on the thin layer of snow. He hit the parking lot with his right elbow and hip. A tingle shot all the way up to his shoulder. He scrambled to the driver's door and lurched inside, locking the doors and glancing at the back seat simultaneously.

Robby stabbed at the accelerator as he put the SUV into gear and it bucked forward. A mile later, he finally slowed down and pulled into a big open parking lot, where he could see in every direction. Most of the crackers found their way into his mouth, but more than a few crumbled and decorated the upholstery before he finished.

It took almost half a bottle of water to wash down the crackers, and Robby realized he'd forgotten to get more to drink at the grocery store. This bottle was packed by his mom back on the island. His house seemed half a lifetime away from his stolen SUV sitting in an empty parking lot.

Robby sighed.

He could try to find a convenience store now, but he decided to get on the highway and make some progress first. The signs for the entrance ramp stood just up the road. Robby brushed himself off and put the vehicle into gear.

# CHAPTER 6: GOVERNMENT CONTROL

FIVE MONTHS EARLIER...

Dear Karen,

It's funny that I was just recently writing you about meeting new people. I've met a bunch of new people recently. Well, I've only actually met a few, but I've certainly seen a bunch. That new plant growing out back has commanded the attention of a determined and humorless branch of the federal government. I'm not exactly sure what their organization is called. They haven't given me very much information. They're positioned all around the house, and they ran a bunch of trucks out back to deal with the vines.

I'm not allowed to leave the house for anything. Every night, someone comes in and restocks the kitchen and drops off the mail. I found out if I leave my outgoing correspondence on the counter, it's gone the next day, as long as it's stamped. They haven't yet snuck in and stolen my pad of letters to you, but I wouldn't put it past them. I know what you would say—"Sounds like your dream life." I miss going to the store though, and I miss talking to the toothless woman at the gas station. I even miss dealing with Phil on the phone. He was supposed to approve my estimate, but I haven't heard a word from him. It will probably reduce my odds of getting more work, but I may have to call Phil.

You're probably wondering how a silly little vine out back made me a prisoner in this house. There's really not much more to the story to tell you though. One day they showed up and asked me about the vine, and then later the same day they were crawling all over the place. I'm not supposed to contact anyone about it because it will "cause a panic." I guess they're right about that part. I am a little panicky about the whole situation.

Somehow my computer is still able to create a "secure" connection to my clients, but when I trace the packet flow I can see it going right through their servers. I wish I knew how they managed that little trick. I can't get an unadulterated connection to anything on the internet. If I try to get a message out, I'm certain they'll block it before it even leaves the property. They've jimmied the phones as well. If I call someone I can hear a delay before the person responds. I tried to tell Stavros to stop by, but he said there was static on the line and hung up. I called him back and was able to talk to him with no problems, as long as I didn't mention the vines or the government visitors. Hell, they may come in and tear up this letter, even though I don't have anywhere to send it.

I miss you terribly, but I'm glad you didn't stick around for this. You'd go crazy, trapped in this house.

Much Love,

Brad

BRAD WOKE UP TO the alarm, same as a normal day. He didn't reset the alarm, though. Before the casually-attired government guys took over his property, Brad used to wake up just long enough to set the alarm forward for another half-hour of sleep. Now he pushed his legs over the edge of the bed at the alarm's first warning. Wearing pajamas every night became habit as well.

The only window where he'd drawn the blinds was in the

bathroom.

He didn't talk to himself anymore as he walked through the house. Whenever he passed a window he cut his eyes sideways to spot the closest government guy. He often turned off the television right in the middle of a program and peered out the window to track the progress of the men. They sent trucks back and forth to the back pasture, until they'd carved deep grooves in the lawn by the gate.

When he read a book, he kept his finger in the crease between the pages to mark his place; his attention drifted so often he read at a snail's pace.

Herm knocked on the door at four in the afternoon. He always knocked at four. For the first few days, Brad was too angry to let Herm in. He blamed Herm for the arrival of the rest of the government guys. Herm was the first, and lied to him back when the vine problem was a very small part of Brad's life.

Herm always opened with the same question—"How have you been, Mr. Jenkins?"

"Why don't you tell me? Any plans to get the hell off my property any time soon?" Brad usually asked.

"We're working as fast as we can," Herm would always reply.

They placed the back deck strictly off-limits to Brad. The government guys installed a lock between the handles of the French doors to make sure Brad didn't even try to go out there. Brad was dying to see what they were doing with the hole under the garage. From time-to-time he could hear them using heavy machinery—jackhammers and excavators from the sound—back there. The garage was sealed as well. Brad didn't see the government guys move his truck out of the garage, but he imagined they probably pulled it out late one night. He couldn't imagine his garage still had a floor, with all the noisy digging going on back there.

Brad toyed with the idea of drilling a hole through the wall of his mudroom so he could peek into the garage. He reasoned that even if they discovered him doing it, he'd probably get at least a few seconds to look at what was going on. He even went to the cellar and got his cordless drill. He put it in the bottom of a cardboard box and carried it up to the mudroom, leaving it on the floor next to the garage wall. The idea bothered him, though—he didn't want to know what they were doing. He simply wanted them to leave him alone.

Three sides of Brad's house had a pretty big yard. In front, his lawn extended nearly half the distance to the road. The pasture the government guys drove their big trucks through was at least an acre and a half, and the lawn out back, down to the pond, was nearly as big. Back before the government guys took over the chore, Brad would set aside a solid two-and-a-half hours each summer week for mowing.

The side yard though, the one just out the door from his laundry room, only measured a few paces before the woods started.

Brad measured the steps in his head over and over, as Herm stood there for his four o'clock visit. He pictured throwing open the door, sprinting to the woods and then running. After a small uphill climb, he'd be descending down a steep bank to the creek. The creek wound north and west until it met up with the river at the big marsh. If he took a left at the marsh, he should pop out behind the burned down Cartonio place.

"Mr. Jenkins?" asked Herm.

"Pardon?" Brad asked.

"I trust you've found your kitchen well stocked?" asked Herm.

"Well, no, actually," Brad said. "You people have accurately replaced what I've been eating, but I don't buy the same exact things every week. I would be getting lots of fruit this time of year —apples, pears, peaches. The apricots are no good anymore. They're all bland and unripe."

"Would you prefer to make us a list?" asked Herm.

"How am I supposed to know what's good? I have to see the selection in person," Brad said.

"I'm sorry. We'll try to work something out," Herm said.

"Yeah, I bet," Brad said.

Herm nodded, shrugged, and turned for the door. He stopped with his hand on the knob as if he wanted to say one more thing. Herm let himself out, leaving the thought unspoken.

Brad tried to act casual as he gathered his laundry. He put his sneakers in the bottom of his basket, along with his Swiss army knife, wallet, and a bunch of other things he thought he might need. In the laundry room he loaded his clothes into the washer and left everything else in the basket. The government guys never looked like they were actively watching him, but he wanted everything to look perfectly normal, just in case.

In the living room, Brad turned on the television and waited for his laundry to finish. If he could just get to the woods, he was certain he could find his way. His nearest neighbor, Butch, lived about seven-tenths of a mile to the north. He'd have to run longer though, assuming his path through the woods would meander more than the road. Brad figured his stamina would carry him at least a mile or two. His last serious foray into running was years ago, but he stayed in good shape.

If he cut a little to the east, he could find the snowmobile trail, which the riders kept pretty clear. Brad didn't want to risk it—the government guys could easily stake out those trails. In fact, he thought, they might have a guard on those trails, just to keep any random four-wheelers from finding their efforts at the vine patch.

Brad wondered how far he could get before they spotted him. With a little luck, he thought he might get away from the house unnoticed. He left the television on and made his way back to the bedroom to do a little surveillance. From the window in his master bath, he could see the outside of the laundry room door. He sat on the toilet and pushed up a corner of one of the blinds. Nobody was posted outside the laundry room door. In fact, he couldn't see anyone posted on that side of the house at all.

When the buzzer for the washing machine sounded, Brad had been staring at the television for several minutes. He debated whether to make his break now, or wait until the laundry was out of the dryer. It would be more natural for him to take a long time in the laundry room after the dryer was done—he always folded his laundry there—but he was tired of waiting. He knew he wasn't a good actor, and the longer he stayed in front of the television, biding his time, the more likely they would grow suspicious he was plotting something. The laundry required attention and the sun was setting. He figured his best chance had arrived.

Brad strolled to the laundry room and flipped on the light. He moved around the corner so he couldn't be seen from the living room windows before he dug to the bottom of his laundry basket and pulled out his good running shoes. It only took a few seconds to get ready to bolt.

He moved the clothes to the dryer and started it up. It tumbled and hummed as Brad stared at the door knob. All he needed to do was reach out and turn, then he could sprint for the woods. Brad wondered why he couldn't get his hand to reach for the door. Was this a kind of learned helplessness, he wondered.

He clenched his teeth and took a deep breath. He lunged for the door and grabbed the handle, pulling and turning as hard as he could. The door sprung open, letting in the soft evening light. The air pulled in by the outside door slammed shut the door to the living room behind Brad. He winced at the noise, but slipped out onto the porch as quietly as possible. He pulled shut the door behind him and turned to face Herm.

Herm stood there in his slacks, boat shoes, and golf shirt, on Brad's lawn, and regarded Brad with narrowed eyes. A pair of men in sandals and shorts flanked Herm. They held their hands behind their backs, probably hiding weapons, Brad thought.

"Would you join me inside, Mr. Jenkins?" asked Herm.

Brad sighed and glanced at the woods.

"Sure," Brad said.

Herm followed Brad back into the house through the laundry room door. They sat opposite each other on the couches in Brad's living room before Herm spoke again.

"Believe it or not, I've been in your position before," Herm said. "I've been held captive, and it wasn't in nearly as nice a place as this." Herm waved at Brad's living room.

"For doing nothing?" Brad asked. "For just happening to have property where these vines appeared? You think that's fair in this country?"

"For the greater good, we all may be called upon to make sacrifices," Herm said. "That's what living in a society is all about."

"Spare me," Brad said.

"We debated moving you to a facility," Herm said. "It would certainly be easier than keeping all these guards posted around your house. But, in the end, we decided it would be less stressful for you to stay here. You're a solitary type anyway. You seem to be happiest when you're here."

"I am happy here," Brad said, "but I do enjoy the freedom to *leave* here, occasionally."

"Understood," Herm said. "And this will be temporary."

"Perhaps," Brad said. "But back to your statement from a second ago. I think I know why you kept me here instead of shipping me off to a prison cell. At least I can narrow it down to one or two strong possibilities."

Herm didn't answer, so Brad continued.

"You're either afraid I've been contaminated, or contagious, or whatever, or maybe you just don't want me to have the chance to tell anyone else what I know," Brad said.

"If we were afraid of contagions," Herm said, "then the men stationed here would all be wearing the appropriate gear."

"Maybe the ones out back are," Brad said.

"And maybe I wouldn't be sitting here across from you," Herm said. "I do have a strong self-preservation streak, despite my occupation."

"You've been exposed already," Brad said. "I saw you touch the vine out back."

"So you did," Herm said. "Back to why I'm here: can I assume you're not going to try any more heroic escape attempts?"

"I'm not sure," Brad said. "Can you tell me how you knew I was going to make an attempt today?"

"There are two reasons I'm good at my job," Herm said. "First —I prepare. Second—I'm very good at putting myself in someone else's shoes, so I can think as they would."

"So you just tried to think like I would and you found yourself considering a mad dash from the laundry room?" Brad asked.

"Nope," Herm said. "I just prepared for it. You went to the laundry room, so I took a walk around back. It's the same thing I do every Sunday when you're doing laundry. I stay out of sight of the bathroom window, of course."

"That's very discouraging," Brad said. "You've given me an explanation which leaves no hope of improving my plan."

"You could always just change your plan to go along with this brief occupation until our work is done," Herm said. "By the way, the tech guys out in the van over there really enjoyed your attempt to create a new communication channel by embedding encrypted data in regular images. What's that process called again?"

"Steganography," Brad said.

"Nice touch using graphic pornography as the carrier. The guys were shy about the files at first until they noticed the size of the images seemed too big for the quality. I think you got a little greedy with the payload," Herm said.

"If you're through trying to win me over through compliments, I think I'd like my house back now," Brad said.

"Sure thing," Herm said. He stood in his odd way—rising up with his leg muscles without pushing with his arms. "Just try to accept our presence. The time will pass faster once you do. And please don't drill any holes through the wall in your back room— we've got tarps hung around our area, so you won't see anything."

Brad tried to hold his face perfectly still while he waited for Herm to leave. Once the tall man shut door behind himself, Brad got up and closed all the blinds in his living room. Then he went through the rest of the house, closing those windows off from the outside world as well.

✪ ✪ ✪ ✪ ✪

In the basement, to the left of his workbench, Brad kept leftover lumber and building supplies from various projects. After Herm thwarted his escape attempt, Brad found himself in the basement, cataloguing his stockpile. He grabbed his measuring tape and headed back upstairs to make a list.

His brain churned away at two different tasks: on one level, he moved through his house, taking measurements of each window and door; on a higher level, Brad analyzed his own actions. He wanted to board up every window—cut himself completely off from the government intruders on his property. They set up command tents in his back yard, and parked trailers just over the hill in his back pasture, but it was still his house. If they would deny him any access to the outside world, then the most Brad could do was deny them any access to his world.

Brad boarded up most of the downstairs windows before he stopped for dinner. The guards positioned around the perimeter of the house didn't flinch as Brad pounded nails through the sheets of plywood fitted to the window trim. When he ran out of scraps, Brad stole sheets of plywood from the attic. They'd been stacked up there for a year, waiting for Brad to get around to replacing the creaky flooring up there.

Just before boarding up the last window in the dining room Brad paused, resting his hands on the top edge of the plywood. He stared down his long driveway towards the road. He tried to remember the last time he'd seen a car drive down the road. His road never was very busy, but he started to wonder if he'd seen even a single civilian drive down the road since the day the government guys arrived. The window he was about to seal offered the best view, so Brad set the plywood down and fetched a camera from his office closet. It was a cheap webcam—one he'd purchased for video conferences. Brad set it on the bottom window frame and ran the cord out the bottom before positioning his plywood.

Brad worked through the night, finishing with the skylights before his normal breakfast time. Instead of sealing the skylights completely, Brad built a small frame to hold the plywood several inches below each skylight. He cut the plywood extra large and painted it white, hoping to reflect some sunlight down into the room through the gaps on the perimeter. As the dawn light filtered in, he discovered his blockade let in plenty of illumination for him to move around comfortably, and enough to read at close distance.

For most of the outside doors, Brad removed the handles and boarded them up completely. For the front door and the door to the garage, Brad constructed sturdy, removable blockades.

Brad flopped down on the couch with a box of cereal. He snacked and enjoyed his gloomy cave. His eyelids started to drift shut when he heard a noise at the door. The handle turned and the door pushed in a quarter inch before hitting the wooden bracing.

Brad smiled. The edges of the door let in bright morning sun, and in the thin band of light Brad saw a small note push through the crack between the door and the frame. The door was pulled shut, holding the note a few inches over the height of the door knob.

Brad pushed to his feet and shuffled over to grab the note. He turned on the kitchen light so he could read the handwritten text.

Dear Mr. Jenkins,

We've done our best to find you a variety of food this time. We also took the liberty of providing you several days of supplies, so you won't have to "unlock" your door too often for us. If you need anything, don't hesitate to leave a note or send us an email.

Thanks,

Herm

Brad crumpled the note and tossed it in the garbage can under the sink. He looked at the close-to-full basket and pulled out the trash bag before going back to the living room to remove the barricade from his door.

Dear Karen,

I've disconnected everything. You're my only connection with the outside world. Yes, I realize it's an imaginary connection, but still. I downloaded tons of information first. I filled the whole server with as much information about survival and whatnot I could find. I've stockpiled most of the food they've given me. I just eat the fresh stuff that would go bad anyway and ask for more dried food and canned stuff each time.

I found three of their bugs. I don't know why they wanted to listen in on me, it's not like I talk aloud much. When I found the first one, I didn't move it or try to break it or anything. Instead, I rigged up a RF sensor to detect what frequency they were using. With my homemade bug finder, I was able to find the other two. I don't think they have any video surveillance, which is weird. They might be tracking me through the walls with thermal imaging, but there's not much I can do about that.

Speaking of heat, the furnace has started coming on at night. It must be getting cold outside. I wish I hadn't cut the cable TV. I really wish I could watch the news just to find out if the world's still turning. Sometimes I hear the casual soldiers through the walls—digging next to the garage or backing a truck up the driveway. I had one camera pointed out front, but last week they painted the window black. I tried drilling a hole through the wall to the garage, but Herm was telling the truth. They've hung tarps around whatever they're doing in the garage. I couldn't see a thing through my hole. It didn't last long. Somebody filled it in during the night.

Maybe I'll go outside the next time they drop off food. I'm sure they'll just usher me back inside, but at least I might get a chance to talk to someone for a few minutes. I've lost track of the days, but I think it's been at least a month. My phone says it's October 18th, but they might be messing with it.

Much Love,

Brad

The house was still shaking when Brad fully woke up. He reconstructed the event as he rubbed his eyes. A giant "boom" jolted him upright, and he threw off the blankets, ready for action. His closet light gave the room an amber, pre-dawn feel. He'd slept with the closet light on for several weeks.

Three dusty coins vibrated off his bureau and bounced on the floorboards. The shaking died away slowly, until Brad wasn't sure if it had stopped or if he just couldn't sense it anymore. He put on his clothes quickly, but as quietly as possible. The closet light flickered twice. On his nightstand, Brad's notebook sat flipped open to a page with a couple quintets of tick marks. He added one

117

to the collection before shutting off his closet light.

In the dark, Brad moved to the doorway and pushed away the blanket he'd hung over the doorway. His hand found the door knob and he held his breath as he pushed the door open a quarter inch. When he saw no light from the hallway, he exited his bedroom as quietly as possible and slipped past the blanket hanging in the doorway to the kitchen. All his rooms were now divided by blankets in the doorways.

The kitchen had a little light—some from a crack between the plywood and the top of a window frame, and some which seeped in from the living room skylights. He walked through the kitchen and living room quickly, finding his way past the blanket to the back hall. He spread his arms and trailed his fingers down both the walls, counting the doors so he'd know when to expect the door to the mudroom.

Brad let himself into the mudroom and closed the door behind himself. The french doors to the back deck normally let in a lot of light, but today they were black. Brad inched around to the door to the basement. On the wall, just next to the door, he kept a flashlight in case he needed access to the basement when the power was out. He pointed it towards the french doors and turned on the light. In the upper left corner the plywood didn't make a good seal with the frame, but the glass there was dark.

Brad set the light down and moved to the door to the garage. All the other noises came from the garage area, so he assumed the boom that had woken him up had happened there as well. The door to the garage was barricaded much like the front door. Brad disassembled the brace and unlocked the door. He picked up the flashlight, put his hand on the knob, and then turned off his light before pulling it open.

Light streamed in, making Brad squint. Instead of the inside of his garage, Brad's eyes were drawn to a dark gray sky spitting big flakes of snow through jagged holes torn in the roof of his garage. Tattered blue tarps pooled around a pit in the floor of his garage, where his truck used to be parked. From the hole, thick mud had vomited up, coating the interior of the garage. One of the garage doors had a huge splat of mud right in the center which had hit with enough force to punch the door halfway off its tracks and into the driveway.

Brad shut the door and locked it. He sat in the dark and replayed in his mind everything he'd just seen.

"They blew it up?" he whispered to himself. He clapped a hand over his mouth.

He put the bracing back in place to seal the door shut and turned off his flashlight.

Back in the living room, Brad crouched on the floor and peeked out the front door at his driveway. A box of provisions sat on the porch; the top was dusted with snow. A couple of vehicles were parked in the driveway, but he saw no soldiers and no footprints in the fresh snow. He got to his knees and opened the door enough to pull the box of supplies into the living room before shutting the door most of the way again.

Brad rose to his feet and took a deep breath. He slipped through the door and stood on his porch. Looking around for signs of life, Brad stuffed his hands deep in his pockets and shivered as the wind gusted. Snow swirled in the corner where the garage met the side of the house. Three steps led down to the short path to the driveway. Brad looked left and right as he rushed to the nearest car—a tan sedan might have been the same one Herm arrived in months before.

Brad tried the door. When it opened the warning chime told Brad the keys were still in the ignition, but he leaned in and verified they were there. After one more glance around, Brad turned the key. The sedan's engine fired up immediately. Brad shut it off and pocketed the keys.

He glanced back at the house.

Out of nowhere, Grandpa Joe flooded back into Brad's memory.

"They're trees when they're standing," Grandpa Joe had told him. "That's when they're safe. You can never trust them once you put the saw to them. Do you know why?"

"Why?" young Brad had asked.

"It wakes them up," Grandpa Joe had said. "Once they're on the ground, they're called lumber. You know why?"

"Why?" young Brad asked again.

"Because they walk," Grandpa Joe had said. They were standing next to a felled pine. Grandpa Joe held his de-limbing axe over his shoulder and he motioned for Brad to back up. As Grandpa Joe worked his way down the tree, his sharp axe liberated the trunk from all the branches propping it up. With each swing, the trunk twisted and wriggled, working its way to the ground. "You take your eyes off this thing for one second and it's gonna roll over your ankle and snap off your foot. You understand?"

"I think so," young Brad had said.

Brad shook his head to clear away the memory and he dropped into a crouch next to the open car door. A loud "Tock!" came from the backside of the garage. Brad shuffled across the snowy driveway to the edge of the car as another "Tock!" sounded.

The garage doors rattled. The one which bulged out looked like it was about to fall. Brad ducked even lower, with just his eyes above the edge of the hood. As he watched, the roof of the garage—what was left of it—began to shake and rattle. A sound like giant rocks scraping together came to him through the snowy air. "TOCK!"

Brad felt reality swimming away and another memory of Grandpa Joe tried to surface. He shook his head and pushed away from the sedan, sprinting for the house. The "TOCK!" sound came once more before he slammed the door shut behind himself. As soon as the door was shut, and the next echoing TOCK was muffled, Brad felt the intrusive memories start to fade. He pressed his back to the door and reached up over his left shoulder to turn the lock.

The next TOCK sounded like it came from the driveway. Brad scrambled away from the door and put all the bracing back into place—locking the door tight. The living room windows near the driveway began to rattle in their frames. He moved to the couch and pressed his hand against the plywood covering the windows. The whole wall was shaking. The picture frame next to the door bounced against the wall. Brad tiptoed away from the couch and crouched over near the bookcase on the far wall. He watched from across the room as the undulation moved slowly down the wall, towards the kitchen.

The plates in his kitchen cabinets began to rattle when the rumbling suddenly stopped. Brad took a deep breath and waited. Just as he exhaled, a new sound began. This one was less of a rattle, and more of a movement of air; like his house was a big violin, and something was moving a giant bow across it.

Brad covered his ears. The luffing sound hurt his ear drums, like driving around with just one back window open. Brad moaned, but couldn't hear his own voice. He doubled over on the floor. He thought his head might implode with the pressure, and he was beginning to have trouble inhaling. Brad crawled on hands and knees, under the blanket-barrier to the hall, and down the long hall to the back of the house, while the noise in the living room slowly faded.

He stopped at the door to the mudroom, and sat in the absolute darkness as a mixture of new sounds rang out from the front of the house. One noise lasted several minutes and sounded like a giant hunk of metal being dragged across concrete. Brad felt the next sound in his teeth, like he'd bitten into a big chunk of styrofoam. Brad cringed and plugged his ears again.

He squinted and curled into a ball for several minutes until the noises stopped. Brad removed his hands from his ears and lay on the floor, relieved by the silence. He crept back to the living room, stopping frequently to listen for any distant sign that the sounds were returning. When he'd heard nothing for a while, he peeked past the blanket into the living room. Based on the intensity of the sounds, he expected to find destruction, but his living room looked normal in the soft glow from the partially-blocked skylights.

One picture next to the door was slightly askew, but even the kitchen seemed intact. In the hall to his bedroom, the crack between the plywood and the window frame looked bigger—more light seeped in. Brad approached cautiously, but eventually pressed his eye right to the crack. Once his eye adjusted, he had a pretty good view of the driveway.

The car he'd crouched behind just minutes before—maybe Herm's car—had turned ninety degrees, leaving big sweeping tire-streaks through the fresh snow. Whatever turned the car left no tracks at all. Brad scratched an itch on the side of his head and found his fingers sticky with fresh blood. He turned his hand slowly in the light coming in through the crack and wondered about the dark red blood.

Brad made his way back to his bedroom. In the bathroom mirror he found the source of the blood. A small trickle escaped his right ear, and ran down to his cheek before ending in a smear. Brad sat on the edge of the tub and dabbed at the blood with a glob of wet toilet paper. He gently brushed his fingers together next to each ear. He could still hear okay, but felt a low throb from the right side of his head.

"Just the essentials," Brad said to himself.

He jumped up and moved with purpose over to the closet. From the top shelf on the left, he pulled down a backpack. Back in the bathroom, he shoved in various pills and a few toiletries. At his bureau, he dressed himself and then stuffed a few extra socks, shirts, and underwear into his backpack. Most of the space in the backpack he filled in the kitchen. He added easily portable food and bottled water to his stash. Brad finished his preparation in the living room, where he kept his hiking boots next to the wood stove. He took a deep breath and listened for any more driveway sounds before he un-blocked the door.

✪ ✪ ✪ ✪ ✪

Brad didn't even set both feet on the porch before he turned around. He'd forgotten how cold it was outside, and the swirling snow made it seem even colder. He ran back through the house to get his coat, hat, and gloves. This time he left the house and quickly broke into a hunching jog. The snowfall was heavier. He could barely see across the driveway through the swirls of snow, and his feet swished through a few inches of fresh powder. He circled Herm's car to get to the driver's door. What he saw stopped him short once again.

The back of the car—now facing the house—looked fine, but the front part was utterly destroyed. The edges of the wound were smooth and shiny. The front left quarter of hood looked like it had been flattened under a giant weight. Vital fluid still dripped from severed hoses and stained the fresh snow.

Brad scanned the driveway for another vehicle.

He found a big Humvee about fifty feet towards the road. It sat unmolested by whatever had destroyed Herm's car, but he couldn't find any keys. He looked around for his own truck, but it was nowhere in sight. More trucks were parked down in the field, near the back gate that led out to the vine patch. Brad put his hood up, to keep the snow from blowing down the back of his neck, and loped across the field. He found the doors unlocked, no sign of the casually-dressed government guys, and no keys.

By the time he reached the last vehicle, he'd given up hope. He reached in the cab, felt for the ignition, and jerked his hand back when he hit the keyring. Brad smiled. He jumped in, slung his backpack on the passenger's seat and turned the key.

Nothing.

No lights, no bells, not even a click from the solenoid. Brad sighed and turned the key on and off to no avail. His smile returned when he noticed the gear shift lever. He pushed the clutch to the floor, put the Humvee in neutral, and turned the key again. It still didn't make a sound. Brad grabbed his pack and jumped back out into the snow.

He slammed the door and then froze, suddenly aware of how much noise his frustration caused. With a nervous glance in each direction, he hunched over and jogged for the trees at the west edge of the field. A band of trees separated his fields from the road. When he got to the cover of some low-hanging pines, Brad crouched and surveyed his property. He sat at about a ten-second sprint from his front door. Through the thick falling snow, his house looked strange to him, with all the windows boarded up from the inside. The windows on the front of the house, the side which faced towards the road, looked even more strange—Brad was close enough to see the opaque paint on each pane left by the government guys.

From his hideout, Brad could just see the corner of the excavator parked behind his garage. He considered running—he had supplies and warm enough clothing to brave the storm. Downtown Kingston Depot was about an hour away on foot, the few times Brad had walked it. But those were nice summer walks, not panicked winter escape attempts. The yellow-orange paint of the excavator drew his eyes through the snow. He could only see the corner of the track, but it looked weird. It angled up towards the sky, like the other end, the end he couldn't see, had fallen into the hole back there.

As Brad thought and watched, the snow changed. The nice, organized flakes gave way to big, sloppy piles of snow that fell in dense clumps. Brad could barely make out the dark shape of the house through the wall of falling snow. Even under the thick boughs of the pine tree, Brad's shoulders were becoming dusted with snow as he tried to decide what to do. The government guys— or rather, the lack of government guys—drove Brad back towards the house. All their vehicles were there, but he didn't see a trace of any of the men, not even a footprint in the snow except his own. He wanted to know where they'd gone.

Staying along the edge of the woods, Brad circled his house. Around back, he saw the excavator had indeed fallen into a hole near the deck. It wasn't the same hole Brad had investigated. This was a new pit, rapidly filling up with snow. The nose of the excavator disappeared into this sinkhole.

Around back near the laundry room door, Brad found a pair of sunglasses right on the edge of the woods. The two arms were stuck in the snowy grass and the lenses faced directly up towards the sky. He dusted the snow from the glasses and then stuffed them into his jacket pocket.

The snowfall increased even more. When Brad came back around to the driveway, he could barely see ten feet. Between the drifting snow and gusting winds, he couldn't even walk in a straight line. Brad gave up his thoughts of hiking towards town and trudged back towards the house. He brushed most of the snow from his clothes before he pushed back through the front door.

Dear Karen,

I should have gone when I had the chance. I was afraid to be outside—I think someone or some thing took all those government guys. If they could all be scooped up without a trace, what chance do I have? I figured I was safe in here when they all got "disappeared," so maybe it's safe in here now. Maybe they were taken by the same thing that ate Herm's car.

I peeked out a few hours ago, and it's gotten even worse. It's still snowing like crazy and there must be two feet already. I'll never make it to town in this stuff. I did manage to scrape off some of the paint on the front windows so I can watch the road. I haven't seen any cars or even a plow go by. But it's been so long since I've seen or heard traffic on the road, I think they might have closed it.

I've still got that old snowmobile in the cellar. I'm going to head down there and see if I can get it running.

The power just flickered again. I've got my headlamp around here somewhere.

It's out for real now, I think. It's been about five minutes. I'll get a fire going in the wood stove before I go downstairs, just in case it stays off. I have to take down the barricade I have on the laundry room door. I moved the wood pile out to the north side of the house last spring—I probably told you already.

I'm glad you talked me into keeping the wood stove. You were right.

Even though all the government guys are gone I still can't use my cellphone. I even tried it out in the yard. No signal.

I'm not exactly sure what day it is, but I think it's around the end of November. If I kept up writing to you every Tuesday, I could just count back. Sorry. Anyway, I'll want to get the snowmobile out there as soon as the snow slows down. You know how storms are this time of year. We could easily lose all the snow-cover in just a day or so, and then I'd be back to walking into town.

I love you, and I hope wherever you are, you're looking down on me and sending happy thoughts my way.

Much Love,

Brad

Brad got the old snowmobile running in less than an hour. Age mellowed the beast—the ornery machine usually required days of loving attention before it's sputtering coughs turned into a sustainable purr. Brad merely changed out the plugs, gas, and oil, and he started it with a few dozen violent tugs.

He stored the snowmobile on a large wooden pallet, so he could move it around with a special jack. With the engine still running to charge the battery, Brad wheeled the snowmobile on its pallet over towards the door. A terrible thought crossed Brad's mind as he removed the lumber boarding up the outside door—what if the door was completely blocked from the outside with piled dirt from the garage excavation? His fear grew stronger, the closer he got to opening the door.

This door opened right near the underside of the deck, right near where all the dirt was piled. Brad didn't want to risk letting in an avalanche of dirt, so he bundled up and let himself out the mudroom door so he could evaluate the situation. When he opened the door to the deck, he let in another type of avalanche, albeit a small one. The piled snow spilled in through the door.

Part of the deck was nearly clear—a strong wind blew away most of the snow—but against the side of the house, the drifts piled nearly up to the door handle. The snow plastered the side of the abandoned excavator. Brad could only see a few orange-yellow parts sticking out from the buried machine. Brad held the railing tight and descended the stairs into the ocean of snow surrounding his deck. In spots, he found himself up to his waist. His going was slow, but he spied good news about the basement door. The wind kept clear the area just outside the basement door, and the dirt pile didn't block it either.

Brad swam back through the snow and jogged down the interior stairs to where the snowmobile still hummed. His feet stirred up clouds of exhaust. Brad tugged the door open and lined up his snowmobile carefully before driving it out of the basement. He closed up the basement before much snow could blow inside and plotted his course. He wanted to get the snowmobile to the front porch, where it would be accessible, but still have some cover from the weather.

Breaking trails was never easy, but even worse that day with the amazing depth of accumulated snow. His snowmobile was built for comfort, not for trailblazing. Brad wrestled the heavy machine through the drifts and away from the sinkhole which nearly swallowed the excavator. He ran the engine at full speed and pulled the handlebars back, just to make headway.

Brad was panting and sweating inside his jacket by the time he'd parked the snowmobile on the front porch. He made several attempts, packing down the drifts with each pass, before he could get the snowmobile up the stairs. He left the snowmobile with the tracks facing out towards the front yard while the snow continued to fall.

Back in the living room, the wood stove made quick work of melting the snow from Brad's clothes. His short trip around the house convinced him that waiting for the snowfall to end was the right plan. The blowing and falling snow reduced visibility to just a few paces. While he waited, Brad busied himself with the fire. He got his best snow shovel from the wall of his ruined garage, pausing briefly to watch the snow filter in through the gaping hole in the roof. It took the better part of an hour for Brad to carve out a path from the laundry room door over to the wood pile. By the time he reached the stack of wood, inches accumulated at the start of his path.

He filled the wood rack in the living room and then stacked even more firewood next to the chimney. Water pooled on the tiles as the snow melted off the wood. Brad rested around dusk. Every hour throughout the night, Brad woke up to check the snow. He wanted to leave as soon as it abated, but it came down strong all night. Dawn filtered in slowly through the thick clouds. Brad shoveled the path to the woodpile several more times. He didn't anticipate sticking around long enough to need much more firewood, but it gave him something to do. The snow on either side of his path was now piled up to shoulder height. He tossed each shovelful higher than the last. Brad's shoulders ached with each throw.

Brad ate light meals next to the warm wood stove. He melted snow in buckets next to the stove, so he could fill the toilet tank. His water came from a well, so with no power, he needed to supply the toilet manually.

Around noon, Brad felt trapped inside his dark living room. He strapped on his backpack and decided to take his chances with the low visibility.

The snow mounded around the front porch so he could drive his snowmobile right from the porch onto the snow. His heavy machine packed down the powder, but it stayed afloat on the surface as long as he kept his speed up. Brad navigated to the end of the driveway mostly by memory. He could barely make out the trees on either side of the path, but he knew the twists and turns well enough to stay out of the woods.

The road sat buried—unplowed and untraveled. Brad tried to guide the snowmobile to the widest expanse ahead, but soon found himself riding down the sloping shoulder into a gully. He fought the machine's tilt, leaning far out to the side, to keep it from rolling him off. Brad followed the shoulder for a several slow minutes, thinking he could use the angle as a guide, but soon found himself plunging forward into another gully. It didn't make sense to him—he couldn't imagine how the road could turn ninety degrees.

Brad turned right and continued until the new gully veered even further right. That's when Brad figured out he was way off course. He turned his snowmobile around in a tight loop and backtracked to his own driveway. An hour on the machine, and he found himself no farther than the end of his driveway. Brad goosed the snowmobile and fled back to his house, convinced again he would have to wait for the heavy snowfall to end before he could escape his property and make his way to town.

Dear Karen,

This snow is unbelievable. It's still coming down. There has to be at least six feet of snow out there now and it's still falling. I've still got the laundry room door cleared, and I've moved a lot of wood into the laundry room. If you thought it looked cluttered before, you should see it now. It's stacked from end to end with firewood.

I broke the dryer, too. Not that it was very useful since the power's been out, but it was a bit of a crisis for a few minutes. I came in through the door with a sling full of wood, and one of the big pieces slipped out. It dropped straight on the section of gas line that comes up through the floor and goes to the dryer. It probably would have been fine, if I'd left it alone, but I thought I could un-crimp the copper tubing. When I tried to bend it back into place, the pipe split and propane started to flood the room. I shut the door to the living room pretty quick— I didn't want gas to get to the wood stove—and opened the back door. But with five feet of snow, getting to the propane tank was impossible. The pipe split before the cutoff valve, so I didn't have any way of shutting it off except out at the tank.

I couldn't climb through the snow from the laundry room door, and I didn't want to let the laundry room fill up with gas while I shoveled my way around, so I wrapped the pipe with some tape and dug my way out through the kitchen window. The snow already covered the lower half of the window in there. You know how the snow slides down from the corner of the house where the two roofs meet in a valley? Well all the snow sloughed off the roof and collected there. It didn't take me long to dig down to the tank though. I ended up hanging out of the window far enough to reach down to the cutoff valve. So the stove is out of commission too until I re-plumb the gas line for the stove. I think I can just figure out a way to take off the "T" fitting where it splits to go to the dryer, but I'm a little nervous about working with gas lines. Meanwhile, I've been doing all my cooking on the wood stove. It's fun this way—I have to admit—more like camping.

I'm also keeping a ramp clear for the snowmobile so I'll be able to use it when the snow stops. Actually, it's easier than I thought it would be. I just go out every hour and pack down the ramp leading from the front porch so I can get it up to the level of the snow. I took down some of the plywood from the windows and jammed it in between the railing and the snow bank to keep the front porch from filling up with snow. It's drifting pretty deep up there. Once it gets to the roofline, I think the porch will become like a cave and I won't have to worry about so much snow blowing in down the ramp.

You get into a place where you're just reacting to the latest disaster, and figuring out how to survive. It rarely occurs to me to even wonder how this could be happening. It seems like ever since this summer, I've just dealt with whatever comes along and adapted to it. Makes me think, what other things could I have adjusted to? Horses, kids, dinner parties, dancing—none of those could possibly be as weird as what I've been dealing with, and yet I'm perfectly able to roll with these changes, so why not those? I guess it's just because I wasn't offered a choice by the casual government guys. They just showed up and took me prisoner. Same with the snow. Anyway, for the millionth time, I'm sorry. I hope you know.

Love,

Brad

# CHAPTER 7: ROBBY LEAVES MAINE

ROBBY SLOWED TO A stop on the highway with the green metal bridge crouching before him. The road deck stood high above the banks of the river, so big ships could navigate the river below. The tree tops were below Robby on either side. Bridges made him nervous, he decided. Heights made him nervous now too, although they never did before. He inched the vehicle forward until he passed under the big green bridge trusses.

He saw few cars on the road, but with the metal guardrails on either side hemming the wrecks in, they forced him to weave around. With sixty miles under his belt, Robby felt pretty good about the SUV. He'd allowed himself to ramp up to almost fifty miles per hour on the highway. Now, with only thin rails between him and the drop into cold Piscataqua River, ten miles an hour seemed too fast. Robby opened his window a few inches. The cold air felt good on his sweaty brow. Robby gripped the wheel tighter.

Up ahead, several cars piled up against the concrete barrier. The barrier separated the northbound and southbound lanes. The bridge had three lanes of travel and a wide breakdown lane, but the cars took up most of that space. Robby guided his big vehicle all the way to the right side of the bridge to even have a chance of getting by.

The view to his right terrified him, so Robby focused on the wrecked cars. The two on the left appeared empty, but Robby suspected if he checked closer he would find an exploded-eye corpse collapsed behind each steering wheel. In the third car from the left, Robby saw at least two people slumped together in the front seat. The lump in the back seat might have been a shoulder—Robby couldn't tell. In the car immediately next to Robby, the back seat held a boy about Robby's own age.

The boy wore a dark sweater over a collared shirt. His eyes splattered the top half of the window, but the boy's face slouched against the bottom of the pane. The boy's nose and cheek pressed against the inside of the glass. His mouth hung open, flattened on the left side, like a capital D.

Robby inched by the trunk of the car. He glanced to his right several times to verify he wasn't going to hit the guardrail, but it bothered Robby to look away from the boy's gaping face. Despite the exploded eyes, Robby couldn't shake the feeling the boy was staring right at him. Worse, actually, it seemed like the boy looked just over Robby's shoulder at some terrible menace that his gaping mouth wanted to warn Robby about. Now Robby split his attention in three directions. He stared at the boy, stole glances to the right to make sure he wasn't going to hit the guardrail, and spun around frantically to make sure nothing was sneaking up behind him from the back seat.

Robby tried to catch his breath and settle down, but it wouldn't come. His panting brought even more panic. The right front tire of the SUV hit the curb and Robby jerked the wheel to the left. With no room to spare, the adjustment forced Robby's SUV to tag the corner of the boy's wrecked car. The jolt shifted the boy's corpse and the boy's face slid down the window a little farther. The boy's hand was pressed right against the glass, like he was either banging to get out or executing the world's slowest wave. Robby held his breath and stared at the boy's hand.

When had the boy's hand moved to the glass, he wondered.

Before, only the boy's face had been visible—where had the hand come from?

Robby's SUV idled forward, shaking the boy's car even more. For the first time, Robby looked past the boy to the front seat and saw the dead bald man turned in his direction as well. Robby's brain invented the upcoming scene in double speed. He imagined the gory occupants of the boy's car scrambling towards his SUV and banging on the windows while dark clots of half-dried blood oozed from their eye sockets.

Panic overtook Robby's legs and he jabbed the accelerator. The SUV bucked back to the right and up over the curb as the back tires squealed. Robby didn't—couldn't—look away from the dead boy's car until the SUV's right quarter panel began to grind into the guardrail. He jerked the wheel back to the left and stomped on the accelerator. The wrecked car deflected the back of the SUV until the right rear tire made contact with the curb and the SUV shot forward, clearing itself of the constriction. Robby steered frantically, trying to keep between the center wall and the guardrail. He locked his knees as the SUV continued to accelerate. Robby focused all his attention on his arms, not realizing he was standing on the gas pedal.

Up ahead a car towing a rental trailer had rolled into the right guardrail and stood nearly perpendicular to the road. Robby nudged the wheel left and then overcorrected back to the right, trying to target the thin gap between the center wall and the trailer while he continued to accelerate. The side of the rental trailer read "Wyoming," in big sweeping letters. Under the state name, a bronco bucked, kicking its back legs towards the gap where Robby aimed his vehicle.

His common sense returned a split-second too late. Robby lifted his feet and stomped both onto the brake pedal. The tires chirped briefly before the throbbing anti-lock brake system kicked in. The vibration of the pulsing brakes ran up through the steering wheel and numbed Robby's hands.

It wouldn't stop fast enough—he would hit either the trailer or the divider between the north and southbound lanes unless he threaded the gap perfectly. Robby aimed slightly more towards the wall. As the trailer and wall rushed towards him, Robby strained his legs against the pulsing pedal, thinking if he could somehow press harder he would stop faster. His left bumper hit the wall first and straightened out the SUV. From the sound, it seemed the whole left side of the SUV was being peeled away from the frame. Robby gritted his teeth as the SUV finally came to a stop.

He'd wedged his vehicle right between the center wall and the trailer. Robby applied the gas. The rim of his front tire ground against the concrete, so he turned the wheel to the right to get some distance. On his right, the trailer shook as Robby nudged past. Up ahead, the road looked totally clear. Robby sighed with relief as he finally pulled by the trailer and left the sounds of grinding metal behind him.

He traveled almost two seconds before his spirits fell again. Although the grinding sounds diminished, a new rumbling sound took its place. Along with the new sound, the wheel of the SUV pulled to the side and resisted Robby's attempts to drive straight. Robby stopped again, shifted to park, and took off his seat belt. He leaned out the driver's window and then the passenger's—he saw a flat tire on either side. The right rear tire merely looked deflated; the front left tire appeared shredded.

# CHAPTER 8: BRAD LEAVES HOME

Dear Karen,

Each day it gets colder. Each day the snow gets deeper. I used the rest of the plywood on the path out to the wood pile. When the snow banks grew higher than my head, it got too difficult to keep shoveling the path out. So, one day I took the plywood out there and wedged it into the walls above my head. The first day I could still see cracks of light between the sheets and a blue halo around the plywood where some light was leaking through. But after just one day, the tunnel was completely dark. Who knows how much snow is packed above my tunnel?

I do know how much snow has drifted out front. I could park the snowmobile on the second floor if it would fit through a window. If it gets much deeper, I might have to. I wonder what's happened to the rest of the world. I bet everybody has moved into emergency shelters at the schools and public buildings. That's where I would go, if I could. They're probably finding it easier to keep big places operational. I haven't been able to get any stations on the radio. Reception always was pretty bad here, but you'd think I would at least get the emergency broadcast system or something.

The living room is still pretty comfortable thanks to the wood stove. I kept the blankets up between the rooms—they help keep the heat concentrated.

The pipes burst in the extremities of the house. I went down to the basement yesterday with a flashlight and I could see ice blooming out from several joints in the heat and water pipes. Oh well—looks like a complete re-plumbing job when this whole situation gets resolved. Insurance should cover at least part of it. Assuming the insurance companies don't all go out of business when this storm is done.

For the moment, I've managed to keep the pipes to the septic system from freezing. I think they're beginning to clog though. The water threatens to backup and overflow every time I flush. On top of the house the chimney sits in a little bowl of snow which has melted and refrozen into ice. I went up there to make sure it wasn't going to get blocked and kill me when the exhaust backed up. I haven't seen anything coming or going from the hole out back by the garage. I wonder if the hole is still in use? I figure it has been abandoned, since I haven't seen or heard anything, but who knows?

The snow's still coming down at a crazy pace. Although, I went out the other night to work on the snowmobile ramp and it let up for a couple hours. By morning it was a full-on blizzard. I can't survive here until spring. I only have enough wood for a few weeks, and food for about twice that long at my current starvation-level diet. What's going to run out first is the light. I get a little from the fire when I leave the doors open, and there's a faint blue glow from the upper windows during the day, but with a few more feet of snow I think it will be as dark as a cave in here. I'm saving the candles for then. I'm also going to need a way to get fresh air in here. The fire is sucking up all the oxygen. I'm considering punching a hole through the metal roof on the back part of the house.

I would do anything for a view of the horizon, or the night sky, or even just to look up at the clouds without seeing snow. I read somewhere that people need to be able to un-focus their eyes and look at something far off. They need to be able to do that every so often so they can relax. I believe it's true. I don't know how those researchers at the south pole manage to make it through a single winter. If the snow ever stops I'm going to climb up high enough so I can see something so far away I can't tell what it is, you know? I'm sick of only seeing things close. Everything's so close. Only the fire seems infinite. I stare at it for hours some nights, like it was the best TV show ever made. I stare at it and think of nothing at all.

Love,

Brad

BRAD WORKED ON HIS list for four days before he finally left the house. The snow stopped a week earlier. It switched to freezing rain in the middle of the night, layering his jacket in crunchy ice before he got back inside. In the morning, he cursed the rain. It made his snowmobile ramp into a treacherous sheet of ice.

Before the rain, his ramp was packed down by countless trips through with the shovel, and bolstered with pieces of plywood layered down. The ramp led up from the front porch up to the surface of the snow. Where he'd stopped shoveling and laying plywood, you could sink into the drifts like quicksand. You really needed to swim more than walk, he'd found out. He also found he could keep the snowmobile afloat in the fresh powder if he was careful. His snowmobile was long, and powerful. He usually rode established trails. Riding in the fresh snow required a lot of effort and a lot of standing.

His education began when he took the machine out into snow about ten feet deep. As soon as he left the ramp, he thought the sled would be lost forever. He almost rolled it over and couldn't move it an inch. Brad eventually consulted a book from his library. He read it while perched on the side of the sled's half-buried seat.

Within a few hours, he wrestled the snowmobile back upright and cut a few trails through the yard. With the wind and continued snowfall, his tracks disappeared by the next day.

Now, the ice changed the whole equation. Brad tried to climb the ramp and slipped immediately. He spun as he fell and slammed his shoulder into the hard ice. He tried to chip through the it with his shovel and found it too thick to break up easily.

The top task on his list was to figure out a way to get the snowmobile up the ramp. The rest of the entries were items to pack for the trip.

The snowmobile took a day. Packing took the other three.

Over the years, Brad trained himself to find a quick solution instead of a perfect one. It was essential to staying profitable as a contractor. Most of the companies he worked for employed people who could engineer a really good long-term solution to their problems. The only issue was budget. Often, Brad found, a really good long-term solution to the problem was way outside the budget allowance for the project. And, Brad found, a lot of companies didn't really need a good long-term solution, they just needed a cheap, short-term fix for a problem that would go away in the near future.

Of course, a lot of solutions took longer than anyone wanted to admit, but that was a different issue.

That's how Brad made his money—he presented options. He evaluated the situation, figured out what the "right" solution should be, and also figured out what the "right now" solution could be. His clients paid him for that skill—the ability to see an imperfect solution which would fix a problem soon, rather than a perfect solution which would fix a problem eventually.

When trying to free his snowmobile from the porch and get it up the icy ramp, Brad almost fell into that perfect solution trap. His first approach consisted of melting grooves in the sheet of ice to line up with the tracks of the snowmobile. Then, as he tried to climb the ramp, the bumps in his snowmobile tracks would interface with the grooves in the ramp, and he could climb. It was a perfect solution which would be durable, repeatable, and take forever to complete. Brad abandoned the idea quickly.

His next idea was to use his chainsaw to cut through the ice. He didn't know how well it would work, but he'd seen ice sculptors use chainsaws before, so it seemed plausible. Unfortunately, his chainsaw had disappeared when his garage exploded in mud.

Brad returned to the ice ramp with a sledgehammer and a lot of aggression. By the end of the day he'd broken up enough patches of ice to get traction to the top of the ramp. He left the snowmobile parked on a flat spot in the snowfield.

The day was overcast with low clouds, but without the falling snow, he could finally see more than ten feet. Brad looked back at the house and gaped at the sight. Only the peak of the roof at the front, and the peak of the garage were visible. The rest of the house was a white mound of nothing. It was only a guess, but Brad figured the snow to be at least twenty feet deep if not more.

"Jesus," he said, exhaling.

As slippery as the ramp was, the ice up on the flat wasn't so hard to navigate. The freezing rain left the surface bumpy, like the individual drops froze before they could spread out too much. Brad walked up to the peak of his roof and saw that hot air from his chimney created a bubble beneath the snow. The top of it was still open, but if the snow continued it might close up, suffocating Brad's fire.

On the edges of his clearing, some trees poked out of the top of the snow, but most were just more white mounds. In some directions, the view looked like rolling dunes in a pure-white desert.

Brad hauled his essentials up the ramp by hand and lashed them to the snowmobile. He wore a lot of his food provisions on his back in a hiking pack. In the morning he didn't bank the fire, but instead left a note for the next person who might find his house.

He set out at dawn, or at least as early as he could see clearly.

## CHAPTER 9: SOUTH IS DEAD

ROBBY LET OUT A long, slow sigh. He turned around and sat on the center console so he could look back at the wrecks behind him. Behind the Wyoming trailer with the bucking bronco, Robby saw the corner of the boy's car in the distance. Robby wondered if the boy's face had slipped farther down the window, or if the boy's hand still perched in the same position, or if it had mysteriously moved again.

His stare didn't shift, but his hands found a box of cheesy crackers from the back seat. Robby crunched them by the handful while he considered his options. He could replace one flat with the spare, but did it matter? Would changing just one tire even help?

None of the cars stopped on the bridge looked heavily damaged. In fact, on his trip, Robby saw a lot of cars pulled over with exploded-eye corpses but only a few looked like they'd been in a big crash. He theorized they'd made some attempt to pull over just before their deaths and then rolled to a gentle, post mortem stop. This assumption led Robby to the depressing idea that most of the vehicles on the road would have remained running until they eventually ran out of gas.

He hadn't confirmed this idea. The thought of getting close enough to one of the exploded-eye corpses to see the gas gauge was not even slightly appealing to him. At the other side of the Wyoming trailer, another idea waited for him. The car hooked up to the trailer also had a bike rack attached to it. Two full-sized mountain bikes and a kid's bike—pink with handlebar streamers—were lashed to the trunk. Robby gathered everything he could fit in his backpack, and grabbed the keys to the SUV before he let himself out to stand on the bridge.

The wind blowing up the river bit at his skin. Robby zipped up his coat until the zipper hit the sore spot on his neck. The sore spot made him think of his father. He felt naked walking up the slight slope of the bridge deck to the wrecked car. The bucking bronco painted on the trailer stared at him with a half-crazed eye. The horse gave the impression of brown, but it was really composed of colorful strokes of random colors. Rings of blue and purple made up its flared nostrils and streaks of red flowed down the horse's chest like blood. Robby focused on the bikes and tried to ignore the horse mural.

When Robby approached the back of the car, he just stared at the bike rack. He figured they would be locked to the rack, and he would need the driver's keys to unlock them. He almost couldn't believe his luck—they weren't locked. The bikes were merely lashed to the rack with nylon straps. In minutes, Robby unhooked and rested them against the side of the trailer.

Both of the adult-sized bikes looked good, so Robby chose the one with the pack of tools and pump clipped to the frame. He coasted down the slope of the bridge and waved goodbye to the SUV as he passed. It felt strange to ride a bike without a helmet. Robby didn't pedal, he let gravity take him down the road and looked back and forth carefully, watching for any sign of danger. He felt stealthy on the bike, but less insulated than in the SUV.

He planned to trade in his bike for the next functional car or truck he could find.

Not far down the road the first exit led to Market Street. Robby rolled down to the stop sign and rode up onto the sidewalk of a fairly big road. Just up the road he found small neighborhoods mixed with clusters of businesses. A little farther, Robby found a shopping mall with a bunch of cars grouped near the entrance to the Best Buy.

He let his bike slow to a stop and put his feet down. When he saw movement over by the store, he hunched over the handlebars.

Robby shuffled the bike over to a clump of bushes decorating a concrete island in the parking lot. He laid the bike down and crept between the evergreen shrubs.

Past all the parked cars, color lined the sidewalk next to the Best Buy. Closest to the door, behind some velvet ropes, people had set up tents; farther away, they had sleeping bags and lawn chairs. The movement which caught Robby's eye was the flap of a big purple tent, fluttering in the breeze. The whole line looked messy and disorganized against the clean facade of the building.

Robby's family never shopped on Black Friday. Their Thanksgiving always consisted of dinner at Grandma's followed by his mom and grandmother working on little projects around the house. Grandma never asked for help, but she worried around the edges of something until someone would come to her rescue. That someone was always Robby's mom.

Robby had seen the lines of people on TV though. He'd seen them camped out on the news, waiting for the big post-Thanksgiving sales. Now, witnessing the line of shabby tents and chairs, Robby saw them in real life. Or, perhaps "real death" would be more appropriate, he thought.

Even from his distance, Robby saw that these would-be shoppers suffered the same fate as everyone else south of Portland —the sitters all sat with slumped heads and eye goo on their jackets. Most of the others were splayed out on the sidewalk. One unlucky man in a black jacket and a black cap had fallen forwards. The velvet rope propped him up under his armpits and the stanchions on either side leaned towards him, like drunken buddies propping up their passed-out friend.

Robby stood up and glanced around, feeling stupid for having ducked because of a tent-fly flapping in the wind. He rolled his bike down the aisle of the parking lot over towards the group. He figured this would be an easy place to score another vehicle.

He started scanning the clump of cars looking for a nice, big, new-looking vehicle. With a few candidates in mind, he looked down the line of corpses, trying to determine which body belonged to what car. He decided to try to correspond each car's parking lot position to the place of the person in line.

He couldn't see the occupants of the first tent, but guessed from the big double-wide tent that the people belonged to the first tan minivan. The third guy was easy. His wheelchair matched him nicely with the van in the handicapped spot. Robby thought about going directly for the wheelchair guy's keys. The van looked capable and sturdy. Then he remembered a thing he'd seen on TV —people in wheelchairs were likely to have their vehicles retrofitted with hand controls. Robby didn't want to learn something new; he was still getting comfortable driving a normal car.

Robby walked past the handicapped van and paused at the travel lane to look both ways before crossing. He smiled at his habit—who was he expecting to drive by? Robby pushed the bike and then stopped quickly when the bike made a weird sound. The freewheel clicked twice and then made a weird "swooshing" sound. The sound stopped almost as quickly as the bike. Robby leaned down closer, but didn't see anything wrong with it.

He pushed the bike forward again, waiting for the familiar click from the rear tire. Once again, as soon as he heard the second click, he heard a swoosh. He stopped the bike again, and the swoosh was followed immediately by a complementary "whoosh."

Without moving the bike, he heard it again. "Swoosh-whoosh."

Robby realized the sounds weren't coming from the bike. He looked up. His eyes tracked down the length of the line towards the corner of the Best Buy.

A giant puddle spilled down from the sidewalk into the parking lot. As he watched, another wave of liquid gushed from around the corner of the building and joined the puddle. The crest of the new flood made the swoosh sound, and it spread out into the puddle with the whoosh sound.

To Robby—an island boy—the flowing liquid was the tide coming in on gentle swells. Despite the volume of fluid coming in with each swell, the puddle didn't seem to be growing. At least it wasn't growing in diameter. If anything, instead of getting wider, the puddle was getting deeper. Robby backed up. His feet seemed to move on their own until his body was mostly hidden behind the van. Robby peered around the side to watch several more swells bring even more height to the center of the puddle. It sloped down towards the pavement on the edges, but in the center the puddle looked about knee-deep. Robby glanced around in all directions, looking for the best angle of retreat. When he didn't see anything else dangerous-looking behind him, his curiosity returned his gaze back to the liquid.

The swells stopped coming from around the corner and the edges of the puddle pulled in a little tighter. The pavement around the puddle where the liquid retreated was still dark with moisture. Robby watched the swelling liquid change direction and head towards the back of the line of corpses.

Except for his winter jacket, the last guy in line would have looked perfectly at home on a beach. His big folding chair had cup-holders built into both armrests, and the man slouched deep into the seat. His head slumped over to one side, as if his last margarita finally caught up with him. The man's gloved hands flopped over the armrests and dangled at his sides.

The fluid in the puddle seemed to slosh from front to back in slow motion. First, the trailing edge would rise up and the front edge of the puddle would pull back a little. Then, with the whoosh sound, the liquid flowed to the front, inching closer to the sunbathing corpse. Robby watched the slow sloshing fluid and remembered his grandmother's living room. On one of the end tables she'd kept several knick-knacks. Robby's favorite—the one he could stare at for an hour—was a little wave machine. It had a layer of clear oil and a layer of blue water and it sat on a fulcrum. Touching one side of the device would start it tipping back and forth so you could watch a wave travel from one end to the other and then back.

Robby stared transfixed at this real-life wave machine as it overtook the sunbathing corpse.

For a minute he forgot about the bike, about looking for a car, and about his missing parents. Robby simply remembered his grandmother's living room and the wave machine as he watched the slow-motion liquid slosh over the sunbather corpse's legs. It looked like the liquid would just move past the corpse, but then the chair started to sway. The sunbather's arms swayed as the chair rocked from side to side. The shaking became even more violent and the corpse's head flopped back and forth. When the sunglasses flew from the corpse's face, Robby ducked a little lower. With each rock, the sunbather slumped lower. Robby thought it almost looked like the liquid was tugging at the sunbather's legs. The chair stopped rocking when the sunbather corpse slipped all the way out of the chair and disappeared into the liquid.

Robby couldn't see much of the next corpse. Only the feet poked out from behind a gray and red tent. The liquid barely even took two swells to envelop and then move past those feet. When the fluid moved up the line to the next corpse, the feet were gone. The original sunbathing corpse disappeared without a trace as well. Robby squinted over the distance at the sloshing fluid. It looked perfectly clear, but it absorbed two adult corpses.

Robby glanced in every direction, suddenly feeling exposed.

Movement on his right caught his eye and he retreated to the far corner of the car to hide from this new threat. At the front of the store, near the double-wide tent, another pool of sloshing liquid formed just inside the big glass doors of the Best Buy. Every time the liquid pulsed, it rose higher on the inside of the glass door. Robby didn't see where the leak started, but soon the liquid gushed from the bottom of the door and started to pool on the sidewalk outside the store. This pool looked bigger than the other, and it was a lot closer to Robby. As soon as the puddle completely migrated to the sidewalk, it started sloshing towards the tent.

The pool at the head of the line moved faster than the other. It nearly rolled the big tent over with its first assault. The tent poles sprung free with the tent flipped up at a forty-five degree angle. They bent over into parabolas from the tent fabric, but when they tore loose from the corners, they pointed straight into the air. Without its poles, the tent collapsed and bunched up in the sloshing tide. The poles fell backwards, landing on either side of the wheelchair. They were quickly joined by the next wave, which swept over the base of the wheelchair.

Robby watched the liquid flow around the feet of the wheelchair man. When the fluid receded, Robby saw what was left of the wheelchair man's useless legs. Instead of leaving behind wet shoes and cuffs, the fluid left behind nothing. The wheelchair man's pants simply ended below the knee. Nothing, including the fabric of the wheelchair man's pants, remained. Before he could blink, he saw the next wave slosh up to the wheelchair man's waist. Robby couldn't see the man's lower body—the fluid sloshed but continued to obscure the wheelchair man's lower body—but suspected it disappeared to wherever the legs went. He figured the legs were gone because the wheelchair corpse suddenly became unstable in his chair. As the liquid sloshed, the wheelchair corpse's body wavered and then toppled over into the fluid.

One arm remained above the surface of the fluid for a second, and then the whole wheelchair corpse disappeared. The liquid pooled around the wheelchair still looked clear.

Robby had seen enough. He glanced back to the end of the line and discovered that the original puddle had overtaken about a third of the line of corpses. If they kept moving towards each other, within minutes the two puddles would run out of corpses to absorb and would collide somewhere in the middle.

Robby slid his bike back from the front of the van and backed away slowly from the Best Buy. He tried to keep the knot of parked cars between himself and both of the puddles, but that soon proved impossible. Even though they moved closer together, Robby couldn't shield himself from both puddles. He made his choice and moved from behind a little Toyota.

If it had eyes, the puddle farthest away at the back of the line could have seen Robby as he snuck across the parking lot to get away from the carrion-feeding puddles. When Robby reached the sidewalk, he threw a leg over the bike and strained at the pedals to pick up speed.

At the next intersection, under the dead traffic lights, Robby saw a trail of dark, wet pavement running down the center of the road. He couldn't see the puddle that left the wet trail, and couldn't even guess where it was headed, but he still didn't want to cross the trail. He imagined even touching the damp pavement might summon the swelling fluid.

Robby took a chance and steered his bike to the left. A few dozen yards down the new road, the wet trail veered off and intersected a storm drain. He slowed the bike and put his feet down to consider the trail. He would have to jump the curb to ride on the sidewalk unless he wanted to cross the trail. It seemed like a stupid chance to take.

Robby took off his gloves and tucked them under his armpits so he could blow on his cold hands. It wasn't as chilly as Maine, but the wind cut right through the gloves and froze his fingers to the handlebars. The smallest whisper of a sound made him take his hood down so he could hear better. He tilted his head—the sound came from the curb. He took a couple of timid steps closer to the wet streak on the ground. The sound wasn't the same swoosh-whoosh from the Best Buy. This sound reminded Robby of a squeaky hinge on a door in a haunted house.

"Hawn-ned howse," his mother would have said. Halloween had been her favorite holiday by far. Their house always sported the most intricate Halloween displays—from spooky spider webs in every doorway, to the rounded gravestones in the side yard. Robby remembered the corny epitaphs his mom composed and then inscribed in chunks of styrofoam before she painted them to look like weather-worn rocks.

Robby's dad liked the simple ones—"Here lies Fred. A rock fell on his head."

But his mom enjoyed writing more abstract verse. "Herbie found a dime and ate it. It made him constipated. Then he died." Robby remembered standing over her shoulder as she composed the verse, carving it into the foam with her paring knife.

"You're going to run out of space," Robby said. "How will you finish it?"

She didn't answer—his mom just completed the thought with those last three words—"Then he died." That cracked her up. She'd laughed for five minutes at the sudden change in tone of that particular epitaph.

The memory of decorating with his parents warmed up Robby from the inside. He wanted to sit down and remember their faces. He wanted to wrap himself in a blanket of memories. He thought about lowering himself to the ground so he could stare off at nothing and remember better times. The sound—weird screeching like a protesting metal hinge—was the only thing bothering him. He wondered why it didn't stop. It just kept going.

The sound of the bike clattering to the pavement snapped Robby back to the present. His mouth hung open as he looked at the bike lying on its side. The back wheel spun, producing a slow tick, tick, tick. Its rhythm almost lulled him back into his trance. He shook his head and glob of spit flew from his lower lip.

The front tire of the bike was touching the wet streak on the pavement. But it wasn't just a wet streak anymore; near the tire enough liquid stood to smooth out the surface of the asphalt. The fluid looked deepest right around the bike's tire. The whole bike jerked and Robby heard a hissing sound from the front tire. The rim settled into the puddle as the tire deflated.

Robby reached for the back wheel so he could pull the bike away from the swelling puddle. When he gripped the metal rim of the tire, his fist closed hard around it. His hand clenched against his will, like his fingers were magnetized. One of the spokes dug into the webbing between his index and ring fingers. Despite the pain, Robby couldn't relax his grip. His arm throbbed with the effort of his clasping hand. Numbness started to spread up Robby's arm from his hand. Robby gave up on trying to let go of the rim and instead pushed back with his legs to pull his arm from the bike. His grip didn't waiver, but he pushed his way to his feet.

The bike pulled away from the puddle until the front tire was just about to break contact with the water. At that point, the liquid seemed to exert some kind of force on the front tire. As Robby pulled and leaned away from the puddle, the bike held him from backing away. He lifted the back half of the bike off the ground with his pulling as the puddle held the front tire.

Robby grunted with effort. Where it gripped the rim his hand felt ice cold. The gloves he pinned under his armpits fell to the pavement as he raised his left hand to tug on the wrist of his right. The numbness in his right arm worked its way up to his shoulder.

Robby sprawled backwards when the puddle gave up its grip on the front tire of the bike. His hand immediately came free of the rear rim and he hit himself in the forehead with his cold right hand. Robby flew back a couple of feet and landed on his back on the asphalt. As soon as he hit, he scrambled backwards with his legs and left hand. He held his right arm to his chest. Pins and needles stabbed his right arm as the feeling rushed back into the limb.

The bike looked to be free of the puddle now, but Robby didn't want anything to do with it anymore. He got to his feet and backed away without taking his eyes off the part of the puddle that ate the bike tire. The fluid was still collecting there; it grew deeper each second. Before he could get any farther away, he noticed the liquid ebbed and flowed, like back at the Best Buy.

Pain came with the return of feeling to his right hand.

Robby turned and ran from the liquid trail on the pavement. He crossed the sidewalk and kept going, running full-speed across a scrubby vacant lot bordering a gas station. The station had a little convenience store and Robby pressed himself flat against the side of the building while he tried to catch his breath. He rubbed his hands together. The feeling started to return to his cramped right hand.

The faint wet streak down the middle of the road was just barely visible from the store, but Robby kept his eyes locked on it as he backed around to the far corner of the building. The back wall of the store had two steel doors and a narrow alley between the store and a tall stockade fence. He jogged down the length of the building.

On the other side, he found a vacuum machine with a big "QUARTERS ONLY" sign and a corpse face-down in the parking lot. Just past the dead guy, Robby saw a beat-up truck. He sprinted the few steps to the corpse and gave him a big shove to roll him over. The exploded eyes still shocked Robby. He could barely take his eyes off the man's face as he patted down the guy's pockets, looking for keys. No keys. Robby rolled his eyes and let out an exasperated sigh. He tucked his hands in his own jacket pockets and looked around for another body to search.

Robby looked at his own right hand and flexed his fingers. His hand still felt a little numb, and his palm was red where he'd gripped the rim, but it looked okay. It felt like an electric current, but without the buzzing sensation. Robby had shocked himself experimenting with electricity, and this was almost the same feeling.

He glanced back at the corpse's right hand. The man's hand was closed around on something. Robby ignored the exploded eyes and went right for the fist. The corpse's fingers gripped a set of keys. Robby smiled and pried them free from the cold fingers. The chain didn't have a fob for unlocking the doors, but the truck was the only nearby vehicle, and the key said Ford just like the grill of the truck.

Robby found the truck unlocked. The key fit the ignition and the truck fired up.

"Yes!" Robby said. He slammed down the door lock on the passenger's side and then took care of his own door before he turned to look around. The truck was just a two-seater, so he didn't have to worry about something jumping up from the back seat, and the bed of the truck was empty. Robby adjusted the seat so he could reach the pedals.

He dropped the transmission lever down to drive and cranked the wheel around. He took a hard right on the asphalt to stay as far away from the wet streak as he could. When he straightened the wheel out, he floored the gas and nearly lost his grip on the wheel as the old truck burst forward. He took the next turn a little fast. The truck swayed and felt out of control. Robby stabbed the brakes and tried to wrestle the vehicle back under control. He took his feet off of both of the pedals and let the truck slow down and straighten itself out instead of fighting it.

"That's more like it," he said, smiling. He adjusted the rearview mirror. "Now let's get the hell out of here."

Robby accelerated gently and leaned back.

This road was mostly empty. Only a couple of derelict cars remained in the travel lanes, so Robby didn't have to weave at all. He reached down and turned on the blower. It made a chirping, bad-bearing sound, but warm air leaked out from the vents and made the noisy truck a lot more pleasant. He read the signs carefully—he could get back on the highway up ahead and continue his southward trek. The skies were packed full of sooty clouds, but to the south they looked brighter. He thought it possible he might even find clear skies before the sun went down completely.

The gas gauge showed more than a half tank of gas. Robby turned on the radio just loud enough to hear the static and hit the seek button. The frequency display spun quickly up through the numbers without pausing. He watched as the numbers worked up through the low hundreds. A shadow across the road caught his eye just before the explosion. As the shadow crossed under the front of the truck's hood, Robby realized it wasn't a shadow at all. The dark pavement was a wet spot.

The front tires of the truck fired off at the same time. They blew out with a spectacular bang. The idiot light on the dashboard of the old truck—the one to remind Robby to fasten his seat belt—was dark during the trip up until this point. At the very instant the information could no longer help, the light flashed on.

The tires didn't just explode—they actually stuck to the road where the pavement was stained dark with fluid. Robby figured this out as the back of the truck started to rise. The truck's momentum was forcing the engine down towards the pavement, and the rear up in the air.

Robby tried to brace himself against the steering wheel, but his arm strength was no match for his own inertia. He flew forward into the wheel. Like the seat belt warning light, the truck's airbag was sluggish to respond. Robby's chest almost made contact with the top of the wheel when the vinyl under the horn sprung out of the way of the inflating bag. The airbag's deployment was almost as violent as the sudden, jolting stop, so Robby was now thrown backwards and his momentum deflected upwards.

His head hit the roof of the cab and he left a streak of skin and hair on the headliner.

The rear wheels of the truck floated almost three feet over the ground before they reached their apex and started to fall back to the pavement. Robby fell backwards too after his encounter with the late but overzealous airbag. He fell backwards at the same speed as the truck, so it seemed like free-fall to Robby, like he would never hit the ground.

When the truck hit the ground and Robby hit the seat, his arms and neck rag-dolled and he bounced on the old seat springs. On the second bounce, his jaw clacked shut, and his left incisor drilled a perfect hole through the edge of his tongue. Blood filled his mouth as he blinked hard, trying to hold on to his senses, and batted the airbag out of the way.

Movement on Robby's left drew his attention. The dark streak of moisture across the road led up over the curb and then disappeared into the grass embankment next to the road. The movement turned out to be a swell of liquid returning to the wet track. It seeped out of the grass and produced a bubble of fluid moving towards the front of the truck. The first swell only looked about five inches high, but on its heels, the next swell could have touched Robby's knees if he'd been brave or stupid enough to stand in the street.

The fluid looked the same as the carrion wave back at the Best Buy, but it didn't move at the same lazy speed. This wave had a purpose. It pushed across the westbound lanes as Robby's mouth filled with blood. He grabbed for the door handle, but the door wouldn't budge.

"Shoot," Robby said. His pierced tongue turned the word into "Thoot," and blood and spit spilled down his chin. He banged at the door with his shoulder. It seemed like it wanted to open but the upper corner was hanging up on the frame—newly bent from the accident, Robby figured.

He hit the button to lower the window. The motor sounded sick, but the window began to slowly open. He pressed the other button too. The passenger's window started to descend as well. It went faster. Both windows stopped when the wave impacted the truck's wheel. All the lights on the dash extinguished as well. He jerked his hand away from the switches, afraid to touch anything after his experience with the bike. His window was only halfway down; the other window was a little lower.

Robby dove across the seat and grabbed for the passenger door handle.

The front of the truck dipped, dropping Robby into a six inch free-fall. Stretched across the seat, he pulled the passenger's door handle and pushed with his other hand. The door groaned, but moved a little. He pulled his legs up and thrust them back against the side of the driver's seat for leverage.

The front of the truck lurched again, dropping another foot.

Robby wailed away at the door. It sprang free and flew out of his hands. The door swung wide open, hit the limits of the hinges and bounced back. He caught it with stiff arms and held it open as he scrambled across the seat. The floor mat of the truck, where his feet would have been if he'd been riding shotgun, changed color and then disappeared completely. Where the wheel-well should have been, he could now see clear through to the pavement. As the pavement grew and the floor mat disappeared, Robby realized the whole front of the truck was falling at a steady pace now.

The driver's side was disappearing faster, so the truck tipped to that side. By the time Robby climbed out through the passenger's door he could almost stand on the side of the truck. He surveyed the pavement quickly. The front edge of the truck was eroding into the puddle of liquid, but the rear still sat over dry asphalt. He leapt to the rear.

He only needed to push himself a few inches to the rear to get clear of the puddle. But with the truck falling, and his pulsing adrenaline, he misjudged the jump. His right foot and hand landed on the dry asphalt, but his left foot came down right on the edge of the puddle. It was more than just a wet spot on the pavement now, but still only an inch or so deep where his foot landed.

The pain scared him because it was like nothing he'd ever felt. The numbness when he'd gripped the bike wheel earlier felt like an electric shock, but where his foot touched the liquid, it felt like a lightning strike. He screamed and tugged at his leg. On the second pull, his knee popped and his foot slipped free from his boot and sock. When Robby's bare foot pulled out, the boot sunk into the liquid and disappeared before his eyes. The fluid swelled around the spot, and the puddle was instantly several inches deep there.

The last of Robby's sock vanished. The fluid swelled and then extended a runner towards his bare foot. He sprang to his feet and ran. His naked foot slapped the pavement as he sprinted. After a couple dozen steps, he looked back over his shoulder. The truck silently upended—the front half was now completely gone and the bed and rear wheels stood straight up in the air. The puddle rapidly ate the rest of the truck. It looked like the truck was sinking into a hole opened up in the pavement, but Robby thought the puddle was somehow absorbing the truck's matter. It wasn't like acid, he thought. With acid there would be a sizzling or a smell. The puddle was just dissolving things. Selectively. Back at the Best Buy it hadn't absorbed any of the tents or chairs, but here it consumed everything.

Where the puddle ate his shoe and sock, the puddle struck out after Robby. A thin line of liquid flowed and paused, flowed and paused. It zig-zagged a little and Robby realized the puddle was flowing from spot to spot where his feet had fallen as he ran. He ran up the grass slope to the parking lot of a strip mall. His foot was already starting to feel numb from running barefoot on the pavement, but he knew he didn't have time to worry about his foot. He glanced back. The stream picked up speed; it now gushed after him. The front of the wave was about half-a-foot deep, but behind the leading edge, he saw some swells which looked at least knee-high.

He thought about his mom. Barefoot running would not have been a problem for her. She'd always gone the whole summer without shoes. She would sometimes sit on the front stoop and file down her callouses, leaving a fine white powder of skin on the flagstones.

He slapped himself in the face. Hard. He recognized that weird nostalgia from the last time he'd been close to the liquid. This was not the time for childhood memories. He started jogging across the parking lot. There was only one car in the lot—parked outside the fabric store—and he didn't see any corpses around, but he headed that direction anyway.

He gulped in the cold air through his mouth. He forced himself to jog faster. He couldn't see the flow of the liquid anymore, that was back down the embankment on the road surface, but he sensed the slight hill wouldn't slow it down. His bare foot ached and threatened to cramp each time he lifted it.

Robby reached the car and tugged on the driver's door. The handle snapped back. The door was locked. He pulled back and thrust his elbow against the window, but his elbow just bounced off the glass. He looked back over his shoulder. Back at the edge of the parking lot, the liquid was cascading over the curb, forming a pool on the asphalt where Robby had paused to think about his mom.

"Come on," Robby said. He smacked the window with the palm of his hand and then jogged away from the car parallel to the strip mall. His stride became uneven, favoring his bare foot. A hot knife of pain poked at his right side, under his ribs. He gasped, trying to breathe through the pain.

At the end of the mall, he found a short downhill slope and then another parking lot belonging to the next strip mall. He didn't look back. He barreled down the hill and kept running, scanning the lot but not seeing any cars in this lot either. He almost ran right past the cars tucked along the side of the end store. They were parked behind a concrete block wall, right next to the dumpsters. Even after he saw them he kept jogging. For no good reason, he turned and jogged over to peek around the wall. That's when he saw the green-shirted employees who had gone outside for a smoke break before their eyes exploded and they collapsed in a pile with unlit cigarettes in their hands.

He kicked his legs back into a sprint and instantly regretted it. He stubbed his toe and stumbled the rest of the way over to the bodies. He didn't hesitate at all with the corpses. He rolled the men over and clawed at their pockets. From the three men he came away with two sets of keys and a lighter. He ran to the nearest car—a brown Chevy compact car with New Hampshire plates—and fumbled through the keys. The key with the bow tie fit the door and popped up the lock. He jumped in and cranked the engine as he pulled the seat lever and rocked it forward. The engine caught and he pulled the shift lever into reverse.

The car looked clean but stunk of cigarette smoke. Robby spun the wheel and backed around. He heard a thump from the rear when he backed over one of the smokers' legs. He shifted to drive and pulled around the cement-block wall.

He stood on the brakes, screeching to a halt—the liquid flowed down the hill between the two parking lots and turned the corner to follow Robby back to the smoking area. He stopped less than ten feet from its edge. Robby clutched the gear shift and chunked it to neutral and then reverse. The Chevy's engine wound up like a toy as Robby backed up down the alley next to the mall.

The lot extended back behind the building. He turned the wheel just a touch and slowed to a stop. Behind the mall he saw a long access road and loading docks dotting the back wall of the mall. He paused to see what the liquid would do. Now that he saw an escape route, he wanted to see how smart it was.

The trail of liquid approached the smokers and pooled around them. A fresh branch continued over to where the Chevy had been parked. He watched the corpses dissolve into the puddle—they went quick, without much of a swell of fluid—but the liquid didn't follow the tire tracks of the Chevy. It swelled and ebbed where he had run, but couldn't track him in the vehicle.

He wanted to leave while his luck still held. Before he hit the gas again he pulled the seat belt over and buckled himself in. With the rearview mirror adjusted so he could keep an eye out for the liquid, he drove carefully down the access road. It felt good to get his bare foot off the pavement. The foot still felt numb, but at least it wasn't on cold pavement anymore.

At the far end of the mall, the access road looped around the building and back out to the main parking lot. He slowed and crept the car out slowly back to the main lot. The other end of the lot was so far away that Robby couldn't even see the flowing liquid pursuing him. He found an exit down to the main road on his side of the lot so he steered for it.

Down at the parking lot exit, Robby paused for several seconds and scanned the road in both directions. He couldn't see anything of his old truck back to the west, and he didn't see any sign of wet pavement in either direction. He headed east, towards the highway.

He drove slowly, nervously looking for any signs of damp asphalt. His spirits lifted when he saw the entrance ramp to the highway. He was anxious to start moving south again, regardless of how much his new vehicle smelled of smoke, or how bad his foot was starting to hurt. He rolled down the window and spat a mouthful of salty blood out the window. He probed his swollen tongue against his teeth, wincing at the puncture.

The southbound entrance was first. It swept to the right and gave Robby a long acceleration lane uphill to the level of the highway. Long shadows from the streetlights stretched across the road. He stopped at the first one. He knew it must be a shadow, but the dark pavement could have been wet in that shadow. He crossed it at a crawl, ready to jump out of the Chevy at the first sign of trouble. Nothing happened.

He accelerated again and drove through the second shadow, although he still braced himself when his tires crossed the dark patch of asphalt. The highway here was mostly clear. This part of the road had soft, grassy shoulders and the few deceased cars had veered off the travel lane when their drivers expired.

✪ ✪ ✪ ✪ ✪

Robby saw the wet trail across the highway from quite a distance. He'd been watching for it. On the other side of the center divider, it looked like the trail blocked the northbound lane as well. Robby put the car in park and left it running. He made a quick stop at the trunk of the Chevy, where he retrieved the jack handle from underneath the spare tire. Then he limped over to a gray Volvo, run aground on an embankment on the right side of the road.

The exploded-eye corpse behind the wheel of the Volvo was a man—Robby guessed he was about his father's age, which meant about forty-something. The guy looked short. He wore wire-rimmed glasses with little circular lenses, which were now covered from the inside with eye-goo and blood.

Robby stood on his right foot. On his left foot, only his toes touched the cold grass.

"What size do you wear?" Robby asked the corpse through the Volvo's window. His lacerated tongue felt thick in his mouth, but it also felt good to move it around. "I'm about a nine. Does that sound right?"

Robby swung the jack handle and smashed the glass next to the corpse's face. He raked out the remnants of the window with the end of the bar and then leaned his head through the window so he could figure out the lock. The door wasn't even locked. Robby laughed and tugged at the handle. The Volvo emitted a low "bong, bong, bong," to let Robby know he was opening the door with the ignition engaged.

Robby tried not to step on any of the auto glass with his bare foot as he knelt next to the car to untie the corpse's shoes. The guy wore ankle-high hiking shoes. Robby approved. He pulled the left one off the man's foot and held it bottom-to-bottom with the sole of his foot. It looked a little big, but better than nothing. He thought for a second and then took the sock as well before he moved on to the next foot.

"I think these might fit," he said to the corpse. "Thanks."

Robby stuffed the socks down into the shoes and slung them over his shoulder to head back to the running Chevy.

"You know what?" he asked, turning. "I've got one more question for you."

Robby smiled—he liked the way his voice sounded on the quiet highway.

"This will just take a second," he said as he approached the Volvo again, dropped his new shoes and jack handle on the roof, and reached past the steering wheel. "If you've got enough battery to sound that bell, maybe you've got..."

Robby tried to turn the key off, but it wouldn't turn past a certain point. He wrinkled his brow and thought through his limited knowledge of cars and driving.

"What's wrong with this thing?" he muttered under his breath.

He heard his father's voice in his head. *"Gotta be in Park, Robby. Key won't turn unless it's in Park."*

"Ah," Robby said. "Pardon me, sir."

Robby leaned in farther and tried to move the gear shift lever towards the dash. It went as far as neutral and then stopped.

"What now?" Robby asked.

He heard his father's voice again. *"Foot on the brake. Think, bub."*

"No shit," Robby said to the corpse. He felt like he was playing Twister with the gray Volvo and the barefoot corpse.

"Left foot, brake," he said. He slid his bare foot alongside the corpse's feet and depressed the brake. Then the gear shift slid easily up to Park. With that accomplished, Robby turned the key off and then back on. When he pressed it into starting position the Volvo's engine fired to life. The gas gauge climbed slowly until it reached three quarters of a tank and then it leveled.

"I'll be damned," Robby said. He clapped the corpse on the shoulder and turned the car off.

He grabbed the shoes and jack handle from the roof and turned to hobble back to the Chevy. It took him less than two steps to reconsider. The Chevy was smelly, small, and unreliable-looking. Aside from some eye-splatter, the Volvo looked clean and efficient.

"Thank you sir, I believe I will," Robby said. He wrestled the corpse out of the Volvo and dragged it a couple of feet away from the door. The man's glasses flopped back up onto his forehead, and Robby stepped briefly on an uncomfortable piece of glass, but otherwise the procedure was quick and easy. Robby slid behind the wheel and found he didn't even need to adjust the seat. He backed away from the embankment—the sure-footed Volvo didn't slip at all on the grass—and made a big u-turn across the southbound lanes. He stopped one more time to shut off the Chevy, but he kept the jack handle from the trunk. Before retreating north, Robby took a minute to put on the new shoes and socks. They fit even better than he'd hoped. He used his old sock to mop up some of the eye-juice splattered on the inside of the windshield and then tossed it through the shattered window.

Robby drove north in the southbound lanes until he got to the first police turnaround where he could switch to the northbound lanes. Even though the cars were off the road, it bothered Robby to head towards the fronts of other cars and see the backs of all the signs.

He took the first exit and probed some of the local roads looking for another way south. Robby didn't get far. Before long he found a wet streak of liquid across each road. The highway seemed like the only road safe enough to travel on, and he would have to go back to the north.

He kept a close watch for any more damp pavement. It got harder to be sure as the sun went down. The headlights tried to turn on automatically, but Robby found the override and turned them off. He didn't know what kind of attention they might draw, and he didn't want to find out.

Soon he came to, and traveled over, the bridge back to Maine. He passed the bucking bronco U-Haul, and then the wrecked car with the little boy in the backseat, but they were both in the southbound lanes. Robby observed them like animals at the zoo—sure, they might be dangerous, but they were way over there. He convinced himself they presented no immediate threat to his side of the bridge.

"We've gotta stop soon, Volvo. It's getting dark, and I need some shut-eye," Robby said. He shifted his eyes quickly from mirror to mirror as soon as he finished the sentence. Somehow it felt natural to talk to corpses, but completely creepy to talk to an empty car. Robby decided to keep his mouth shut and hoped the crawling-skin feeling would subside soon.

He drove north until he found a rest stop. The parking lot had a decent number of cars, and scattered corpses here and there. Most of the bodies were in a loose grouping near the visitors center door. Robby pulled right up to the curb near the door and shut off the Volvo as he peered around in the fading light. He saw no sign of carrion-feeding puddles ready to wreck his car and eat his shoes. He listened to the still evening, but didn't hear any city-wrecking tornadoes within earshot. The corpses would have unsettled him even a few hours before, but now they seemed almost comforting. With corpses still around, the puddles must not have arrived, or so went Robby's deduction.

Robby flipped down the visor and slid aside the door to expose a vanity mirror. A light flicked on, but Robby turned it off with the switch. He'd intended to use the mirror to get another view of the highway behind him—he wanted to be able to see every direction at once—but once he caught a glimpse of his eyes, he couldn't look away. His eyes, framed by the little mirror in the visor, looked just like his Dad's eyes.

He heard his dad's voice in his head again. "*Go on inside. You can get something to eat and use the bathroom."*

Robby tested his punctured tongue against his teeth and glanced over at the small pile of bodies near the door.

*"They won't hurt you. You've seen plenty of bodies today. Nothing to be afraid of."*

Robby grabbed the keys from the ignition and took one last look at his eyes in the mirror before opening the door. They still looked like his father's eyes, and they still glowed with a confidence Robby didn't feel.

*"Robby?"*

"Yeah?" he asked aloud—responding to a question only in his head.

*"Look in the trunk. This car is tricked out and well cared for. You'll find an emergency kit with a flashlight in the trunk."*

His father's voice was right. Robby found a kit of useful tools and a flashlight in the trunk. He moved the kit to the back seat of the Volvo and took the flashlight to the door of the visitors center. The new shoes felt weird to walk in. They were comfortable, but weird. His left foot still felt a little sore, but Robby was able to walk without much of a limp. He rounded the corpses and pulled open the door to the visitors center.

He didn't need the flashlight until he got to the bathroom door. The big glass wall on the front of the building let in enough of the fading light for Robby to get around.

In the bathroom, Robby tried to not swing his flashlight around too much. The dancing shadows created by the moving beam made the dead people seem to shift. A guy near the urinals had shot an impressive double-shot of blood from his eyes against the tile wall before he slumped to the floor. Another man had fallen forward into a urinal. His chin was propped up on the porcelain scoop.

Robby stepped over the arm of a man who had flopped backwards while washing his hands. He approached the nearest stall. After using the bathroom, he made his way quickly out the door.

At the far end of the lobby, a small convenience store sold snacks, newspapers, and souvenirs. Behind the counter he found shopping bags. He filled a couple with shirts, sweatshirts, food, and water. They didn't sell socks. Shoes were one thing, but the thought he was wearing a dead man's socks still bothered him.

He stood examining the coffee mugs, thinking about nothing at all, when he heard a noise outside. Robby shut off the flashlight and listened. His eyes adjusted rapidly to the low light, but all he could really see was the outline of the glass doors at the other end of the building. The noise had been a muffled thump, like a bag of sand landing on a wooden floor.

Robby shuffled slowly towards the doors in the dark. He slid his feet along the floor, conscious he would hit a corpse or two on his way out. The only sound he made was the crinkling of the swinging plastic bags which held his supplies. Robby inched his way over to the doors in the dark. He stepped over several corpses on the way, but he did it without having to turn on his flashlight. He stood by the door for several minutes looking out into the evening. The clouds diffused enough of the moonlight so he could make out shapes in the lot. The Volvo sat near the curb, waiting for Robby. He took a deep breath and pushed through the doors. The three corpses near the outer door let him by with no mischief.

Robby got back in the Volvo and shut and locked the doors. His eyes, blinded by the dome light from the vehicle, took several seconds to readjust to the dark.

*"You should move away from here, Robby,"* his father's voice counseled.

"In case that liquid shows up and tracks my footprints?" he asked, looking up to the visor mirror.

*"Exactly,"* he heard inside his head.

With the headlights off, Robby drove very slowly to the far end of the lot. He backed the Volvo into a spot bordered by a patch of grass meant for walking dogs. He shut the car off and checked again to make sure the doors were locked.

The clouds overhead moved fast. Robby could tell because an occasional break in the clouds let through bright, sharp moonlight. The view changed from soft blue to sharp black and white until the next set of clouds diffused the light again. Before him, the lot looked like a very complex model built by a very morose child. It possessed all the right elements—cars, buildings, people, trees—but it looked too still in the moonlight. It was an underexposed still-life.

Robby ate chips on the right side of his mouth and draped sweatshirts over his legs like miniature blankets.

He glanced up every now and then to look for his father's confident eyes in the visor mirror. It was too dark to see the resemblance, but Robby looked anyway.

"*I trust you've abandoned your local extinction idea,*" his father's voice asked.

"Yeah," Robby whispered in the dark. "It was just a working model. I told you that. Just a theory to test and use for decision-making until more evidence could be collected."

"*And what does your evidence tell you now?*"

"Looks like something or someone malevolent has decided to take over," Robby whispered.

"*Thing? Or things?*" his father's voice asked.

"Yeah, it does appear different forces are at play here. At home we got lots of snow and people disappearing into the air. South of Portland, I found lots of bodies and less snow. In New Hampshire, no snow at all and a carrion tide dissolving all the people it could find."

Halfway through explaining to himself, Robby stopped speaking out loud and just thought the ideas in his head.

"That stuff was like a liquid cleanup crew. Like a wet cleaners instead of a dry cleaners. It also seemed to be a trap to catch any stragglers. I wonder if it eventually formed a grid to catch all the leftover people like me who didn't have their eyes blasted out," he thought.

Robby drifted off to sleep with one hand on the steering wheel and the other on the gear shift. A potato chip sat on his chest.

## CHAPTER 10: BRAD TRAVELING

THE SNOWMOBILE MOVED EASILY over the ice as long as he kept it pointing directly up or down a slope. He ran into trouble when he tried to ride along the side of a snow dune. Then, the back end of the sled wanted to slip down the hill faster than the front. Brad checked his compass and map often, but he had trouble finding enough landmarks in the deep snow to keep him on course.

He intended to find the highway and follow it south. After half-an-hour of following what he thought was his road, Brad conceded he had no idea where the highway might be. He should have crossed it, if he'd stayed on course. Near his house, the highway ran almost east and west. So, if he traveled roughly south, southeast, as he intended, he should find it or even cross it.

He thought perhaps he did cross it and just didn't know. In his mind, it would be easy to spot—a big swath of smooth snow, dotted with overpasses and marked down the center with a hump. But, with the random drifts and rolling dunes, perhaps it wouldn't be so obvious.

Brad let the engine of the snowmobile idle as he consulted his map.

Instead of looking at the roads, Brad paid more attention to the contour lines and shading of the map. Those he tried to align with the hills in the distance. He smiled as he squinted at the distant hills—he felt more relaxed being able to see the horizon.

The real key to his navigation turned out to be the waterways.

They cut through the landscape, leaving big ribbons of troughs. The river was frozen over and snow accumulated on top, but far less snow than on the banks. As a result, when Brad finally came upon the river he figured out exactly where he was. The curve of the river, the way it narrowed before the dam, and the hump of the bridge let him triangulate a specific spot on the map. Once he figured it out, Brad was able to make sense of some of the other bumps and curves of the snow dunes.

On the far side of the river, Brad saw a thin black line in a wall of snow. He identified the line as the top windows of the old mill. The snow drifted dozens of feet deeper than he believed earlier.

Brad angled his snowmobile towards the hump of snow covering the old bridge so he could get a closer look.

He made his way carefully down the slope to where he thought the bridge started. Somewhere under snow was a green bridge consisting of overhead steel trusses, holding up the road surface over the falls. The snow mound looked solid from a distance, but up close he saw bumps and holes aligned with the steel trusses beneath. It didn't look at all safe enough for his snowmobile, even with the icy shell on top of the snow. On either side of the bridge, the snow sloped down way too steeply. Brad imagined getting safely down to the frozen river—assuming the ice there was thick enough to support the loaded snowmobile—but he didn't know how he could get back up the other side.

Brad looked up and down the river.

The next closest bridge was east and a little north, but it was a local road. He could get across the river, but then he wouldn't have any good landmarks to follow on his trip south. To the west, the next bridge was where the highway crossed the river. He'd have to track a ways back north to get there, but then he might be able to recognize and stay with the highway as it turned south.

Brad turned the snowmobile around in a wide arc and headed north and west, keeping the dip of the river valley on his left shoulder, always within sight.

As he made his way through neighborhoods and across town, Brad didn't see many landmarks punching up through the snowpack. He saw treetops here and there, and the occasional peak of a roof, but most of civilization was buried under a thick white blanket.

The bridge where the highway crossed the river was easy to spot. The black hole beneath it drew Brad's eye. As he traveled up the shore of the river, keeping the sharp drop-off on his left, he saw a black dot approaching. Above it, the big mound of snow blended in with the gray horizon, but the black was unique in this landscape. Around the edges, as he got closer, Brad saw the hazy blue of translucent snow.

To Brad, It looked like a portion of clear night sky existed just in one spot, and it entranced him. As he drew even closer, he discerned two distinct black spots, separated by a thin line of white.

He let the snowmobile slow to a halt as he considered the scene. The river headed about northwest here, and from his map he saw the train tracks veered away from the river's edge to head almost north.

Looking northwest, the river valley stopped suddenly where the highway bridge crossed. Beneath this bridge the snow left deep caves—Brad's black patches of night sky.

"They're just snow caves, under the bridge," he told the idling snowmobile. "There's nothing under there, I'm sure." After all, he didn't see any tracks away from the black holes, or any disturbance in the snow at all. But he couldn't take his eyes off those black spots, and couldn't convince himself there wasn't something living down there where the light didn't seem to penetrate.

Brad started the snowmobile moving again, but wished the whining engine didn't make so much noise as he followed the river up to the bridge.

The bridge made a big double hump across the river. Brad felt better once he was aligned with the highway and couldn't see the black caves under the bridge anymore. His instinct told him to line up with the center of the double hump and go right down the middle of the bridge, but his memory rejected that idea. If he remembered correctly, each direction of the highway had its own separate bridge. That little dip of the double hump might just be a suspension of ice and snow, supported by nothing. Brad needed to aim for the rounded top of one of the humps to make sure he would stay over pavement. On either side, the snow dropped off a good fifty feet to the bottom of the river valley. The last thing he wanted to do was plunge fifty feet into whatever was at the back of the black cave.

Brad chose the hump on the right and steered for the center. The highway beneath was two lanes with generous shoulders on both sides, but the top of the hump looked dangerously small to keep his snowmobile centered on. Brad thought about how easily the back end would slide if he missed his mark and aligned with either edge of the hump. He started slow, but as the banks fell away on either side he found himself speeding up, trying to get across faster. The bridge straddled the five hundred feet of the river, plus a bit extra on the sides where the banks swept down to the edge.

Through his weeks of battling the snow, Brad learned how to stay warm. He left no skin exposed. His flannel-lined pants were tucked into his waterproof boots, which kept the snow from reaching his wool socks. Over the pants and over the boots he wore snow pants bought years earlier for snowboarding. On his torso, Brad wore layers. The top jacket snapped into his snow pants. A special, breathable scarf wrapped his lower face and tucked under his hood. Goggles covered his eyes. The yellow lenses gave definition to the snow shadows and the tight band around the hood made it move with his head as he turned. Two-part gloves covered his hands—the inner for warmth, and the outer for the waterproof layer extending with cuffs over his forearms.

Because of all this protection, Brad didn't notice the strength of the wind until about a third of the way across the bridge. A gust rocked his snowmobile and caused the back end to slip left, towards the cleft between the lanes of the highway.

Brad slowed, trying to get the snowmobile under control. He immediately recognized the mistake. With no power driving the snowmobile from the back, the skid intensified. Brad stood and shifted his weight to the right—that kicked the rear end even farther to the left. Brad goosed the throttle, but with his weight shifted to the right, he couldn't steer into the skid. When he pushed the right handlebar away, he moved his weight to the left. He had a high center of gravity because of the backpack full of food. The snowmobile rolled up onto the left ski and threatened to tip over.

Brad didn't have any choice. He lowered his weight down to the seat and steered to the left to regain control and keep the snowmobile from rolling. The sled straightened out and shot down into the cleft. Brad felt like his heart would beat right out of his chest. He pictured the bridge in cross-section. As he remembered it, the northbound and southbound lanes of the highway shared nothing in common except perhaps foundations at the river's surface. Between the two humps of snow covering the traffic lanes, the snow and ice must be suspended above nothing. Perhaps the wind created a drift held up by nothing more than melting and refreezing ice until after weeks the drift spanned the gap. Then, maybe ice capped the whole delicate structure, giving it the illusion of a solid surface.

Before Brad reached the lowest part of the cleft, he heard the first crack. It sounded like a rifle shot echoing in a canyon. Worse than the sound, he *felt* the crack send a shockwave up through his snowmobile. Brad hunched lower behind the windscreen and opened the throttle all the way. The back end of the snowmobile danced as the tracks tried to drive the skis faster over the ice. Brad didn't try to steer—the machine headed for the upslope to the northbound lane and he let it go. He figured he would try to regain control just as soon as he wasn't hovering on thin ice over a chasm of death.

The slope up to the northbound bridge broke under the pressure of his skis. They dug into the ice and turned the front of the sled away. Brad reengaged his arms and tried to steer against the rebuff, but the skis wouldn't bite. Behind him, another rifle shot crack cut through the noise of the engine and made the hair on the back of Brad's neck stand up.

Brad steered back to the right, to try to climb back to the southbound lane. He was about two-thirds of the way across the river at this point, but had no thoughts about reaching the other side. He just wanted to reach the safety of pavement somewhere beneath his snowmobile.

With the third echoing crack, Brad saw evidence of the damage to the ice. A jagged white line shot out like lightning from beneath his snowmobile and ran down the length of the cleft. He felt the ice sag as he tried to climb the slope back up to the southbound hump.

The rear end of the snowmobile jumped to the left when a chunk of ice gave way. Brad looked back over his shoulder to see the snow and ice falling away, revealing a white hole which disappeared into blue depths. Somewhere down there he knew he'd find the black if he fell. He would find the night-sky black in that cave, and he would find out if something lived down there.

Brad leaned to the right to balance out his sled as he tried to climb the side of the hill while still moving forward. His right hip floated just inches over the ice, but he kept the snowmobile from rolling.

He never made it back to the top of the southbound bridge's hump.

The hump had a slight lip on it, and every time Brad tried to angle the snowmobile to crest it, the back end of the sled would skid.

Brad panted and sweat soaked through his shirt as he fought the machine, but before he could summit the hump, it disappeared. The ridge line marking the lip simply faded into the snow, and instead of climbing back up on the hump of the southbound bridge, Brad found himself on a flat stretch of ice with no hump to fight. Brad looked back and saw the bridge behind him.

He let the snowmobile slow to a stop. In between the lanes, giant holes opened up in the ice leaving snowmobile-eating chasms. Brad took a deep breath and it shuddered out of his chest. His breath felt thick. He clawed the goggles from his face and wiped the corners of his eyes with his glove.

"That *sucked*," he said. He giggled into the back of his glove while looking at the holes through the ice. The edges of each hole looked blue, but even at this distance he thought he could see the black down there somewhere.

"Guess I'll come back over the bay," he said.

Brad put his goggles back on and turned his attention south. Since he'd found the highway, he thought following it would be fairly easy. He could see the dip of the center divider and then the banks on either side of the lanes. Plus, farther down the road, he could see the next overpass. The outline was subtle, but trackable.

Behind him, another crack rang out and made Brad flinch. He turned, expecting to see another hole opening up, but it still looked the same. Brad kept watching as he eased the snowmobile back into motion. He glanced back several times until the bridge passed out of sight behind a hill.

✪ ✪ ✪ ✪ ✪

The overpasses became Brad's best landmarks. They gave him an opportunity to pin down his exact location on his map. The big one, where the two-lane entrance from Route 1 crossed over and integrated with the highway, cost Brad about an hour to navigate around though. The underside of the bridge stood filled with snow, and the slope to the top stood too steep to climb. Brad needed to find his way around. He used the exit and entrance ramps, eventually.

The highway turned due south just before Freeport. Brad dug out a can of orange marking paint he'd packed in one of his bags. He tucked the spray can inside his jacket to warm it up. Then, after Brad found a way around the overpass for Route 125, he kept his eyes open for any landmarks on his left. In Freeport the high school sat in a lot which basically abutted the highway, and Brad wanted to test his theory that the schools might be emergency housing for storm survivors.

Along this stretch of road, trees lined the highway. Brad couldn't see the trees for all the snow piled on top of them, but they made the highway seem like it was carved into the snowscape. He rode along with the sound of his snowmobile reverberating off the walls of snow on either side. Brad tried to get on top of the snow wall on his left, but the snow was unstable underneath the ice. He punched through little air pockets so often, jolting the sled's ride, that he was forced to return once more to the snow-covered highway. When he saw a break in the wall to the left, he decided to leave the highway and try to find the high school.

He took the can of spray paint from his jacket and marked an arrow on two of the snow-covered tree mounds before he left the road. The orange paint stood out well amidst all the white. Brad kept the can at the ready and laid down a mark on the ice every time he was forced to make a turn around an obstacle.

The map didn't give him any clue. What finally pointed him in the right direction was the shape of the baseball diamond. Its geometrically perfect fences ended at the looming backstop and snow-mounded bleachers. Brad had to drive over to the dugout and orient himself down the third-base line before he could point to the series of lumps belonging to the high school.

Brad drove around to the front of the gym to hunt for any signs of life.

He found nothing.

Around the side of the gym, Brad made his way to the front of the building. He stood on what should have been the front lawn of the stately high school, looking up at was surely the front facade. He didn't expect anyone to still be there—he figured anyone would have evacuated south weeks before—but he thought he would at least see signs that people had sought refuge from the snow there. He found nothing.

Brad took a side street away from the high school and found the big municipal parking lots which serviced the multitudes of summer shoppers who came to visit Freeport's outlet stores. In town, the wind swept big snow banks against the sides of buildings and down the streets, making everything a jumble of unfamiliar shapes. Brad steered his snowmobile to the top of the highest snow hill to try to get his bearings.

He found an interesting shape which reminded him of his own house. Just downslope from his perch, Brad found a bowl of ice surrounding a cluster of chimneys. The exhaust from the chimneys had melted the falling snow enough to keep this area clear. As he rounded the bowl, he made another discovery—part of the melted snow had kept part of the building exposed. Brad found a dormer with a set of windows looking in on a business office.

Brad's curiosity turned into excitement when he realized he'd found entry into L.L. Bean—a huge retailer of outdoor gear. He shut off his snowmobile, smashed through the window, and found himself in the penthouse office of the hiking and hunting mothership. Brad considered himself pretty well decked out, but knew he could easily upgrade all his gear in this one store.

Walled offices lined the perimeter of the floor. The center was divided up into cubicle space. Brad guessed it served as a call center at one time, but not too recently. Most of the desks had no personal items, just a dead computer, stapler, and roll of tape. Brad left his backpack at the window and led with one of his flashlights as he explored the empty floor.

In the very center, he found elevators and a door to the stairs. Brad propped open the door with a fire extinguisher and took the stairs down into the retail space. The next door was three flights down. Big windows in the staircase showed layer after layer of packed snow against the glass. Halfway down the bottom flight, he saw a layer of gray in the pristine snow, like soot had fallen from the sky along with the white flakes.

Brad pushed through the heavy door and found himself standing behind an information desk in a section dedicated to fishing and archery. He dragged a display rack of fishing line over to prop open the door and then swept his flashlight around the cavernous store. The inside of the store featured tons of exposed beams and hanging canoes and other merchandise. As Brad's flashlight beam swung through the space, the shadows danced and spun two stories up on the tall ceiling.

Next to a stand of fishing poles, a split rail fence divided the shopping area from a nature scene with a standing black bear. It looked like pretty good taxidermy to Brad, but the dusty fur detracted from its realism.

Brad shined his light in the bear's glass eyes and leaned on the fence. "Can you do me a favor, Baloo? Can you keep this door open for me?"

The sound of his voice in the emptiness of the place gave him a chill. These aisles expected dozens if not hundreds of milling shoppers to animate the space. Without them, it seemed haunted. Brad busied himself making a mental list of survival gear he could use and set about finding the items. The store had multiple floors and twisted and turned over a city block, but Brad only needed to hit a couple of sections to find what he needed. He passed by the giant aquarium. A few fish darted to the corner, away from his light. They fed on their dead cousins.

"Why aren't you frozen?" Brad asked the fish behind the glass. The fish didn't answer. They only stared back with bulging eyes and flared mouths. The fish didn't answer him, but he found his answer as he looked for a parka in his size.

In the men's outerwear section, Brad set his flashlight on top of one of the display cases and pointed it at a stuffed bobcat which sat on a cubby case filled with jeans. Its shiny eyes weren't looking at Brad. Worse—the eyes seemed to have just turned away every time he looked up at it, like it had been studying Brad and then looked away nonchalantly just before he caught it in the act.

He removed his gloves, goggles, and jacket, bracing himself for the cold of the icy tomb, but found the temperature moderate. It wasn't just the lack of wind—Brad gauged that the inside of the store was at least in the forties, if not higher. He removed his cap and listened. He couldn't hear any machinery. Brad grabbed what he needed and dressed quickly. He added a headlamp just above his goggles. He glanced back at the bobcat several times as he left its section.

Back at the stairwell, the door stood propped open by the fishing line rack.

"Thanks, bear," he said. "One more favor? If you see a bobcat, try to slow him down until I get out of here?"

Brad glanced back in that direction as he spoke. His headlamp reflected on some shiny object at the far end of the store and Brad imagined the bobcat crouched there, waiting for the right moment to sprint after him. Brad moved the display and let the door swing shut behind him. It clicked as it closed, but not before Brad heard some sliding noise, like claws on a tile floor. His new clothes were too well insulated for the store. Sweat stood out on his brow and he unzipped several layers while he pounded up the stairs.

At the top of the stairs he burst through the door and kicked aside the fire extinguisher. He had a moment of panic when he couldn't remember where he'd come in. He'd gotten turned around during his exploration and expected the window in the wrong direction. He found it again by covering his headlamp and shutting off his flashlight. Brad jogged for the faint glow of sunlight through snow which marked the exit.

The door to the stairwell clicked shut.

Brad turned and braced himself for a bobcat attack. There was nothing there. He climbed out through the window and felt more comfortable when he mounted his snowmobile and started the engine. Brad drove back up to the top of the building to scan for the best direction to get back to the highway. He initially intended to head back to the high school so he could backtrack to where he'd left the highway. With his new stolen binoculars, he picked out one of the dashes of orange paint he'd left to mark his trail.

Brad pulled the binoculars away from his eyes. A dark shadow passed by the hump he identified as belonging to the high school. He caught the smallest glimpse of it before it disappeared behind a snow drift. Brad slung the binoculars and turned his snowmobile in the direction of Route 1. The drifts from all the stores made the road hard to follow, but he preferred that to facing the implied unknown of the momentary shadow he'd just seen.

Fortunately, he kept his speed low and didn't flip his snowmobile when his ski punched through the crust and hooked a power line. For a second, the line looked like a giant snake. Brad wrestled the sled backwards—not wanting to touch the twisted black cable—until he pulled the ski free from the line.

✪ ✪ ✪ ✪ ✪

Once he got back on the highway, Brad wound the snowmobile back up to a decent speed. He still slowed for bridges and overpasses, but mostly to check the map and verify his location. The next significant crossing came just a few miles south of Freeport, where the highway crossed over Route 1 in Yarmouth. Here the two roads switched places, with the highway hugging the coast and Route 1 pushing inland for a while. Brad found the location of the overpass, but it didn't look right—he couldn't find any drifts marking the buildings he knew in the area. He expected to see at least a big mound to his left, where a map store featured a giant blue globe in the lobby.

Instead, Brad found flat snowfields in both directions. He could see the line of Route 1 trailing north, mostly because it cut through the hills in a straight line, but to the south it just faded into the flatness. A little farther south he found the bridge where the highway crossed the river, and he saw up the river where the other bridges crossed, but aside from the gentle swells and dips of the terrain, he saw no features. Towards the ocean, Brad saw nothing but frozen white plains.

In the middle of the bridge Brad lifted the binoculars. With these he could see dark water—at least one sign that the whole world wasn't frozen over.

✪ ✪ ✪ ✪ ✪

By mid-afternoon Brad found himself in Falmouth. He took his time navigating the ramps and overpasses, trying to find the safest way around them. His work was complicated by the diminishing snow. Here he saw the tops of trees poking out from the drifts, and even the peaks of a few houses up on the hill. Where the highway passed close to the marshes, he saw open water not far off the coast. Brad stopped next to a spot where the retreating tide left a muddy bank. He ate lunch while watching the lapping waves.

To his south, Brad saw buildings of Portland—whole buildings —without a trace of snow on them. He took care on the bridges which led into the city. They were covered with just enough snow to make the footing for the snowmobile unstable. He found hardly any crust here, like the ice had given up somewhere around Falmouth.

With the lack of snow, Brad expected to find other signs of life. He kept his eyes peeled for animal tracks, smoke from chimneys, or even birds, but he saw nothing. He slowed down as he entered town. The snow only measured a few inches deep—just barely enough to keep riding the snowmobile without worrying about damage to the skis. Brad killed the engine the first time he heard them scrape.

Brad removed his goggles and took down his hood. The whistling wind blowing across the cove was the only sound he heard. He didn't see a single car in either direction. The highway was deserted. He stepped off the snowmobile and stood in the middle of the southbound lane of the highway. The few inches of snow was covered with just enough of a crust to not blow away.

He stood at the north end of Maine's largest city. The city looked intact, but utterly uninhabited. From his position he saw all the tallest buildings of the city. On his right, the city's muddy cove bordered perfectly still neighborhoods.

Brad started walking.

He followed the highway down to a grocery store. He still carried plenty of provisions, but he wasn't looking for food. He was looking for signs of human activity. He approached the store through the adjacent park, stopping at a bench to use his binoculars. Someone had broken out the window next to the door. Brad approached cautiously. He found various footprints leading in and out of the store, but most of the prints seemed to belong to one set of shoes, slightly smaller than his own.

The store was dark inside. When he turned on his headlamp, Brad found the fist-sized rock inside the circle of broken glass. A cart, flipped on its side, lay past the rock. He wrinkled his nose as he stepped carefully over the glass. Even with the cold, aisles of past-due perishables assaulted his senses. Brad took a quick tour through the store. In the realm of canned goods, he found a couple of shelves which looked suspiciously empty. The store's inventory of soup, beans, sauce, and canned vegetables had been hit hard. The baking supplies looked fully stocked.

On the other side of the store, Brad found the chips, snacks, and other junk food diminished as well. He grabbed a couple of items for himself, stuffed them in his big pack, and then exited. The footprints led to tire tracks.

At the end of the parking lot, the tracks headed off in various directions. Brad picked a direction and walked down the tire tracks. The snow crunched under his feet and he whistled a tune to go with the rhythm. Under a dead traffic signal, the tracks split up again, heading in all three directions.

"You've been busy," Brad said to the tracks. He crouched to study them further. It looked like the vehicle had only gone straight through the intersection once, to the left a couple of times, and the majority of trips had gone to the right. Except for his own, he saw no footprints to go along with the tire tracks.

Brad took a right and walked down the middle of the road. Local businesses and office buildings flanked him on either side. He walked between a set of fast food restaurants, and rubbed his stomach through his jacket.

He interrupted his whistling for another comment to nobody. "Oh, what I wouldn't give for a hot burger right now. Give me a large fry, no, two, and a large shake," he said.

At the next block the tracks branched again. Brad stopped and turned in a slow circle.

"I get it," he said. "You don't want me to know where you're going, so you've gone everywhere. Is that it? Either that or you've got business in every part of town. Well I know one place you've visited quite a few times."

Brad left the main drag and wound down side streets until he came up behind a house which faced a grocery store. He stood on the front porch for several minutes. The brick porch featured pretty, understated columns holding up a solid roof. The panes on either side of the door were frosted, but by kneeling on the porch swing Brad could see into the living room. The house looked clean and spare. Under-stuffed furniture sat on oriental area rugs and hardwood floors. The walls and trim were white, but the moldings had a fancy, old-school design.

Brad went back to the door and cocked his elbow to break through the glass panel next to the door handle. He couldn't do it. He felt compelled to knock first. Brad knocked and then stood there, looking around to make sure he was still alone, feeling foolish while he waited to see if anyone would answer.

"Okay," he whispered, "I'm breaking in."

He tapped the glass and then lined his elbow up. His eye

landed on rocks lining one of the flower beds right next to the porch. Brad smiled as he fetched a rock.

"No sense ripping my new jacket," he said as he got ready to smash the window with the rock.

Before he thrust the rock forward, he reached out with his right hand and tried the handle. The door opened and swung inward.

"I'll be damned," he said. Brad pitched the rock back into the yard.

He left the door open a crack. The temperature was lower inside the house than out. He took a quick tour of the first floor— nice dining room, living room, kitchen, bathroom, den. When he made it back to the entry, he climbed up to the second floor. Upstairs he found bedrooms and bathrooms. The house had nice views of the cove and the city in the distance. Out front the maples would block most of it in the summer time, but this time of year they would have a glittering view of the city lights every night.

Brad smiled to himself as he stood in the master bedroom—if he ever lived near the city, this would be the kind of place he'd like to have. Around him, everything pointed to life suddenly interrupted. A glass of water and a folded magazine stood on the nightstand. A pair of pants lay draped over the back of a chair. In the master bathroom, a towel was hung over the shower curtain rod. Brad took off his glove and ran his hand over the top of the bureau. He found some dust—enough for his finger to leave a trail —but probably less dust than on his own bureau at home.

Brad visited the rest of the bedrooms. The family had two girls from the looks of the rooms. One girl had a serious odor problem in her room, but Brad guessed it was from the dead ferret in the aquarium. At least it looked like a ferret. Brad only saw a fuzzy lump of moldy fur in the corner. He found plenty of signs of them, but no actual residents.

In the kitchen, Brad found the stairs to the cellar. He turned on his headlamp and his handheld flashlight, but he barely needed them down there. Three walls of the house had window wells which let in plenty of light into the unfinished space. Despite having concrete walls and floors, the cellar looked very neat. Aside from the furnace, water heater, and other appliances, Brad found some workout equipment and well-organized plastic bins of books.

Brad locked every door, even the cellar door, and checked the locks on all the windows. He removed his backpack in the living room and moved the couch away from the front window. From this window he saw the best view of the grocery store. He planned to camp out in the house until he spotted the owner of the vehicle and the small sneakers, assuming they were the same person.

Brad pulled up an austere chair, and snacked on food from his pack as the light faded from the winter sky. The throw blankets from the living offered little warmth, so Brad fetched a down comforter from the non-smelly girl's room. He wrapped his legs and stayed awake for as long as he could. The clouds glowed from a moon which Brad couldn't see. Every now and then, he spotted a break where he could see the stars. While he stared at the night sky, his eyes drifted close and Brad fell asleep.

He woke once in the middle of the night and found his way to the back porch to relieve himself. He didn't use a light—he didn't want to be spotted or to ruin his night-vision. When Brad returned to his seat, he thought he saw a glimpse of brake lights on the other side of the cove. He stayed up for hours, staring at the spot and hoping to see more, but he saw nothing. He eventually slipped back to an uneasy sleep and didn't wake up again until the boy broke into his hideout at dawn.

## CHAPTER 11: BRAD AND ROBBY MEET

ROBBY PUSHED OPEN THE door and shined his flashlight into Brad's eyes. Outside, the clouds on the horizon glowed with the dawn.

"What do you want?" Robby asked. His tone was flat, rather than inquisitive.

Brad jerked awake and held up his hand in front of the light. A package of cookies slipped from his lap and landed on the floor.

"I'm sorry," Brad said. "Is this your house? I didn't think anyone was home."

"What do you want?" Robby asked again.

"What do you mean?" Brad asked. Even without being able to see Robby completely, he got enough of an impression from Robby's stature, frame, and voice to guess that he was young. "Hey, kid, do you mind not shining that thing in my face?"

Robby lowered the beam to Brad's feet and then swept it quickly around the living room. Robby returned the beam to Brad's chest. Brad saw Robby's silhouette, but not his face.

"Why are you watching the grocery store?" Robby asked.

"I saw tracks there. I wanted to see if anyone would come back," Brad said. "Do you know how long it's been since I've seen another person? Since before Thanksgiving."

"Where were you living?" Robby asked.

"Kingston," Brad said. "Where were you living?"

Robby ignored Brad's question. "How much snow did you get there?"

"What's with the questions anyway?" Brad asked. "How about we go back and forth? You know, with me answering one question, and then you answering one question? Like a real conversation?"

"I'm from an island off the coast. You don't know it," Robby said. "How deep was the snow in Kingston?"

"I didn't exactly get a chance to measure it, but it was pretty fucking deep. Pardon my French," Brad said. "Not as deep as Freeport though. Maybe about twenty feet?"

"And Freeport?" Robby asked.

"No, no," Brad said. "My turn. Where did everyone go?"

"I have no idea," Robby said. "Why did you come from Kingston down to here?"

"I couldn't keep living up there under twenty feet of snow, could I? As soon as the snow stopped I came south to find out where everyone went. Were they evacuated or something?"

"No, they weren't evacuated," Robby said. "So, as you said, you haven't seen anyone since Thanksgiving, correct?"

"As I said," Brad confirmed.

"If you decide to stay here, you can have that grocery store," Robby said, pointing. "If you decide to leave, there's a parking lot up on Forest Ave. If you see a car with the windshield wipers up, it's driveable and the keys are in it. There will be a syphon in the back seat. If you see a parked car with the gas door open, you can assume there's no more gas in it. You'll have to syphon from another to fill your tank."

"Wait, son, wait," Brad said, sensing the conversation was coming to an end, "how long have you been alone?"

"What makes you think I'm alone?" Robby asked.

"Well, then how many people are there?" Brad asked.

"I have no idea," Robby said. "Some people are living here where the snow is only a couple inches deep, but most people live alone. If you go south or west, you'll find dead bodies. Go too far away from the snow and you'll find worse. Watch out for any standing water or even any wet spots. They're dangerous."

Robby started to back out of the door, pull it shut behind him.

"Wait, wait," Brad begged, "where will you be?"

"I'll see you again," Robby said.

"Hey, get back here! What day is it?" Brad yelled as Robby clicked the door shut.

From beyond the closed door he heard Robby's yell. "Friday, January sixth."

Brad threw off the comforter and bolted over to the door. He pulled it open and followed the boy's footprints across the neighbor's yard and over to a side street. A couple of stop signs away, he saw a red car taking a right turn.

✪ ✪ ✪ ✪ ✪

Brad spent a week in the Dead Ferret house before he saw the boy again. He intended to grab one of the cars from the Forest Avenue lot and head south. He found the cars just as the boy said he would —two near the corner of the lot had the windshield wipers raised, keys in their ignitions, and syphons in their back seats. Brad took the nicer of the two vehicles and started out for the highway.

Lots of tracks led down Forest Avenue, but none veered onto the entrance ramp for the highway. Brad puzzled about that as he too continued past without using the ramp. He continued on Forest until he saw a set of tracks turn off onto a side street. His curiosity got the better of him and he followed. The tracks led up the side street, and down another, zig-zagging through the streets past businesses and houses. At the next major road he found so many tracks leading to the bridge to South Portland that it almost looked like the road had been plowed.

In South Portland, Brad saw a wrecked vehicle for the first time. He got out to investigate.

A woman's curly hair pooled over the steering wheel of the compact car. The car sat with two wheels up on the curb, but had little damage where it rested against a utility pole. Brad knocked on the window even though the hood of the car was cold when he took off his glove and touched it. The curly hair still didn't move when he knocked again.

He tugged at the handle, but the door was locked.

Farther south, Brad found a big truck in a ditch with unlocked doors. When he pulled the door open, a man in a flannel suit slumped to the side, held in place by his seat belt. The air from the truck smelled bad. The man behind the wheel had an open mouth and black, crusty holes where his eyes should have been. His tongue looked gray and swollen. Brad shut the door to the truck and walked slowly back to his own vehicle. As he drove around South Portland, he saw several more wrecked cars and although he slowed for each one, he didn't bother to check out the people inside. From what he could see from a distance, they'd all shared the same eye-bursting fate.

Brad made his way back to the ferret house that night.

He explored his local neighborhood. Although he found no corpses—eyes burst or not—he did make several other discoveries. Right next door he liberated a round heater from a sewing room over a garage. This house also yielded two big blue cans of kerosene. The round heater drove the living room temperature of the ferret house up to eighty degrees one evening. Brad slept in his underwear that night for the first time in months.

The one thing Brad didn't find was any other real live people. He followed tire tracks through the snow, but never found any footprints leading to a house, or saw any cars driving around. He got good at rolling up on parked cars and siphoning off their gas when he got low. Brad always remembered to leave the gas doors open on cars he drained.

Then, finally, a week after he'd moved into the ferret house, Brad walked up to the parking lot to find the boy standing next to one of the parked cars.

"Hi," Brad said, raising a hand to the boy when he was still a few dozen yards away.

Robby lifted a hand back, but waited until Brad drew closer before he spoke.

"Do you want to come have dinner with us tonight?" Robby asked.

"Sure," Brad said quickly. "Where?"

"You know where the Denny's is?" Robby asked.

"The one right up there?" Brad asked. "There's not another one, is there?"

"That's the one," Robby said. "We'll be there at four."

"Great," Brad said. "Can I bring anything? How many people?"

"The clocks in these cars are both right," Robby said. "You don't need to bring anything. See you at four."

"Excellent," Brad said. "See you then."

Robby turned and snaked between some parked cars, heading towards the back of the lot.

"Wait," yelled Brad, "what's your name?"

"I'm Rob," he called back.

"See you tonight, Rob," Brad said. "My name is Brad."

Robby didn't turn around, but lifted a hand to wave and acknowledge Brad.

✪ ✪ ✪ ✪ ✪

Brad cleaned himself up the best he could. He used an outdoor turkey frying rig to heat up several gallons of water and then dragged the water inside to the bathtub. He found fresh clothes in a house behind his Dead Ferret house. The men's clothes in the Dead Ferret house hung comically large on Brad. But, the guy who'd lived in the house behind the Dead Ferret house must have been just Brad's size.

He bathed and shaved, amazed at how much better he felt about himself when he finished. His hair hung down over his forehead, but he managed to sweep it back with some mousse from the bathroom cabinet. Brad changed twice. He settled on a red golf shirt. It had a collar, but didn't look too fancy. Over the shirt he wore a thin grey sweater to match his thick grey socks. He wore flannel-lined chinos which fit okay in the waist. He rolled up the cuffs so they didn't drag when he walked. Brad finished the ensemble with a nice black jacket—zippered, but nice enough to wear indoors if it was cold.

He went upstairs to look himself over in the master bedroom's full-length mirror. Before, he'd looked like a homeless person. Just what you'd expect in a post-apocalyptic hellscape, but not the best way to make a first impression. He preferred to look capable, together, but not too prosperous. He wanted to look able to take care of himself, but not somebody you'd envy. He'd lost a lot of weight—he saw it in his face now that he was clean-shaven. His cheeks didn't have grooves in them, but they showed noticeable shadows where the grooves were staking out their claim. Brad reminded himself to smile a lot—smiling hid the shadows.

Brad walked up to the Denny's. Taking a car from the lot felt cumbersome, and Brad wanted to feel unencumbered in case he wanted to get away quickly. He took his pack, loaded with survival supplies, and tucked it behind a bush about a block away from the restaurant. He got there too early—almost thirty minutes too early—so he walked around the side streets for a while. He found the local jail. It sat in a tidy brick building near the train tracks. His watch read three-fifty we he got back to the Denny's. Brad went inside.

Two kerosene heaters—not the same as Brad's, but the same idea—warmed the place up to about sixty. Brad took off his outer jacket and kept on the black one. It wasn't toasty, but it was comfortable.

"Hello?" he asked the room. The only light inside came from the flames of the heaters and the late afternoon light through the windows. The door was unlocked, but someone had drilled out the lock, so it would remain forever open. One table with four chairs had a tablecloth and candles. Brad sat down and lit the candles with a book of matches he found on the table.

The swinging door from the kitchen opened and a young woman stepped into the dining room. She looked like a schoolteacher to Brad. More accurately, she looked like one of Karen's friends—Brad couldn't remember her name—who had taught fifth grade. Brad immediately thought of this woman as a teacher, just because of her resemblance to a woman whose name he couldn't remember. She wore shoulder-length brown hair and a windbreaker over a bulky sweater. Both the windbreaker and the sweater hung down over her black corduroys. When she pushed through the door she looked down at her feet, and her eyes seemed buried in dark hollows. She brightened considerably when she looked up and spotted Brad at the table.

"Are you Brad?" she asked.

"Yes," Brad said. He half rose from his seat—wanting to seem polite, but unthreatening.

She approached quickly with her hand outstretched.

"I'm Judy," she said as she shook Brad's hand. "Robby will be here in a bit."

Robby entered through the front door a few seconds later. An older man followed Robby. Brad figured this guy to be in his sixties. Brad was forty-two, and hoped he could move as gracefully as this guy did when he reached that age.

"I see you've met Judy," Robby said. "This is Ted," Robby gestured at the older man. "Ted and Judy, this is Brad."

Brad shook the older man's hand as they all moved into position around the table.

"Judy called you 'Robby' just now," Brad said to Robby. "You said your name was Rob earlier. Are you a Rob or really a Robby?"

"He *prefers* Rob," Judy said. "But he only seems to answer to Robby."

Robby smiled and blushed a little. Brad liked him more in that moment than in their previous two encounters combined. The kid had seemed too serious before, like he was trying to act like he thought an adult should.

"Does everyone like pancakes and sausage?" Robby asked.

Judy nodded. She took a seat next to Brad.

Ted stood behind a chair and held the back of it as he spoke. "I'm just here for introductions. I'll leave you to dinner. Brad," he extended his hand again, "I'm sure I'll see you again soon."

"Okay?" Brad said, shaking the man's hand.

Without further explanation, Ted waved and then left by the front door.

"Pancakes?" Robby asked Brad again.

"Yeah, sure, absolutely," Brad said.

Robby turned towards the kitchen.

"How can I help?" Brad called after Robby.

"Just have a seat and I'll be right back," Robby said as he propped open the swinging door with a high chair.

Brad sat down reluctantly and smiled at Judy.

"I wish I could help with something," Brad said. "We can't just let the kid do all the work, can we?"

"Don't worry about it," Judy said, smiling. "Robby likes to cook for people every now and again. He prefers not to have an audience though."

"Oh," Brad said. "So you've known Robby for a while then? Are you related?"

"No," she said, smiling. "I've only known him for a month or so. We met at the grocery store."

"Oh," Brad said. "So where were you living when everything happened? Were you in Portland."

Judy put her hand on the table between them, as if she could pin the conversation right there, on the tablecloth. "Do you mind if we wait until Robby comes back before we talk about how we all got here? He's heard it all before, but we always like to make sure everyone is present when we talk about recent history. 'More ears pick up more details,' he says."

"Sure, sure. That makes sense," Brad said. "How about farther back? Can we talk about what we did before?"

"Of course," Judy said. She smiled and looked down at her hand as she withdrew it to her lap. She touched her ear before she began to speak. "I used to work in marketing for a little company downtown. We did things like direct mail, emails, magazine ads, you know—increasing brand awareness and stuff."

"Cool," Brad said. "What was the product?"

"I don't know," she said, smiling a tight, close-lipped smile. "I mean I do, but I don't really. I'd only worked there a couple of months, and it seemed like we were just selling air."

Brad smiled and nodded. "I think I've worked for that company too," he said.

"What do you do?" she asked.

"I was a contractor," he said.

"Like construction?" she asked.

"No, nothing so practical. I did computer stuff—web stuff and programming," he said.

"Sure, okay," she said. "Good work?"

"Not really," he said. "But it paid the bills."

Judy nodded and pushed a wrinkle out of the tablecloth with her finger. Brad was careful to keep his hands on his lap, one on each thigh. It was a trick he used whenever he spoke in public. With his hands on his thighs he would keep his feet flat on the floor and sit up straight. If he slouched, he tended to stammer. Good posture brought clear speaking.

"I'm just wrapping up," Robby yelled from the kitchen.

"Is everything okay with the other guy? Ted?" Brad asked.

"I think so," Judy said. "He doesn't like gatherings. Or, I mean, he likes them, but he doesn't like to stay. He just wants to be introduced and then he usually heads on his way."

Robby came in holding a serving tray with both hands. He brought plates, utensils, and a big stack of pancakes.

"They've got a great gas grill out back, so we like to do gatherings here," Robby said as Brad stared at the pancakes. To Brad, the pancakes looked like civilization, and smelled like heaven. He kept his hands in his lap as Robby and Judy passed around the plates, silver, and food. Robby doled out equal portions to everyone, and Judy used her fork to put two of the pancakes back on the center stack.

Brad wanted to dive into the food, but waited as everyone fixed their plates just so.

"You wouldn't believe how long it's been since I've eaten any decent food," Brad said.

"It shows on your face," Judy said. "No offense."

"None taken," Brad said.

As soon as Robby lifted his fork, Brad tore into his stack of pancakes and savored the authentic maple syrup. That syrup hadn't come from a Denny's. Brad would have bet a thousand dollars on it if money still meant anything. That syrup came from someone's backyard maple tree.

"This is fantastic," Brad said.

"Thanks," Robby said. "It's one of the few things I cook well."

"I'll say," Judy said. She and Robby shared a smile. Brad couldn't tell if her statement was a compliment, or a light-hearted jab.

"So did you guys wait to talk about how we got here?" Robby asked through a mouthful of food.

"Yes, are we waiting for Ted too?" Brad asked. "Judy said we should all be here, but I'm dying to know what you guys know."

Robby nodded as he chewed. He wiped his mouth and set down his fork before he replied.

"No, we don't have to wait for Ted," Robby said. He pushed away from the table and went to the counter to grab three bottles of water. After he drank, he told Brad and Judy his story.

Judy nodded at all the right spots, but it was clear she'd heard it all dozens of times. Brad listened closely to Robby's account of Thanksgiving on the island. The boy's story seemed to have coherent details and no exaggeration, but it was hard to take everything Robby said as a gospel truth. Brad wondered how much of the story was colored by Robby's age and lack of experience. Robby told everything, including how he met Judy and the days leading up to the dinner they all were currently sharing.

Brad quickly understood the wisdom of this approach. With Robby's entire story told from his perspective, there was no blended viewpoint. When Judy began, she told all of her details even though some of her story shared many of the same elements as Robby's. They both told of snowstorms, TV and radio broadcasts fading to static, and people disappearing. She attempted to drive south, but turned back when she found all the wrecked-car corpses lining the roads.

"I wasn't scared," she said deliberately. "I wasn't. I mean I wasn't scared of the dead bodies, but I thought there was probably some plague or something that infected everyone south of here. I figured it would be safer to come back here. Everyone was gone here, but at least there weren't dead bodies everywhere."

Brad nodded. Robby stopped eating while he listened to her account.

"I saw a couple of people who looked like their eyes had burst," Brad said. "It was like they'd been exposed to low pressure or something, and their eyes just popped out. I mean, not popped, but burst." They sat for a second before he spoke again. They all nudged their plates away. "I'm sorry, you were right in the middle of your story."

Judy picked up the thread again with how she returned to her apartment and figured out how to survive. After a few weeks, she met Robby in the grocery store. Here, apart from the times they'd been alone, her story and Robby's were fairly identical. They both had sketchy descriptions of their daily activities. Brad sensed plenty of room in there to hide many details, but he didn't probe with questions.

When Judy and Robby turned to Brad for his side of the story, he started immediately after the explosion that woke him up. He left out any account of the casually-dressed government guys, spinning rocks, killer vines, and fugue-like flashbacks. He started with the snow, and how it was almost immediately too deep to make any attempt at escape. The beginning of his story stumbled, but everything flowed better once he started talking about the snowmobile journey.

Robby didn't move an inch while Brad talked. As soon as Brad finished, Robby rose, took their plates and headed for the kitchen.

"I have to at least help with cleanup," Brad said. He stood and dabbed his mouth with his napkin before dropping it on the chair. Outside, the sun went down, leaving them on a little island of flickering light provided by the candles and heaters.

"I'll come too," Judy said. "I swear he has night vision."

Brad followed Judy to the kitchen. They used the glow of the candles and headed for the dark door. Judy fished a small flashlight from her pocket just as a light in the kitchen came on and gave them something to navigate towards.

In the kitchen, Robby lit a bright lantern and set it on one of the stovetops. On another burner, a big pot held simmering water.

"I've got to go," he said and pointed as they entered the kitchen.

Judy nodded as Robby headed towards a back door. Brad saw a dim rectangle of light as Robby let himself out into the evening.

"Where's he going?" Brad asked.

"He means go," she said. "You know? You want to wash, rinse, or dry?"

"I'll take rinse," Brad said. "Back at the Dead Ferret, I just toss them in a barrel."

"The Dead Ferret?" Judy asked. She tested the temperature of the water in the big pot with her finger and then hefted it to the sink.

"It's just what I call the house where I've been crashing," he said.

"Gruesome," she said, flashing him a thin smile.

"I'll call it the D.F. then," he said. "Seems presumptuous to call it home. I don't know how long I'll stay there anyway. Nothing in the closet fits me. I might look around for a place with more light."

"You can draw another pot of water from the barrel over there," she pointed.

"Is this potable?" Brad asked, eyeing the large white plastic container of water near the door. "I haven't been washing dishes because I didn't want to use up a whole lot of good water. I figured it was more precious than the dishes themselves."

"We pump our own from a well," Judy said from the sink. She was scrubbing the syrup from the plates with hot soapy water.

Brad set the pot down on the floor next to the white tub. A hose came out of the top where a thumbscrew was mounted. When Brad turned the plastic tap, a little water flowed from the hose below. The stream petered out rapidly.

Robby came through the back door as Brad tried to puzzle out the water barrel. Brad could smell the hand sanitizer Robby rubbed between his young hands.

"It's pressurized," Robby said. "You pump it up here."

"Like a keg?" Brad said.

"I guess," Robby said.

Robby followed Brad back to the sink. Brad rinsed the dishes and handed them to Robby to dry. The light from the lantern was bright, but lit everything from behind, so most of their movements happened in the shadows. Robby seemed to see everything and helped Judy and Brad get the dishes perfect before he dried them and set them back on the prep counter.

"So, you saw a layer of black soot in the snow strata?" Robby asked.

"In Freeport? Yes," Brad asked and answered.

"Tornado?" Judy asked Robby, as the boy hung up the towel.

"I think so," Robby said.

"What's that?" Brad asked.

"You remember how I told you about my boat trip?" Robby asked. When Brad nodded, the boy continued. "I saw clusters of tornadoes tearing apart some of the cities along the coast. I'm guessing Yarmouth was one of those. You said you couldn't see any signs of any buildings in Yarmouth, and you also mentioned a layer of soot in the snow in Freeport. I think when the tornadoes tore apart Yarmouth, they put down a layer of soot in Freeport."

"Yeah, I wanted to ask you more about that," Brad said. "These were sentient tornadoes?"

"Controlled by something," Robby said. "Not necessarily intelligent themselves."

"Sure," Brad said. "That makes sense. I mean, it challenges the imagination, but anything's possible, right?"

"Given enough energy," Robby said.

"I don't believe that," Judy said. She folded her arms. "Can we go back in the dining room? It's cold in here."

Robby didn't reply, but immediately moved towards the door, picking up the lantern on the way. Brad and Judy followed him back to the dining room where the heaters felt pleasant. Judy moved her chair closer to a heater and sat down. Robby put the lantern on a table of one of the booths.

"Should we close the curtains or something?" Brad asked. He walked over to the booth next to the one where Robby left the lantern. "You could probably see that light from across town."

"We haven't found anything in town here to be afraid of," Judy said.

"Yet," Brad said. He stared out the window, not sure what he was looking for, but feeling exposed nonetheless.

"Right. We haven't found anything to be afraid of yet," Robby said. "What are you afraid of?"

Brad spun and faced Robby. "As far as I know, there are only four people left alive in the world. What am I *not* afraid of would be a better question."

"There's a bigger group of us spread around. You'll meet everyone the next time we have a big meeting. Come tell us again what happened before the snow fell," Robby said as he sat down at the table again. He propped his head up on his hand.

Judy pretended to look over at the flame of the heater, but she watched Brad out of the corner of her eye.

"Okay," Brad said. "Not much to tell, really. I was working on a contract. My boss didn't call me when he was supposed to. It started to snow on Thanksgiving Day, then my internet went down, then TV and radio, and then the power."

"Cell phone?" Robby asked.

"That went out," Brad started and then stopped. "That went out the same time as the TV and radio."

"And you didn't try to get to town then?" Robby asked.

"I tried, sure," Brad said. "But the roads were already too bad to drive. Nothing had been plowed. Besides, I figured nothing would be open on Thanksgiving Day."

"How far do you live from Kingston?" Robby asked.

"I'm not sure what you're getting at," Brad said. He forced himself to stay seated and return his hands to his lap.

"We just want to hear as much of your story as we can," Robby said. "The more we know, the closer we get to figuring this thing out."

"Yeah, no pressure," Judy said. "Just anything you can remember."

"Why are you two so convinced that there's anything more to tell?" Brad asked. "Neither of your stories contained anything particularly interesting before the snow started to fall. Why should my experience have been any different?"

"One of the guys who I first met in Portland, after I came back north, had been evacuated from Kingston Depot *before* the snow started," Robby said. "He said the National Guard moved in almost a week before Thanksgiving and removed everyone."

"On the news last fall they downplayed the whole thing," Judy said. "At least they did at first. They started by saying some people were asked to leave their homes because of a groundwater contamination. Later in the week, just before the storm, there was a story that there was more to it. They showed pictures of Kingston Depot on the news—Army and National Guard trucks were everywhere."

"I wasn't evacuated," Brad said. "But, then again, I live out in the country. My nearest neighbor is over a mile away."

"On the Meadow Road, right?" Robby asked.

"Yes," Brad said after a moment.

Judy nodded. "That's where they said it started."

"I also heard there was a similar thing going on up north of Augusta, but that Kingston Depot was the biggest. My parents never really talked about it. It was just something happening on the news," Robby said.

Brad frowned and looked down at his hands.

"Well, I don't know what to tell you," he said. "Maybe they didn't know that I live out there, or maybe I was fine because I don't have city water. Who knows?"

"And you didn't go into town that week, or happen to see the news?" Robby asked.

"I was busy working," Brad said. "When I get busy, everything else just falls away. Just ask my ex-wife. She'd tell you, if she were still alive."

"There's a chance she's still around," Judy said. "You never know."

"No," Brad said, "she died years ago."

They sat through an awkward silence. Brad wanted to change the subject, but knew they might construe that as an admission that he had something to hide. He thought he could feel their eyes on him, but when he finally looked up, Robby and Judy were looking elsewhere.

"Do you have any theories on what happened?" Robby asked.

"I don't think I have enough information for a good theory," Brad said.

"Doesn't have to be informed to be good," Judy said.

"The whole thing is just puzzling," Brad said. "More so now than before I talked to you guys. I thought everyone just left, or evacuated, or whatever. Then, the other day, I saw the corpses for the first time. So I figured some people didn't make it out. But now you guys are saying that most of the people just disappeared into the sky. Evaporated or at least became invisible, right? Well that puts it right in the realm of some brand new force. Something we've never seen or heard of before has now acted upon our neighbors. It's too much of a coincidence to believe that it doesn't have anything to do with the coordinated tornadoes or multi-story snowfall. So that means that this new force has powers many times greater than anything we've ever heard of."

"So you're thinking aliens," Robby stated.

"I didn't say that," Brad said. "Just a force."

"Or Rapture, right? Why not Rapture?" Judy asked. "Why can't your great and powerful force be God?"

"I'm just not a religious person," Brad said. "That's always been stuff I was asked to believe with no physical manifestation. When something inherently physical happens, religion is not my first thought."

"But it all fits, doesn't it?" Judy asked. "I'm no Bible scholar, but people disappeared into the sky, and we're left here with Hell on Earth."

Robby took in a deep breath. Brad looked over at the boy and wondered how previous conversations on this subject between Judy and Robby had ended. Robby didn't look exasperated, but he wasn't exactly nodding in agreement with Judy's proposal.

"So you think we're the only wicked ones?" Brad asked. "Everyone else ascended?"

"Perhaps," Judy said. "Or maybe that part was just misunderstood. Lost in translation, you know? Maybe it's not about good people get Raptured and the bad people stay here to witness the battle. Maybe God just has another purpose to leave us here on Earth for a while."

"So what's the difference then between my theory and yours? Either way, we've got an ultra-powerful force changing the landscape around us. Whether it's God or not, how does that affect what we do from here?" Brad asked.

"It changes everything," Robby said. Something was different about his voice when he spoke these words. Brad looked up at Robby and for the first time wouldn't have characterized him as a boy—he would have Robby said was a young *man*. When Brad's eyes met Robby's, the young man continued. "Because I'm going to fight it. And if it's not God, then I'm going to win."

✪ ✪ ✪ ✪ ✪

Brad got back to the D.F.—the Dead Ferret house—a little after nine. After living so long in isolation, he didn't want the conversation to end. It seemed like after they went their separate ways, he would never see Robby and Judy again. Before they left for the night, he helped Robby shut down and refill the heaters, and retrieve the half-full water keg. They strapped it in on the back of the truck next to an empty barrel. Robby could have done the work himself—he had a lift-gate on the back of the truck and used a dolly to move around the barrels, but Brad enjoyed making himself useful after enjoying their hospitality. He made tentative plans with Robby to meet up the next day.

Judy vanished while Brad and Robby did chores. Brad only saw her again as Robby got in the truck and honked the horn. Brad waved as Judy appeared from across the parking lot and climbed into the driver's seat. He couldn't tell for sure at his distance, but in the light from the cab of the truck, it looked like Judy had been crying.

Brad wondered about that as he walked home.

Brad slept well that night, feeling that somewhere reasonably close to him other people slept as well. He finished brushing his teeth in the morning and when he heard the horn of the same truck outside the D.F., Brad ran to the window and saw Robby sitting behind the wheel. When he smiled, toothpaste dripped down Brad's chin and onto his gray sweater. He changed it out for a hooded sweatshirt and dressed as fast as he could. He checked the window several times as he pulled on his coat and boots, hoping Robby wouldn't get impatient and leave.

He jogged across the lawn to the beat up old truck.

"Hi," Brad said, waving through the truck's windshield.

"Come on in," Robby said, waving. His voice was drowned out by the truck's engine.

Brad slid into the passenger's seat and wondered if he should offer to drive. Robby looked uncomfortable behind the big steering wheel. When Robby put the truck into reverse, Brad strapped on his seat belt and tried not to look nervous.

"I thought I'd show you where we get water," Robby said.

"Cool," Brad said.

"Do you know your way around?" Robby asked.

"Mostly, sure," Brad said. "A bit."

"There's a spare map behind your seat," Robby said.

Brad reached back and grabbed a magazine-shaped book of local maps. He flipped through the pages and saw several annotated spots. He located his own house and saw it already bore a star and the letters "D.F."

"Ha," Brad barked a laugh. "You've marked me."

Robby smiled as he turned onto the main road. "Wouldn't want you to get lost. Check out page D-three, you'll see where we're going."

"Vyermin Labs on Hardwick Lane?" Brad asked. The map showed a small square and the label for the business. It sat on a small side street, not far from the airport.

"Yes," Robby said. "They're an environmental engineering firm. The facility is on city water, but they've also got a deep well with a tremendous capacity. We'll fill up these barrels in minutes." Robby pointed to the bed of the truck where Brad saw a half-dozen of the white water kegs.

Robby wasn't exaggerating. When they pulled up to the big garage attached to the office complex, Robby backed in and they moved the barrels down next to the pump. Robby started up a portable generator wired into a breaker panel next to the frost-free hydrant. The outlet pipe on the hydrant filled the white barrels with a smooth, steady stream. It took less time than filling six glasses of water at a sink.

When he'd filled the barrels, Robby unwrapped two sterile containers and took samples from the first and last barrel. He beckoned Brad to follow him and led the way into the main building, putting on a headlamp as he walked.

"Should we shut down the generator?" Brad asked.

"No, it runs the stuff inside as well," Robby said. He pointed at the extension cord which snaked in the door from the garage and down the hallway of the facility.

Brad had forgotten his headlamp, but found a flashlight in his jacket pocket. He didn't need it for long. The lights were on in the lab where the young man led him. The black countertops, glassware, and lab equipment were only familiar to Brad from his college chemistry lab.

"What are we doing, exactly?" Brad asked.

"We test the water quality to make sure it doesn't have any chemical or biological contamination. It doesn't take very long," Robby said.

"Oh," Brad said.

He watched Robby work. The young man moved around the lab confidently. He donned gloves and took smaller samples from the two cups. Some he loaded into a centrifuge—a word which Brad pried from the back of his reluctant memory—and some he loaded into a big machine which looked like a laser printer.

When the machines were loaded they hummed and spun. Robby and Brad took seats and waited

"Who taught you to do this stuff?" Brad asked.

Robby pointed to a shelf near the back of the room. "This lab is ISO certified, so all their processes are documented. The water quality tests are documented right over there. It's really pretty easy to follow. I think it has to be, to pass the audits."

"So you learned the process from those books?" Brad asked.

"Yeah," Robby said. "I can show you. I mean, after you follow them a couple of times it's pretty easy."

"That's okay," Brad said, "I trust you. But how did you even know to do this?"

"Do what? Test the water?" Robby asked.

"Yeah," Brad said.

"It just made sense," Robby said. "We have to test the water. It's the most important resource. We could go around drinking bottled water for quite a while, but eventually that's going to run out, and it's not really convenient for showers and washing and stuff."

"Seems like there must be a million wells around here though," Brad said. "I had one at my house. If I had just hooked up a generator, like you have here, I could have pumped all the water I wanted."

"True, but they all come from the same aquifer," Robby said. "And you don't know how long you could continue to trust the supply."

"I've been using it for years," Brad said. "I don't know why I wouldn't keep using it."

"Well, before you were relying on the community to some extent," Robby said. "If your neighbor discovered a problem, you'd be more likely to investigate your water supply. We don't have many neighbors now."

Robby had a way of explaining things so it didn't sound like he was lecturing. He delivered his statements in a way that made them seem like ideas he was formulating that moment. But they were so well constructed, they didn't invite as much argument as newly minted ideas. Brad imagined the young man in a situation where adults would have no reason to listen to his opinions. He figured Robby had developed this method of explanation as a defense-mechanism so he could get his ideas across to hostile adults. Brad admired his diplomacy.

"You mentioned something funny about the water down in New Hampshire," Brad said. "Does that have something to do with your caution?"

"Yeah, the liquid. I guess," Robby said.

The centrifuge shut off and decelerated as the timer beeped.

"These tests weren't designed to detect that kind of thing, but who knows," Robby said. He got to his feet and waited for the centrifuge to stop spinning before he plucked one of the test tubes from the device. From the sample, he prepared slides for different machines.

Robby showed Brad what to look for, and how to gauge the results based on photos and tables in the books he laid out on the counter. All of the tests came back negative, and Robby cleaned up quickly. Brad considered himself a quick study, but he didn't really pay much attention to Robby's instruction. As carefully as Robby explained it, Brad didn't see much of a need to learn the process. He figured it was harmless obsession for the young man, but not really a necessary use of time.

As if he sensed Brad was merely humoring him, Robby let Brad in on his theories as they made their way back to the truck.

"I figure it's best to consider ourselves under attack," Robby said.

"Yeah?" Brad asked. "Still?"

"Yes," Robby said. "I could come up with a lot of ideas about what happened, but I've decided to focus on the one which requires the most caution."

"Makes sense," Brad said. He held open the door to the garage for Robby, whose hands were full with the next batch of testing supplies he would leave in the garage.

"The more I think about it, it must be aliens, and they're here to colonize Earth," Robby said. "But you argued against aliens last night."

"I just didn't want to put a label on it," Brad said. "What's the point of putting a label on something we don't understand?"

"Because like I said last night, it changes what we decide we can do about it," Robby said. "Let's say your force is something that's always been around. It's the force that caused the last ice age, or killed off the dinosaurs."

"Or brought life to this planet," Brad said.

"Sure," Robby said. The young man wheeled the dolly over to one of the barrels. "Could you tilt that back?"

Brad helped him muscle the barrel onto the dolly.

"But what are we supposed to do if there's a giant omnipotent force that wrecks the planet for us?" Robby asked.

"Or fosters it," Brad said. "People were doing a pretty good job of wrecking the planet. Maybe this force is the planet itself."

"Exactly," Robby said. "That's one of the things I considered too. So there's this giant force which has always been around and it sweeps through and changes everything. That doesn't leave us anywhere to go."

"How so?" Brad asked.

"Well you've proposed a force which can't be defeated, or at least it doesn't have a motivation we can defeat. You're already at checkmate," Robby said.

"But maybe we don't have to defeat it," Brad said. "Perhaps the job is done now and we can start rebuilding. But in your model, we can't afford to sit back and wait to see what happens. We can't assume that the cause of all this was a benevolent force that means to just hit a giant reset button on the planet," Brad said.

"Yes, that's what I think," Robby said.

"And we can't just assume all the changes are done? We can't assume that knocking out almost everyone on the planet is good enough for these aliens?" Brad asked.

"Well, I'd counter that with the example of the dinosaurs," Robby said.

"What about them?" Brad asked.

"If all this is the same as the dinosaur extinction, then I think it's pretty clear what our fate will be," Robby said. "I mean, you don't see any of them still walking around, do you?"

✪ ✪ ✪ ✪ ✪

After they loaded up the truck, Robby drove through a neighborhood bordering the marsh. His driving still bothered Brad. It wasn't just the way Robby pulled the seat all the way up to reach the pedals, Robby ignored all the stop signs, rolling through intersections with barely a glance. Robby turned a lot. He turned down side streets that didn't have any tire-tracks at all yet in the thin snow.

"Why do you do that?" Brad asked eventually.

"Do what?" Robby asked.

"You keep turning down side-streets that don't have any tracks on them. Are you trying to throw off an imaginary pursuer?" Brad asked.

"No, not really," Robby said. "Well, kinda. I mean, yes, I don't want to have all the tracks pointing exactly where I'm going, but I'm also trying to see all the parts of town to see if there's anything else going on. That's how I found you—I saw your footprints and I just followed them."

"Oh," Brad said.

"It's getting hard to see anything over near where you live. There are tire tracks everywhere," Robby said. "But there are only a few tracks of people on foot. Everyone drives everywhere."

Robby turned onto a street and joined the tire-tracks already there. On the left side of the street, little one-story houses sat on small lots with short walks leading down to the street. On the right side, the houses were spaced far apart, and their back yards ended with marsh trailing down to the river's edge. These houses stood two or three stories high. Robby backed down the long driveway of a tall house with an attached garage. As he approached, he punched a button clipped the visor and the garage door began to lumber up. Using his mirrors, Robby guided the truck into the garage and then punched the button to lower the door again before he shut off the truck.

The truck's engine ticked as it cooled in the big garage.

Robby opened his door before he spoke. "This is where I live right now."

"Oh," Brad said. He got out of the truck. "Nice place."

The garage was clean and spacious, lit only by the bulb of the garage door opener and the two windows on the back wall which looked out to the marsh.

"Where does your power come from?" Brad asked. He couldn't hear any generator running.

"There's a big bank of batteries and an inverter in there," Robby said, pointing to a door in the direction of the house. "It's charged by solar on the roof and a generator I run once a day."

"Cool," Brad said.

Robby removed a hose from the wall and uncoiled it carefully. One end had a submersible pump attached. Robby removed the cap from a barrel and dropped the pump and hose down into it. The other end of the pipe connected to a pipe mounted on the wall.

"This pump runs on two-twenty, so I have to run the generator," Robby said. "It's noisy."

Robby had a talent for understatement, Brad decided. When Robby started the generator and engaged the pump, the sound was deafening. Communicating through yelling and hand gestures, Brad indicated that he was going to step outside.

Brad exited the garage through the side door out to the lawn. Many footprints led to the right, around the back of the garage.

Behind the building, under the overhang of the roof, someone had brushed the snow off a granite bench. Brad sat down and looked over the marsh. Inside, he heard the motor of the generator level off and he guessed Robby had shut off the pump to move it from one barrel to the next.

At his feet, Brad found scattered gray cigarette ashes, but no butts. He looked closer at the footprints leading to the bench. They looked too narrow to belong to Robby. In fact, on some of the prints, the imprint from the heel looked no bigger than a silver dollar. These prints were from women's shoes, Brad concluded.

After a few more cycles of the generator's engine, the sound ended abruptly. Brad wandered back inside, wondering when the feeling would return to his numb backside.

"Sorry," Robby said. "I guess I'm just used to how loud it is."

"You ought to wear earplugs," Brad said. "That's probably ruining your ears."

Robby nodded.

"Where does it pump to?" Brad asked.

"A big tank in the attic," Robby said. "The plumbing in the house is convertible. It can either run on city water, or gravity-fed from upstairs."

"Smart," Brad said. "How did you find this place?"

"I drove around looking for solar panels, and then picked the best one," Robby said. "Want to see inside?"

"Definitely," Brad said.

Up a few stairs, a door led into a mud room. Robby took off his shoes as he entered and Brad stooped to do the same. The tile floor felt warm under Brad's feet. He took off his jacket and hung it on a hook next to Robby's. To their left, the kitchen opened up into a big family room. The whole back wall had big windows which looked out over the marsh and the river. Despite all the glass, the house felt warm and snug. Brad instantly felt more comfortable than he had in a month.

"You want some toast?" Robby asked.

"Love some," Brad said.

Robby picked out four rough-cut slices of bread from the cutting board and inserted them into the toaster on the counter that separated the kitchen from the sitting area.

"Judy makes the best bread," Robby said.

"She lives here too?" Brad asked.

"Yeah," Robby said. "Is she out back smoking?"

"No," Brad said. "I didn't see her, at least."

"She's probably upstairs," Robby said.

"It's so warm in here," Brad said.

"Yeah," Robby said. "There's a furnace downstairs that works on wood or oil. All the heat is radiant underfloor stuff. It's nice, but it means you can't sit next to the radiator if you're really cold."

"So you've got quite a setup here," Brad said. He walked over to the island and pulled out a tall stool.

"It was all pretty much like this," Robby said. "I just found it this way."

"But it seems like you've made it a priority to create a comfortable life," Brad said. "It's not at all what I expected."

Robby took a tub of margarine, some jam, and bottled water from the refrigerator. Brad accepted the drink.

"What did you expect?" Brad asked.

"You've been talking about aliens, and wiping out the last of the people, and fighting back," Brad said. "I thought most of your energy would have gone to that."

"We still need the basics though, right?" Robby asked.

"Fresh bread, refrigeration, and radiant heat hardly seem like the basics," Brad said.

"Like I said," Robby said, "this place was already set up."

The toast popped up and Robby fetched two medium-sized plates from the cupboard and a knife from the drawer. He slid one plate towards Brad and pulled up a stool in front of the other. Robby waited for Brad to butter his toast before he took the knife to apply jam to his own.

"This is good," Brad said. "Thank you. And thank Judy, wherever she is."

"Probably upstairs," Robby said. "So you were saying—I shouldn't have heat?"

"No, that's not what I meant. I'm just saying it doesn't look like your priorities are centered around fighting. Shouldn't you be doing reconnaissance? Studying the enemy? Trying to lie low and stay off the radar? Band together with allies? Stockpile weapons? Hell, even figure out what weapons would even work against an invisible enemy that controls the weather?"

"What else?" Robby asked.

"I don't know what else," Brad said. "That's the point though, isn't it? How old are you anyway? You're clearly very smart, or you've had a lot of help figuring out how to get this house running and how to test water and everything, but do you know anything at all about mounting a resistance?"

"I'm still working on the 'studying the enemy' part," Robby said.

"How's that?" Brad asked.

"I'm working on establishing a bond of trust with a potential source of vital information," Robby said. "And I'm fourteen."

Brad took another bite of toast as he thought about Robby's answers.

"This source of vital information—how are you establishing a bond of trust?" Brad asked.

"I showed him where I live and I fed him toast," Robby said.

When Robby smiled, Brad broke into a laugh.

"Let me show you the basement," Robby said.

Brad stood at the top as Robby led the way down the dark stairs. He gave Robby some space. Something about going to the basement with the young man seemed a little off. Robby hadn't been excited to show off any other parts of the house. After they arrived in the kitchen, he didn't even bother to show Brad the rest of the first floor. If Robby had turned around to beckon Brad, or shown any concern that he wasn't following immediately behind, Brad would have fled. Only because Robby didn't slow at all, Brad walked down the stairs.

When he reached the bottom of the steps, Robby flipped a switch and fluorescent fixtures lit the room with a cold blue and yellow light. The basement had no windows or doors, so only their flickering illuminated the big open space.

At one end, past the open-riser stairs, sat a giant furnace and a wall of tightly-stacked wood. At the other end, Robby stood in front of a long white stretch of wall, white except for the symbols. Brad leaned against a column and looked at the mural of scrawled shapes.

"What is it?" Brad asked.

"I think it's the reconnaissance you were asking about," Robby said.

"How's that?" Brad asked.

"You remember the part of my story where we went to check on the neighbor?" Robby asked.

"Sure, through the snow? Where your Dad's friend was snatched?" Brad asked.

"Yes," Robby said. "But it was before that. We went to check on Mr. Dyer, but he wasn't home. My dad searched the house, and he found something like this in the cellar under the house."

"And you found the same thing here?" Brad asked.

"No," Robby said. "This is my recreation of what was under Mr. Dyer's house. I drew this copy."

"All this?" Brad asked. He swept his arm and indicated the wall. The wall was enormous and the mural covered almost all of it. Brad gauged that the stretch of symbols must have measured twenty feet long and stood at least four feet high. "Did you have a picture? Did you transcribe it? How did you do it?"

"I did it from memory," Robby said. "I have a really good memory, always have. There were two-hundred-and-seventeen shapes on the wall. I think I've got almost all of them perfect, but a couple on the edges are still a little fuzzy to me."

"How can you know you have it correct?" Brad asked.

Robby ignored the question. "See this one here?" he asked. "It's almost the Japanese symbol for god. And this one is almost the Egyptian hieroglyph for god."

"So who drew it in your neighbor's cellar?" Brad asked.

"I think Mr. Dyer drew it there using the blood from his dogs," Robby said.

"Ugh, no," Brad said. "That's terrible."

"I know," Robby said. "My dad didn't want me to see, but I think that's what it was."

"Why did you draw it here?" Brad asked.

"Well, I put it on a sheet of paper, but it has to be big. I believe the relative size of the shapes to each other makes a difference, but more than that, I think the actual size of the shapes themselves is important," Robby said.

"That's impossible," Brad said. "Size changes with perspective."

"I know," Robby said. "I can't quite explain it, but I think that if the characters aren't the right physical size and shape, they have no meaning or perhaps the meaning changes."

"So you have a really good memory," Brad said, sweeping his hand at the mural, "and a you're able to exactly judge and reproduce the size of things."

"It was trial and error," Robby said. "I used that."

Robby pointed to a milk crate in the corner of the basement. On top of the crate, sat a projector. Next to the box, Brad saw a coiled extension cable.

"I drew the symbols on a laptop, hooked it up to the projector, and then blew it up until it seemed like the correct size," Robby said.

"And all this means what? What meaning have you found in all this? Mr. Dyer draws a bunch of crazy scribbles on his wall with dog's blood, and you call it reconnaissance?" Brad asked.

"Yes," Robby said. "I haven't figured out the whole thing, but I think that somehow Mr. Dyer came across information about the attackers."

"And instead of just leaving a note or telling someone, he used this crazy writing to communicate this information?" Brad asked.

Robby looked at the wall, scanning the symbols, like they held the way to convince Brad.

"Look, I'm not questioning your belief in this stuff," Brad said. "I'm just a logical person, and I need to see logical explanations for things. Show me what you've figured out. What does it say?"

"I'm not sure," Robby said.

Brad took a step closer to the wall and let it fill his whole vision. He felt bad about grilling the kid. Clearly Robby was trying to make sense of the end of the world, and the disappearance of his whole family, and he needed something to hang his hat on. The boy, young man really, needed a puzzle to figure out. He needed some kind of riddle to occupy his mind so he didn't go crazy. Brad could respect that.

Brad took a deep breath and blinked his eyes hard. His breathing and his heartbeat began to slow as he stared at the wall. The edges of the mural were fuzzy in his peripheral vision, but that was just fine. They needed to be fuzzy, he thought. It only made sense that they were fuzzy. The whole mural just seemed to make perfect sense as Brad stood, swaying slightly, and stared. Brad forgot about the snow, the rock creatures, the killer vines, the casual government guys, and the black hole under the bridge. That hole was the last thing he forgot about, but he forgot about the hole too.

The next thing Brad knew, someone shook his shoulder.

"Brad? Brad?" Robby asked.

Brad shook his head and turned towards Robby.

"What?"

"What were you thinking about?" Robby asked.

"I don't know, what do you mean? Nothing, I guess," Brad said.

"For ten minutes?" Robby asked.

"What do you mean?" Brad asked.

Robby held out a camera. Brad had a question on his brow as he reached out and took the camera from Robby. The display showed a single video stored on the camera. When Brad started playback, he saw a ten-minute movie of himself, standing and staring at the mural. During the course of the video, Robby circled Brad with the camera, filming his blank stare from every angle. Brad never moved except for the gentle sway of his balance.

"This thing did that?" Brad asked, holding up a hand to block his vision of the mural.

"Yes," Robby said. "It seems to only happen at this distance. See the mark on the floor?"

Brad looked down and saw that under his own feet was a little cross of electrical tape stuck to the concrete floor.

"So you maneuvered me down here so I could experience it for myself?" Brad asked.

"Yes," Robby said. "I thought it would be the only way you'd believe me."

Brad thought about this for a second, and then turned his back on the mural.

"Do you mind if I get out of here?" he asked. Brad started to walk for the stairs before Robby could answer.

"It won't hurt you," Robby said. "As long as you don't stand in that spot, you'll be fine."

"I'm guessing it won't do anything to me when I'm upstairs then," Brad said as he climbed the stairs.

Robby shut off the lights and then followed him up. Brad pulled his chair back up to the island while Robby shut the door to the basement.

"So that's one of the reasons why I think there's something special about this series of shapes," Robby said. "It seems to hypnotize anyone who looks at it from that exact spot."

"Awesome," Brad said. He ran his fingers through his hair and took a deep breath. "So what connects it to the apocalypse?"

"It tells the story of the aliens," Robby said. He pulled a sheet of paper from his back pocket.

Brad held up his hands. "Whoa, is it safe to look at that thing?"

"Yes," Robby said, "perfectly safe. The story starts from the center. They've got a multi-pronged attack. This describes the center area, where they'd prepare the ground and then cover the whole thing with snow. In that area they purged the animals. I think that was supposed to include us. Then, outside the center area, they describe converting big patches to resources."

"Resources?" Brad asked.

"Yeah, like an energy harvest area," Robby said. "When the time comes, the resources will move to the center. I think this part mentions the liquid cleanup crew down south. Snow in the center, then a ring of corpses, then a ring of clear area."

"Where are you getting all this?" Brad asked. "All I see is random symbols."

"It's not all in the shapes themselves, it's the relationship of the symbols and their physical dimensions," Robby said. "I don't know if I could explain it."

"So why are you showing it to me?" Brad asked.

"Because I still think you have information you're not sharing. That information might be crucial to figuring this all out," Robby said.

Brad let out a big sigh. "Still? What is it? Why do you think I have information?"

"You were there," Robby said. "You were there in the middle of the deep snow, and you're the only one to come out of there since Thanksgiving Day. Everyone else either fled that day or just disappeared. What did you see?"

"I'll tell you about two more things, and that's it. And I don't care if you believe me or not," Brad said.

Robby nodded.

"I didn't tell you about the vines and the rock monster, and that's it. Wait, well three things," Brad said, "because I also had the casual government guys for a while. And the hole under the garage. Okay, let me start back with last summer."

Brad started at the beginning and surprised himself with the amount of detail he recalled from months before. He told Robby all about his first walks when he discovered the vines, and then even backed up to tell him a little about the contract he'd been working on before the whole vine thing had started.

When he'd made it up to Herm showing up for the first time, Judy entered from the garage and took a seat. Brad started to greet her, but she motioned for him to keep talking. She smelled of cigarette smoke. Brad continued his tale and told them everything right up to the explosion from under the garage. Then he found himself repeating parts of the story they'd already heard. He trailed off.

Robby was looking at the counter, propping his head up in his hands.

Judy rose and fetched the three of them soda from the fridge.

Brad pulled the tab on his can and held it to his mouth before sipping. The carbonated bubbles felt good bursting on his upper lip. He drank and the soda tasted good—complete.

"Thank you for telling us that," Judy said. "It must have been difficult to share."

"It actually feels good," Brad said. "But does it really help? Are you any closer to understanding the riddle of the end of the world?"

He directed this question to Robby, who still sat silent—focusing on the countertop.

"Robby?" Brad asked.

"He's in his deep cycles," Judy said. "It doesn't happen often, but when it does you have to let him come out of it on his own."

Brad raised his eyebrows and took another sip. The sugary soda was going straight to his head.

## CHAPTER 12: ASSEMBLY

ROBBY AND TED CONVENED a meeting of all the people who lived within radio distance of Portland.

"I want to hear what the new people have to say," said the smelly guy sitting next to Brad.

Brad couldn't remember the smelly guy's name, so he focused his attention on Ted, who stood over near the row of stools.

"I do too," Ted said. "I'm sure we all do. But I believe it's important for you all to hear what Rob has to say. He told me what he's been thinking about, and I think we should all hear his ideas."

"Facts first, then conclusions," said the smelly guy.

"I agree," Judy said. "Let's hear from the new people."

That startled Brad—he thought that Judy would automatically be on Robby's side. Brad looked around the room. Most of the two-dozen people seemed to agree with Judy and Smelly.

"Fair enough," Ted said. "Brad? You want to start us out?"

Brad scanned the room before he realized that Ted was talking about him.

"Oh, sure," Brad said. He glanced at Robby and asked—"From the beginning?"

Ted said, "Yes," and Robby nodded.

Brad started his story from the walk where he'd first seen the vines. A tickle started in the back of his throat when he told the people how he'd found the hole under his garage. The tickle turned into a cough as Brad told of the casually-dressed government guys and how he'd boarded up his house from the inside. His voice was overworked—virtually no use for months followed by days of non-stop talking took their toll. Brad stripped several details of his story near the end so he could finish and sit down.

"Thanks, Brad," Ted said, rising to his feet again. "Who else? Frank, could you introduce us to the new person at your table?"

Brad followed Ted's eyes to the guys sitting just beyond Smelly. Brad hadn't met any of these people yet. When everyone arrived, Brad was busy with Robby and Judy in the kitchen, preparing pancakes for dinner. Now, the guy behind Smelly pushed back his chair and pushed himself up, not quite all the way to his feet. He wore a blue tank-top, camouflage pants, and serious black boots.

"This is Luke," Frank said. He motioned to the man on his left. Frank started to sink back down in his chair and then rose up again. "He's been traveling down south awhiles, and then he appeared up'ta my ranch last week."

Luke cleared his throat. He looked like the template from which Frank had been cast. Like Frank, his head and face possessed no hair except a couple days of stubble. But Frank's shave looked new—the skin of his scalp in the lantern-light glowed pink. Luke's head glowed with a deep tan.

Luke didn't stand. He pushed back his chair and relaxed down into the seat a bit before beginning his speech.

"Things are diff'rent down south," Luke said. "Not like up here a' tall. I mean further south than the eye poppers." Luke hooked a thumb over his shoulder. "Down there you got things that hunt."

"From the beginning," a woman said from the next table. A couple of people mumbled their agreement.

"Settle out, Tib, I'm gettin' there," Luke said. He took a deep breath through his nose, flaring his nostrils. "I didn't actually see the begin, not like most folk. I had some time off work, so I headed out in the hills, tryin' to get a deer. I live down-state Mare'land. Western edge."

He folded his hands on top of his belly. Luke looked up at the ceiling. He seemed to be aware that everyone was looking at him, but he avoided locking eyes with them.

"I set out 'round three or four. Good and dark out there. No big towns around or nuthin'. No light pollution a' tall. All I had was my gun, a six-pack, and the brightest goddamn spotlight you've ever seen, but I wasn't using any of them at the time," Luke said.

"I was just hiking in the dark. I got about half-aways up Brandette hill when I heard some rustlin'. Sounded like a buck thrashin' his rack, marking out a spot, so I got down low. But the noise, it just kept getting louder and louder, like there wasn't just one buck, but two or three or four, and they were having it out with each other. Pretty soon, thrashin' turned into a pounding, like a stampede. That's when I used my light," Luke said.

"As soon as my eyeballs dialed in, I could see more than a dozen of 'em, and they were barreling down the hill right at me. Usually when a big light hits them and they stop dead and just stare at me," Luke said.

"Jacklighter," Brad heard someone mumble, but Luke didn't seem to notice.

"But they just kept coming—bucks in front, does in back. You never see them all herded up that time of year. I slid over so I was mostly blocked by a big oak tree and just watched 'em run. I shut my light off after they passed by. Didn't even take a shot. I figured I wanted to hike up the hill, figger out what was drivin' 'em. I guess they wasn't the only ones, too, 'cause on the other side of those deer I didn't hear nuthin' in those woods. No birds, raccoons, · squirrels, possums, nuthin'. Honestly? I didn't even know what I expected, but I didn't expect such a ... such a *void*.

"So I kept climbing. I kinda gave up on looking for some monster, chasing all the sounds away, but I wanted to get to the top. All them hills are covered with trees, but on the south side of Brandette, there's a little cliff where you can see a ways. I had to move real slow because I was coming from the other side and it was dark—just starlight—and I didn't want to fall over t'other side of the cliff. Took me almost 'til dawn to get all the way up there.

"I don't know how all the deer knew it was coming," Luke said, "but when I got up there, I saw what scared them away."

Luke folded his hands behind his head as he talked. He still looked up at the ceiling while the eyes of everyone else were locked on him and his story. Brad glanced over at Robby; the young man leaned forward, perched on the very edge of his chair.

"Up above me, the sky was full of stars, but in the distance... It looked off in the distance like the sky was disappearing altogether. Looking into it almost hurt my eyes," Luke said. He shut his eyes, like they still hurt now.

"Was it black?" asked his compatriot, Frank.

Brad rolled his eyes—when Frank prompted for an answer he must already know, this seemed more like a sermon than a story.

Luke might have sensed he was losing his audience. He lashed out at the interruption—"No, Frank, you asshole, I already tole you it weren't *black*."

Luke sat up straighter, put his hands on the table, and glanced around to a few people in the room, locking eyes with them for a brief second to recapture their trust and then he looked down at his hands.

"It weren't black," he repeated. "The sky just weren't *there*. It's like a TV in the ol' days. When you didn't get signal, you'd get fuzzy snow, ya know? Not black, just no signal. What was worse— it weren't just the sky. The 'no signal' was starting to creep down over the hills across the valley. Down the slopes it spread out in these little fingers. Least I think it did, coulda just been the terrain that made it look that ways. It was almost like watching the sunrise, but in reverse, and slower. We've got a tall ridge out to the east, so the sun always lights up the peaks first and then rolls down the hills. Well that morning it looked like the hills were being eaten from the top down. I just stood there watchin' with my jaw hangin' open.

"When a couple of big black shapes passed overhead, I got movin'. At first, I crashed down the hill like the deer, but then I remembered what I was standin' on," Luke paused while everyone wondered about his statement. He once again controlled their full attention. "Those hills are made of nuthin' but pure limestone—all shot fulla holes. I turned west, and ran up hill for a little bit until I found the entrance to a cave they call 'Fat Man.'

"They call it that because you have to be right skinny to fit in the entrance. It's like about this high," Luke said, spacing his hands about a foot apart, "for the first five feet and then it turns straight up. It ain't too hard to find 'cause it's right at the base of a big maple what's split at the base—looks like a female with her legs up in the air.

"I went in rifle first and shimmied all the way in. I didn't stop until I got to the first room, where you can stand up. When we were kids we called it the 'Altar Room.' We'd go in there to drink beer and have herbal picnics. I turned on my light and found it pretty much how we'd left it back when I was in high school. There's some candles on the ledges on the wall, and in the middle there's a great big flat rock—the altar—with a bunch of bat bones on it," Luke said.

At the mention of the bones, the woman he'd called "Tib" let out a tiny sigh of disapproval.

"Yeah, kids catch 'em and then burn 'em up on the altar," Luke said. "You don't know better. I didn't keep my light on long though. I had just sat down when I heard a noise comin' through from the entrance. It kinda sounded like wind, but it was too steady. It was like a high-pitch train whistle or something. Gave me a chill. I didn't even notice when the noise stopped, but then I was hearin' different sounds and the first one was gone. The new ones sounded like 'swish,' only real fast. There was something menacing 'bout these new sound. Made me flinch back. Like the sound of a circular saw would if you all of a sudden didn't quite know where your fingers were."

Frank smiled and nodded. Brad watched his head dip up and down.

Luke continued. "With the lights off in a cave, you get real sensitive to noises, and these ones really bothered me. I fished out my lighter so I could make sure I was still alone. I mean it seemed like the sounds were coming from outside the cave, but with those sounds it was damn hard to tell. I grabbed one of the candles stuck on a ledge in the wall, lit it up, and then started shimmying even deeper into the cave. The cave goes back a ways before it gets serious. I waited around one of the turns to see if the noises would stop."

"What do you mean 'serious'?" Ted asked.

"You can just *walk* through the beginnin' of it," Luke said.

"Then you get to a point where you have to chimney between two walls to get to the next room."

Ted and several other people still seemed perplexed by the answer, so Luke continued his explanation. "You put your back against one wall and then put your feet against the other—they're only about three feet apart. Down below, the crack goes down forever. Can't see the bottom. You just shuffle sideways and it's called chimneying. That's what I mean by serious—serious climbing and risk to life and limb are involved."

Luke took a second to reorient himself in the story.

"So I waited and waited. I blew out the candle for awhiles, then lit it up again. It's hard waiting in the dark. You don't know how long anything takes in a cave, and I didn't have a clock except on my phone, and it had gone blank," Luke said.

"When? When the deer stampeded? When you ran to the cave?" Ted asked.

"The clock? I don't know for sure. I didn't think to check it until I was in the cave. First time I checked it, it was blank," Luke said.

As Luke continued, Brad watched Ted. The older man handed something to Robby; more accurately, he pushed it into Robby's hand as Robby focused on the storyteller. Robby took it and flipped it open without looking down. It was a small notepad.

"So, like I said," Luke said, "I don't have an idea of how long I crouched, but it felt longer than hell. The gap between the swish noises got bigger an' bigger, until it seemed like they were about to stop. I crawled back to the altar room without the light and then waited even more. I wanted to get out. Now that I look back, I almost wanted those noises to still be goin' when I got outta there. I wanted to see what they were, you know? Curiosity. Nuthin' more. Had I known, I woulda just sat right there." Luke shook his head slowly.

"I crawled out," Luke said. "One of them whoosh sounds went by as I crawled out from under the rock. The sun was up by then, but the sky looked funny. I ran through the woods as quiet as I could and tried to head for where I'd parked my truck. I got a hot stitch in my right side, and I could barely breathe, I was runnin' so fast, but I didn't slow down until I saw a little patch of my red truck through the woods. Then WHOOSH! One of those things came down right on top of me. I heard it comin', and I got tangled up in a branch so I was falling when it grabbed my back. The thing lifted me about a foot or two by my back and then somethin' off to the north exploded."

Luke picked up his glass and took a sip of water. He ran his tongue over his lips while everyone watched.

"I guess it was just dumb luck that the thing got distracted. I suspect the loud noise drew it away. I never did find out what blew up, but it sounded pretty damn big. After the boom, I could hear stuff falling—crashing back to the ground—for several seconds. I figured out later that the way the thing picked me up was weird. It didn't touch my jacket or my shirt, but it just grabbed ahold of me —just the flesh. I found three big scrapes and a chunk of meat missing from my shoulder, but my clothes weren't ripped one bit."

"Did you get a look at it?" Ted asked.

"I did," Luke said. "I did. I don't know what to tell you, though. When it let go of me, I was fallin' back to the ground, but I flipped over enough to see. It was like a hole in the world. Wherever the thing was, nuthin' else was. I can't tell you more than that."

Brad was watching Robby this time and saw him pass the notepad over to Ted. The older man barely glanced down and then asked a question. "What was the size of the hole?"

"It's a good question," Luke said, "but I can't answer it. I'd hafta assume how far away it were, you know? If it were ten feet up, then I 'spose it was only 'bout five, six feet across. But if it were fifty feet up, then maybe thirty feet across. Because it wasn't a thing, it was like an absence of anything."

"But it had claws," Ted said.

"I never said claws," Luke said, wagging his finger. He turned his finger over to Robby and asked, "Boy, why don't you just ask me your questions directly?"

Robby straightened up and tugged his shirt down before answering. "It wasn't a question, and it wasn't from me."

"The hell it wasn't," Luke said. "I'll finish the rest of my story without y'all questioning my account, if you don't mind." He paused and swept his eyes around the room.

Brad wanted to hear the rest of the story. He felt Luke didn't have cause for indignation, but he really didn't care either way. He just wanted to hear the rest of the story.

"Like I said, I hit the ground like a sack of dumbbells, but I didn't even feel the pain in my back yet," Luke said. "I rolled to my feet and got running again. This time I hunched over, kinda looking up over my shoulder. I drove the same way—I hunched down in my seat and looked up through the windows. Nearly ran my truck off the road a couple of times. I was so busy lookin' up and drivin' fast that I'm not sure how I made it down to the main road in one piece. I went straight for town; I didn't even stop at my house. I didn't know yet, but I was soaking my shirt with blood.

"When I got to the center of town, everything was deserted, but I didn't think much of it. It was still early, a'course, and Thanksgiving and all. Down near the Sheriff's office there's a Sevum-'Levum—always open and always a deputy or two hanging 'round. Not this time though—the place was empty. Door was wide open, lights on, nobody home. I went back around the counter and I nearly jumped outta my skin when the light shut off. I figured someone out back shut 'em, but then I saw out the window— everything had gone off. Exxon sign across the corner, red lights, *everything* was off. I figured the power went out.

"I went through a ton of buildings and I couldn't find a soul. Hell, I couldn't even find a dog or a cat. The whole town had just emptied out. I've got to take a break if y'all don't mind," Luke said. "My throat's givin' out."

Luke got up and headed for the door. After a couple of seconds, Frank got up and followed him out to the parking lot.

Brad turned to Judy, who gripped her coffee cup with both hands.

"That's crazy," Brad said to her. "I can't imagine what attacked him."

"Sheila has a similar story," Judy said.

"Oh? Who's Sheila?" Brad asked. He glanced around the room. A few people left their tables to move around or wander outside, but most of the twenty-four people still sat at their tables. Several people who started out the evening sitting alone now joined one of the tables with two or three people. Brad sat with Judy, and on the other side Robby and Ted were loosely associated with their table.

Judy pointed her coffee mug at a woman who stood to gather some plates and take them to the kitchen. "She's Sheila. See her limp?"

Brad couldn't help but notice the limp.

"When one of the things grabbed her it nearly split her right calf in two. She's got about three pounds of tape holding her leg together," Judy said.

"Whoa," Brad said. "The way you and Robby described it, it sounded like people were just vanishing into thin air."

"Robby was on an island," Judy said. "Sheila was down in Mass, and it sounds like Luke was down in Maryland or whatever. Who says they experienced the same kind of thing?"

"I guess," Brad said.

"I saw a couple of people disappear with my own eyes," Judy said. "I couldn't begin to say what actually happened to them."

"But I thought you were a proponent of the whole Rapture concept. If you knew about Sheila, then why all the talk about people being raptured?" Brad asked.

"How do you know the rapture doesn't happen that way?" Judy asked.

"Swooping down on people and nearly tearing them apart?" Brad asked.

"Just their physical manifestations, right? Transformation can be both destructive and constructive, don't you think?" Judy asked.

"I guess I've never thought about it," Brad said.

"Isn't it funny?" Judy spoke to her coffee mug. "The world ends and as far as we know every single person within a hundred-mile radius gathers at a shitty Denny's for what amounts to a status meeting. I can't tell you how many marketing campaign meetings I sat through just wishing the world would end so I wouldn't have to endure even one more second of formless conjecture. Now I've willingly subjected myself to listening to some hillbilly messiah spin a yarn about his heroic journey."

"Humans need human contact," Brad said. "They can try to isolate themselves, but eventually they gather together."

The door to the parking lot swung open and Frank entered, followed by Luke. They took their seats as the chatter at the tables died down.

Nobody spoke for a moment and then Ted broke the silence. "You have the floor, Luke."

Luke nodded and cleared his throat.

"I wandered 'round for a few days 'fore I figured I should make my way to a city to see what's what. I headed east through Maryland and parts of Virginia. I traded cars coupla times. The truck made so much noise that I just felt conspicuous. Down there the roads are empty. There's no cars anywhere 'cept in parking lots and driveways, so it was pretty easy going. I din't have any problems at all until I got to the suburbs of DC. I'd already been through Hagerstown and Frederick, and everythin' was the same as out west, so I kinda figured nothin' would be new. But I got up one morning to leave Gaithersburg and I realized there was a glow on the horizon in the direction of DC.

"There was no smoke at all, but this glow. And I know it couldn't have been real, but I thought I could feel heat coming from that direction too. The first time I saw it I was crossing the Cabin John bridge. I mean, the whole time I was thinkin' somebody prolly left a teakettle on or somethin' and the city was burning down. I figured as soon as I saw flames or smoke, I'd just turn around. But when I saw those flames runnin' up and down the Potomac river, I din't know what to do.

"It wasn't like the whole river was on fire or anythin', but there were these bands, like ribbons of fire strung out across the water from bank to bank. They'd zip up and down stream, crossin' each other, breakin' up and then formin' again. Some of them were blue and green, but most were red and orange, and they was bright. It was hot just to look at them. Even from up on the bridge I could feel sweat breaking out on my forehead. While I was sitting there, just idling in a little BMW I'd picked up, I saw one of those ribbons break off a piece of fire and head over to the shore. Once it hit ground it zipped up through the tops of trees like a fuse. It din't burn the trees up, but it traveled across them from limb to limb. When it got really close to the bridge, I couldn't see it anymore. I was about to jump out to look where it went when it flipped up over the rail and started burnin' right on the road surface at the end of the bridge.

"It was still just a single piece of flame, like a little column from a candle, but about ten feet high. I put the Beemer in reverse and eased into the gas, hoping the fire wouldn't notice me. My eyes was locked on the flame, but movement in my rearview caught my eye. Directly behind me, two flames came up over the rails and were milling around. Before I could step on the gas, those little torches zipped over and started to burn up the back of my car. It went from a nice fall day to Africa-hot faster than I could yell. I got out of the car and ran right for the edge. I guess I was ready to jump over the edge, but I din't have to.

"Those flames only cared about the BMW, and they only cared until it stopped running. They din't torch the thing, really, or make it blow up. One of them went around to the hood, disappeared under the engine and then the next thing I knew, the BMW was shut off. I was still grippin' the railing of the bridge as the flames wandered away. One went back over the edge of the bridge and through the woods. The other one made its way to the other end of the bridge and joined the first flame. They were both orange and red, but when they joined together they burned hot and blue, like a butane torch. I could feel the heat double when they combined.

"I didn't go much further into the city. The flames were everywhere and if I even started a car, they'd show up and put it out. I rode a bike for a while, but they caught on and snuffed that too. They burned up the tires and fused the chain to the chainring. So I walked and walked.

"The first living thing I saw was a horse. He was stomping around his paddock, lookin' half-starved and thirsty. Really fancy house and barn and pastures right there inside the beltway. I din't know such a thing existed, but I guess when you have money anything's possible. I found him some hay and managed to draw some water with a hand-pump—got him squared away. In the barn they had a whole harness and cart thing, but I was afraid the fire would come after that too. I tried him with the saddle though. That bastard horse is so big, it's like riding a damn couch, but he's good under saddle. The two of us went north—the fire seems worse to the south and west—and we came all the way up through Pennsylvania, New York, and then east through Massachusetts until we turned north and ended up here.

"I found a place though—a big farm in the hills of upstate New York. I mean to go back and settle there. It's got good visibility and a herd of horses who din't disappear like everything else. I figured I'd throw it out there. Thought maybe some of you would go with me," Luke said.

"To where? New York?" Ted asked.

"Yes, that's what I said," Luke said.

A low murmur spread through the group as if they, like Ted, were just starting to grasp Luke's proposal.

"Why is New York better than here?" asked Sheila, straightening up in her chair.

"Like I said, there's horses there and a farm on a hill," Luke said. "There's a pond out back the horses drink from, and pastures. There's plenny of room for a summer garden, and a greenhouse next to the barn. The place still has life in it."

"That might just make it the next target," Ted said.

"Like we're not a target here?" asked Frank. His voice sounded a little frantic.

Luke patted the table next to Frank to settle him down. "I covered a big chunk of ground in the past couple of months, and I've only seen a couple signs of life. There's a band of scattered souls here, where the snow is only a coupla inches deep, and then there's this pocket down in New York. You folk up here are livin' right on the edge. You got corpses a few miles south, and lord-knows-what up there in a snow drift covering most of the state. Personally, I'd prefer to put some distance between myself and those things."

Another wave of whispered comments swept through the crowd, but to Brad the approval seemed to shift towards Luke.

Ted stood and waited until the sound died down and the eyes turned back to him. "Thank you Luke and Brad for sharing your stories. I don't see any other new faces tonight, so I'd like to get back to what I was saying about Rob's ideas. He has some thoughts about our situation and he'd like to share them now."

Brad looked over at Robby, and followed Robby's gaze over to Luke. Luke folded his arms and settled into a deep slouch.

"I agree with Luke," Robby said. "I definitely want to put some distance between us and the corpses and whatever is up in the snow."

Robby waited a breath before he continued.

"But the world we knew has ended. We have to assume it ended *everywhere*. We can't ignore the strange forces that brought us here. We can continue to be victims of it, or we can try to find a way to stop it. I suggest we first drive out the cause of the world's destruction, and then we can sneak off to New York and settle in the hills," Robby said. As he spoke the last sentence, he looked directly at Luke, as if his statement were an accusation.

"How you gonna fight things we don't even understand?" asked Luke. "Have you seen the columns of fire that chase down anything mechanical and burn it up? Have you seen the smart water trails that eat up anything that touches them? What about Brad's rock monster? You have a way to drive out rocks?"

"I do," Robby said.

During the verbal sparring, Brad had felt solidly on Robby's side. But Robby's last statement went too far. In Brad's opinion, the young man possessed the preposterous confidence only youth could grant.

"Huh," Luke said, voicing the group's doubt.

"The short version is this—we go south and gather as many corpses as we can. We'll need at least a several hundred; a thousand would be better. Then we head northeast. We'll find the main encampment somewhere near Kingston. That thing wants to use the corpses, but not yet. By bringing them early, we'll be able to drive off whatever brought the snow, the rocks, the fire, and the cleanup liquid."

"This ain't some movie, kid," Luke said.

"Rob," Judy said. She waited until he locked eyes with her before she continued, "There are some problems in life that don't

225

have a solution. Sometimes you just have to get by the best you can."

"Let me walk you all through the steps of my deduction," Robby said. He looked around and continued, "I wish I had a whiteboard. I could draw it all out for you."

Luke rose and backhanded Frank's shoulder.

"Me and Frank are leaving in the morning," Luke said. "I know how to get past the water things, how to avoid the fire creatures, and I'll take us out to the ranch in New York. Only bring what you can carry. We can get most of what we need on the way. We'll meet up at the Jetport parking lot at ten tomorrow morning. Who's coming?"

At first, only Frank and Luke raised their hands, but they were quickly joined by the loners on the outskirts of the group.

"We're going to need you to help fight these things," Robby said.

"Boy, you don't know what yer even up against," Luke said. "C'mon now, who else wants to look up at night and see the stars, or see the sun out in the daytime. I've heard you've seen nothing but cloudy skies here for months. Well, back at the ranch, it was sunny and pleasant."

A few more people raised their hands, including Judy and the woman Luke called "Tib."

"Good, then," Luke said. "Let's go get ready."

Luke and Frank headed for the door and most of the other hand-raisers followed behind. Judy stayed in her seat.

"Hey, guys," Robby began, but Ted put a hand on his shoulder and Robby stopped.

Sheila moved over to Brad's table and leaned over towards Judy.

"You're not really going with them, are you?" asked Sheila.

"Yeah," Judy said, "I think I am."

"I hate to say it," Sheila said, "but I just don't think that guy is safe. I don't trust him."

"What's safe?" Judy asked. "Safe ended a while ago. I'm sick of being here. I want to go away from here."

"What about Robby's idea?" Brad asked, injecting himself into the conversation.

"I can't follow his logic," Judy said. "He's always right, but I just don't have the energy for all that. He's full of fight. Let him fight."

Robby and Ted conferred with each other until Robby heard his name.

"It's not time to give up yet, Judy," Robby said. "I know you want to go back to the way it was, and we still can."

"I'm not giving up," Judy said to him. "I'm just moving on. I don't even think I want my old life anymore. I just want something different than all this. What are we still doing here? There's nothing left. I'll be out by the truck."

Judy pushed back from the table and fished a pack of cigarettes from her pocket before she put her coat on.

"We're losing a lot of people, Rob," Ted said.

After the hand-raisers left, fifteen people remained including the people at Brad's table. When Judy got up, several others stood and started to put on their coats as well.

"We really need everyone's help," Robby said to the room. "If you can just stick around for a few more minutes we can start making our plans."

Smelly, silent since the beginning of the meeting, was one of the people preparing to leave. Before he walked away, he addressed Robby. "You know I'm in for anything, Rob. Just get me on the radio when the time comes."

"I'd like to talk this through with you right now, Glen," Robby said.

"I'm going to get moving," Glen said. "You just give a shout on the radio and I'll help out however I can."

"You guys want to pull up chairs and we'll start hashing out some details?" Ted asked the others. His invitation spurred people to action, but not the action he requested. Even more people grabbed their coats and made their way to the door. Two women who'd been sitting together in the opposite corner conferred in their seats and then came to join the table with Brad, Robby, Ted, and Sheila.

Brad introduced himself and found out their names were Lisa

and Romie.

The door closed behind the last of the defectors and then crashed back open. A burly man in a grimy sheepskin coat flipped around a chair and sat backwards while uncapping a bottle of whiskey.

"Good to see you back, Pete," Ted said.

"Took me five minutes in the parking lot to figure out that Luke guy is an asshole," Pete said. "I wonder how long it will take the rest of them to piece it together. Probably they'll figure it out just west of Standish."

"I hope so," Ted said. "Or else it will be a long trip back."

"So what are we talking about here?" asked Pete. "You said you want to get a thousand eye-poppers up to Augusta?"

"Yes, that's about right," Robby said.

"You're talking about a thousand dead bodies. Maybe one-fifty pounds apiece on average," Pete said. He spoke quick and low, counting on his fingers. "That's gonna be about a hundred-and-fifty-thousand pounds. Maybe seventy-five tons, give or take, that about right?"

"Yes," Robby said. "And I think..."

Pete interrupted—"We can get some of those Bombardier one-eighties; probably some trailers on skids too. Might get close if we all drove." Pete counted around the table. "All of you can drive, right? Put seven of them in a convoy and run up the interstate?"

"What's he talking about?" asked Sheila.

"Can you drive?" Pete asked her.

"Of course," Sheila said.

"Ever been on a snowmobile?" asked Pete.

"Maybe," Sheila said. "When I was a kid, I guess."

"This is just like one of those, but much bigger," Pete said. "It's like a big tractor on treads. They use them to groom ski trails and such. We're going to round up seven of them and drive a bunch of dead bodies up north."

"But why?" asked Sheila. "You just jump in and start planning, but we don't even know why."

"That's little-man's department," Pete said, pointing to Robby.

All eyes turned to Robby and the young man cleared his throat.

"We're going to take back Maine," Robby said. "And if the assumptions prove true, the whole planet."

"Take it back from who?" asked Sheila.

"It's my conclusion that the Earth has been impregnated with a planet-sized organism," Robby said.

The group sat silent.

Brad looked around the table at each of the people. Ted and Pete both looked at Robby. Lisa and Romie both looked down at their laps. Sheila, her eyes twinkling in the lantern-light looked up towards the ceiling. She eventually broke the silence—"A what?"

✪ ✪ ✪ ✪ ✪

Brad woke up startled. His arm shot out from under the pillow, and still numb from being pinned under his head, swept the contents of his end table to the floor. He slipped out of his bed and fumbled around on the floor for the travel alarm clock. As soon as he had it in his hands, he realized it wasn't ringing.

The sound that woke him up came from the handheld radio on top of the dresser. When it buzzed again, Brad snatched it with his good arm—the not-numb arm—and stared at it until a voice came from it.

"I'll head over now. I've got some gear I can give them. It might help them out on the road," the voice said on the radio. Brad recognized the voice as Ted's.

The travel alarm read seven, but it felt way earlier. Brad and the others had stayed up most of the night talking and planning. First coming to terms with Robby's theories and then slowly scrutinizing his plan. They'd talked until the kerosene heaters ran out of fuel and Pete started rubbing his temples and complaining of a headache. Robby presented his evidence like a dissertation. He cited details from everyone's personal stories. Robby's memory was so perfect that Brad recognized the pauses and phrasing of Judy's speech as he quoted her story. In the end, Robby's outlandish theories seemed like a logical explanation.

Brad dressed quickly in the dawn light.

Luke had said he wasn't leaving until ten, but Brad wanted to be there early so he could say farewell to everyone headed for New York. He'd just met most of them, but felt a tight bond with the other survivors. Brad made it halfway across the yard to his truck before he stopped and turned around. Up in the closet of the master bedroom, he'd stashed a bag with the few sentimental items he'd taken from his house. In addition to that stuff, he packed a couple of shirts and some socks and underpants. As he exited the Dead Ferret House this second time, he shut off the valve to the heater, drained the hose on the water keg, and stored his food supplies in the empty refrigerator.

"I'll be back tonight," he told himself, but he prepared to be away indefinitely.

At the airport, he followed the convergence of tire tracks to the staff parking lot, which sat a few hundred yards away from the modest terminal. Robby and the rest of his people parked in a line at one end. Brad left his truck parked at the curb and walked across the snow-dusted grass to where Ted and Pete stood. They watched as the travelers consolidated possessions into a few vehicles.

For the road, they'd chosen some rugged Toyota Land Cruisers. The vehicles looked several years old, but in good condition. Frank and the smelly guy were strapping fuel cans to the roof racks while other people packed their bags into the backs of the trucks.

"That's a lot of gas for a few hundred miles," Ted said. He didn't direct his comment over at the vehicles, but he said it loud enough that they would hear.

"It's heating oil," Frank yelled back. "We're not running off with all the gas in town."

"What the hell do they want with that?" Ted asked, much quieter.

"You can run them diesel Cruisers on number two oil, if you don't mind the red stains," Pete said. "It's what I'm putting in those Bombardiers."

Aside from the Land Cruisers, Frank also packed some bags into the back seat of a four-door pickup truck. Hooked to the back of this truck sat an enormous horse trailer with its back doors standing open and its ramp extended. Brad saw that the front of the trailer was stocked with bales of hay. He also noticed the well-stocked gun rack in the back window of the truck.

Brad looked up at the sky. It looked like a lousy day for traveling. The clouds formed two distinct layers. Up high, it looked like the clouds were moving slowly from west to east. Lower, much closer to the ground, a spotty layer of sooty clouds moved fast from east to west. The weather had remained roughly the same every day that Brad had been in Portland. They always had clouds, and they never had any precipitation. Oppressive, impotent, charcoal-grey skies every day made him understand why so many people were choosing to go west with Luke and the promise of sunny days in a pastoral setting.

Brad saw Ted point and followed his finger to the vehicle approaching from the far side of the lot. When the car pulled up next to the closest Land Cruiser, Brad recognized Judy behind the wheel. She got out and pulled a tiny backpack from the passenger's seat. Robby walked over and said a few words to her and then the two of them walked away from the crowd to talk in private.

Brad zipped up his coat and stuffed his hands in his pockets.

"I'm cold," Brad said to Ted and Pete. "I'm going to see if I can help. I need to move around to warm up."

Brad walked over to the nearest people—he didn't remember their names—and watched them moving cases of canned goods from the back of a hatchback to the rear of a Land Cruiser.

"Hey," he said.

The nearest guy, the one with the long beard and the red flannel jacket on over his coat, grunted.

"You need help moving stuff? I'm freezing just standing around," Brad said.

"Then don't," said Beard.

"Sorry?" Brad asked.

"Nobody asked you to stand around," said Beard. "Just be on your way."

"Oh," Brad said. He walked back over to where Ted and Pete were standing.

"Harris hates everyone," Ted said. "Don't take offense."

The three men turned their attention over to Robby, who returned to the group with Judy. Robby and Judy hugged briefly and then she got in the back seat of one of the Land Cruisers and shut the door.

Robby came over to Ted. "She agreed to take a radio, and she'll stay in touch as long as she can."

"Or as long as they let her," Ted said.

"If she decides to come back, she can use the radio to link back up with us," Robby said.

Pete interjected—"It would be real useful if we could set up repeaters when we head north. Her radio is not going to do her much good once we've made some distance."

"We'll be back this way," Robby said. "If she doesn't come back, we can track her down in New York."

"Any luck on finding out exactly where they're going?" Ted asked.

"She didn't know," Robby said. "None of them seem to know for sure. Not even Frank."

"Here comes the man who does," Ted said. He pointed his chin off to the north.

Sitting straight up with his shoulders back, Luke appeared at the far end of the parking lot riding an enormous chestnut draft horse. The horse's blond mane fluttered back from his regal head as he trotted towards the group. Luke didn't bounce in the saddle, but bobbed up and down with every other stride of the horse. Brad took an involuntary step backwards as the horse and rider approached. The horse seemed impossibly big as it approached.

Luke rode back and forth behind the line of cars before he edged the giant horse alongside the trailer. Luke kicked his right foot from the stirrup and swung his leg over the neck of the horse, sliding from mount facing away from the horse. He held a hand protectively on his sidearm as he dropped to the ground. Luke looped the reins over a hook on the side of the trailer and greeted the people who came to get a closer look at the horse.

Brad approached in a wide arc, careful not to step directly behind the horse. He stopped a few feet away from the horse while Luke unbuckled the saddle. Robby stepped past Brad and went to the horse's head. He reached forward and up to stroke the horse's nose.

"He's beautiful. What's his name?" Robby asked Luke.

Luke flipped the cinch over the top of the saddle and stood on his tiptoes to hook the stirrups over the horn. He pulled the saddle and blanket down into his arms.

"I call him Cincinnati," Luke said. "Pardon me." He ducked around Robby and carried the saddle to the front of the trailer.

Several people stood on either side of the horse, but Robby was the only one close enough to touch the big animal. Luke returned with a small stepladder and a brush.

"You want to brush him out while I get the trailer ready?" Luke asked Robby.

"Sure," Robby said with a big smile.

As Robby climbed the ladder to start at the top of the horse's back, Brad walked back over to Ted and Pete.

"That's one big goddamn horse," Pete said.

"Robby likes him," Brad said.

"Robby needed a reason to be close to Luke. I wouldn't conclude anything other than that," Ted said.

"You know, I think I can smell the horse from here," Pete said.

Ted raised his nose to the air and shielded his eyes while looking up. "I don't think that's the horse you're smelling," Ted said. "I think something is on fire."

The radio clipped to Ted's belt let out a squawk, followed by Lisa's frantic voice. "Robby? Robby?"

"Lisa, this is Ted," Ted said. "What's going on?"

Robby, still on the step ladder, stopped brushing. Ted started walking towards him so he could hear the radio.

"Is Robby there?" Lisa asked through the radio. "Can you tell him he has to get back to his house right away? Actually, tell him not to come to his house. Tell him to come to our house, and tell him to come the back way."

Robby climbed down from the ladder and took the radio from Ted. He leaned against Cincinnati's broad side as he spoke into the radio – "Lisa, what's the problem?"

"Your house is on fire," she said.

"I'll be right there," Robby said. He handed the radio back to Ted, folded up the ladder, and leaned it against the trailer before setting the brush on top of it. "Can you tell Luke and the others I had to take off?" he asked Ted.

"We'll be right behind you," Ted said.

✪ ✪ ✪ ✪ ✪

Robby squatted down on his haunches in front of Lisa and Romie's big picture window. Down the street and to the right, through the scattered branches of two big fir trees, he could just see the flames. Above the trees the sky was marred by a thick black column of smoke.

"That's why he was late," Ted said as he paced around the coffee table. "I bet if we went over there we'd find hoof prints leading up to the house."

"Why the hell would he ride a horse over here to set a fire?" asked Pete.

Brad sat in a small flower print chair near the door. Romie and Lisa sat side by side on their couch. The door opened and Sheila let herself in.

"I heard you guys on the radio," Sheila said as she came through the kitchen into the living room. "What's going on?"

"Luke burned down Robby's house," Ted said.

"Oh my god, why? Is everyone okay? Is Judy okay?" asked Sheila.

"Yeah, she's over at the airport with those guys," Pete said. "Unless they've left already. You know, she was late to the party too. Robby, was Judy still at home when you left the house this morning?"

"Yeah," Robby said. He spun around and sat on the carpet, hugging his knees to his chest.

"So what's the damage?" asked Sheila. "Where are we at?"

"No harm, really," Robby said. "Just personal stuff. I mean it's all stuff I collected in the past few months anyway."

"It's an attack, is what it is," Ted said. "Plus all your notes and maps. What about your recreation of the alien message on the wall in the basement? That's all gone."

"I've got electronic copies of all that stuff," Robby said. "And I remember it all anyway."

"It's good you've got copies, but you've got to remember—if something happens to you, it doesn't matter how good your memory is. The rest of us will be in the dark," Ted said.

"Maybe we shouldn't stay here," Romie said. "Plenty of people know we live here. We should go hide out until they're all gone."

"You think they'll come after us?" asked Lisa.

"Why not?" Ted asked. "All we know is this: at least one of them is trying to hurt us. For all we know, several of them wish us harm. Did you see all the guns that Frank and Luke were packing?"

"Frank had a bunch," Brad said. "I only saw one on Luke."

"They had guns?" asked Sheila. "What for? What do they think guns are going to help with?"

The group fell silent, but the tension in the room built anyway. Sheila started to chew at her fingernails and Ted sat down on the edge of a table and rocked back and forth.

Robby stood up and addressed the group. "Romie's right. We shouldn't stay here. I don't think Luke's crew is coming after us, but if the fire spreads, it might attract other attention."

"You mean from the thing up north?" asked Romie. "I thought you said it was still gestating."

"Yes," Robby said, "I think it is, but I'm talking about the forces that were deployed to prepare the area. There might be versions we haven't seen yet—things like white blood cells. Things that will show up to counteract any destructive forces; fire, for instance. I've got another place set up. It's downtown. It will be closer to the bridge anyway. We can start executing the plan from there."

"Is it safe?" asked Lisa.

"Safe as anywhere, I guess," Robby said.

They didn't wait long to find out if Robby's theory about the white blood cells would be correct. The men and women piled into three cars and left after Romie and Lisa gathered a few things they thought they'd need from their borrowed house.

✪ ✪ ✪ ✪ ✪

They followed Robby to the third floor of a downtown parking garage. From there, a covered walkway led to a well-appointed apartment building. Robby had equipped several adjacent dwellings with portable heaters and water. He ran a generator in the atrium to provide basic electricity.

Robby and Brad pinned maps to the living room wall while Ted, Sheila, and Pete ventured out to collect their possessions from their temporary homes. By the time the three of them returned to the apartment, Robby and Brad finished reconstructing the plans and Lisa and Romie joined them in the center apartment.

Although they'd discussed the plan, this marked the first time they'd all seen Robby's map laid out. Robby and Brad constructed a mural on the wall of high-detail topographic maps showing the terrain from Portland to Waterville. The highlighted route stretched about seventy-five miles—north from the coast to deep inland.

Ted scratched the back of his head as he studied the map. He traced his fingers up the gently waving dotted line. "You've told us it will be using our own infrastructure as the scaffolding for its growth, right?"

"Correct," Robby said.

"But why wouldn't it just use the rivers?" Ted asked. "Our roads follow the rivers for the most part. I don't see why the thing wouldn't grow into them."

"I don't know exactly," Robby said. "But if this thing has tried to colonize Earth several times before and it was unsuccessful, we should look for the man-made differences. Since the origin of the planet, it's had natural features like these rivers. I assume if it could use the rivers, it would have done so back in the time of dinosaurs or even earlier. Since it didn't gestate then, I'm guessing it needs things like roads to thrive. Maybe it waited until our civilization tamed the landscape enough to make it suitable."

"There are a lot of guesses in there," Pete said.

"You bought in last night—has your opinion changed?" Brad asked.

"Not substantially," Pete said. "Just stating the obvious."

"Well, we can try the highway up to here," Robby said, pointing at the center map. "This is where the train tracks diverge from the highway. It's several miles south of Brad's house. If everything looks okay north of there, I'm fine continuing on the highway. If not, we can backtrack to the rails."

"Fair enough," Pete said. "I can even go ahead on a fast snowmobile to scout. Make sure everything is kosher."

"I object," Ted said. "For one thing, we'll need everyone driving a rig if we want to do this in one trip. And second, I don't think we should split up for any reason."

"I'm with Ted," Sheila said. "Everyone together."

"Okay, okay," Pete said. "Just thinking out loud, that's all."

"What about the people?" asked Sheila. "We have to get a thousand of them you said?"

"I have no way to come up with an exact number," Robby said, "but I think a thousand will do."

"Any particular people?" asked Sheila.

"No," Robby said. "The first thousand corpses we can find will do."

"I've been thinking—we need to respect them," Ted said. "We need to remember that they were our neighbors."

Romie waved a hand at Ted. "They're just meat now. What difference does it make?"

"We're human," Ted said. "We have certain rules we live by so we can respect life. You wouldn't want us to drop into chaos, would you?"

"This is an emergency situation," Romie said. "And we've all lost people."

"We'll certainly respect the dead," Pete said. "Let's just not go crazy here. At the heart of the matter, we're going to have to collect, and then haul those bodies across a big chunk of real estate. There's only so much respect you can pay when you're loading a body on the back of a big sled."

"As long as we remember them as people," Ted said. "I used to live down in Saco, before all this happened. I moved up here because I couldn't stand to be around all those eyeless people. Everywhere I'd go, I'd see someone and it wouldn't register who they were. It's hard to recognize someone when their eyes are blown out, running down their face." Ted lowered his head and sat down on the edge of a chair while he rubbed his temples. "I wished I could give them all a decent burial, pay my respects, but what could I do?"

Romie rolled her eyes and shifted forward. Lisa put a hand on her shoulder to stop her from interrupting Ted's confession.

"I got a backhoe running and figured out how to dig up our plot for my Marie, but then I just left the rest of them," Ted said.

Pete crouched down next to Ted. "If Robby's plan works, then we'll be paying them the ultimate respect, because they'll be the ones who save everything."

"I suppose," Ted said.

"And even if it seems a little undignified to be piled up, you've got to remember—respect comes from the intentions. It comes from *our* intentions," Pete said. He rose to his feet and found a particular spot on the map. "I can start lining up the seven Bombardiers right here, on this bridge. It's right on the edge where the snow starts to get deep, so we should be able to drive pickups with the bodies right up to them."

"Shouldn't we use something bigger than pickups?" Brad asked. "That's going to be a lot of trips."

"We'll need to use maneuverable vehicles to collect the bodies," Robby said. "So I think big pickups or moving vans are probably the way to go."

"I can't lift a body," Romie said. "At least not a big one. Maybe a dead kid or something."

Lisa gave Romie's arm a light smack.

"What?" asked Romie.

"We'll go in pairs," Brad said. "One strong person per pair."

"I know a place where I've seen a few big trucks," Sheila said. "I'll get them over to the garage so we can start first thing in the morning. Ted? You want to come with?"

Ted was still looking down at the floor, not making eye contact.

"Sure," he said. He rose and headed for the door. Sheila waved to everyone and followed him out.

"You have the list from last night, or did it burn up?" Pete asked Robby.

"Burned up," Robby said, "but I can remember it."

"Good," Pete said. "I've got some stuff to add to it."

"You guys want spaghetti for dinner?" Lisa asked.

"Sure," Brad said. Pete and Robby agreed also.

"Good," she said. "Romie and I will make dinner."

"How did I get conscripted?" asked Romie. "I hate making pasta."

"Just come on," Lisa said. She took Romie's hand and led her to the door. "We'll be back."

✪ ✪ ✪ ✪ ✪

By the second day, Brad and Romie achieved a decent working arrangement. Despite her objections to lifting, Brad found that Romie could easily shoulder her share of the burden. For the first day, they cruised the streets, stopping at derelict cars and pulling out the drivers. Most were easy to extract—their slumped bodies were stiff from the cold and Brad slid them out to the street with one hand. Then, he took the shoulders and Romie the feet. Together they transported each body over to the moving van and loaded the person into the back.

For the heaviest bodies, they sometimes stopped to rest. For anyone even moderately fat, they used the van's lift-gate to elevate the person to the van's height.

Brad found he liked Romie a lot more when she wasn't talking. She looked to be a few years older than Brad, and carried a sour expression on her face matching the band of extra weight she carried around her midsection. While they drove, he wished they had a way to play music in the moving van, so she wouldn't feel the need to fill the silence with her angry commentary about everything that crossed her mind. Only when they were carrying a body, did Brad actually welcome her diatribes as a distraction from the horror of the dead.

It didn't matter how many corpses he saw, something about the dead appalled Brad's eyes. He couldn't see them as chunks of meat, as Romie professed. He couldn't see them as former friends and neighbors, as Ted described. To Brad, the corpses looked like broken puppets; like marionettes with the strings cut. He kept imagining them fluttering their eyelids over empty sockets, or working their jaws up and down in hitches and jerks. Each time he touched a corpse, he expected their hand to reach over and grab his arm.

Only Romie's constant talking kept Brad rooted to reality.

"You think the birds would be back at least," she said as they hauled a middle-aged guy out from a convenience store.

"Back?" Brad asked. Since they carried a corpse, this was one of the times he wanted her to talk. He gripped the guy under the armpits, and the man's head flopped back and kept hitting Brad in the knees.

"Yeah," Romie said. "I mean after a fire, or a flood, or something, you always see birds on the scene right away. It's been months and there isn't a bird around. Where are they? Did that thing really kill all the birds in the whole goddamn world?"

"Maybe the birds are afraid of something?" Brad asked. "Or maybe the food is better somewhere else?"

"It's like Noah's Ark, you know?" she asked.

Brad did not know what she meant, but he kept his mouth shut figuring she would continue. He was right.

"They gathered up all the animals two-by-two," she said. "I don't believe in any of that horse shit, but it might just be a story they put around something half-remembered. What if almost everything disappeared, like now, and they just made up the story about the flood and Noah's Ark to explain it all away?"

"The genetic record would reflect it," Brad said. "DNA would be less diverse."

"Oh, so we're taking as gospel the word of a whole lot of scientists not smart enough to survive the apocalypse? We're the ones who got through it. Doesn't our survival give our opinions just a tad more weight?" she asked. She didn't wait for a reply. "So I think the kid is right. This thing he's talking about has tried to take the Earth before. The birds ain't coming back, because they're all dead. Maybe there's a couple around, like us."

"Or like Luke's horse?" Brad asked.

"If you ask me, I wish Luke hadn't made the cut," she said. "He strikes me as a jackass."

When they got to the back of the moving van, they didn't bother to engage the lift-gate; the guy was too small to bother. They moved into their positions and swung the man like a hammock: one, two, three times. On the third, they both let go and his stiff body skidded quickly to a stop in the bed of the van. Brad jumped up to drag the corpse towards the front of the vehicle with the other bodies. When they had a few more up there, Romie would clamber up to help him stack.

"So everything is dead, right?" she asked, but didn't really ask. "At least everything that used to move around is. Seems to have left all the plants. I wonder if there are any fish left. But how long are the plants going to last if there aren't any animals around? I mean, maybe the plants don't really care about animals, but the bugs, they must need the bugs to pollinate all the flowers. That's how they reproduce, right? So maybe we make it until summer, then the grocery stores start to run out of food, and then we're done."

"There aren't very many of us," Brad said. "I don't think the grocery stores are going to run out of canned goods."

"Yeah, but we can only get to so many of them," Romie said. "There's too much snow up north, and worse things down south."

Brad jumped back down to the pavement and scanned around the parking lot. They'd grabbed the body of the clerk and the one shopper they'd found in the convenience store, and the few cars around them were tapped out.

"Plus," she continued, "who knows what kind of climate changes we can expect going forward. Are we even going to have seasons anymore? If all the plants die, will we have oxygen?"

"Romie?" Brad asked.

"You know, Robby is relying on that thing not even being aware of us. What did he say? When a bird makes a nest in a tree, do you think it's aware of the bacteria living on the branches?" she asked.

"Romie?" he asked again.

"What?" she asked.

"Do you have any ideas of where we could hunt for more bodies? Or should we just start going door-to-door?" Brad asked.

"Yeah—Chinese place over near the mall," she said.

"You sure? Everyone died on Thanksgiving. Do people go for Chinese food on Thanksgiving?" Brad asked.

"Any holiday," she replied. "I bet there's thirty of them over there. Let's go."

Brad rolled down the cargo door and climbed back into the cab. Romie was already strapping herself in.

"So what do you think of his theories?" she asked Brad as he started the engine.

"Who? Robby?" Brad asked. He knew what she was talking about but the question just fell out of his mouth. He was shocked she actually asked him a question that she expected an answer to.

"Yes, Robby," she said. "Who else?"

"He certainly presented a compelling case," Brad said. "There's no real way to verify some of what he said. A lot of it was based on the interpretation of those runes he found in a basement. When I looked at those things there was definitely something interesting going on. It made me feel fuzzy just to look at the symbols."

"Hmmm, yeah, well..." Romie started, but Brad cut her off for once.

"And the fourth dimension stuff seems a little outlandish. I'm an engineer and a software architect. Spatial reasoning and higher math are not foreign to me at all, but I've always been taught that *time* is the fourth dimension. He said these things can move through three-dimensional space without continuity because they exist in four or more dimensions," Brad said as he slowed for a stop sign. He knew he shouldn't bother to heed the sign, but it was hard to break the habit.

"I remember," agreed Romie.

"So it would be like if you or I were interacting with creatures that lived on a sheet of paper. We could pick up and move to a different spot and they'd be oblivious to how it happened. Robby says that's how these creatures manage space travel. For them, all the points in the universe are essentially connected through the higher dimensions," Brad said. He glanced over at Romie, who was looking straight ahead. He continued—"I guess I can visualize that, but it seems like if that's the case, we would have had contact with them before."

Now Romie spoke up. "Exactly. He said we *have* had contact before. We just didn't recognize it, or it was too long ago. Their idea of an hour or a year might not be the same as ours. What if they don't live from one moment to the next?"

"I suppose," Brad said.

"But you didn't answer my question—what do you think of his theories? Like about how to drive this thing off?" she asked.

"Well, I guess to me it's the same question," Brad said. "If he's right about the extra-dimensional beings and the planet-wide organism, then he may very well be right about the immune response of dumping a thousand bodies into the embryo. No way to tell except giving it a try, you know?"

"That's exactly how I feel," Romie said. "I believe him. I just wish we didn't have to go a hundred miles north to test it out."

"I'm not sure I'd go that far," Brad said.

"What? Not all the way to Augusta?" asked Romie.

"No, no, it's just that you said you believe him," Brad said.

"And I do," Romie said. "He's a trustworthy kid."

"Yes he's trustworthy," Brad said, "but I'm thinking that *if* he's right about the planet-wide organism, *then* dumping bodies into it might be the appropriate thing to do."

"But you're not convinced?" asked Romie.

"Not entirely, no," Brad said.

"Take a right up here. It's faster," Romie said.

They bounced along in silence for a little while. Every so often, usually during a turn, they could hear the bodies shift around in the back of the truck. Romie guided Brad to pull up next to a giant restaurant. He backed the rear of the truck up near the doors and they climbed out.

Romie opened the front door of the restaurant and held it open until Brad dragged a sign with a metal base over to prop it open.

They repeated the process with the interior door. This time Brad used a chair. Romie strapped on a headlamp and started off to the right, but Brad just stood there at the door. He didn't like the way the light from the doors seemed to die out so quickly.

The restaurant was huge and almost industrial-looking to Brad. The red and purple swirls of the carpet were probably designed to hide stains, but they also confused Brad's eyes. The panels of the high drop-ceiling looked dusty and old, even from a distance.

"Come on," Romie said from her little pool of light, "there are two over here."

Brad put on his own headlamp and joined his partner.

"Let's get this fat one first," Romie said. "I swear my back's never going to make it to the end of the day."

Romie flipped up the tablecloth and grabbed the man's ankles while Brad worked his hands into the man's armpits. They lifted at the same time and started a slow shuffle towards the door. The guy looked fat, but he wasn't too heavy. Brad and Romie had no trouble getting him to the lift-gate. With him loaded, they went back for the woman at the table.

"I used to come *at least* once a month," Romie said as they slung the woman up into the bed of the truck. "It's a pretty good value if you stay long enough."

"Why?" Brad asked. The lady-corpse had long hair, and Brad had already stepped on it twice. He dragged her to the front of the truck by her feet so it fanned out behind her.

"Value? Because they only bring out the good stuff once every couple of hours. Crab legs? Forget it. You have to be here for a while before you're going to see any of those. It's like they know I'm coming and they only bring out the good stuff just before I show up. It's all gone by the time I get my seat," Romie said.

They followed their headlamps back inside, past the table where they'd found the first couple. Romie walked between two long buffet stations and then stopped. Brad almost ran into her back.

"Something's been here," she said. Her voice was low—nearly a whisper.

"Like what? An animal?" Brad asked.

"You tell me," Romie said. She turned to the side so Brad could see. In front of her, on the floor, sat a rough pile of chicken wings. Next to those, Brad saw several egg rolls littered on the carpet. Romie scanned the big room with her headlamp, but the meager light couldn't reveal much of the room. Romie dug around in her pocket and pulled out a little flashlight. That was better, but Brad didn't see much more than round tables to the left and square ones to the right.

He looked back to where the door stood out as a bright white rectangle of light. Suddenly those dozen paces seemed far away.

"Let's hurry up so we can get out of here," Romie said.

Brad slipped between two of the buffet units and crossed the walkway to the tables. Before rounding the first table, he tripped and landed on his hands and knees. Looking back, he saw black pants and a white jacket—he'd tripped over a fallen waiter. The waiter's outstretched arm offered a pitcher of spilled water.

"I got one here on the floor," Brad said to Romie, who stopped on the far side of the table.

Brad flipped the waiter's torso and grabbed him under the armpits. He glanced down at the face and then looked away, but the image burned into his vision. The corpse's eyes had exploded just like the rest, but he had no sign of gore on his cheeks. The waiter had big, white teeth though. He had a rack of giant, white, piano-key teeth. When Romie finally lifted the waiter's dead legs, Brad got up the nerve to look back down. His lips were missing— that's why Brad could see the corpse's teeth so well. Something had taken the lips and part of the cheek. The edge of the wound was jagged, but clean. No blood or gore stained the rest of the skin.

Romie let out a yelp and dropped the legs. The body slumped and tugged on Brad's shoulders, but he kept his grip. At least he kept it until he looked where Romie's headlamp was pointing. She was staring at the corpse's groin. There, the black pants had been pulled down a bit. The waiter's white skin nearly matched the tone of the white jacket he wore. In the low light, Brad understood why neither of them had noticed earlier. But in the groin area, the white ended. There Brad could see the stringy, shiny edges of muscle where the skin and sex organs had been removed.

Brad dropped the corpse's shoulders and backed up.

"There's something in here with us," Romie whispered. She whipped her headlamp around the room.

"Over here," Brad said. "We'll go together. Back-to-back."

Romie stepped over the mutilated corpse and joined Brad. They matched steps and moved towards the door.

Brad saw the shadow first. When Brad stopped moving behind her, Romie turned her head and saw it too. Something standing just to the right of the doors cast a fuzzy shadow on the pavement between the restaurant and the truck. Brad thought about the gun tucked safely in the glove compartment of the truck.

"Out the back?" Brad whispered.

"Fuck that," Romie said.

As if they'd agreed, they resumed moving towards the doors. Brad scanned the area surrounding the door for anything he could use as a weapon. He found nothing. Brad led the way and the two side-stepped through the doors. Outside, a short, stocky man stood a couple of paces from the back of the truck.

"Hello?" Brad asked.

The man didn't reply. He flipped his bangs to the side, reached up with a grimy finger and rubbed his teeth. Romie passed behind Brad and moved towards the driver's side of the truck as the two men stared at each other. Brad lost the staring contest. His eyes darted to his right, to the gaping black hole that was the entrance to the Chinese restaurant.

"Can I help you?" Brad asked.

"What are you doing?" the man asked. His voice was so low that Brad could barely hear him. He slurred the four words together into one.

Brad took a second to reply. "We're clearing out the bodies," he said, gesturing to the back of the truck.

"For whom?" asked the man.

"What's your name?" Brad asked. "My name is Brad."

"And I'm Romie," she said. She circled around the truck and around the dirty man. Brad spotted the handgun she held at her side.

They waited for the man's response. His eyes seemed to take inventory of the scene, darting around from place to place, again and again.

"Nate," he said, finally.

"Nice to meet you, Nate," Brad said. "Are you here alone? I mean, do you live with anyone else."

"Yes," Nate said.

"Which?" Brad asked.

Nate shook his head from side to side violently. He shook it so hard that Brad could hear the man's cheeks flapping against his teeth. Romie took a half step back but kept the gun pointed only at the pavement.

"I'm sorry," Nate said. "It's been a long time since I've talked to anyone. I must look like a crazy person."

"No," Brad said, "not at all. But you did startle us a bit because we only saw your shadow at first."

"Sorry," Nate said. "You never answered my question—for whom are you clearing out the bodies?"

"Oh," Brad said. "I don't know. I mean, we're clearing them out for everyone, I guess. We thought it would be..." he trailed off, not knowing how much he should tell the dirty man.

"Respectful," Romie said from her position. She kept her distance. Brad moved a little closer to Nate as they talked.

"Yes, that's a good word for it," Brad said. "It's the least we could do."

"I'm not sure I understand the point," Nate said.

Romie and Brad exchanged a glance.

"Maybe we should be on our way," Brad said. "I'm guessing we'll see you around."

"Probably not," Nate said. "It's been months and I haven't seen you before." Nate ran a slow gaze from the ground back up to Brad's eyes. "I guess we travel in different circles."

"Well..." Brad started and then didn't know how to finish.

"So where are you taking them?" asked Nate. "To, you know, be *respectful*."

"Mass grave," Brad said.

"Where? In case I want to pay *my* respects."

Brad looked to Romie.

"A patch of woods off of 114," Romie said.

"Got it," Nate said. "Patch of woods."

"Okay then," Romie said. She moved in a careful, sidestepping circle around Nate, back to the cab of the truck. Brad waved and walked to the driver's door. They both closed their doors quickly and immediately locked them. Brad turned the key and prayed the moving van would start. Nate still stood next to the door of the Chinese restaurant as they pulled away.

"Well that was a bust," Romie said. "Lots of corpses in there. We could have finished off the day."

"What a creepy guy," Brad said. "I hope we don't meet up with him again."

"I get the feeling we will, somehow," Romie said. "Take a left up here in case he's watching. I want him to think we're headed south."

"Sure thing," Brad said.

Until they'd rounded several turns, Brad paid more attention to the rearview mirrors than the road in front of them. Romie called out turns and led them back around to Route 1 before they turned north again. They passed cars of the dead—veered off to the side of the road—but they were all empty. The doors hung open revealing empty seats. Another team of corpse collectors, probably Ted and Sheila, had already harvested this area.

"Hey," Romie said, snapping her fingers. "Take a right up here. Old folks home."

"Good idea," Brad said.

They finished their quota with an easy pile of withered, graying corpses. Some of the old women, dressed in sweatpants and shirts, smelling like salty chicken soup, were so light that Brad could have carried them on his own. They doubled their speed when Romie realized they could pile two bodies on a wheelchair and move four corpses at a time.

They headed north towards the rendezvous point with their truckload of death.

Brad followed the tracks of other trucks north on the highway through the snow. Weighted down with the corpses, the big moving van didn't have any problem with traction. Before it got too deep—still less than a foot of snow—Romie pointed out the line of sleds parked up ahead. Each flat sled was about twenty-five feet long and attached to a huge, tracked vehicle, the Bombardiers Pete acquired.

When he saw them pulling up, Pete waved Brad up to the front sled where the other two moving vans were also parked. Sheila and Ted were pulling bodies off the back of the van and carrying them over to the sled. As soon as he got Brad to the right spot, Pete jumped up on the sled to help Robby stack the corpses.

They were working on the second row of bodies. They'd already secured the first row with thick yellow straps.

Brad jumped down from the driver's seat and walked over to where Ted and Sheila were lifting the body of a fat man in a bathrobe. They'd stomped down a path through the snow between the van and the sled, but Brad was cutting a new path through the powder as he approached.

"Can I take over for one of you guys?" Brad asked.

Sheila answered, "We're fine, but you might want to help Lisa." Sheila pointed her chin at the back of the van. In the gloomy interior, Brad saw Lisa dragging another body to the back edge of the moving van. Brad used the handle mounted on the side of the van and hoisted himself up onto the deck. He blinked at the darkness—eyes still squinting from looking across the snow—and helped Lisa slide another heavy man by his bathrobe.

"Who's that?" asked Lisa.

"Who?" Brad asked. He looked up to see her pointing south, down the highway.

A dark figure stood in the snow about a hundred yards from their position.

"Nate," Brad said, under his breath.

"Who?" asked Lisa, but Brad was already jumping down from the back of the moving van. Brad caught up with Ted and Sheila as they tossed their corpse up to Pete and Robby.

"Hey, guys," Brad said. When he had their attention, he continued. "I think this guy might be trouble." He didn't point, but motioned with his eyes in the direction of the dark figure standing in the snow.

Pete dropped to one knee on the deck of the sled, bringing his head level with Ted's.

"Who is it?" Ted asked.

"I'm not sure," Brad said, "but it might be the guy Romie and I just met over at the Chinese restaurant."

"So you talked to him?" Ted asked.

"If it's the same guy, yes," Brad said.

Robby climbed down from the sled and tromped off, cutting a new line through the snow. "I'm going to go meet him," he called back over his shoulder.

"I'm right behind you," Brad said.

As Brad walked away, he heard Sheila and Ted arrive at the conclusion that a two-person greeting party was probably enough. Brad glanced around for Romie—he hadn't seen her since they pulled up to the convoy—but she wasn't with the group.

Brad caught up to Robby as the boy slogged through the snow.

"Did you see where Romie went?" Brad asked Robby.

"She's still in the truck you guys pulled up in," Robby said.

Brad confirmed as they walked by the other moving van. Romie was still sitting there in the cab. She slid over to the driver's side and she looked focused on the side-view mirror. She nodded to Brad and Robby as they walked past.

"She's watching that guy," Robby said softly.

"Yup," Brad said.

"What did he say to you before?" Robby asked.

"Not much. He wanted to know where we were taking the corpses. I don't know how he followed us. We went south and then looped back around before coming back here and we didn't see him the whole time. When we left him, he was on foot in a parking lot. There was a cannibalized body in that restaurant. He might be responsible."

Robby didn't comment. They'd crossed about halfway to the man. The dark figure, who Brad still assumed was Nate, didn't move. He stood between the tire tracks left by the moving vans. He flicked his long hair out of his face with a toss of his head. Robby and Brad stopped about ten feet away from him. It was Nate.

"Respectful," Nate said.

"Hi, I'm Robby."

"Nate," said the dirty man. A breeze brought his odor to Brad. Nate smelled a bit like the nursing home corpses. It was a smell Brad had begun to associate with cold neglect. Brad traced Nate's footprints through the snow. He hadn't arrived on the highway; he came from the west.

"Hello again," Brad said.

"Patch of woods?" asked Nate, gesturing to the sleds off in the distance behind Robby and Brad.

"It's a long story," Brad said, "and, frankly, we didn't think you needed to know."

"You could have said that," Nate said. He tilted his head down towards the snow and then started violently shaking it, as he'd done outside the Chinese restaurant. Again, he kept going until they could hear Nate's cheeks slapping against his teeth.

"Are you okay?" Robby asked.

Nate stopped instantly and looked up at the young man.

"Are you? Should any of us be, after all this?"

"We have to load these deceased onto these flatbed sleds there," Robby said. "You're welcome to help or we can talk with you while we work." Robby gestured back to the group who stopped working to watch the conversation.

"I'd like to know what the hell you're doing first," Nate said.

"We're taking all these people up north," Brad said.

"Why?" asked Nate.

Brad looked to Robby.

"We think we can get rid of the thing growing up there," Robby said. "If we trigger an immune response, we think we can get it to go away."

"That's a hell of an odd thing to say," Nate said.

Robby shrugged.

Brad wanted to argue in Robby's defense. He wanted to put the young man's theory in context to convince Nate why he should take it seriously. But the silence seemed to belong to Robby and Nate alone; it wasn't Brad's to break.

A light breeze kicked up swirls of snowflakes, taking the hard edge off of the fresh footprints. Since Brad arrived in Portland, he hadn't felt much wind. In fact, he wondered if he'd felt any wind at all. In Portland, everything was still. None of the snow drifted or melted under the perpetually gray skies. Could this breeze be the first breath of air he'd felt in a month?

Nate broke the silence. "Seems like grave robbery to me."

"They weren't buried," Robby said. "And we're going to inter them up north."

"In a patch of woods, right?" Nate asked.

"Like he said, you didn't need to know so they made the choice to tell you a lie. We're not making any apologies for what we're doing here. It's the right thing to do," Robby said.

"And if I help you move some of those dead, will you explain further what you intend to do with them?" asked Nate.

"Certainly," Robby said. He turned and swept his arm towards the sled. "After you."

Nate nodded and shuffled between Robby and Brad. As short-and-stocky Nate passed by, Brad caught a bigger noseful of the man. He smelled like he looked—greasy and sour. Robby and Brad followed him back towards the sled. As they passed Brad's moving van, Brad looked up to see if Romie was still in the cab. He didn't see her.

When they'd approached to a few dozen paces from the sled, everyone stopped working and grouped together to greet the new arrival.

"This is Nate," Robby said.

"Hi," Nate said, waving.

Brad stepped forward to make the introductions. "Nate, this is Sheila, Lisa, Ted, and Pete."

"Where's the other one?" asked Nate.

"Pardon?" Brad asked.

"The thick woman who was with you in the truck. Where did she get to?" asked Nate.

"Oh," Brad said. "I'm not sure. She must be around here

somewhere."

"I'd like to talk to her again," Nate said.

Brad glanced around the group to see if anyone else found this statement peculiar. Only Lisa seemed concerned; or at least *more* concerned. Ted's eyes hadn't slowed since Nate walked up. Ted scanned up and down Nate's body, like he was just waiting for the new man to pull out a concealed weapon. Even Pete, who seemed to like everyone, displayed guarded, half-turned-away body language.

Robby broke the silence. "Nate's going to join us for a bit."

"We're hustling these citizens from the truck there over to this sled," Pete said, pointing.

"Why don't you help us on the sled?" Robby asked. "We could use a hand keeping all the deceased in one place until we get the straps up over them."

"Sure thing," Nate said.

Brad walked with Sheila, Lisa, and Ted over to the truck while Pete and Robby brought Nate up to speed on how they were stacking the corpses. After a brief consultation, Ted and Brad volunteered to carry the bodies from the truck to the sled while the women worked inside the truck. Brad caught pieces of the conversation between Robby and Nate as they worked to pile up the bodies on the sled.

"... and Brad experienced the same thing up his way, but he waited out the first part of the storm." Robby told Nate. "If you look on a map, you can see concentric circles around where this thing is gestating. In South Portland, you happened to be in the protein-rich area. It's like the albumen of an egg. In some zones all the biological material was removed, but down in your zone..."

Brad walked away before Robby finished his sentence, but Brad had heard his theories before. Robby related the whole Earth to a giant egg, where the embryo was from an enormous alien species. Before planting its egg, the aliens prepped the Earth by destroying as much of the population as possible and then released antibodies to take care of the rest. Robby equated his plan to scrambling the contents of the egg.

When Brad and Ted carried the next body over to the sled,

Robby was talking about the antibodies.

"We call them the 'Elementals' because we've seen solid, liquid, air, and fire. The solid was Brad's rock monster. I saw the liquid down in New Hampshire and destructive wind. A guy up from Virginia described the fire creatures, and the aether is the thing that snatched up everyone on Thanksgiving Day," Robby said.

Nate grunted something Brad couldn't hear.

Robby replied, "No, I don't. But it could be something passed down through oral history from a much earlier time."

After their last Denny's dinner, Robby had shared some of his research with the small group. He'd found copies of scientific articles which theorized that a mass extinction had nearly killed off the human race seventy-thousand years earlier. Based on genetic evidence, the worldwide human population had been reduced to just a couple-thousand individuals. Most scientists blamed the earlier crisis on a supervolcano, but Robby showed the group eerie similarities between that event and their current situation.

"Why are we bothering with this guy?" Ted asked as he and Brad walked back over to the truck.

"What do you mean?"

"It's clear to me that Nate is up to no good. Why are we bending over backwards to explain what we're doing?"

"It's not terribly strange," Brad said. "I mean, he's getting the same information we all got when we signed on, you know? It seems reasonable."

"But we were already part of the group," Ted said. "We made a conscious effort to seek out other survivors and then form into a network. That's how we all came together. If this guy was living this close, he must have known there were other people in the area. How many months did he know about us and yet he never tried to make contact?"

The men were now standing back at the truck. Lisa and Sheila dropped another body over at the edge of the moving van and listened to the conversation. Back at the sled, Robby, Pete, and Nate were strapping down a row of bodies.

Lisa offered an observation. "Some of us tried to make contact several times before we found a welcoming party."

"You're talking about when you met Lyle? I think Lyle had problems before all this started. It was just bad luck you ran into him first," Ted said.

"Yes, that's my point," Lisa said. "Maybe he did try to join up, but he ran into somebody like Lyle first."

"That's no excuse," Ted said. "He should have tried again."

"And here he is," Lisa said. "He's here, and he appears to have reached out to join up with us. Seems like the only difference between him and us is timing."

The four stood and watched Robby explaining something to the newest member of their loose group.

"Let's keep moving," Brad said. "It feels like it's getting colder out here." He tugged on the shoulders of an old corpse and waited for Ted to grab the man's ankles. Brad tried to keep his own shoulders back as they lugged the body over to the sled, but his upper back always wanted to hunch forward. A dull ache settled into the space between his shoulder blades.

"Why didn't you guys pull up closer to the sled?" Brad asked. "We could have just slid them right from the truck."

"We did with the first one. It got stuck and we didn't want to waste a bunch of time to move it out of the way. The shoulder drops off too fast on the other side of the road," Ted said.

"But we could have just unloaded to one of the other sleds," Brad said.

"I just work here," Ted said, smiling. "Those guys make all the decisions."

The men reached the sled and started their gentle, swinging, three-count automatically. On three they slid the corpse onto the deck of the big trailer.

"We almost done with this truck?" asked Pete.

"I think just a few more," Ted said.

"Can one of you guys get the next one backed up right here?"

"You read my mind," Brad said. "I was hoping we wouldn't have to haul them by hand this time."

"Great," Pete said. "Back right up here, please."

Brad nodded and headed back down the road. He circled around the left side of his moving van to look for Romie's footprints. He hadn't seen her leave the vehicle, but the passenger door was pointed away from the group, so she could have snuck off. The snow on her side was undisturbed. Brad continued around the moving van, leaving his own set of prints. He checked out the back to see how much room he had to turn the big truck around, and then came back to the driver's door.

He climbed in expecting to find Romie in the cab. She was crouched down in the cargo area behind the front seats.

"You okay?" Brad asked.

"Are you?" Romie asked. "That crazy guy hasn't attacked you all and eaten your privates?"

Brad closed his door and started the moving van. He strapped himself in with his seat belt and reacquainted himself with the mirrors.

"We don't know he was the one who desecrated the body in the Chinese restaurant," Brad said. "Maybe it was an animal or something."

"Animals don't know shit about zippers," Romie said. She'd used this same line earlier as they'd driven north to rejoin their compatriots.

"Well Robby's giving him a tryout," Brad said. "He might be perfectly normal."

Brad pulled the gear shift down into reverse and eased off the brake as the van's alarm beeped rhythmically.

"Sure, he might be," Romie said. "He might also follow us until we fall asleep and then murder us all. Did you ask him how he happened to follow us here? We went south for five miles and then looped back around. Then we spent an hour at the nursing home. How did he find us again?"

"He probably just watched the bridge," Brad said. "He probably saw us go south this morning and was ready to follow us back north over the bridge."

Brad shifted into drive so he could straighten out the moving van before making his approach in reverse. He centered the sled in his two rearview mirrors and shifted back to reverse.

"The hell is that?" asked Romie.

"What?"

"That," Romie said. She pointed slightly to her left, through the windshield. Brad shifted to park. On the side of the highway, facing directly towards them, an abandoned car rested half on the pavement and half in the ditch next to the shoulder.

Brad followed Romie's pointing arm and stared at the car. It seemed like an ordinary car—a dark-brown Chevy sedan with its driver's door propped open. Brad hadn't witnessed any people disappear, but he pictured it from the descriptions of those who had. He imagined the driver pulling over with eyes glazed over and mouth slightly ajar. The driver probably stepped all the way out of the car before being sucked up into nothingness. He turned to Romie, wondering why she was suddenly interested in this car.

"Look. There," she said, jabbing her finger at the car.

When Brad looked back he finally understood. Peeking around the rear corner of the car he saw a small head. Two intent eyes locked onto his for a moment before the head disappeared again behind the bumper.

"Is it a kid?" Brad asked.

"I think it is. A little girl," Romie said. "Come on." She slipped past the passenger's seat and slid out through the door.

Brad shut off the truck and followed her through the snow.

Romie walked towards the car and held out her hand like she was approaching a stray dog. "Hello? Are you back there?"

Brad hurried to catch up with her. He pulled alongside as Romie rounded the back of the car.

"Hey there," Romie said as she dropped to a crouch with one hand on the trunk of the car. "What's your name?" The child retreated when Brad moved into sight. The kid shuffled backwards until the far side of the car and then sprinted around the corner.

"She's headed for the others," Romie said. "Hey! There's a kid coming your way." She shouted in the direction of the sled. Brad ran after the child, sprinting through the slippery snow around the van. Nate jumped down from the deck of the sled as the child ran up. The kid threw arms around Nate's leg.

Nate bent and hefted the child to his chest. He whispered in the kid's ear and clutched tight.

"So you know her?" Romie asked, arriving at a jog.

The others arrived and formed a semicircle around Nate and the child.

"Him," Nate said. "His name is Brynn." Brynn's face remained buried in the space between Nate's neck and shoulder. Brad understood why Romie had thought Brynn a girl. The child wore pink sneakers, red leg-warmers, and a purple jacket with a fur-lined hood. Long, curly hair poked out from the edges of Brynn's hood.

"Come on, boy," Nate said. "Introduce yourself to the people."

Brynn shook his head without removing his eyes from Nate's shoulder.

"He's shy," Nate said.

"Why didn't you mention him earlier?" Ted asked.

"You didn't ask, and I hadn't gotten around to it," Nate said. Brynn was too big for Nate to hold for long. "I'm going to put you down now," Nate said to Brynn. "You'll be okay."

He set the boy down on the edge of the sled. Brad thought the child somehow shrank in Nate's arms. He seemed so helpless, sitting on the edge of the sled next to the stacked bodies. Brad was terrible with guessing ages, but figured Brynn was about ten. Brynn folded his hands into his lap.

"He was supposed to stay back in our truck until I came to get him later. Weren't you?" Nate asked Brynn. The boy didn't acknowledge the question, he simply stared back at Nate.

"Does he speak?" Ted asked.

"Ask him yourself," Nate said.

"Brynn? Is that your name?" Romie asked. The boy glanced at her and then back to Nate.

"You stay out of the way, boy," Nate said. "We've got to move some more of these people. We won't take too long, I promise."

Brynn did as he was told. He moved off to the side of the road, cleared away the snow from a section of pavement and spent his time lighting books of matches. While they moved the bodies, the group held a whispered debate about Nate and Brynn. Romie and Lisa shared the opinion that Nate and Brynn should be welcomed into the group and invited back to the apartment building they all shared. Ted maintained his distrust of Nate.

"Are you and Brynn coming back with us tonight?" Robby asked Nate. "There's plenty of room at the building where we're staying." Ted approached and stood at Robby's side, ready to revoke Robby's invitation as soon as he got a chance to speak.

Nate beat him to it—"Thanks, but no. We've got a place to get back to. Stuff to take care of. We'll be back in the morning if you're going to fill the rest of these sleds."

"Yes," Robby said. "We'll meet you here two hours after sunrise, if that's okay?"

"See you then," Nate said. "Nice to meet you all."

Lisa waved, but nobody said goodbye. Nate whistled to Brynn and the two trudged off through the snow walking south on the highway until the overpass, and then over the embankment and down the hill.

✪ ✪ ✪ ✪ ✪

The group compared notes after their first day of collecting corpses. Their second day proved much more productive. Ted and Lisa rounded up nearly a hundred on their own and the unloading was so smooth that all the teams managed to fit in a second gathering trip. By the fourth day, they'd exceeded Robby's quota of one thousand bodies.

Nate showed up each morning and helped them unload and stack. He never went with the collection teams. While they were out, Nate disappeared with Brynn only to show up just as a team returned with a full moving van. Ted remained wary, but the rest of the group warmed to Nate and Brynn. The boy rarely engaged with anyone except Nate. He stayed away from the others, usually focused on burning something with his endless supply of matchbooks.

Pete strapped tanks of diesel fuel to the tractors and to the sleds they would pull. It wasn't as volatile as gasoline, especially in the cold, but Pete still got nervous whenever Brynn and his matches strayed too close to one of the tanks. He approached Nate several times who would then scold Brynn until he moved farther away with his pyromania.

On the fourth day, as they strapped the last of the corpses to the final sled, Nate finally accepted the invitation to dinner. He and Brynn followed the group's convoy over to the apartment building they shared.

The only fresh thing they cooked was the bread, which Lisa set to rise as soon as they returned. Everything else came from cans, but they prepared a good variety of fruits, vegetables, and two kinds of canned ham. Ted opened a bottle of wine while Robby showed Brynn the assortment of soda he'd collected. With the generators running, they had lights and music. Pete hooked up a propane tank for the oven and a camp refrigerator.

Sheila prepared a selection of cheese and crackers while they waited for the bread to bake. The group took up positions in the living room of the largest apartment. Through the big French doors to the balcony they could just see the spot on the highway where they'd loaded the sleds. Nate perched on the big couch by the coffee table. He sat on the edge of his seat, ready to jump up if need be, or perhaps just to spare the couch from his dirty clothes. Sheila gently suggested that Nate could change into Pete's extra clothes—they were about the same build— but Nate declined. Next to Nate, Brynn folded himself deep into a corner of the puffy couch. His arms were crossed tight. Brynn's hands looked empty without matches. Nate had relieved him of all his packs of matches before he allowed him inside.

A silence formed when Robby shut off the TV over the bar. He'd started a DVD of a kid's movie, but Brynn wasn't interested in watching. Sheila set her tray of cheese on the table and Nate broke the silence.

"So you're leaving in the morning?" Nate asked.

"Yup," Pete said. He turned in his chair to glance over at the highway where the tractors were parked.

"I guess you're not going to need this setup anymore then?" Nate asked.

"I suppose not," Pete said.

"Wait a second," Romie said. "We'll be back. We're not leaving forever, are we?"

"If we do make it through this thing—this morbid corpse delivery job—why would we want to come back *here*?" asked Pete. "All the places we could go? We could move to Cape Elizabeth and have the best ocean-side property available."

"There's eye-poppers down there," Lisa said.

"Not so many as there used to be," Pete said. "And it wouldn't take much effort to clear them out. Haven't we learned that?"

"I like this place," Romie said. "It's south of the snow and north of Robby's Elementals."

"Why did you say you called them that?" asked Nate.

"What?" asked Romie. "Elementals? I thought Robby explained."

"I only gave him a rough outline," Robby said. "I didn't really give him much background."

Robby jumped down from his barstool, grabbed his bottle of pop, and moved to the small couch, next to Brad.

"Did you see anyone disappear, Nate?" Robby asked.

"No, but Brynn did."

Brynn nodded his head.

"Have you been south? Did you see any of the moving water or the columns of fire?" Robby asked.

"No," Nate said. "Oh, the bread smells good." He closed his eyes and seemed to relax a little, but his back didn't get any closer to the couch.

The aroma of the fresh bread reached Brad. Lisa had made her sourdough, and Brad's mouth was already watering for it. He stuffed a cracker and a big hunk of cheese in his mouth.

Robby ignored the bread comment and continued his explanation. "I'll go back to the beginning. In ancient Greece, they believed everything was made up of combinations of five elements: Earth, water, fire, air, and aether."

"I've heard of that," Nate said. His hand slipped forward and snatched a cracker from underneath a piece of cheese. He handed it to Brynn before reaching for one of his own.

"They also believed that spirits inhabited those elements. Those were called the Elementals. We've seen or experienced things which seem to fit this pattern. I saw sentient tornados and water. A guy named Luke from Virginia saw columns of fire patrolling the roads," Robby said.

"I saw a rock monster," Brad said.

"And several of us saw people snatched away to nothing," Lisa said.

"Aether," Nate said.

"For lack of a better explanation," Robby said. "That's how we've characterized the disappearance."

"And which Elemental made everyone's eyes pop out?" asked Nate.

After a short silence, Robby said, "It's just a framework we've hung theories on."

"And Elementals hate corpses?" asked Nate.

"I think of the Elementals like an immune system. They were let loose to clean up the area so something could gestate on or in the planet. We're going to take the corpses up to the embryo and infect it with biologic material it's not ready for yet."

"Why do you think a thousand will be enough?" Nate asked.

"Based on the area it cleared, and my estimate of the survivors, I think it needs about eight-thousand square miles with less than ten tons of animal material. We're going to drop over five times that amount right into its lap," Robby said.

"It just occurred to me—it cleared out live animals, and we're going to hit it with dead ones," Brad said. "What if corpses have no effect?"

"The clearing it did was on a budget," Robby said. "For a certain radius it took out everything, then left a ring of the burst-eye corpses, and then cleared out everything again. If it could deal with dead bodies, it wouldn't have cleared everything out before the snow came down."

"Sounds like a big butt-load of conjecture," Nate said.

Brynn snickered and then clamped his mouth shut and twisted his face down into the arm of the couch.

"A lot of Robby's documentation and evidence was lost in the fire," Ted said.

Nate didn't respond other than to shake his head and frown.

"Where are you from, Nate?" Lisa asked.

"Originally? Texas," Nate said. "I've been living up this way for a long time though. I like it up here, at least I did until, you know. I've thought about heading back south one of these days."

Brynn shot him a glance and then snuck a hand forward to grab another cracker. He took one with cheese on it. Lisa leaned forward and pushed the platter to closer to Brynn, but the boy took his one cracker and sat back again. He held his cracker in both hands and began to nibble around the edge without disturbing the cheese on top.

"Did anyone tell you about Luke's group?" Lisa asked. "They headed down towards New York a couple of weeks ago."

"Yeah," Nate said. "Robby and Pete told me about him. I might try to follow their tracks south once I'm done with you guys. Might be safer to follow in the tracks of someone, you know?"

"Robby, have you heard anything else from Judy?" Lisa asked.

"No. She checked in by radio the first night, but she hasn't checked in again. They're either out of range, or the radio's broken, or maybe... I don't know," Robby said.

An uncomfortable silence grew in the room.

"Nate, are you going to help us drive the tractors up north?" Brad asked.

"Why not?" asked Nate. "Trucking up into the land of forty-foot snow drifts? Sounds like my kind of fun. Beats sticking around here. Besides, I've never been afraid of a little snow."

"I don't mind saying—I'm a little scared," Brad said. "I don't know if it's one of the Elementals, but there's something up there. I was moving fast on a snowmobile. I worry about what might catch up with us when we're dragging those sleds."

"What about you, Robby?" asked Nate. "You worried?"

"No," Robby said. "I'm only worried about what will happen if we don't stop that thing from maturing."

Lisa jumped up and strode to the kitchen. Seconds later, her voice called out from the archway. "Bread's ready. It will cool off while everyone fixes a plate."

Brynn was the first up. He launched from the couch, planted a foot in the middle of the coffee table, and bounced over the opposing couch on his way to the kitchen. Nate smiled and stood with the rest of the group. The men and women filed through the arch to the smell of fresh bread.

✪ ✪ ✪ ✪ ✪

Nate and Brynn left soon after dinner. The boy ate a huge amount of food in a short time. He looked half-asleep as Nate guided him towards the door. They declined offers to stay in an adjacent apartment and said they'd return shortly after sunrise.

After they'd left, the seven men and women reconvened in the big living room to talk about the departure. Brad was the last to join the group—he had volunteered to wash the dishes after dinner.

Pete was mid-sentence. "...with me. Put Brynn in someone else's tractor. There's no reason not to keep an eye on him."

"I'm not comfortable driving one of those rigs anyway," Robby said. "Why don't we ask Nate to drive one and I'll ride along?"

"You've seen the inside of one of those snow tractors. It's not even as hard as driving a car," Pete said, "and you're plenty good at driving. You'll be fine."

"I had no problem with it," Sheila said. "Besides, we'll be going so slow that if you get into trouble, you just back off the throttle and wait for Pete to come help you."

"Exactly," Pete said. "Nate will ride with me, and Brynn can ride with one of the women. He seems to like girls better anyway."

"I still say we should leave tonight," Ted said. "Makes me antsy, just waiting around until morning. Those tractors have lights on them. Why can't we get underway?"

"I'd like one more night in a bed, if you don't mind," Romie said. "I'm not anxious to try to stay awake after eating my weight in canned food."

"We should at least have a guard out there with the vehicles," Ted said. "I'm going out there. If you hear two shots in a row, I need help." Ted pushed up from his chair and headed to his room. He returned with a backpack, sleeping bag, and thick jacket.

"See you all in the morning," he said.

"I'll be out to check in with you in a couple of hours," Brad said. "Don't shoot me."

"Stay well-lit with a flashlight, and I won't." Ted said, smiling.

"We'll be there at sunrise," Robby said.

"Night, all," Ted said, closing the door behind himself.

Pete moved to the sliding-glass doors and looked down in the direction of the highway.

"Can we go over the list one more time?" asked Lisa.

Romie practically bellowed. "That's it for me. I'm hitting the sack. A decent bed for the last time in a long time, I'm sure." She kept talking as she moved towards the door. "If your shower hadn't burned down with the rest of the place, I'm not even sure I'd be going with you on this little errand. I miss showers." She closed the door behind her, but the others could still hear her complaining as she made her way to the apartment down the hall that she shared with Lisa.

"I wish we had enough people to drive in shifts so we didn't have to stop," Sheila said. She'd been sitting on a stool at the bar, but when Romie left she'd moved to her spot on the small couch. The four seated people—Sheila, Lisa, Robby, and Brad—leaned in closer to each other now that their number was diminished. Pete stayed at the glass door, still looking for Ted.

"Luke's probably got the rest of them all killed by now," Pete said.

Robby's head dropped. The young man looked down at the floor.

"I'm sorry, Robby. I didn't mean it. I'm sure Judith is fine," Pete said.

"Call her Judy," Robby said. "Her brothers used to call her Judith when they'd tease her."

Pete nodded. He turned back to the view and then reached for binoculars from the end table.

"Hey," Pete said, "kill the light, will ya?"

Brad dimmed the lantern until the mantle glowed cherry-red.

"Yup," Pete said, peering through the binoculars out into the night. "That's him. He's headed for the tractor in the middle."

Sheila swirled her mug. Just a trace of coffee clung to the

bottom. "I'm never getting to sleep tonight unless I have something a little harder." She stood and made her way to the kitchen.

"Maybe you should lay off the coffee?" Lisa called out.

"It's decaf," Sheila said. Her voice carried easily from the kitchen. She came back with a fresh cup of coffee, topped off with enough creamer it glowed in the dim light. In her other hand she carried a bottle of Irish cream.

Brad squinted to see the bottle she set down on the table. "Is it still good?" he asked.

"Says two years after opening," Sheila said. "Tastes good and smells good, too," she added, holding the bottle under her nose.

"Let me get two fingers of that," Brad said, holding out his glass. His first sip was barely a drop, but he liked the taste. He drained his glass in two good mouthfuls. Heat bloomed in his belly.

"What do you think, Robby? You want to get drunk for the first time?" asked Sheila.

"I'm off to bed," Robby said. "I'll make a hot breakfast in the morning."

"Don't go to bed. I didn't mean anything by it. I swear," Sheila said.

Lisa put her hand on Sheila's shoulder.

"It's okay," Robby said. "Night."

Robby disappeared down the hallway to his room.

Pete wrapped the cord around the binoculars and took a seat next to Brad. With a sigh he stretched to reach a coffee mug from an end table. Pete wiped out the mug with a bandana before pouring himself a generous helping of whiskey.

"Ted get settled?" Lisa asked Pete.

Pete shrugged as he took a gulp of whiskey. "He's in the middle tractor. I don't know how settled he is."

"Isn't he the one who said we should always stay together?" Brad asked.

"Yup," Pete said.

Brad poured himself another half-inch of the Irish cream.

"He misses his wife," Sheila said. "Marie."

"Does he think he's going to find her out there?" asked Pete.

"Don't be cruel, Pete," Sheila said. "He's heartbroken."

"Aren't we all?" Brad asked.

"I haven't had time to be heartbroken," Lisa said. "I don't know about the rest of you, but just surviving takes up most of my time. And hauling corpses for Robby, of course."

Pete muttered a single "huh" into his cup as he took another sip of whiskey.

"I wonder what the others are doing right now," Lisa said. "You know, the people who went with Luke."

"What was the name of Robby's friend? Judy?" asked Sheila.

"Yes," Brad said. "Judy."

"They were so close," Lisa said. "You could almost see Robby's place from where me and Romie were living, and Robby and Judy went everywhere together. They were really close. I can't believe he wasn't more broken up when she decided to go with Luke instead of coming with us."

"He's just a boy," Sheila said. "Kids that age don't get upset about anything except zits and video games."

"You know him better than that," Lisa said.

"I know the face he chooses when he's around us," Sheila said. "But I don't pretend to know who he really is. You can't really know someone if they haven't even figured out who they are yet."

"You sound like my former brother-in-law," Pete said. "He was always saying inscrutable shit."

"All I meant was that Robby hasn't lived long enough to know how he really feels about anything. Don't you remember how morally ambiguous the world was when you were a teenager?" asked Sheila. "Robby's a little too young to get broken up about Judy leaving."

Brad shifted in his seat and rolled his mug between his hands. "I think he was really upset; *is* really upset. He's just good at hiding it."

"Does that mean we shouldn't trust him?" asked Lisa.

"I never said that," Sheila said. "I still think his reasoning is sound."

"I do too, or I wouldn't be here," Pete said.

Brad sipped his whiskey and thought about Pete's statement. He didn't share the man's sentiment. He'd told Romie that Robby's theories could only be proven through testing. Trust in the reasoning didn't enter the equation. So why was he risking his life? Brad chose to stick with the group because they seemed like good people, and he'd rather be with them than be alone. The world had become a dangerous place with little hope of survival. Why *not* risk his life? Wasn't every potential move in this new world a risk?

"I used to have a girlfriend from college who lived in this building," Sheila said.

Pete raised his eyebrows and cocked his head.

"Not that kind of girlfriend, you pervo," Sheila said. "Kendra lived down on three. Sometimes I'd come over from Westbrook and spend the night on her divan. We'd walk down to the Old Port on a Friday night."

"Party girls," Pete said.

"This part of town was so wholesome back then," Sheila said. "Even the homeless guys were pretty decent. Kendra tripped on a curb on Chapel Street one time. She busted her knee up really bad. One street person ran and got a cop to call an ambulance. I mean he didn't really *run*, he kinda shambled up the street, but still. What a nice town. In Westbrook they would have stabbed us, robbed us, and left us for dead."

"I used to hang out in Westbrook," Pete said. "The drunk girls were the ones you had to watch out for the most. They'd kick your ass."

"Yeah, but we didn't want to have to," Sheila said, laughing. Before long Brad and Lisa joined in the laughter. Pete mimed being scared of Sheila and that kicked off another round of braying.

Lisa snorted one last laugh and then set her mug down on the table. "I can't stay up drinking all night if we're leaving in the morning. Good night."

Pete stood with her and showed her to the door. He waved a silent goodbye to Brad and Sheila before heading off towards his bedroom.

"I'd better go check in on Ted before I hit the sack," Brad said.

"I don't want him to think he's on his own tonight."

"Everyone needs to be on their own sometimes," Sheila said. "In fact, I plan to be all alone with Mr. Bailey for a few minutes before I retire." She tipped her mug and nodded at the contents.

"I'll see you in the morning then," Brad said. He took a candle from the bookshelf and found his way to the coat closet. Hoping to hold on to the warmth in his belly, he wrapped himself in a thick coat, scarf, hat, and gloves—more than he'd need against the night air.

"Take care," Sheila said eventually. She'd become preoccupied with the view out the windows.

Brad stretched the band of his headlamp over his hood and tested the light before leaving the apartment. He turned the knob to be sure it was unlocked before pulling the door shut.

In his room, with his blankets pulled up to his ears, Robby stared at his bedroom door. Just enough light from the cloudy night filtered through his curtains to allow him to see. He had slid the dresser, filled with the clothes of a husky teenaged boy, against the door before he crawled into bed. Robby did this every night. Logic guided most of Robby's actions, but not this one—not any of the desperate things he did to feel safe enough to fall asleep.

He counted to forty-three before he stole a glance over his shoulder at the window. No eyes were looking back at him through the window. Nothing he could see was trying to get in.

Robby clutched the visor mirror to his chest. It was the mirror from the Volvo he'd adopted down in New Hampshire. It was the mirror where he'd seen his father's eyes looking back instead of his own on that night outside the rest stop. When sleep wouldn't come he knew he could always look in the mirror and see his father's eyes.

He counted to thirty-eight before he pushed down the covers to make sure the closet door was still shut. Robby returned his eyes to the dresser and reset his count back to one. If he could count past forty-three before feeling compelled to look at the window, then perhaps he could eventually get some sleep.

*Four. Five. Six. Seven. There's nothing in the window. My window is at least forty feet above the street.*

More than two-dozen times he'd told his story—recounted to another survivor how he'd ended up living in Portland after the big storm—but he'd never mentioned what happened the first night at the rest stop in the stolen Volvo.

*Eight. Nine. Ten. Eleven.*

He didn't even allow himself to think of that night except when it crept back in around the edges of normal thoughts as he tried to fall asleep.

*Twelve. Thirteen.*

It was the curse of his treasured mirror. He held onto it because reflected in the small vanity mirror, his own eyes looked just like his dad's. But the mirror also reminded him of that night; of what happened when he'd drifted off to sleep while watching his dad's eyelids slowly droop closed.

*Fourteen.*

If he could hold off until forty-four, then he was making progress against his compulsion to check the window.

When he held the mirror, Robby heard his dad's voice in his head. *"You're being silly, Robby. You know that, right?"*

*Fifteen. Sixteen.*

All he wanted was to go to sleep and give himself over to dreams he could easily forget in the morning.

"Yes, Dad," Robby thought.

*Seventeen. Eighteen. Nineteen.*

Robby fell asleep.

The hallway was cold. It almost felt colder than outside. Brad walked right past the stairwell next to the elevators. Those stairs didn't have any windows. Going down those stairs at night felt like descending into a deep cave below sea level. At the bottom level he would pause, afraid to open the doors, afraid seawater would rush in and drown him.

Instead, Brad took the walkway to the parking garage and used those stairs. With open doorways at each landing, and big windows looking out to the cloudy night, he wouldn't need his headlamp to find his way down. Brad brushed a gloved hand lightly down the bannister as he wound down the stairs to street-level. He paused at the second floor landing to look out the window. Across the street, in the direction of the highway, a brief flicker of light caught his attention. It was gone before he could pinpoint the origin.

Before exiting the stairwell, Brad tightened the scarf around his neck—adjusting it to cover the lower half of his face—and braced himself for the wind. The hinge squealed as Brad pushed open the door and stepped out into the night.

Brad walked up the sidewalk and stayed close to the building on his left. Most of businesses had awnings, so the old snow on the sidewalk was intermittent. He crossed in and out, from dry pavement to a thin crust of trampled snow. He and the others had walked the streets dozens of times since moving into the apartment building, so individual footprints were impossible to distinguish except for the odd stray.

Brad stopped when a set of footprints veered from the others and headed off across the street. He stopped and stared. There was something strange about the footprints. The clouds didn't offer enough light for any detail. Brad looked up and down the street before turning on his headlamp. Once he did, he knew why the prints looked strange. First, the prints were too small. The stride matched his own, but the length of each print was tiny. Brad hunched and followed the prints as they dropped over the curb and headed diagonally across the street. On each left print he could see a perfect print of the sole of the shoe. On each right, the print was twisted; smeared by a foot that turned as it lifted.

Brad shut off his light and crouched in the middle of the street while he waited for his eyes to readjust to the dark. He wondered if Brynn had left the prints. Brynn's feet would be small enough, but Brad couldn't remember if Brynn had walked with a limp. He doubted it. Brynn had leapt over the table to get to Lisa's fresh bread. Wouldn't he have noticed if Brynn had limped while making the jump?

Brad shuffled across the street and ducked into a doorway. The footprints continued up the street a few feet away from him and then disappeared under an awning. They didn't reappear on the other side. Either the owner vanished or they entered the building. Given all the vanishings, either explanation seemed reasonable to Brad. The thin layer of snow hadn't melted or really drifted in the past couple of months, but it had blown around enough to soften the edges of other footprints and tire-tracks. These prints were so crisp. They had to be recent.

Brad looked back towards the apartment building. He could fetch Pete and they could investigate the tracks together, or he could just wait for morning and not wake anyone else up. He glanced in the direction of the highway. Brad took his first step back towards the apartment building.

The sound of a child sobbing stopped him. It seemed to come from the building where the footprints ended, but it was so quiet that Brad couldn't be sure. He turned back to look, but kept his feet moving in the direction of his temporary home. Warning klaxons fired off in his brain. His instincts told him to run—run from the weird footprints, and run from what sounded to be a child in distress. Brad stayed calm and moved cautiously, back towards his building.

On the building to Brad's right, a door fired open with a bang and a huge hooded figure emerged.

"Get down," a gruff voice ordered.

Brad raised his hands but kept backing away.

"Motherfucker," said the hulking figure. "I said get down."

Brad couldn't see the weapon in the man's hands, but he heard the click of a shell sliding into the chamber of the pump-action shotgun. Based on the stance of the dark silhouette, Brad assumed he was the target of the gun.

Brad stopped, but didn't have a chance to follow the order to get down. Just as he stopped, feet planted on dry pavement under the awning of a jewelry store, another man tackled Brad from behind. Brad's arms shot out to take the worst of the impact with the sidewalk. His face came to rest just inches from the shotgun man's shoes—black Chuck Taylors with green laces. The stock of the shotgun plowed down into the back of Brad's head, knocking him unconscious.

## CHAPTER 13: UNDERWAY

ROBBY WOKE FACING THE window. It was too early—the sun hadn't come up yet. Until he heard the door knob turning behind him, he couldn't figure out what had roused him. Robby flipped over and threw back the covers in time to see the door pushing inward, stopping only when it hit the dresser.

He lay paralyzed with fear. He had nowhere to run.

"Robby," Pete called from the other side of the door. "Robby, wake up."

"Yup," Robby said. He flew out of bed, shaking off his fear. "Give me a minute. I'll be right there."

Robby's door drifted shut and Robby heard Pete moving down the hall. Pete was talking to someone else out there, but Robby couldn't make out what they were saying.

Robby jumped into his clothes. He had laid out everything he needed the night before, and even in the nearly dark bedroom, he dressed quickly. He shoved the dresser aside enough to open the door and jogged down the hall. He found an assembly in the living room.

Sheila and Lisa sat on the big couch and Ted and Pete stood. Pete stopped talking when Robby walked in the room.

"Tell Robby what happened," Lisa said.

"Brad's missing," Ted said. "I was on my way back over here when I saw tracks on Pearl Street. Two sets that I'm sure weren't there when I went out. One of them could have been Brad's. Both sets disappeared near an insurance building on the north side of the street."

"He left to go check on Ted hours ago," Sheila said.

"He never showed up," Ted said.

"Something has happened to him," Pete said. "Ted showed me the tracks. They end at an awning for an insurance building, like he said. We'll start at that building; see if we can track him down."

Their heads snapped around and Lisa grabbed her chest as the front door swung open. Romie strode in, letting the door swing shut behind her.

"What's going on over here? I thought we weren't getting together until sunrise," Romie said.

"Brad's missing," Pete said. "We've got to find him."

"I told you guys not to trust that Nate guy," Romie said, waggling her finger in Robby's direction. "He shows up and suddenly people start disappearing. You think it's a coincidence?"

"Was there a sign of struggle?" Sheila asked Ted.

"I couldn't see any," Ted said. "But the tracks ended at dry pavement, so who knows."

Pete stepped forward into the center of their loose group and raised his hands before speaking. "We can stay in contact with radios and break up into teams of two. We'll start with the insurance building and work outwards."

Sheila began to stand, but stopped when nobody else moved. The rest of the group didn't respond or move to comply. Pete's eyes jumped from person to person, looking for agreement.

"Wait a sec, Pete," Romie said. "We've still got six people. We need to get to hauling those bodies or at least start redistributing the seventh sled."

"Yes," Robby said. "I'd be more comfortable if we could at least offload half of Brad's sled to the rest. We've got some margin for error, but I'd rather not lose a whole sled."

Pete's voice started at a reasonable volume and rose to a shout. "Are you people kidding me? We're going to move on and LEAVE BRAD BEHIND?"

Robby tightened his jaw, but didn't respond.

Lisa was the first to answer. "Pete, listen. We've all lost a lot of people. All we can do is keep going. If we finish this mission, we have a chance to gain back some stability, but right now we're living in a very unstable world."

"Are you seriously conflating the big extinction with what's likely happened with Brad? Like Romie said, it's probably that Nate guy who got him. We can stop Nate. We don't need a big plan. He's just one guy," Pete argued.

"By the same argument," Lisa said, "we can't afford to let one man stop us from finishing this. We don't have any guarantee that Robby's plan will work, but it's the only plan we've got to take this world back."

Their heads snapped around once more as the door swung open again.

"What are we arguing about?" asked Nate. Brynn stood at his side with one arm around Nate's waist.

"What did you do to Brad, you son of a bitch?" Pete yelled as he lunged for Nate. Ted stepped in his way and restrained the big man.

Nate took a step backwards and pushed Brynn behind himself. "What's your problem?"

"Let me see his shoes," Pete said, still struggling against Ted. He was pointing towards the feet of Nate and Brynn. "I want to see his shoes."

"Calm down, big man," Nate said. "We didn't do anything." He kicked off one of his shoes and flicked it over towards Pete. Pete didn't bend to grab it.

"Not yours," Pete said. "His." He pointed towards Brynn's feet.

Nate bent down as Brynn raised one foot. He plucked the shoe from Brynn's foot and tossed it to Pete. The shoe bounced off Ted's arm and Pete dropped to grab it from the floor. He flipped it over and ran a finger over the tread. He narrowed his eyes and tossed the shoe back towards Brynn. He kicked Nate's shoe back as well.

"Are we exonerated? Can we come in now?" asked Nate. He picked up his shoe and ushered Brynn towards the couch. "Can someone tell us what's going on here?" Nate sat down and untied his shoe so he could fit it back on his foot.

"I'll be right back," Robby said. He walked back to his room while the others brought Nate and Brynn up to speed on the night's events. He squeezed back through the door and opened the bottom drawer of the dresser. Under the sweatpants, he found his thick envelope. He bent the papers, stuffed them in his back pocket, and returned to the living room.

"Did you check his room?" asked Nate. "Did he leave a note or anything?"

"If there is a note, I'm guessing you planted it there," Pete said to Nate.

"When, Pete?" asked Sheila. "I was here on the couch all night. When could Nate have snuck in and left a note in Brad's room? You, Ted, and Robby are the only ones who have been down the hallway."

"I'll go look for a note," Ted said. He gave Pete a stern look and headed down the hall.

"So we'll just go find Brad and ask him what happened," Nate said. He finished tying his shoe and stood up.

"Wait," Robby said.

Nate sat back down.

"We need to head north. We can't be distracted by losing a member of the group," Robby said.

"So we're all just expendable?" asked Pete. "We're not looking out for each other anymore? What's the point of banding together if we can't trust each other when we need help?"

"We've banded together to accomplish something we can't do on our own," Robby said. "We're trying to help *everyone*, not just the people in this room. We have to be willing to make hard decisions and sacrifice."

"So if I disappear tomorrow, you're not going to spend one minute looking for me?" asked Pete.

"You're the only one who can keep those tractors moving, Pete," Romie said. "We'd spend at least *one* minute looking."

Ted came back to the living room empty-handed. "Nothing."

"I'm not going," Pete said. "I was willing to risk my neck, but only because I thought we were watching each other's backs."

"Okay," Robby said. "Nate, can we assume you'll drive one of the rigs?"

278

"Yup," Nate said.

"Great," Robby said. "Is everyone else in?"

Nobody responded. Their eyes shifted around, stopping short of eye-contact. Sheila looked down at the table where the empty bottle of whiskey still sat.

Robby pulled the envelope from his back pocket. "None of us are indispensable. I've rewritten all the notes I lost in the fire and pulled together all my theories. If I'm lost, I expect you all to proceed without me so I recorded everything I expect to lead us north and what to do when we get there. Lisa? Would you keep these notes?"

"Yes," Lisa said.

"So you're in?"

"Yes," Lisa said.

"I'm in," Ted said.

"I'll go too," Romie said.

"Good," Robby said. "We really need at least six drivers or this trip will take forever. Are you coming, Sheila?"

She didn't answer. She shifted her gaze from the table to the window, where the sun was just starting to brighten the sky.

"Brynn can mostly drive," Nate said. Brynn didn't say anything. "We'll have to show you how these things operate, but you can handle it," Nate said to Brynn.

"That's a good fallback position, but if we can I'd like to..." started Robby. He was cut off by Pete.

"Fine, I get it. I'll go," Pete said.

"You're sure," Robby said. He said it more like a statement than a question.

Pete nodded his head.

"Sheila?" Robby asked.

She dragged her eyes from the window over to Robby.

"What? Of course," she said.

"Good," Robby said. "We're back to seven, and with Brynn as a backup. Let's get moving."

Brynn pushed the slider another sixteenth of an inch to the right, raising the temperature in the cab of the tractor yet again. Robby unzipped his coat the rest of the way, trying to stay ahead of the sweat beginning to form under his clothes.

"It's good to talk to another kid," Robby said. He'd been trying for an hour to strike up a conversation with Brynn. "It sucks talking to adults all the time."

When they were loading up the tractors and getting ready to head off, Nate and Brynn approached Robby. Nate made Brynn state the request—Brynn wanted to ride with Robby. This was his chance to finally learn something about Brynn. He figured since Brynn wanted to ride with him, they would talk. This assumption proved to be incorrect. Brynn hadn't said a word to Robby since climbing in the cab.

"You talk like an adult," Brynn said.

Robby was startled by Brynn's sudden statement. He almost forgot to answer.

"Yeah? What makes you say that?" Robby asked.

"Pull over. I gotta pee."

"Sure. Well, wait, I can't really pull over. You remember how much trouble we had with the soft snow near the edges of the road before? I'm afraid if I veer off this course at all we'll get mired again."

The journey started very slowly that morning. Just north of Portland, the snow became incredibly deep—ten to twenty feet in spots—and it got worse as they continued north. Pete, at the head of the convoy, guided the group along the right side of the road. There, the crown of snow on the northbound lanes looked a little less deep. The massive tracked vehicles punched right through the snow, bogging down to a crawl.

Pete radioed back that he would scout a better path. About halfway back in the line, Robby didn't see Pete until he crested the hump of snow which followed the highway north. Pete was nearly swimming in the snow until he reached the top, where the crust had some integrity and supported his weight. After they maneuvered the tractors up to the top of the hump, they moved much more easily.

"Pull over," Brynn repeated.

"Like I said, I can't. I can stop if you want to just go off the side or something. Nobody will watch."

Brynn shook his head.

"You want a cup or something? You can go in the back seat?"

Brynn shook his head.

"What do you want to do?" Robby asked. The boy wasn't offering any suggestions. They rode in silence while Robby considered the problem. The cloud cover was even thicker here, north of the city. It was about noon, but the sky had the same grey, gloomy look it always did. Robby wondered if anyone else needed to go to the bathroom and then he thought about the women of the group. They couldn't just leave the tractor in gear and piss out the window. That's what Nate said he would do when the time came. The women might also want to pull over, but how would they?

Robby picked up his radio handset. "Anyone else need a bathroom break?" he asked.

Lisa's voice came over the radio first, but she was interrupted by Romie. "Sure do."

"Me too," Lisa said.

"Already taken care of," Pete said.

Robby turned to Brynn. "Grab those snowshoes from the back seat and start putting them on." He sensed Brynn would really want some privacy. Brynn slid over the seat and started to rearrange the food and gear to make enough room back there to maneuver.

Robby kept his speed until he saw Nate's sled in front of them start to slow. Before embarking they agreed to maintain a certain distance between tractors at all times. The line of tractors stopped. Brynn threw open the back door, aligned the edges of his snowshoes on the step and then jumped down into the snow. After a quick roll, Brynn was back on his feet and reaching up to close the door behind him. Robby grabbed the other set of shoes and made his way onto the track to put them on. Ahead, he saw Nate rounding the back of the corpse-loaded sled in his boots; gingerly putting each foot down so he wouldn't punch through the crust of packed snow.

Robby cinched the last strap and paddled his snowshoes over to Nate.

"Brynn have to pee?" Nate asked.

"Yeah," Robby said.

"I should have warned you—Brynn needs privacy," Nate said.

"No worries."

Robby slipped out of his snowshoes, climbed up the back of Nate's trailer, and stood on the seat of the snowmobile lashed there. From the head of the convoy, Pete was whisking an even pace towards them. The big man showed his dexterity on snowshoes. Romie, Lisa, and Sheila formed a group to walk towards a small clump of branches—the tops of trees sticking out of a deep mound of snow. Brynn was disappearing over a snow bank at the edge of the road.

"I don't see Ted," Robby said as he dropped down from the back of the trailer. He tried to land light on his feet, but he sunk down to his knees. Nate helped pull him out of snow.

"He radioed that he was going to stay in his cab—you didn't hear?" asked Nate.

"Nope, but I left pretty quick to put on my snowshoes."

"I don't know if those things help or hurt. I've never had much use for them," Nate said. "Pete's the exception. He moves like a goddamn gazelle on those things."

Robby nodded. He collected his own snowshoes from the back of the trailer and debated whether he should put them back on. Instead, he decided to use his break wisely and he moved a few paces away from Nate and turned his back. As he urinated in the snow, he heard Pete and Nate greet each other.

"Hey," Pete said.

"Pete," Nate said.

"Any problems with the rig?"

"Nope."

"How 'bout you, Robby?"

"No problems, Pete," Robby said, walking back to the two men.

"If either of you see any change in engine temp, let me know right away," Pete said.

"You expecting any?" asked Nate.

"Always expect problems and you'll never be surprised by them," Pete said.

"Fair enough," Nate said.

Pete walked over to the other side of the trailer and looked up and down the highway. "Who's with Brynn?" he asked.

"Nobody," Robby said.

"Jesus," Pete said. "I thought we decided we should always stick together when we're not in the tractors?"

"He's right over there, I'm sure," Nate said, pointing in the direction of Brynn's footprints.

"That's what we thought about Brad," Pete said. "Fuck." He shuffled off, following the tracks.

"Wait, Pete!" called Robby. "Brynn needs privacy."

"I'm not going to watch or anything," Pete called back over his shoulder.

Brynn was spared embarrassment. He crested the snow bank before Pete got there. Pete waited for Brynn to catch up and then the two came back to Robby's tractor together.

"There's an overpass just north of here," Nate said. "Do we have a plan? Just go under, like the last one?"

"Nope," Pete said, shaking his head. "Brad told us the snow was right up to the structure. I figure we'll have to find a way around."

"He also said he found a thick crust from Falmouth north," Robby said.

"On a snowmobile, it might have seemed thick," Nate said.

"We're making terrible time," Pete said. "We're not going to make Kingston Depot before sunset."

"I say we hole up in Freeport," Pete said. "Brad said we can get into the L.L. Bean. We'll follow his tracks there if we can and stay the night."

Robby bowed his head and considered his plan for several moments.

"Probably worth checking out," Nate said.

Brynn shed his snowshoes and climbed on top of the snowmobile lashed to the trailer. He turned the handlebars back and forth, grinding the skis on the deck of the trailer. Pete, leaning back against the edge of the trailer, reached back and stilled the skis. Brynn let go and stood up on the seat.

"Women coming back," Brynn said.

"Wave them over here," Pete said, turning his head to address Brynn.

Just as Romie, Lisa, and Sheila rounded the corner of the sled, Robby looked up from his concentration.

"I'm a little wary of following Brad's path," Robby said. "But as long as we're cautious…"

"What are we talking about?" asked Lisa.

"Let's go back and run it by Ted," Pete said. "So we don't have to repeat ourselves."

✪ ✪ ✪ ✪ ✪

Everything took longer than they thought—navigating around overpasses, refueling, crossing the river. Even following Brad's snowmobile tracks was a chore. In some places the wind scoured all tracks and left an icy flat plain. In others it looked like the tracks were only hours old.

They used the GPS to get close, but in the end the sunset reflecting off of jagged glass led them to the spot where Brad had broken into L.L. Bean's retail headquarters. With the line of tractors and trailers parked at a safe distance, Pete poked around in the snow with a ski pole and found a row of shattered windows. He pointed his flashlight inside and found the top-floor offices of the retail store. He waved everyone over and they climbed inside as a group.

Between headlights and handheld flashlights, more than a dozen beams cut through the entombed office.

"Jesus," Lisa said. "Why didn't Brad just turn around and leave?"

"He was cold, and this was the first he'd seen of civilization since leaving his house," Ted said.

"I bet they sell heaters downstairs," Pete said. "Let's go get one going." He motioned to Ted and they headed towards the door next to the elevator.

Lisa turned back to the windows, where Robby was still looking at the snow that had drifted in through the broken panes.

"Why would Brad break so many windows getting in here?" Lisa asked.

"He only broke one getting in. This one," Robby said. He pointed his light towards the floor where it glittered off shards of glass. "These windows were all broken outwards. That's why we found the glass on the snow out there."

Robby led Lisa back to the rest of the group, who followed Pete over to the stairwell door.

Ted picked up a fire extinguisher from the carpet. "He used this to wedge the door open," Ted stated.

"I'll do him one better," Pete said. He produced a screwdriver and hammer from somewhere inside his coat. He popped the hinge pins from the door in seconds and then opened the door halfway before pulling it off and setting it on its side.

"Take it easy, Pete," Romie said. "What did that door ever do to you?"

"Better safe than sorry," Sheila said.

"Always expect problems, and you'll always find them," Nate said.

Pete whipped his head around and shot his light in Nate's face until Nate raised his hand to shield his eyes.

"Let's go," Ted said.

"We could just stay here," Lisa said. "Camp in the corner and then head out in the morning. Why do we have to go deeper into this tomb?"

"Supplies, heat, snacks," Pete said.

"What do you think, Robby?" Lisa asked.

"I don't see a reason not to," Robby said.

Pete turned the beam of his flashlight down the stairs and led the way. As they descended the flights to the bottom, they mostly focused their beams on the snow packed against the windows. One whole side of the staircase was floor-to-ceiling windows, and the snow layers varied in color and consistency. At the bottom landing, Sheila ran her gloved hand down the glass where some of the layers of snow looked brown and black.

"All that snow out there," Sheila said. "If this glass breaks we really are buried."

"There are other ways out of here," Pete said. "But if the glass hasn't broken yet, it's not going to in the next few hours. I'm going to set up camp."

They turned the last corner to the door. The bottom corner of the thick, metal door was peeled back, exposing a hole so big that Robby could fit through it. Ted kneeled down and pointed his light at the hole. Lisa crouched next to him and the two looked through.

"What would bend a door?" asked Lisa.

Pete reached forward and turned the handle. It turned smoothly. He let go and let the door latch again without opening it. He scanned his light around the seams of the door. Aside from the corner bent out of shape, the door looked to be in perfect condition—nothing to indicate it had endured any stress.

Pete reached for the handle again and gripped it before Sheila stopped him.

"We're not going in there," she stated.

"Why not?" asked Pete.

"There's something in there that can tear open doors, that's why," Sheila said.

"No, that's not necessarily true," Pete said. "Whatever was in there, looks like it left. If anything, it might be dangerous to be anywhere *except* in there."

"You can't believe that," Sheila said. "Where would it have gone? Is there anywhere for it to go? No, it must have come into this stairwell and then returned back through this hole. It's just not safe."

"It really could be anywhere," Nate said. "The whole world is currently full of scary shit, you can't exactly live your life trying to stay away from it."

Brynn moved over next to Ted and touched the twisted metal. Just below the handle, a thick crease marked the start of the bend. Below that, the door looked almost like crumpled paper or a dog-eared page that someone tried to smooth flat. Even where it was bent, it hadn't been compressed at all.

"Careful, Brynn," Lisa said.

Ted continued to shine his light through the gap into the retail store.

"I'm going in," Pete said.

"Right behind you," Nate said.

"Stop trying to help me," Pete said.

Nate threw his hands up in an exaggerated shrug and backed away from Pete.

"What do you think, Robby? This trip was your idea," Sheila said.

The stairwell seemed to shrink as everyone's headlamps and flashlights turned to Robby. He stood in the center of the group, looking down towards the bent door. He swiveled his head and looked back up the stairs.

"I think we should look for a place to settle in for the night. We're no safer out in the tractors. We can at least take shifts here and watch over each other," Robby said.

"Watch for what?" asked Sheila. "And if people start being snatched into nothingness, or if our eyes explode down our face, what then? None of you have been assaulted by one of those things. I almost lost my leg."

Romie came from the back of the group. She pushed past the others, stepped around Ted who still crouched next to the door, and grabbed the handle of the mangled door. "They're right, Sheila. Bad stuff could happen anywhere. Let's find a place to get reasonably comfortable for the night."

Romie opened the door and held it open. Ted and Lisa moved through first, followed by Pete and Nate.

Brynn held out a hand to Sheila. The two moved through the doorway together with Robby close behind. Romie brought up the rear and let the door swing shut behind her. She tested the handle and pushed it open an inch to verify that the door wasn't locked.

"Where to?" asked Romie.

"The camping section is over this way," Pete said, pointing his light to the right. "We can find some air mattresses and sleeping bags over there. Jackets, and snacks, and everything else are back that way."

"Let's stick together," Sheila said.

"Okay," Pete said. "Then let's do a quick sweep through the whole place and then come back to camping?"

"Good," Romie said. "Everyone stay in sight of the group."

They moved through the hunting section of the store. It was decorated to look like a log cabin lodge. The group passed a big stairway flanked by railings made of rough-hewn timbers, varnished to a high shine. Ted pulled off his outer jacket and replaced it with a warm game-jacket, replete with hidden zippered pockets. Nate pulled a crossbow down from a display and loaded it as they walked. Brynn ran a light hand over every garment they passed, but didn't grab anything. Their lights swept beams around the big space as they moved towards a smaller hallway which led to the rest of the store. Here, a rack of canoes lined one wall next to a display of fake trees.

"Wait," Ted said. His lights focused on one of the tree branches. "I thought they had a bunch of stuffed animals on display around here."

"They used to," Nate said.

"So where are they?" Ted asked.

From up ahead, Pete called back. "Watch your step up here. There's ice."

The group shuffled forward. Ted reluctantly swung his lights away from the tree branch and followed the others. Pete stood vigil at the beginning of the icy stretch of hallway. Lisa moved cautiously out onto the ice. It stood about an inch thick at the edge and got a little thicker as she moved farther down the hall. The ice was so pure—with no air bubbles or cracks—it was nearly invisible against the tile floor. Nate pulled glow sticks from a pocket and snapped them as he walked, dropping them every few paces. They lit up his feet and legs with an eerie, green light.

"It's from the fish tank," Nate called back. Most of the group shuffled one foot at a time across the ice, but Pete walked with confidence. About halfway down the hall, they saw what Nate discovered. The giant aquarium built into the wall had shattered, spilling its contents to the floor.

Shards of two-inch thick acrylic, like transparent shark's teeth, jutted from the bottom edge of the aquarium. The surface was shattered the whole length of the tank. Pieces were lost beneath the ice under their feet, but the group could see the glittering edges of acrylic triangles lit up by Nate's glow sticks.

"Look at this," Nate said. He straddled something frozen in the ice, pointing his light straight down.

Robby and Pete reached him first. Nate had found a fish—a long trout with a gaping mouth—lying on the floor under a layer of ice. The head and tail were intact, but the side of the fish was stripped away, revealing bones and gore.

"How did this happen?" asked Pete.

"C'mon, Pete. You know what it looks like, don't you?" asked Nate.

"Yes, I know what it *looks* like, it looks like a bear got at it," Pete said.

"Gross," Lisa said, joining them at the fish.

"But I don't think there are a lot of bear around here," Pete continued. "It must have been cannibalized, or injured itself on the glass?"

"Are there any more?" asked Nate.

"Yeah," Robby said. He wandered a short distance from the trio. "Some heads and other pieces scattered around."

"Come on, Brynn. Let's keep moving," Sheila said. She led the child away from the broken tank. Brynn climbed under a ledge to poke his head up through a glass-encased bubble under the tank.

Everyone else took the prompt and reassembled to continue their shuffle across the ice.

"What could have broken the glass?" Lisa wondered.

"It's not glass, it's a transparent acrylic thermoplastic," Romie said, "and it's very strong."

"So what could have done it?" asked Lisa.

"Nothing I know of would make it shatter," Romie said.

"Doesn't it get brittle in the cold?" asked Pete.

"Nope," Romie said. "It gets soft when heated, but cold doesn't affect it at all."

"Another mystery to add to the pile of mysteries," Nate said.

Ted surprised them all when he spoke again. "No ice over here."

He'd moved onto the carpet in the shoe section. The lip at the edge of the carpeted area was enough to dam the water. The rest of the group moved towards Ted's position.

"Let's sweep the rest of this floor, move to the lower level, and then we can take the front..." Pete began.

"Shhh!" said Ted, raising a hand. The group fell silent, not even daring to breathe. Ted pointed his flashlight over towards the registers. He cocked his head and swept his light in tiny arcs, surveying all the dark corners his beam could reach.

After they'd held silent for almost a minute, Pete spoke. "What did you see?"

"I heard something moving," Ted said.

"That's it," Sheila said. "Back across the fish. Let's get out of here."

Pete frowned.

"Come on, let's see what it is," Nate said. He moved in the direction of Ted's beam.

## CHAPTER 14: CAPTIVE

BRAD WOKE IN THE dark with his head pressed against a cold floor. A thin band of light coming under a door was the only thing he could see. His hands and feet were trussed behind his back, stretching his body into an uncomfortable backbend and tugging at his shoulders. He wriggled on the tiles, trying to free up a little slack on the ropes.

He heard footsteps echo in an open space on the other side of the door and a shadow of moving legs passed through the band of light. Brad held his breath and listened. The steps stopped and he heard a man's voice murmur. It was cut off by another man. The second man spoke louder, but Brad still couldn't make out any of the words.

The door swung open and Brad saw a huge body step into the light streaming through the door. Brad blinked and tried to make out the backlit face.

"Where'd your friends take the little boy?" asked the figure. The voice was deep and scratchy, like the man gargled with steel wool. Brad thought he heard a slight accent, too. Something about the way "little" contracted into "li'l."

Brad began to answer, but it felt like his mouth was glued shut. He ran his tongue around his dry teeth until he could speak. "What friends? What boy?"

The giant man approached and knelt down, and Brad was finally able to see his face. The man was older, or perhaps just well-worn, and he smiled a kind, gentle smile. Clean, silver locks of hair framed his face and cascaded down to his shoulders. He still wore the black Chuck Taylors with bright green laces. The light stubble on his cheeks made him look a little neglected, but not pathetic, exactly. His eyes were complemented by deep wrinkles which seemed to smile.

"Don't fuck with me, asshole," the man said. With only the light coming in through the open door, Brad could barely see, but the man's green eyes seemed to twinkle as he cursed at Brad.

"I don't know what you're..." Brad started. The old man's hand shot out and he backhanded his knuckles against Brad's temple. The hit wasn't hard, but when Brad jerked away he banged his head against the hard floor.

"I don't need a reason to tune you up," said the old man. "This world is beyond reason. It's beyond reason, and retribution, and punishment, and justice. When I say friends, I mean the half-dozen other necrophiliacs you've been partying with. Duzzat ring a little bell for you?"

He punctuated his question with another rap of his knuckles against Brad's skull.

"Who are you?" Brad asked. Brad's eyes locked on the gun holster on the man's right hip.

"My best friends call me Buster," the man said. This time his smile was cold. The lines radiating from his eyes looked flat, and the twinkle disappeared. "We just grabbed you to trade for the little boy. Seemed simple enough, but then your friends lit out at dawn like they didn't even miss you. So now I'm stuck with you and a bunch of tracks in the snow heading north. So where did they take him? He's family, and I don't give up on family."

"Okay," Brad said, "I get what you're asking, but I'm still confused. We didn't have a little boy with us."

"You're beginning to rub me the wrong way, Brad," Buster said.

Brad's eyes darted sideways as he tried to remember if he'd told the man his name.

"That's right," Buster said. "I know who you are, and I know that Peter, Rob, Ted, Sheila, and those other women left you here and took Brynn north. I couldn't give a shit what you and the others do, but when you steal my little boy, I think I deserve an explanation."

"Brynn?" Brad asked. "Who's Brynn?"

Buster rose to his feet and turned to the door. "Hey, Glen? This guy's either really dumb or really stubborn. We're gonna have to work him over to find out. Buster strode to the door and leaned through the frame. He had a quick conversation with someone just around the corner and then returned to Brad.

"We're gonna do you together," Buster said. "Glen's idea, but I think it's a good one."

Brad kicked as Buster grabbed his feet, but as soon as he did, he regretted it. When he kicked his legs, the rope pulled back brutally on his arms, stretching his shoulders until his joints felt like warm plastic about to break.

Buster leaned back and dragged Brad by the feet across the tile floor. He swung Brad through the doorway fast and took a hard right, slamming the side of Brad's head into the jam. When he came to rest again, Brad found himself in a slightly bigger room, stacked with cardboard boxes. From behind, hands grabbed his shoulders and the rope connecting his hands to his feet was cut. The relief didn't last long. The back of a chair slid through the loop his arms made behind his back and Brad was set upright, tied to a wooden chair.

Directly in front of him a woman he'd seen before was tied to a similar chair. Brad had met her only once, at the last Denny's dinner.

"Tib?" Brad asked.

"Christine," the woman said.

"Sorry, I thought I remembered someone calling you Tib," Brad said.

"Luke calls all women Tib," Christine said.

"Shut up, girly." Buster's voice came from just behind Brad's shoulder. "Glen, get out of here for a bit."

Panic broke across Christine's face as footsteps crossed behind Brad towards the door.

"Glen," she said, "don't go. Don't leave me with him. You can't leave me."

Brad heard the door click shut somewhere behind him. He watched Christine's eyes as they tracked the progress of Buster. Finally, Buster came around the chair and into view.

"She's right to be scared," Buster said to Brad with a smile. "She's about to lose a finger."

Christine's chair legs squealed against the tiles as Buster spun Christine around so her back was to Brad. Buster pulled open the flaps of a weathered cardboard box and pulled out a long set of bolt cutters.

"Jesus," Christine screamed, "what the fuck's wrong with you? I didn't do anything!"

"Look," Brad said. "I'll tell you whatever you want to know. What else did you want to know? Where they're going? We're not sure exactly where to go, Robby just said it would be north of Augusta. But you must already know that. Robby told everyone at Denny's."

Christine erupted with a wordless scream as Buster touched the back of her arm with the edge of the bolt cutters. The room was cold, and Christine only wore a white tank top. Brad saw the lines of sinews on Christine's shoulders as she pulled against her restraints. Like Brad, her arms were bound behind the back of the chair. Brad worried that Christine was tugging so hard she would tear cartilage, or dislocate her shoulder.

"I heard about Rob's big plan," Buster said. "Must be a deep, *deep* amount of crazy to convince someone to drag twenty-hundred corpses through the snow. I'm not sure I buy into his explanation one-hundred percent."

"Just get on a snowmobile and you'll catch them. They're not going fast, not pulling those giant sleds. Hell, they wouldn't even hear you coming. If you want to..."

Brad was cut off by another scream from Christine. Buster slipped the bolt cutters around one of her fingers.

"This has to be a mistake of some sort," Brad shouted to be heard over Christine's screams. "We didn't know Brynn was your son. Maybe Nate didn't know either. Brynn doesn't talk much. He's gone through a lot, maybe he couldn't remember who his family was."

Buster turned to Brad. "I said I was his *family*, not his father."

"Right, sorry," Brad said. He was relieved that Buster's attention was away from the finger and the bolt cutters. "Look, I'll come with you. We'll get on a snowmobile and we'll catch them in a few hours, I'm sure. Then we'll figure this all out. You're Brynn's family—everyone will understand that he should be with you."

Buster listened, nodded along, and maintained eye contact with Brad. As soon as Brad finished speaking, Buster compressed the handles of the bolt cutters. Brad heard a squishy pop just before all sound was obliterated by Christine's scream. The sound was heart-wrenching. It contained horror, indignation, loss, and fury. The sound alone hit Brad in the gut and made his teeth ache. It was unbearable and Brad felt his own scream welling up in the back of his throat to join Christine's.

The door burst open and Brad saw Glen for the first time since Denny's. Brad couldn't be sure from his distance, but it looked like Glen had tears welling up in his eyes. Glen waved his arm at Buster with jerking motions and Buster walked over to confer with the man. Christine's scream diminished to a low moan, but Glen led Buster out into the hall so they could talk. The door clicked shut.

Christine moaned.

Brad's wrists burned from the ropes and he realized that the extra strain on the bonds was from his hunched shoulders. He rolled his shoulders back and stretched them out, breathing deep and trying to relax his tensed muscles. Something brushed against the tip of his finger as he stretched, so he repeated the process.

His gaze drifted down to the floor—to the area he'd been trying to avoid looking at. Christine's pinky finger had rolled several inches away when it fell, so it wasn't near the growing puddle of blood dripping from Christine's hand. She tried to clasp her hands together to put pressure on the stump. Just below her bound hands, the blood ran down the rope as it looped beneath the chair to connect with the rope that bound her feet. Someone—Buster or Glen—must have cut her rope and retied it at some point. There was a knot in the rope about a foot below her hands. A similar knot was just above where the rope led from her ankles.

Brad stretched again until he felt the thing brush his hand. It was a similar knot—it had to be. He tucked his feet further under the chair and rounded his upper back into a painfully deep backbend. This was a pain he was accustomed to. He'd spent a year's worth of weekly yoga videos until he could execute a backbend this deep. Stretched to his fullest, he managed to collect the knot between his fingers. He began blindly working on the knot. Sweat stood out on his brow.

Christine stopped moaning.

"They're going to kill you," she said, her voice low.

Brad lost the knot. It swung away from his hands and when he reached for it, it stayed too far away. He needed to relax and let it come back to his hands.

"Glen wants me to be happy, I know he does, but I rejected him once," Christine said. "Neither of them want you, they just want to trade you for Brynn, or at least Buster does. I don't think Glen cares about Brynn either way."

"Shut up," Brad whispered. "I want to hear if they're coming." He tried to focus on the knot. One loop was loosened, but it seemed to only tighten one of the other loops. He tried to picture the knot—how the ropes intertwined—but he couldn't make sense of it. He tugged on the rope and tried to work on the farthest loop.

Footsteps approached outside and he heard a hand settle on the door knob. Arched over he saw the top of the door in the corner of his eye. The knot came loose. Brad pulled and fed the rope through the loop. He sat back down in the chair and slid his feet forward. The rope pulled back on his wrists. The rope was more slack, but the knot still held.

Brad heard the handle turn and the door open. He gathered the slack in the rope and balled it up in his hands.

"You're a lucky woman," Buster said to Christine as he walked past Brad. "I'm not allowed to hurt you anymore to try to get information from him." He turned and looked at Brad before continuing. "I guess I'll have to extract what I need directly from the source."

Buster took a step closer and Brad saw his chance. He thrust his knees back and lowered his head, hoping he could plow into Buster and knock him to the ground. The rope held. Brad only rose up a couple of inches before the rope stalled his momentum and sent him crashing back down into his seat.

Buster laughed. The old man raised a hand to his face and scratched his cheek—considering Brad. Behind the chair, Brad's hands worked at lightning speed, gathering the rope, pulling the knot into his hands, and trying to find the source of the snag. He'd missed a loop, and now having jerked the rope taut, the knot was even tighter. Brad struggled to insert a fingernail in the loop and work it loose again.

"You've already seen the bolt cutters. I think we'll upgrade you to something a little more painful. How's that sound, Mr. Brad?"

"Let me out of here," Christine said. "I have to stop the bleeding. I feel faint."

"You'll be fine for a few minutes," Buster said.

"Glen?" Christine yelled. "Glen—I need you."

"Settle down," Buster said to Christine's back. "He's not completely attached to you. You can't order him around."

"Glen?" Christine yelled again.

Buster waited several seconds before he spoke again. "See? Glen's not at your disposal."

Brad got his finger into the loop and bent his finger back painfully as he tried to loosen the knot. His knuckle snapped and a wave of fresh pain rippled up Brad's arm.

Buster rustled through his cardboard box and shook his head as he considered the contents. He straightened, pulling something from the box, and then turned slowly to reveal it to Brad. Buster held a small propane tank with a screw-on torch.

"Heat motivates," Buster said, "doncha think?"

Brad tried to keep his face still, but he gritted his teeth as he worked a second finger into the loop and then finally managed to work it loose. His face relaxed as he threaded the rope through and then felt it fall away to the floor. He bent his arms at the elbows, testing to be sure his hands were really free this time. No resistance met his pull. He'd managed to disconnect his feet from his hands, but his wrists were still bound to each other, and his ankles were drawn tight as well. Even though he could now stand, he couldn't expect Buster to stand still as he hopped over to him. He waited for Buster to approach.

"Glen, please help me! I'm bleeding, Glen," Christine yelled.

"I could cauterize your stump for you," Buster said. He lit the torch and adjusted the valve until it produced a perfect triangle of blue flame. Christine shut her mouth.

Buster lowered his head and locked eyes with Brad. Buster stalked forward.

The torch hissed.

Brad waited for the older man to get close enough, but Buster held the torch at arm's length and led with the flame. Buster had a gun holstered on one hip and a knife sheathed on the other—Brad couldn't afford to telegraph his attack.

"I'm not telling you anything, you piece of shit," Brad said. He wanted Buster mad—mad enough to get close.

"I'm not sure I care," Buster said. He smiled at Brad. His eyes twinkled.

Buster brushed the flame across Brad's cheek. Brad flinched, but the pain wasn't unbearable. The smell of burning hair—his own burning stubble—filled Brad's nostrils. When Buster moved the flame over to Brad's other cheek, Buster finally leaned in towards Brad.

Brad repeated his move from earlier. He thrust his lower body back, sending the chair flipping backwards, and got his feet under him in a crouching pose. Before Buster could pull back, Brad launched upwards, tilting his head down so the top of his skull would hit Buster in the chin.

Brad connected and heard and felt Buster's teeth slam together. Buster flailed, arms flying through giant circles as he tried to stay upright. The torch sputtered as Buster waved it through the air. Brad felt himself start to topple to the right. His ankles were still bound and he hopped several times to keep on his feet. He angled towards Buster and hopped after the flailing man.

Brad lowered his shoulder and collided with Buster just as the man backed into a stack of cardboard boxes. The two men crashed through the stack, and Buster fell backwards. Brad threw himself down on Buster while bringing his own knees to his chest.

Buster still gripped the torch. As the blue flame ignited Buster's fine silver hair, he tried to shove the torch away.

Brad stretched his already tortured shoulders and worked his hands down below his butt. His wrists strained and popped as he pulled through the pain while trying to keep his weight on the writhing man below him. He got his hands around and past his bound feet as Buster yelled and rolled Brad to the side.

Free from Brad's weight, Buster beat at the flames engulfing his hair.

Brad rose to his knees, gripped his fingers together into one giant fist, and brought them down on Buster's head. For a moment, both men beat at the flames, but after Brad connected twice, Buster's arms began to go limp. Brad continued to beat the older man's head.

Christine's voice hitched through a sob. "What's happening?" she demanded.

Buster rallied and pushed himself up from the floor.

Brad shuffled forward on his knees and threw himself down on Buster, knocking the wind out of Buster with his shoulder. Brad positioned his knees on Buster's chest and resumed beating him.

Buster went limp.

Brad's arms burned with the exertion. He slid forward and brought his knee down on Buster's chin and then repositioned himself to thrust his knee into Buster's cheek. He felt bone split and cartilage crack under his knee. Buster's breath gurgled up through his open mouth and sputtered out his nostril, making snotty bubbles of blood.

Brad fell away and regarded Buster. The man's face looked wrecked. His hair was singed, his nose jutted off to the right, one eye was swelling shut, and his jaw hung to the side like a shutter on a haunted house. Brad kept a cold eye on the man as he brought his feet to his hands and started working on the knot at his ankles. He couldn't reach the knot holding his wrists together, but figured he could reach the one on Christine's wrists.

When he finished with his feet he kicked away the rope and backed slowly towards Christine. He was unwilling to look away from Buster.

Somewhere to his left the torch lit a cardboard box and yellow flames started to grow.

"What are you doing?" Christine shrieked when Brad's hands touched hers.

"I'm untying you so you can untie me," Brad said. The work was difficult with his bound hands, but Brad worked fast. When he'd finished with her hands he held out his own, but Christine turned her attention to freeing her own feet.

Brad ran back to Buster. The man's breathing slowed. Brad kept a respectful distance but reached forward and stole the gun and knife from the man. He shoved the gun in his pocket, but turned the knife around in his hands and used it to slit the rope around his wrists.

Behind him, Christine threw off the last of her ropes and ran for the door.

"Glen!" she yelled.

"Shut up!" Brad said. "Keep quiet."

She threw open the door and disappeared to the hall.

Bright red blood stained the blade from where Brad nicked his own arm. He stood over Buster and considered driving the knife into Buster's chest. Instead, he walked to the burning boxes and kicked the stack away from the other boxes. He found the torch and turned the dial to extinguish the flame.

Brad drew the gun, took one last look at Buster, and moved to the door.

Brad held the gun out in front of him as he stalked down the hallway. The walls, made of cinderblocks, seemed to absorb what little light came through the window at the end of the long hall. He wished he'd taken the lantern from the cardboard-box room, but it was too late now. When he followed Christine out into the hall, Brad closed the door and snapped shut the padlock hanging from the hasp. As far as he knew, Buster owned the only key and he was locked inside.

Brad stopped when he heard the scream. It sounded like Christine. Behind him was Buster's door and the tiny window, mounted high up. Ahead, Brad saw one door on the left and two on the right. He knew the one on the left—at least he thought he did—he thought it was the room where he'd woken up. The scream sounded like it came from one of the doors on the right. Brad brought down each foot with extreme care, trying to make no sound at all as he moved forward.

Sobs followed the scream. The noise came from the second door on the right. Brad pushed the door open with the barrel of the gun. Inside the door a flashlight lay on the floor. It illuminated a grizzly scene. Christine squatted next to a bloody mess. She hugged herself tight, leaving bloody handprints on her tank top and naked shoulders.

When she heard Brad approach, she turned. Her face, twisted in grief, was streaked with tears and smeared with blood.

"Look what he did to Glen," she said.

Brad nodded.

"Are there any more of them?" Brad asked.

"Of who?" she said. Her voice sounded strained and close to panic.

"Of these guys," Brad said. "Your captors—any more of them?"

"I don't know," Christine said. She wiped her face with the back her hand. "I don't think so."

Brad assumed that the blood smeared on her shoulder and face was from the mutilated body of Glen, but he remembered her severed finger. Brad picked up the flashlight and swung it around the room.

"Wait here," he said.

Brad did a quick search of the building. He didn't find any other people and couldn't hear any noise from the room where he'd locked Buster. He wondered if the fire had eaten all the oxygen from the room.

In the room where'd he woken up, Brad found some clothes, a couple of jackets, and a crate full of weapons. After donning his coat, he slung a shotgun bag over his shoulder and added an extra box of shells. Back in the hall, the final door led down another hallway to a door which exited to an alley.

Brad found his way back to Christine.

"Here, put this on," he said, throwing her a jacket. "And then wrap this around your bad hand." He tossed her a cotton shirt.

She moved like a zombie and stared at Glen's corpse more than she paid attention to what she was doing. She bunched the cloth lightly around her stump, not putting any real pressure on the wound. In the light from Brad's lamp, the oozing blood on her hand was black and shiny.

"Let's go," Brad said. "Faster, or I'm going to leave you here in the dark."

She looked up at Brad with anger and sorrow in her eyes.

"Why are you upset? They were holding you prisoner," Brad said, pointing a finger at Glen's body. "Fine. Forget it."

Brad swung his light away from Christine and turned for the door. He turned the corner before she ran after him.

"He *died* for me," Christine said. "Glen never wanted to keep me tied up, it was Buster's idea, and Buster was stronger."

"Fine," Brad said. He kept walking, walking down the hall to the exit. "Keep quiet, I don't want to get jumped again."

Brad pulled the door open, peering through the crack to the outside world before he made his way to the alley. The bricks were bathed in the mellow glow of what passed for daylight in their forever cloudy world. He headed towards the street. Footprints headed both directions were etched in the thin layer of snow underfoot.

Christine looked up and down the deserted alley before she spoke again. "They didn't even really have a problem until you showed up. Everything would have been fine."

Brad shoved the flashlight into the inside pocket of his jacket. He ignored Christine's statement. At the mouth of the alley, Brad paused and leaned his head out to the sidewalk. He wasn't familiar with the street. Christine moved in close behind him.

"Which way is Congress Street? Do you know?" Brad asked.

Christine pointed to the right.

Brad headed left and picked up his pace into a jog. The shotgun bag slapped against his back. Behind him, Christine kept up easily. They turned and headed down a slight hill, towards the highway. The sleds, loaded down with corpses, were gone. When Brad was oriented, he turned again, heading into the deeper snow. They slogged through snow halfway up to their knees before Christine spoke.

"Where are we going?" she asked.

"I'm headed north," he said, blurting his words between breaths. "My friend stashed snowmobiles at a motor pool. I hope one is still there."

"I can drive a snowmobile," she said.

"Good for you," he said.

Brad needed a rest—he wasn't accustomed to jogging through snow and he'd used up most of his adrenaline. He hunched over and grabbed his knees. When the sour pain in the back of his throat abated, he asked, "Why are you following me?"

"I'm coming with you," she said. "We have to stick together."

"Why?"

"It's safer," she said.

"Not for me, it's not," he said. "As far as I know there's another psycho Buster running around looking for you and some little boy. Seems like trouble might be following you."

"That's absurd," she said.

"Maybe it is," Brad said. "It's impossible to know, I guess. Regardless, I'm headed *towards* danger. If you want safety, you're headed the wrong direction."

"You're going to meet Robby and those guys," Christine said.

"Yes."

"Robby has a plan?" she asked.

"Yes."

"Then I'm coming," she said. "I knew I should have gone with you guys before, but I thought Luke knew what he was talking about. I'm not going to make the same mistake twice."

Brad rose to his feet slowly and considered trying to talk her out of coming. He looked her in the eyes.

"I get the feeling you might make bad decisions and then stubbornly stick to them," he said.

"Fuck you," she said.

"Yup. I thought so," Brad said.

He turned away from her angry glare and resumed his trudge to the motor pool. After another half block, they found the trails of the snowmobiles and sleds and they walked on the hard-packed snow. Near the big patches of bare dirt, where the tractors had once been parked, Brad found several parked snowmobiles. He filled the tanks of two snowmobiles with gas cans leaned up next to the big garage. Then, to the back of each vehicle, he strapped extra tanks with the little bit of gas left over.

"You said you can drive one of these?" Brad asked.

"It's been a while," Christine said. "And it's going to be pretty damn cold without any goggles or decent gloves."

"Wrap up the best you can and we'll stop and get warmer gear," Brad said. "Did your finger stop bleeding?"

"A while ago," she said.

"Good, let's follow these tracks to the highway and then move as fast as we can. We should be able to catch up with the others pretty quick."

## CHAPTER 15: REANIMATED

TED WAS HALFWAY DOWN the big, open staircase when his hand flew up with a silent halt command. Lisa, who was following close but looking off towards the upper railing, ran into him and put her hand on the middle of his back to steady herself. Pete, over at the other side of the wide stair, continued a couple of extra steps before he noticed the rest of the group was stopped.

Both of Ted's lights focused on a display to his left. Soon, all the beams concentrated there. The display depicted a scene out of the Maine woods. Fake branches, bushes, and rocks provided habitat for stuffed, mounted animals, or so the placards would lead one to believe. In a whisper, Ted read the signs as he moved his headlamp from sign to sign.

"Raccoon, rabbit, bobcat, red squirrel," Ted whispered. "Where are they?"

"Back there, in the corner," Romie said, about as quiet as she ever said anything. She was a couple of steps above Ted, but she motioned with her light. Ted crouched and peered between the posts of the railing to shine his light back in the corner. A round, black, furry lump, about the size of a beanbag chair, sat near a gray boulder.

"That looks like a bear," Pete said, keeping his voice low. "You think maybe a real bear got in here and ate all the stuffed animals?"

"I haven't seen one mounted animal since we got here," Ted

whispered over his shoulder. "And I'm pretty sure this place used to be full of them. There used to be a big bear over in hunting and fishing, where we came in. That might be it."

"So someone or something moved all the animals around?" asked Lisa.

Sheila positioned herself between Nate and Ted while Brynn walked down a couple more steps to get close to the railing. Robby walked around Ted and Lisa and joined Brynn. They stared at the big black lump.

"No," Ted said, rising out of his crouch. "The mounted bear was standing. If this is a bear, then it's curled up like it's hibernating."

Robby turned and looked up to Ted.

"It's breathing," Robby said. All eyes looked at Robby for a second. Brynn nodded vigorously in agreement.

The rounded ball of black fur grunted and shifted.

"That *is* a bear," Nate whispered. "Get away from there, Brynn." Nate waited for Brynn to scramble to his side before he handed Brynn his flashlight. Nate loaded an arrow into the crossbow and pulled back the string. He held the weapon out at arm's length and gripped Brynn to his hip with his other arm.

The rest of the group tightened into a knot. Most kept their focus on the bear, but Pete and Romie, in the back, looked upstairs in the direction they were headed. The bear grunted again and they saw its head appear from behind a big paw. With its eyes closed it snuffled at the air and then tucked its head back in.

"They don't hibernate very deep," Ted said with his voice low. The group could barely hear him over the dry shuffle of their feet over the wood floor.

Nate and Brynn moved quicker than the huddled group, so they led the way. When they'd moved out of sight of the bear's exhibit, Sheila stopped with a panicked look. She fluttered a hand in front of her face and hunched her shoulders.

"What is it?" Lisa asked in a whisper.

"Keep moving," Nate said over his shoulder. He and Brynn moved slowly away from the rest.

Sheila sucked in a constricted, whistling breath. Her exhale was equally labored.

"Take it easy," Ted said in a low voice. "You having trouble breathing?"

Sheila nodded.

"Close your eyes," Ted said.

Sheila's eyes widened at the suggestion.

"Shhh, just close your eyes and relax," Ted said. "We're all here. We're right here."

Sheila's eyelids fluttered, fighting her as she tried to comply. She finally managed to get them shut and her shoulders fell almost instantly. A long, slow breath leaked from her lungs as she unclenched her teeth. She took a deep breath, collecting it into her belly and then exhaled through her nose. The panic left her face and Sheila opened her eyes.

"Good," Ted said. "Let's go."

Lisa grabbed Sheila's hand and helped her forward. The others drew in around Sheila and moved ahead towards the lights of Brynn and Nate.

From the direction of Nate and Brynn, three noises came out of the dark in rapid succession: a low, angry howl, a loud mechanical snap, and a shriek. Suddenly the beams of Brynn and Nate scattered in random directions, and then repointed back at the group. Dragging Brynn by the arm, Nate scrambled back past the group, hooking a sliding left towards the stairs leading up to the second floor. Just behind him, the others saw the cause of his alarm—a screaming bobcat with a crossbow arrow lodged in its bleeding shoulder was bounding across the tiles towards them.

"Shit," Lisa said as she tried to turn.

The bobcat pounced towards the group.

Pete's knife rang like a tiny bell as he pulled it from the sheath on his side. The big man jumped towards Lisa from the other side.

The bobcat hit Lisa's shoulder and upper back with extended claws. It didn't take much weight to overbalance Lisa, who was mid-turn. Her feet slid out from under her, and her hand slipped from Sheila's. The bobcat took her to the ground as it sunk its teeth into the arm of her down coat. Pete swung his knife down towards the torso of the big cat. His knife struck ribs and stuck, not penetrating much beyond the tip of the blade.

Lisa stifled a scream between her clenched teeth.

Ted flashed a look back at Robby, who grabbed Sheila's coat and dragged her towards the staircase to the upper floor. Sheila flailed and struggled to keep up on her bad leg. Romie looked back to Robby and then forward to Lisa. She watched Ted throw himself across Lisa, grabbing the bobcat around its neck. Pete twisted his knife and brought it back to the ribcage of the bobcat, plunging the blade between its ribs just as Ted wrenched the cat's head backwards.

The bobcat screamed again, spun in Ted's grip, and swiped out a heavy paw at Ted's head.

The paw landed, knocking Ted's head back. A spray of blood spattered Pete's face as he reached for the bobcat. Ted rolled backwards and thrust his arms away, trying to free himself from the claws and teeth flailing at his face.

With his second push, Ted screamed a guttural roar. It was immediately echoed by a resonating, echoing growl from the direction of the lower staircase. The bobcat released its claws and bolted. Pete's knife clattered to the tiles.

Lisa pushed up from under the two men. Pete rolled off of Ted and grabbed his knife. Ted, still dazed, lay on his back. Pete and Lisa grabbed Ted under the armpits and dragged him towards the upper stairs as another loud growl called out.

"I can walk. I can walk," Ted said as he tried to get his feet under him. Pete helped him flip over as Lisa ran for the stairs. Romie, Robby, and Sheila were nearly at the top.

Pain erupted in Lisa's right ankle, slowing her gait to a hitching limp. Robby ran back down the stairs and propped up Lisa's right side. She pulled herself up with the railing and let Robby support her other side. Behind them, Pete and Ted gathered speed as they hit the stairs.

Back toward the lower stairs, the bear grunted and growled again, knocking over a display and shattering glass. From deeper in the store, the bobcat growled and screamed.

Robby got Lisa to the top of the stairs and guided her to the left. Romie and Sheila waved them towards a narrow hallway. Ted and Pete reached them as they rounded the corner and saw Romie and Sheila leading them towards the men's restroom. Against the women's room door a deer was stretched out on its side. Deer guts and blood trailed across the floor.

"In here, quick," Romie said. She held open the men's room door.

The group piled in. Robby helped Lisa around the corner and propped her against the sink. Pete and Ted hurried the door shut and leaned back against it. The door opened to a wall just opposite its swing. Pete braced his shoulder against the door and his feet against the opposite wall.

Ted leaned against the door. He clamped both hands to lacerations on his neck and face. Blood oozed out around his grip.

The men were only leaning against the door for a few seconds before a shuddering jolt hit the door. The bang was followed by pounding. Pete flexed his legs to hold the door shut. Romie leaned in under him and braced the bottom of the door.

"Wait, wait," Romie said. "I hear something."

In between the pounds, they heard a muffled voice on the other side of the door.

"That's Nate and Brynn," Romie said. "Let them in."

They moved out of the way and pulled open the door. Brynn shoved through the gap, followed immediately by Nate, who held his empty crossbow pointed towards the ceiling. Nate turned and helped them press the door shut. Between the four of them, they barely found enough room to all lean on the door.

Sheila broke open a toilet paper dispenser and brought the roll over to Lisa, to help her bandage her scrapes. The cat's claws and teeth hadn't penetrated very far through her jacket; she was in good shape. Robby joined the others at the door. Romie pressed her ear against the door.

"You have pliers, Pete?" Robby asked.

"Shhh," Romie said.

Pete nodded and dug through his pockets until he produced a Leatherman—a folded device with a variety of tools and blades. Robby took it from the man and walked to the handicap stall.

When he returned, dragging the stall door, the four adults held their positions at the door. Romie waved and pointed. Then, they all heard it.

A large animal exhaled and snorted, making a whuff-chuff noise. Through the door they heard long claws click across the tiles as the bear whuffed again. With a grunt, the bear stopped. They heard it snuffle and sniff, and then wet, smacking sounds carried through the door. Rhythmic slurping and chewing sounds mixed with scraping and more grunts. Pete pointed back over his shoulder and then used his hands to mime antlers.

They understood—the bear was feeding on the deer carcass.

Robby pointed at the door and then whispered. "We can prop this under the handle and against the wall."

Pete put his finger to his lips and shook his head "no," and Romie joined him. Robby leaned the door against the wall behind him and shrugged.

"Are you still bleeding?" Robby whispered to Ted.

Ted peeled his hand away from his neck. His palm looked black with blood in the minimal light. It glistened with fresh blood, and Ted clamped it back to his neck before nodding his head.

"I'll take your place," Robby whispered.

Ted pulled his weight away from the door and stepped over the legs of Pete and Nate. He lost his balance and began to wobble before Robby stepped up to steady him. Robby helped him over to the sink next to Lisa. Brynn sat cross-legged under the counter.

Ted swayed gently as Sheila turned to him to help him with his wounds. Before Robby returned to the door, Sheila turned to him with anger written across her brow. "I told you guys we shouldn't have come down here."

Robby left Sheila to care for the wounded and returned to the door. Pete shifted his position so he could press his ear to the door as he held it shut. He motioned to Robby to come close.

Shoulder-to-shoulder at the door, Pete whispered directly into Robby's ear. "We have to find a way to lock this door so we can wait for that thing to go away."

"I think we can prop the stall door between this door and the wall," Robby whispered.

"I don't think it will work," Pete said. "It's too long to fit."

"I mean diagonally," Robby said, "between here and..."

Robby never finished his thought. Despite the combined body weight of four people pressing against it, the door swung inward at an amazing speed. The door caught Nate by the shoulder and spun him around. Pete and Robby were thrown away from it as the door plowed through their shoulders and clocked Robby in the head. Romie—sitting on the floor of the bathroom with her back to the door—was the one who stopped it. The door slid her across the tile until her straight left leg impacted the opposite wall.

Romie let loose a surprised scream as her knee folded backward until the underside of her leg hit the floor.

The door slammed shut again as the three men collapsed against it.

Romie moaned and clutched at her knee, coaxing her knee out of its hyperextension.

The bear whuffed and growled, just outside the door.

"Get out of there," Nate said. He pulled at Romie's arm to slide her away from the door.

Romie rolled to her side and pulled herself along the floor, dragging her legs.

Nate took her spot just in time. His legs were longer, and he braced them against the wall with a slight flex. Pete moved his butt to the wall so he'd have something to brace against as he leaned forward and put his hands against the door.

The door jolted. This time they resisted the push and it only opened an inch or two before slamming shut. They heard a long scrape from the top of the door down to the floor and imagined the bear's strong claws tearing at the door. Another impact shook the door and the hinges rattled as the door slammed back into the frame.

Robby moved his feet back instinctively as they heard the bear sniff at bottom of the door.

A loud boom echoed through the store and the sniffing stopped.

Brynn poked his head around the corner. Romie waved him over and asked him to fetch the crossbow and arrows Nate had dropped in the corner. Pete grunted as another impact almost knocked him off his feet. Brynn helped Romie cock the crossbow and load an arrow and Romie slid closer to the door. She held the crossbow with both hands.

"Let it open a crack," she said.

"Take the safety off," Nate said. He reached forward and clicked off the safety.

"Right after the next..." Pete said. He didn't finish—the bear crashed into the door. Pete grabbed the handle and pulled the door open a crack. Nate held his legs firm to keep the door from swinging in further.

The claws appeared immediately, hooking around the edge of the door and tearing at Nate's jacket.

From her position on the ground, Romie saw a sea of black fur outside the door. She reached the crossbow forward, putting the stock of the weapon right up to the crack, and pulled the trigger. The arrow disappeared into the fur and the bear grunted.

As soon as the claws pulled back, Pete, Robby, and Nate pushed hard and shut the door.

Another boom rang out deep in the store just as the door closed.

"Do another," Nate said.

"I'm trying," Romie yelled. Her hands shook and every time she tried to cock the crossbow, she lost her grip on the cocking rope or dropped the weapon. She paused and took a deep breath. Nate grabbed the crossbow from her hands and loaded it. He set it down on the floor next to Romie.

The bear slammed into the door again. Pete tried to open it a crack once more, but Nate wasn't ready. He held it shut. Romie pulled at the trigger anyway before remembering the safety.

"Next hit," Pete said.

They waited.

Robby wiped at a line of sweat rolling down his forehead.

A third boom from somewhere in the building sounded farther away than the first two.

Sheila came around the corner and all their headlamps moved to her. Her jacket, once a light turquoise, was smeared with magenta streaks of blood. "Ted's not responding," she said. "I think... I think..."

The bear crashed into the door and let loose an angry, frustrated growl. Sheila screamed and ran back around the corner.

"Now!" Pete shouted. He pulled open the door, Nate braced it so it wouldn't open further, and Romie shot another arrow towards the big bear. She aimed this one higher, hoping to land it just under the ribs and up into the animals vital organs. They heard this arrow land. It sounded like a butcher knife sinking into a watermelon.

The bear grunted and slammed into the door several times in row. Each hit was accompanied by another grunt, and each was harder than the last. Nate gritted his teeth and gripped at his thighs. Pete swayed with each hit and looked like a boxer trying to survive the last ten seconds of the round.

An arrow clattered to the tiles as Romie's shaking hands fumbled with the crossbow. Brynn grabbed it and tried to help her.

Between hits, Robby swiped his arm across his face. Not all the moisture on his face was sweat. Some of it was tears, leaking from the corners of his eyes.

"Get it loaded," Pete shouted at Romie.

From around the corner, Sheila screamed again and Lisa started talking, trying to calm her down.

"Give it to me," Nate said. He leaned forward to reach for the crossbow, just as the bear slammed into the door again. The door caught him in the lower back and he straightened with pain.

"I've got it," Romie said. The quivering left her voice. She snapped the arrow home. The bear hit, Pete pulled the door open, and Romie rose to her knees to point the crossbow directly at the bear's chest. The door slammed shut and the bear hit it again, even harder.

They heard two more explosions, one right after the other, from the heart of the building.

Pete turned to Robby. His lamp lit up the tracks of tears on Robby's face. The tears glittered in the wells of Robby's eyes.

"What's that noise? Are you hurt?" Pete asked as the bear crashed into the door again.

"Ready," Romie yelled.

They executed another shot to the bear.

"I don't think it's even hurting him," Romie said as she loaded another arrow.

"I can't hold the door much longer," Nate said.

"You have to," Pete said. He turned back to Robby. "What are those explosions?"

Robby shook his head. "Don't know," he said. He choked out the words.

"My legs are giving out," Nate said. "Somebody needs to take over for me."

"Just hold on, Nate. Romie—aim for the face. Maybe a shot in the face will scare it away," Pete said.

Romie pushed up against the wall and Brynn slipped under her shoulder so she could stand.

"Ready," she said.

When Pete opened the door she aimed her headlamp through the crack and aimed the arrow at the glitter of the bear's white teeth. Pete slammed the door immediately. Romie couldn't see the arrow find its mark.

Another boom rang out; the closest one yet.

Robby pulled back from the door and shrank against the wall. He brought his hands up and clutched them to his face.

"Robby," Pete said. "Robby, get back here."

Robby slumped to the floor and wrapped his arms around his shins, pulling his knees to his chest.

"Lisa! Sheila! Get over here. We need more bodies on this door," Nate yelled.

They heard Lisa say a few more words to Sheila and then Lisa limped around the corner.

"How can I help?" she asked.

"Get over here and take Robby's position. Robby, get the fuck out of the way," Pete said.

Robby didn't move from his place in the corner, but Lisa stepped over Nate and found room to lean against the door anyway.

"You ready to shoot again?" Pete asked Romie.

"Any time," Romie said.

"Next hit," Pete said.

They waited.

"Maybe it's gone," Nate said.

"What do you mean?" asked Pete.

"When was the last time it hit? It's been a little while since she shot it in the face," Nate said.

"Oh," Pete said.

"What do we do?" Lisa whispered.

"Open the door a few inches," Romie said. "Give me another shot at it."

"What if it's just waiting?" asked Pete. "Pull yourself together, Robby." Pete nudged the young man with the edge of his boot.

"Leave him alone," Nate said. "We have to figure a way out of here. Brynn, Romie, see if you can slide the door over here." He motioned to the stall door leaning against the wall.

Romie wasn't much help, but Brynn managed to wrestle the door until it was within arm's length of Nate. Careful not to move his weight away from the door, Nate rotated the door until he could hold its length at a diagonal to the space between the door handle and the corner where the opposite wall met the floor.

"I think this will work," Nate said to Pete. "We can wedge it in like this."

"Yeah and if the door doesn't fit then the bear will barge straight in while we're fucking around," Pete said.

"It's about two good hits from barging in anyway," Nate said. "Come on, let's just see if it fits."

"Fine," Pete said. "Lisa, see if you can get Robby out of here."

Lisa relinquished her position against the door after some hesitation. Robby didn't react when she asked him to get up, but he didn't fight her as she pulled him to his feet. He buried his head in his hands as she led him away. She led him over near the sinks where Robby leaned against the wall and slumped to the floor. He put his hand inside his jacket and gripped the mirror he'd taken from the Volvo.

As they moved away, Nate slid the stall door into position. When he and Pete were both satisfied it might work, the two men inched closer to the corner. The door had about a half-inch of freedom before it hit the heavy steel door handle. The other end sat firmly against the tile floor and wall. Pete leaned over Nate and tugged at the door. It barely moved before the stall door stopped it cold.

"Don't step on it, we don't know if the metal will bend," Pete said. He stretched his leg over and climbed over the door. He reached back and helped Nate make the climb.

"Will it hold?" asked Romie.

Another boom rang out from the other side of the bathroom door. This one echoed down the hallway.

Pete raised a finger to his lips and warned Romie, Nate, and Brynn to be quiet. He motioned for Romie to cover the door with the crossbow and waved Nate around the corner.

Sheila held pressure against Ted's neck wounds, and held him up on the counter to prevent him from collapsing. Lisa crouched down next to Robby with her arm around the young man.

"Can we get out through the drop ceiling?" whispered Nate.

"I doubt it," Pete whispered back. "Fire code. The walls will go all the way up."

"What if we bust through the wall?" asked Nate.

"You have a sledgehammer and a few hours?" asked Pete. "Let's face it—the only way out is through the bear."

"It might not even be out there anymore," Nate said. "At least when it was banging on the door we knew where it was."

They locked eyes when they heard an explosion ring out on the other side of the bathroom door. They turned to see Romie lifting the crossbow to aim it at the door.

"Wait!" Robby yelled. His hands fell away, revealing a face full of surprise and hope.

Romie's ears heard the word, but her fingers were already on autopilot. She pulled the trigger on the crossbow and the arrow struck the door right at the frame. It rebounded and continued its upward, sticking into the ceiling tile at a steep angle. It hung for a second, just barely penetrating the soft tile, and then it fell, flipping in the air and bouncing off Robby's jacket as he approached the door.

He didn't reach for the handle, but Nate reached out and grabbed his shoulder in case he should try anything crazy.

Robby turned his head and listened for a second before he yelled out again.

"Brad?" Robby called.

Puzzled glances spread through the group.

"Robby, are you feeling..." Pete began.

Robby cut him off with a raised hand.

They all heard the response from the other side of the door.

"Hello?" Brad called.

Robby smiled and wiped a tear from his eyes.

✪ ✪ ✪ ✪ ✪

The men swung the door up and hustled Brad in quickly. They tried to close it, but Brad held it open, ushering Christine inside. She moved slowly, raising her feet like she was trying not to step in mud. Their boots left bloody footprints on the tile. Christine smiled when she saw Pete, but her smile disappeared when she witnessed the exasperated look on Romie's face.

As soon as they closed the door, Brad wasted no time trying to get everyone moving again.

"We've got to get out of here," Brad said. "There are wild animals everywhere. We've run into moose, a bear, and a pack of coyotes. I've got a shotgun and plenty of rounds. One of you guys can take my pistol. She won't touch it."

From around the corner, Sheila's voice interrupted—"No. Get away. I've got this."

"Fine," Lisa said. She approached the others. "Ted's dead. Sheila's still trying to stop his bleeding. She's lost it."

"Oh fuck," Pete said.

"Ted?" Brad asked.

"He got hit by a bobcat," Pete said, shaking his head.

"Brad's right," Robby said. "Time to go."

Nate reached forward and took the gun that Brad held out.

"Brynn," he said, "you're with me. We'll bring up the rear. Brad, you lead with the shotgun. Romie, you cover the sides with the crossbow."

Pete pulled Sheila away from Ted's body. When she let go, the man slumped and then slid slowly to the floor of the restroom. His mouth hung open and his face pressed against the tile. Robby returned, slipped Ted's coat off, and covered Ted's face.

Brad led the way out of the restroom and the group passed the bloody bear. It lay near the deer carcass, on its back, with arrows protruding from its chest and belly. The bear's face was gone, wiped away by a shotgun blast. Robby leaned close on the way by to get a look at the brains leaking from the bear's skull.

As they turned the corner, Brad swept the shotgun over the walkway, from the wall to the balcony. He brought his headlamp back to the center and stopped.

"What's the holdup?" Nate called from the back.

"What is it?" Lisa whispered over Brad's shoulder.

In the distance, past the throw of his light, green eyes glowed in the dark. They stared at the group, unblinking.

"I don't know," Brad said.

"Shoot it," Lisa said.

"Closer. I have to get closer," Brad said. He started forward again, slowly, not taking his eyes from the shining orbs. After the group moved about ten feet, the eyes disappeared for several seconds and then lit up again, farther away. The animal moved just when the light might reveal its form. Brad moved past the stairway and the edge of the balcony. Straight ahead, the hall led to the second floor of the hunting department and the stairs leading out. To his right, the floor opened up to a housewares section.

When he'd moved another ten feet, the eyes retreated again.

Nate and Brynn moved past the staircase.

Nate faced the rear, swinging his gun between the stairs, the walkway to the bathroom, and housewares. "What's going on up there?" he called back over his shoulder as Brad paused again.

"It keeps moving farther away," Brad whispered. Pete relayed the quiet message back to Nate.

"This is a trap!" Nate yelled. He pressed his back against Pete and called to the group. "Circle up everyone. It's leading us into a trap."

Sheila panicked and tried to bolt towards housewares. Pete grabbed her jacket and reeled her back in. The group pulled together, forming a rough circle with their weapons pointing out.

Nate called out orders. "Against the wall. Let's move to a defensible position. Let them come to us."

They didn't have time to move.

As an iron skillet banged to the floor, Pete's headlamp turned towards housewares, revealing another set of green eyes. A third set appeared on the stairs, and a fourth popped around the corner behind the group.

"Take any clean shot," Nate said.

He needn't have bothered to speak. Romie took a shot at the eyes coming up the stairs as soon as the form of the wolf crossed into her light. Pete grabbed Brad's arm and pulled the shotgun over to the wolf in housewares. Brad fired a blast at the beast's head, shutting off the glowing eyes with one round. Nate waited for his wolf to leap before he triggered his pistol. He put one slug in the wolf's chest and one between its eyes.

Sheila shrieked at each explosion. She shrank away from Pete and fell to her knees. Brad looked down at Sheila and followed her pointing finger. The wolf up ahead was no longer retreating. The eyes were approaching rapidly, and they multiplied.

Brad swung his shotgun around and fired into the dark at the glowing eyes. They kept coming. He pumped the shotgun. Before they'd left the bathroom, he'd loaded five shells in the gun. Behind him, Christine held out five more. He hoped for time to use them. Brad waited for the animals to get closer.

The eyes slowed and spread out as they passed into the edge of the light. He counted four sets.

"I'm going to need help up here," Brad said.

He aimed at the animal in the middle and pulled the trigger. The thing seemed to sense the shot and it darted left before he'd even felt the recoil. The eyes kept coming. Brad pumped again and figured he was down to two shots.

The wolf circling to the right picked up speed. Brad turned and shot at it. He didn't kill it, but its front leg buckled and it skidded along the floor for a few feet before it picked itself back up into a three-legged limp. The others darted left, running to flank the group. He aimed with more speed than care and pulled the trigger again. He'd forgotten to pump. The chamber was empty. The closest wolf leapt and passed so close to Brad that its hair brushed against his jacketed arm. The fur made a whispering sound against his jacket before Sheila's scream buried the gentle sound. She still knelt on the floor. The wolf hit her in the chest as she tried to raise her arms to block the attack.

Brad pumped his shotgun as Nate turned and shot the wolf as it tore into Sheila. Brad turned his gun on the next wolf, which was leaping towards Robby. His shot tore the bottom jaw from the wolf's face. Robby spun and let the thing sail by. It hit the floor with its front legs splayed and it thrashed its back legs until it ran into the wall.

"Give me one," Brad said to Christine as he pulled back the action bar. He loaded the shell into the chamber, pushed forward, and fired, taking down the next wolf. When he reached back, Christine slapped another shell into his hand. He glanced back to make sure Nate had control of the wolf attacking Sheila, and then he used his next shot to dispatch the limping wolf off to the right. With the next shell, he took care of the wolf with the missing lower jaw. He scanned his light frantically as he loaded five more shells into his gun.

Behind him, Sheila stopped screaming, but breathed with a loud, gurgling sound. Pete and Lisa crouched beside her. Brad continued to scan the darkness as he listened to the conversation behind him.

"The bullet must have glanced off the wolf's bone," Pete said. "It went right through her chest."

"There's nothing we can do for her," Nate said. "Her lung is punctured, and the wolf bit into her shoulder."

"We're not leaving her," Lisa said.

"Nobody said we're leaving her," Nate said. "Just put her arm over your shoulder, Pete, and try to put pressure on the wound."

"We have to move before they respawn," Robby said.

His statement made Brad turn around and face Robby. "You think they'll do that?"

"What's 'respawn' mean?" asked Lisa.

"You have reason to think they'll do that?" Brad asked again.

"Yes, it stands to reason," Robby said. "They were stuffed—just skin and fur—and now they're breathing, bleeding animals."

Pete and Lisa lifted Sheila, who moaned through her gurgling breath. When Pete hugged her close to clamp down on her wound she exhaled a strained sigh. Lisa supported Sheila's other armpit, but Pete took most of the weight because he was taller.

"What's 'respawn' mean?" Lisa asked again.

"It's like in a video game, where the monsters come back to life every so often," Brad said. As he spoke he turned his light back to the darkness, looking for more glowing green eyes.

"Faster," Nate said. "I don't want to find out what happens next around here."

Nate whipped back around when they heard a clattering sound behind them. He turned just in time to see the deer, hooves slipping and leaving bloody footprints, emerge from the hall to the bathroom. It paused for a second, eyes locked with Nate's headlamp, before it turned and trotted off, deeper into the store.

"Deer respawn," Nate said. "Move faster."

Brad and Robby led the group in a fast shuffle. Pete and Lisa tried to move as gently as they could, but Sheila began to convulse and deep red blood spilled from her lips. She couldn't inhale. Pete compressed her chest with another hug and tried to seal the hole with his finger before air could leak back in around her lungs. Sheila managed one more labored breath before her body shook and her head slumped to her chest. Lisa and Pete exchanged a look over Sheila's slumped head, and kept carrying her dead weight.

They passed down a long hallway. A pair of moose lay in giant pools of blood, leaning against the windows which stretched from floor to ceiling. The windows revealed nothing but packed snow. Robby walked closest to the moose, leaning in to get a good look at them as they moved by. Brad kept his attention forward, reacting to every glint and reflection coming from the display cases up ahead. In the hunting department, Brad moved quickly down the wide wooden staircase, sweeping his shotgun in wide arcs to inspect every corner as he descended. He waved to the rest and they hurried down the steps. Pete and Lisa fell behind, struggling to wrestle Sheila down the stairs. They reassembled at the bottom and moved as a group to the utility stairs which led to the upstairs offices. Nate closed the twisted door behind them and caught up with the group at the foot of the stairs.

"We're going to need a hand if we're taking Sheila out of here," he said.

"Is she?" Brad asked.

"Yes," Pete said. "She died back around the moose."

"Leave her?" Brad asked.

"How can we leave her?" asked Lisa. "One of those things will eat her." Lisa shifted Sheila's weight on her shoulder and winced with the effort. She didn't look like she could carry Sheila another three feet, let alone up three flights of stairs.

"Trade with me," Romie said. She held out the crossbow.

Lisa took it, but said, "I'm a lousy shot."

"I'll take it," Christine said. "I'm a great shot. Here, you take these."

Christine gave the bag of shotgun shells to Lisa and took the crossbow.

"Okay?" asked Nate. "All settled? Can we get moving now?"

"Come on," Romie said. She pulled aggressively towards the stairs. Pete struggled to keep up. When they reached the top floor, Pete was panting, but Romie was still strong.

"Put her down for a second," Romie said.

Pete rolled his shoulders back and twisted his neck to find relief for his stiff muscles.

The group moved away from the stairs and gravitated to the broken window where they'd entered. Only a faint glow from the cloudy evening came in through the window, but it was still more attractive than the absolute darkness of the snowbound lower floors. Nate closed the door to the stairs and then got Brynn to help pull a desk in front of it.

"What now?" asked Lisa.

"I say we fire those tractors back up and head north right away. We can sleep when we're dead," Pete said. He blushed and realized his poor choice of words when he glanced down at Sheila's lifeless form on the floor.

"Pete's right," Nate said. "Let's put some distance between us and this place. We're short a couple of drivers, but I can set up Brynn to drive one."

"We're not short," Pete said. "We've got Brad now."

"That's right," Lisa said.

"I can drive," Christine said.

"Perfect," Nate said. "Brynn, you're off the hook."

"Can we find our way in the dark?" asked Lisa.

"Those tractors are rigged with twenty amps of lights per circuit. You could cook a hotdog with those lights," Pete said.

While the others talked, Robby knelt down and pulled Sheila's jacket off so he could drape it over her face. When he stood back up, all eyes turned to him.

"What do you think, Robby?" Pete asked.

"North," Robby said.

## CHAPTER 16: NORTH

PETE WAS RIGHT ABOUT the lights on the tractor—they were almost too bright. As Robby watched the back of the big sled in front of him, the glare reflected off the snowmobile strapped there and the metal frame felt like it would burn his eyes. But every time he blinked he saw Ted's slack face pressed against the bathroom floor, or Sheila's tortured mouth as she tried to pull air into lungs which wouldn't fill. Robby had seen plenty of dead bodies in the past five months, more than most people would see in ten lifetimes, but he'd only seen a couple die directly from his decisions.

The Bombardier tractor was easier to drive than a car. It used a joystick for speed and steering, and Pete was able to coach Christine in its operation over the radios. Robby turned down the volume on his handset as the rest of the group chattered back and forth. He figured they needed to talk to stay awake, but Robby had a co-pilot. He and Brynn took turns steering and napping; neither needed companionship to stay focused.

The miles ticked by slowly according to the odometer on the panel. The tractors pulled the heavy sleds steadily, but not rapidly. Robby held his radio in his left hand and steered with his right. After midnight, the chatter on the radio faded. The group checked in every five minutes. Starting from the front of the convoy, they announced their names in order to make sure everyone was still alert.

"Pete here."

"Christine."

"This is Lisa." Robby thought she sounded the most tired. She slurred through her name.

"Romie here."

"Nate."

"Robby and Brynn," Robby said. He kept his voice low to not wake Brynn.

"Brad in back."

Early on, they talked about taking turns with who would lead the line of tractors, but Pete stayed up front. Robby thought it must be lonely, looking out at unbroken, endless snow and blazing the path north. Robby's GPS worked most of the time. Sometimes the display would simply flash a satellite symbol, as if its view of the sky was blocked. Robby wondered how Pete stayed on course during those outages.

Pete led the line of tractors over a narrow bridge. Robby focused on the sled in front of him. On either side, the snow fell away fast and he saw only darkness. Robby jumped when Brad's voice came on the radio.

"This is where I nearly went over the side. If anyone sees anything weird, jump on the radio," Brad said. The group remained quiet.

Just north of a bridge, Pete's voice came over the radio. "Should we veer off the highway and follow Brad's tracks?"

"Nope," Brad said. "I wandered for miles. The highway gets even closer to my house. Keep following your GPS, if you can."

As they continued, Robby saw Brad's snowmobile tracks veer off to the right. He wondered why the months hadn't erased them. Flurries started about then, and Pete reassured the group that their tractors could operate in a blizzard if required. Fortunately, the snow stopped and they didn't have to test Pete's assertion.

"Everyone look good on fuel, oil pressure, and engine temp?" Pete asked on the radio.

"This is Christine—looks good here."

"Lisa. All good."

"Romie here. Looking fine."

"Nate—good."

"Everything's fine," Robby said. "Sorry. Everything's fine with Robby and Brynn."

"Brad. Looks fine."

Robby looked up at Nate's sled in front of him. Beyond the snowmobile, the bodies were lashed to the sled in a high stack. They were laid with their feet towards the front, and heads near the back. Before applying the straps over the whole pile, Pete and Nate had laid down green tarps. The tarps made it easier for the straps to slide over the pile without binding while they tightened. Robby saw the heads of the corpses, lined up like multicolored matchsticks. Near the top, something flopped with the jostling of the sled. It was the arm of one of the bodies.

They'd lined up all the corpses with their arms at their sides, but this one flopped out and now it bounced up and down with the motion of the sled. The straps were tight, but not tight enough to hold all the arms in place, apparently. Robby tried to imagine how the slight sway of the sled on the churned snow could make this arm flop out. He turned and looked back at the sled full of corpses his tractor pulled. He saw an orderly stack of shoes and bare feet. Nothing seemed unusual.

Robby jumped when Brynn spoke.

"Do you want me to drive now?" Brynn asked, suddenly awake.

"No, I'm okay," Robby said. "You haven't been asleep long. You can sleep longer if you want."

"That's okay," Brynn said. "Where are we?"

"Somewhere near Kingston," Robby said.

"Are we close to where we're going?"

"Maybe."

Robby casually glanced up at the floppy corpse arm in the sled ahead of them. It still bounced.

"Do you have to go to the bathroom?" Robby asked. On his last break, Robby stood on to the wide running board of the tractor and peed onto the rolling tracks. Brynn hadn't gone since they'd started moving again.

"Can I tell you something?" Brynn asked.

"Sure," Robby said.

"I'm not related to Nate," Brynn said.

"I know," Robby said.

Brynn looked at him and then back forward.

"You did not," Brynn said.

"Not for sure," Robby said, "but I figured."

"Why do you always have to try to figure everything out? You're not always so smart. I saw you crying in the bathroom."

Robby nodded and lowered his head.

"Yeah," Robby said.

"So why do you do it? Why don't you just let things be?" asked Brynn.

"Is your name really Brynn?" Robby asked.

"Yes," he said.

"Is anyone from your family still alive?" Robby asked.

"Yes. My granddaddy."

"Why didn't you stay with him?"

"You wouldn't understand," Brynn said. He looked down at his hands and rubbed them together in his lap.

Robby snuck another look at the flopping arm. Now it swung from side to side.

The radio crackled to life.

"This is Pete. How's everyone doing?"

"Christine here. My hand is hurting a lot. I looked through this bag—are there any painkillers in here?"

"Christine, this is Romie. Look in the compartment on the passenger's side."

"Thanks," Christine said.

"This is Lisa. Take the one with caffeine. The other one will make you sleepy."

"Nate here."

"Robby and Brynn."

"Brad in back."

On the panel in front of Robby, the satellite icon on the GPS began to flash. For the moment, the blue arrow hovered over the highway, but soon it would blink out and be replaced with an orange question mark. A few minutes after that, Robby knew the entire map would be replaced with the flashing satellite symbol.

He wondered how long GPS would remain accurate. The satellites might remain in orbit, but he was pretty sure they relied on updates from ground stations to keep them useful.

The farther north they traveled, the less important it seemed that they stick to the highway. Robby suspected that somewhere beneath the snow, the landscape was being transformed to facilitate the growth of the new organism now inhabiting Earth. But the snow was deeper. Robby compared the elevation reported by the GPS to the paper map on his lap and the difference was at one-hundred feet and growing. The contours of the landscape—frozen rivers and bridges, houses and trees—everything was buried so far beneath the snow that it didn't affect their tractors and sleds. Soon they might be able to ignore the GPS completely and use their compass heading alone.

The satellite icon jumped back to the corner of the display and the blue arrow appeared again. GPS lock returned. Robby reached behind the seat and pulled out another warm, sugar-filled soda. He knew the effect wouldn't last forever. When they were younger, he and Jim used to drink a lot of sodas on Saturday nights. They tried for weeks to stay up all night, but they never made it past four in the morning. Eventually no matter how much sugar and caffeine they drank, sleep would overtake them and they'd pass out in front of the television. At some point during the night it always felt like the soda was doing more harm than good. Each sip would wake him up a tiny bit but then hasten the inevitable crash. Robby hoped the little catnaps he'd stolen while Brynn drove were enough to stave off sleep during this trip.

"This is Lisa," the radio reported. Her check-in was out of order and more than a minute early.

"What's up, Lisa?" asked Pete.

"I can't stay awake any longer. I don't know what to tell you. I've fallen asleep at least a half-dozen times in the past few minutes," Lisa said.

"Okay?" Pete said. "Anyone else? What do we do here?"

"Sleep in our vehicles?" Romie asked.

"Let's stop for a minute and talk this through," Nate said.

"Good idea," Pete said. "I'm stopping."

It took a few moments for the slowdown to propagate through the convoy, but eventually Robby recognized the sled in front of him was slowing. He let up off his own throttle and let the tractor slow to an idle. He leaned down and looked at the arm. It stopped swinging.

"Where are we going to meet?" Brynn asked.

"I assume up at the head of the line," Robby said.

Robby pulled on his jacket and began to lace up his boots.

"How long are we going to stop?" Brynn asked.

"While we're stopped, do you want to grab one of the others and go use the bathroom?" Robby asked.

Brynn nodded. He zipped up his jacket and pulled the hood tight.

"Who?" Robby asked.

"Sheila," Brynn said.

Robby tried to think of what to say, but Brynn retracted before Robby could come up with anything.

"Not Sheila, I meant Lisa," Brynn said, blushing.

"Okay," Robby said. "You track her down and let her know when we get up there."

The radio cut into their conversation. "You guys want to meet us up here?" Pete's voice asked from the radio.

"Be right there," Brad said. Robby and Brynn heard the wind whispering behind Brad's voice. A second later they saw him walk by the cab of their tractor. He was headed towards the front of the line.

"Yes, we'll be there in a minute or two. This is Robby and Brynn," Robby said.

The others chimed in soon after.

The cold air on his face woke him up better than the soda. Robby enjoyed the sensation even though the night was uncomfortably dark. Robby and Brynn moved in Brad's wide tracks. As they passed by Nate's trailer of corpses, Robby listened to the tarp flapping in the night wind. They found a pool of darkness between the tractors; a spot where the headlights from their own tractor were blocked by the stack of bodies, and they hadn't yet passed into the grace of the running lights of Nate's tractor. Here, the wind seemed stronger, and the flapping from the tarp a little louder. Robby felt Brynn move closer behind him when the tips of Brynn's snowshoes tripped up the tails of his.

"Sorry," Brynn whispered into the wind.

"You want to jog?" Robby asked.

"Yes," Brynn said.

They shuffled faster. The snow here was easier to walk on. The shoes only seemed to disturb the top few inches of snow and didn't sink down at all. On the island, snow was shoveled or plowed so fast they never saw much call for snowshoes, but Robby had learned the trick at his grandmother's house. Robby relaxed a little when he saw Nate standing near the back of his tractor's cab. Nate was emptying a blue jug of fuel into the tractor's tank.

"You coming?" Robby asked.

"Yup," Nate said. They waited for him while he finished his task and then climbed down into the snow. "You guys go first and I'll walk in your tracks."

The three headed up the line of tractors, passing into the darkness alongside Romie's sled. Robby stayed in front, picking out Brad's tracks with his headlamp.

"I don't think you guys need those," Nate said.

"Need what?" Robby asked.

"Those shoes," Nate said. "Look."

Robby turned back, aware of the sled full of corpses to his side, and annoyed at the delay in the darkness. Nate was using his foot to sweep away the snow from a small area. Robby and Brynn huddled around him to see his discovery. Under about ten inches of powder, a thick, clear layer of ice supported them. When all the snow was cleared away, the ice looked like glass over pure blackness.

"Cool," Brynn said. His hands flew to the straps on his shoes and he shed them with quick motions. With his shoes off, he ran off to the north towards the bobbing headlamps of the rest of the group.

"He has to pee," Robby said to Nate. "He wants Lisa to take him."

"I figured," Nate said. "Let's catch up. These bodies are

creepy."

Nate picked up Brynn's snowshoes and Robby removed his own. They jogged the length of three trailers to find Romie, Lisa, and Christine talking to Brynn. The women decided to head out together to heed nature's call. Nate leaned Brynn's snowshoes against the tracks of the tractor, next to where the women had leaned theirs.

Nate and Robby continued on to meet up with Pete and Brad. They didn't make it very far. After only a dozen steps, they stopped when the wind brought them Romie's scream. The wind also kicked up a swirl of snow, so they couldn't spot the group.

"Brynn!" Nate shouted, but his voice was swallowed by the gust.

Nate sprinted away from the convoy on a diagonal to intercept the group. Robby followed. All he could see ahead of him was the reflection of his lamp in the big flakes of snow. Robby reached up and covered his lamp so he could follow the dim glow of Nate's light ahead of him. The wind brought another panicked cry from the women. Robby couldn't tell who's voice it was.

When Robby caught up with Nate, the man had reached the group. Brynn and Christine were on their knees in the snow. Lisa was on her stomach between them. Nate was straddling Lisa, and the two of them were reaching down into the snow. Robby came up alongside Christine and followed her gaze down.

Lisa and Nate were gripping Romie's hands. Romie was so deep into the snow that only her hands projected up above the loose powder.

"Pull!" Nate said.

"I'm trying," Lisa said.

"What happened?" Robby asked Christine.

Christine didn't answer. She was trying to lean down far enough to grab Romie's jacket. Christine withdrew, pulled off her glove and managed to get a grip on a piece of fabric. On the other side, Brynn tried to help too, but he couldn't reach far enough. Robby circled and took Brynn's place. The four of them managed to tug Romie up onto the ledge of ice. Everyone gasped for air by the time they got her to safety.

Romie was still panting when she started talking. "The ice... It just *ends* there. One second—good footing. The next..."

Robby still wore his snowshoes strapped to his back. He removed one and began tapping out a line in the snow, scraping the powder away from the edge of the ice. He discovered the ledge of ice ran in the same direction as the highway they'd been following with their tractors. Beyond the ledge, the snow was so light and unpacked that it wouldn't support any weight. He couldn't even lay his snowshoe down on the loose snow without it immediately sinking in under its own weight.

Robby left one of his snowshoes with the women and he and Nate took the other to go find Brad and Pete.

They followed Brad's footprints and were halfway up Pete's sled when the lights ahead on Pete's tractor went dark.

"What now?" Nate said, sighing.

Robby and Nate began to jog. They only slowed when they reached the front of the tractor. There they found Pete and Brad leaning up against the front grill. Their headlamps were out.

"What the hell are you doing in the dark?" Nate asked.

"Turn out your lights and see," Pete said. He shielded his eyes against Robby's light as Robby looked him in the eye.

When they switched their lights off, Robby's young eyes adjusted quickly. Nate took several seconds longer to see. Far off on the horizon, on the far edge of the sky, a soft yellow glow lit up the clouds.

"Is it a fire?" asked Nate.

"Could be," Pete said. "If there was anything to burn."

"No," Robby said. "Not fire. That's where we're headed."

"If you like that, you're going to love this," Brad said.

"What?" asked Nate.

"One more second," Brad said. "Keep watching."

The blue light began as a far off glimmer. It looked like a blue shadow of the yellow light on the horizon, but it swelled and travelled towards them. It was barely visible. In fact, when Robby looked directly at the blue glow it seemed to disappear. He only saw it if he looked to the side and experienced the blue glow in his peripheral vision. But it was definitely there. He was sure because it was moving towards them.

"Oh shit," Nate said when he realized the light was about to overtake their position. Nate scrambled back and pushed himself up on the grill of the tractor as it lit up beneath their feet.

"It's the highway," Pete said. "If you compare its path to the map, the glow follows the highway exactly. I think it's coming from the ice."

"It's the circulatory system you described, isn't it, Robby?" Brad asked.

"Yes," Robby said.

"Is it safe to travel on the ice?" asked Pete.

"It's not safe to leave," Nate said.

Nate described Romie's discovery at the edge of the highway.

Pete voiced a concern. "The GPS is only moderately accurate, and mine has been cutting out frequently..."

"Same here," Brad said.

"And if we slip off the edge of the ice, we might just plunge fifty feet into loose snow. We're going to have to send somebody out ahead on foot to make sure we stay on the ice."

"We don't have much time," Robby said.

"Why?" asked Pete. "I don't want to be out here forever, but what's so pressing I have to risk my neck?"

"I'd rather not say," Robby said. "I'll take the front tractor."

"That's not what I mean," Pete said. "I'd rather have none of us take the risk."

"I understand," Robby said.

"We can follow the light," Brad said. "If the blue glow is coming from the ice, then all we have to do is turn off all our lights and follow the light."

"It's periodic, but it does come often enough. We might be able to follow it," Pete said.

"I should still take the lead," Robby said. "My eyes are sensitive. I have the best night-vision."

"But I'm the best at driving these rigs," Pete said.

"Pete drives and Robby navigates," Nate said. "Brynn can drive alone. If we do want to navigate by the light coming off the ice, we better get it done while it's still dark out. We don't have time to lose, and we can't afford to screw this up."

"I don't like it," Brad said. "I can hang back a little so I'll know if Brynn veers off course, but what can I do about it? What if he falls asleep?"

"Just jump on the radio," Nate said.

"Yeah, I guess," Brad said. "I still don't like it."

"Let's top off the tanks while we're stopped," Nate said.

"Definitely," Brad said.

✪ ✪ ✪ ✪ ✪

As they steered carefully north, the pulses of light from the ice increased in frequency, but the sky grew lighter with each passing mile, so seeing the road remained difficult.

"A little left," Robby said.

He and Pete sat in the dark in the cab of the tractor. All the lights—inside and out—were off. The only illumination inside the vehicle was from the yellow glow on the horizon and the faint blue pulses of light from the ice on the highway. Robby took over the duty of starting the roll calls. Every five minutes he would announce his name and wait for each driver to respond. He listened to each of their voices, trying to detect if any were close to drifting off.

The blue glow of the ice was so faint that Robby invested all of his attention. Between pulses he imagined he still saw the light, like his retinas burned with its image. On the horizon, the glow either shifted color, or just appeared different, because it seemed almost white. A flat, horizontal line marked the horizon. Above the line, the clouds reflected the light; below it, the snow stretched out in a dusty gray plane, broken only by the pulses of blue from the ice. Robby concentrated on nothing but the path of the blue pulse. He must have been ignoring his other senses, because Pete surprised him with a question.

"What's that noise, Robby? You hear it?" Pete asked.

Robby hadn't heard, but now he did. The noise was rhythmic, and sounded like a crunch, like potato chips. Each second, in perfect time—crunch, crunch, crunch. After one more pulse to guarantee they were still on-course, Robby spun to look out the back window. His eyes, well-adjusted to the dark, picked out the movement. The sound came from the legs of one of the corpses; the crunch was the crinkling of the tarp as the legs thrust against it. Strapped down horizontally, the corpse appeared to be marching in place.

The radio erupted with Nate's voice. "Hey guys, we got a problem."

"Here too," Romie's voice chimed in.

Suddenly they were all talking. Robby was still looking out the back window, unable to take his eyes from the moving legs. Pete grabbed the radio and cut through the clutter of voices.

"One at a time, please," he yelled. "Nate, go ahead."

"I think some of these dead are starting to not be so dead," Nate said. The radio chirped as he finished his statement.

"What the hell do you mean?" Pete asked over the radio.

"One of them has started to move around. He's still strapped in, but he's moving," Nate said.

"Here too," Romie said.

Christine, Lisa, and Brad all confirmed with their own observations. Brynn stayed silent.

Pete began to slow down the tractor.

"No! Don't stop," Robby said. "Go faster. We have to get them to the source." He leaned forward and resumed his effort to spot the path.

Pete spared a glance at Robby and then lifted the radio. He thumbed the talk-switch. "We're going to speed up and try to get this thing finished before everything goes sideways."

He heard no response for a few seconds.

"Are you serious, Pete?" Lisa asked over the radio.

"Yes," Pete said. He engaged the throttle and the tractor began to pick up speed. Their acceleration hitched unevenly—the tracks skittered on the ice as they tried to pick up speed. The blue streak of ice ahead took a long, sweeping curve to the right. They saw a slight shadow to the right of their path. The ice stood a little higher than the surrounding snow, making it easier for Pete to steer on top of the shelf of ice.

A light in the mirror caught Pete's eye.

"Robby," he said, "what's going on back there?"

Robby tore his eyes from the path reluctantly and followed Pete's gaze to the side-mounted mirror. In the darkness behind them, the line of tractors and sleds swept back in an arc. All were dark—lights off—except the second to last. On that tractor, just the yellow running lights were on, and the tractor veered out of line a bit. As far as Robby could tell, the tractor wasn't in any immediate danger of slipping off the ice shelf, but it would be if it continued to veer.

"That's Brynn's tractor," Robby said. He picked up the radio from the seat beside Pete. "Brynn, are you okay? What's going on back there?"

They heard no response.

"Brad? Can you see anything?" Robby asked.

"Nothing but the back of Brynn's trailer," Brad said. "What's going on?"

"Brynn is veering to the right. Brynn, can you hear me? Brad, slow down a little so you can follow our tracks," Robby said.

Nate's voice broke in over the radio. "Brynn? Listen up—I'm going to scuttle my tractor. I'll be there in a minute. You hold on."

"Nate, don't!" Robby shouted. "We need you in your tractor. We've got the extra person. I'll go find out what's up with Brynn."

"Do something quick, or I will," Nate said.

Robby dropped the radio to his lap.

"I have to go back there," Robby said to Pete.

"What? How?" asked Pete.

"We're not going fast," Robby said. "I'll jump out and then run alongside."

"It might not look fast, but there's no way you could keep up running on ice and snow. You'd slip and get chewed under by the tracks," Pete said. "The ice looks wide enough. We could let the others pass us. Look—you can even see the sides of the road now. The snow drops off on either side. I'm not sure we're still on the highway, but the ice shelf is fairly obvious."

"What about the snowmobile?" Robby asked. Each sled carried a snowmobile strapped to the back, just behind the stacks of bodies.

"You'll never get back there while we're moving, and it's lashed sideways. We have to stop, set up the ramps to the side, and then what? You can ride up next to Brynn's trailer, but how will you transfer to the tractor? It's too high up to climb into the cab from a moving snowmobile."

"We have to do something fast," Robby said.

"Tell the others to pass," Pete said.

Robby picked up the radio and took a deep breath. He held up the radio with one hand and reached the other in his jacket pocket to touch the Volvo mirror he carried. "Christine, you're going to take the lead. Pass us on the right when we move left. You'll be able to see the edge of the road. There's a shadow there. Stay away from the edge and keep your speed even as you pass. Got it?"

"I just keep following the blue ice?" asked Christine.

"Yes," Robby said. "Everyone else, just pass us on the right. Brad, you're going to stay behind Brynn. Drop back a bit so you can stop if something happens."

"Okay," Brad said.

"Good luck," Lisa said.

Pete started moving to the left as soon as Robby got on the radio. The sled lurched behind them and shook the tractor as he shifted its bulk towards the left edge of the ice. Robby's stomach rose and flopped as Pete straightened the tractor again. The sled kept moving left and tugged at the back of the tractor as Pete corrected their direction. Once moved over, Pete dropped their speed. Christine began to pull past them a few seconds later.

"Just follow the shadow, Christine, and move back to the center when I let you know," Robby said. He watched her trailer full of corpses pull by before giving her the okay. Right behind her, Lisa's tractor came into view. Romie was hanging back a little. She seemed to have more trouble than the others keeping her tractor to the edge of the ice and on-course. She swerved towards Robby and Pete a couple of times, and Pete cursed her under his breath.

"Brynn, are you there? We're coming," Robby said.

"Brynn's still on the road," Brad said. "Just barely, but still on."

When Romie finally moved by, Robby let her know on the

radio so she could move back to the center of the road again. Even that move seemed to cause her trouble. Romie's sled sloshed back and forth. She overcorrected her skid and then finally found her mark.

Nate kept abreast of Pete and Robby while Romie weaved back and forth. When he saw enough room, he waved to Robby and then accelerated his tractor fast, pulling up to the back of Romie's sled. When everyone passed, Robby finally had a clear view out his side mirror. Brynn's tractor chugged along with its running lights on, hugging the right side of the ice. Pete slowed to let Brynn's tractor catch up and then he matched its speed.

Robby pressed his face against his window as Pete maneuvered to get as close to Brynn as possible. With only the running lights and the faint glow from the sky, it was difficult to be sure, but Robby thought he saw the tarp covering the bodies at the front of Brynn's sled slipping loose from its straps. It fluttered back. As they drew even closer, Robby saw several of the bodies spilling forward from their stack.

"Tell me how much space I've got," Pete said. The sleds were a little wider than the tractors, so Pete couldn't precisely judge how close he could get before the sleds would collide. Robby gave him a countdown and Pete closed the distance.

With the sleds nearly touching Robby judged the distance between the tractors. He nodded to Pete and climbed out on the running board, slipping past the door before closing it behind him. Nobody sat in the driver's seat of Brynn's tractor.

Pete lowered the window and yelled to be heard over the rolling, clinking tracks. "Reach out and grab the mirror if you can."

Robby tested his weight on the mirror mounted to his own tractor before stretching out for the other one. It was mounted on a long arm to give visibility around the wide sled. Pete had mounted the extra mirrors himself; Robby hoped he'd done it well. Beneath him, the tracks churned up the loose snow. He watched them roll as he reached for Brynn's mirror. The gap between the tractors expanded and shrank. At their closest, Robby's gloved fingers brushed the mirror on Brynn's tractor. He would need several more inches to grip the support bar. Robby pulled his hand back and removed his glove with his teeth.

Robby took a deep breath around the glove in his mouth and let go of his own mirror. He pushed up onto his toes and let himself fall towards Brynn's tractor. His fingers locked around the cold steel and he jumped. The mirror's support bent under his weight, but his feet landed on Brynn's running board and he swung his torso up. Brynn's window was closed, so Robby found nothing to grab. Robby wrapped both hands around the mirror and tried to balance himself as he reached for the handle.

The door was locked, and the tractor looked empty. The throttle was set and locked.

The glove tumbled from his teeth and hit the tracks of the tractor. The tracks rolled forward and threw the glove into the snow before rolling over and chewing it up underneath. Robby banged on the window.

"Brynn! Brynn, are you in there?" Robby yelled.

Over his shoulder, Robby noticed Pete steering away from Brynn's tractor.

"Robby," Pete shouted. Robby heard Pete's voice from two directions—yelled over the sound of the tractors from behind him, and coming from the radio on the seat of Brynn's tractor. "You're about to go over the edge. You have to jump."

The running board shifted under Robby's feet. The sled began to shift off the side of the ice-ledge, tugging the tractor to the side. Robby banged his naked hand against the glass, cursing himself for not bringing something to break the window.

"Jump, Robby," Pete yelled.

Robby looked down at the snow rolling past beneath him. The tractor jerked again and he nearly lost his grip. He'd have to jump far enough so the sled wouldn't run him over as it passed.

"Brynn!" he yelled, slapping at the glass one last time. His bare hand ached in the cold. "If you're in there you have to get out. This whole thing is about to go over the edge."

Robby turned away from the door and set his legs for the jump. Movement caught the corner of his eye and Robby turned to see Brynn's tiny hand appearing to unlock the driver's door of the dark cab. Robby lost no time—he yanked on the door and fell backwards, tugging the door open. All his strength pulled him around the door and up into the driver's seat. Robby unlocked the throttle and eased it back to stop the rig. The tractor shuddered and groaned as the heavy sled kept slipping over the edge, dragging the tractor with it.

The radio erupted with Pete's voice. "Robby, more throttle. Gentle acceleration. You're still slipping."

He nudged the throttle forward and the grinding and shaking intensified. He could feel the tracks slipping on the ice, failing to get traction. Robby clamped his jaw and pushed the throttle a little farther.

"That's it." Pete's voice was nearly drowned out by the grinding. "Keep increasing speed, and don't try to steer left at all. Straight forward."

As the sled's runner began to scrape its way back onto the edge of the ice, the tracks dug in and the tractor bucked with the exertion.

"Robby," Brynn whispered. His voice came from the dark well behind the seat.

The tractor shook and rumbled. The engine groaned under the load. When the sled's runners reclaimed purchase on the ice, the load shifted to the left, twisting the tractor and slamming Robby into the door. With the friction suddenly removed, the tractor shot forward. Robby wrestled the tractor to the left, away from the edge of the ice. They swung left and then overcorrected back to the right when they almost collided with Pete.

"You did it!" Pete called over the radio. "Nice job."

"Good work, Robby," Nate said. "Is Brynn there? Is Brynn okay?"

Robby turned on the lights inside the cab.

"Brynn? Are you okay?" Robby asked. He turned and looked down to find him curled up in the space where they'd packed their food and extra gear. He gripped his knees to his chest and tucked his head down to make himself into a little ball.

"What's wrong?" Robby asked.

"They've come for me," Brynn said. He pointed up.

Robby lifted his gaze towards the back window of the cab. He scrambled backwards away from the rear window, throwing his body against the dashboard of the tractor. His numb hand accidentally landed on a switch, killing the interior lights.

The image from the window was still burned in his eyes—a dozen or so eyeless faces were pressed against the glass. Robby fumbled with the switch until lights inside the cab came back on. The dead didn't respond to the light, but they were moving. Their hands groped and slid across the surface of the glass. Some pressed their lips against the window, giving Robby an intimate look at the insides of their mouths. All of them, whether their faces were pressed against the glass or not, were smiling with big, toothy grins.

Robby remembered the throttle just as Pete's voice came over the radio. "Robby, what are you doing? You're headed for the edge again."

He spun and sat on the very edge of the seat and regained control of the tractor's heading.

"It's okay, Brynn," Robby said, trying to get control enough to keep his voice from shaking. "They're not trying to get us. They're not real people, they're just shells."

Robby picked up the radio. "Brynn's fine. Everything's under control here. One of the straps gave way and we've got some... um..."

"Should we stop?" Brad radioed from behind.

"No," Robby said. "Keep going as fast as we can. We have to get to the light."

"Put Brynn on the radio," Nate said.

Robby handed the radio down to Brynn. He didn't look around to see if Brynn was reaching to take it. He didn't want to risk looking at those hungry, eyeless, grinning faces. Brynn took the radio from his hand. When the boy's hand brushed his, the skin on Robby's hand crawled and sent a ripple of goosebumps up through his arm.

Nate's voice came over the radio. "Brynn? Are you there, Brynn?"

After several long seconds, Robby heard the click of the send button and Brynn's soft voice whispering into the radio.

"I can't hear what you're saying," Nate said, cutting in.

"They're here for me," Brynn whispered louder. "You said they wouldn't be able to get me, but they're here for me."

"I'm so sorry," Nate said. "You're okay now. Robby is there. He's going to take care of you."

"He's just a boy," Brynn said. "He talks like a grownup, but he's just a boy."

"He's smart," Nate said. His voice sounded small over the radio; not nearly as strong as he sounded in person. "Don't you worry. We're almost there and then we'll be together again. I'm sorry. I shouldn't have left you on your own."

"You couldn't have done anything," Brynn whispered. "They're all here for me."

Up ahead, Pete pulled up behind Nate. Robby increased his speed until they re-formed their convoy.

Pete's voice cut into the conversation. "How's it going up front? Christine, are you okay? Still keeping to the center?"

"Yes," Christine said after a few seconds. She left space between her phrases, like she expected someone to cut in. "It's getting easier to follow the ice. There's not as much snow up ahead."

As they moved forward, Robby became aware of what Christine meant. Not only was the snow's depth falling away on either side of the ice, but the thin layer of snow on top of the ice was decreasing as well. The miles rolled by under their tracks and the landscape changed. The snow on either side of the ice fell away and they drove their tractors down the middle of a wide path of blue-glowing ice. Robby's shoulders ached, but he couldn't stop hunching them forward. He would take a deep breath and try to relax his muscles, but soon they'd be bunched up again, burning hot from tension. Under the tarp on the back of Pete's sled, the corpses writhed and squirmed, held down by the heavy strap. Here and there an arm would wrestle its way out of captivity and flop around. Robby sat on his bare hand until it warmed up, and then kept sitting on it. Occasionally the radio in Brynn's hands would crackle to life and the team announced their status, but it happened less and less often.

Eventually, Christine broke the monotony.

"I can see the top of the thing that's giving off the light," Christine said. "It's like a ball, mostly under the ice. It's so pretty, but so cold. It's bright, but not as bright as the sun. You can look right at it. What should I do?"

Robby reached back and Brynn put the radio into his hand.

"Christine?" Robby asked. "Does the ice keep going right to the edge of the ball?"

"Yes," she said. "As far as I can see."

Through the side windows of the tractor, Robby saw other paths made of ice, all converging ahead of the tractors. They all pulsed at once with the same blue glow. Somewhere down in the snow, perpendicular to their road of ice, a line of orange light pulsed just before the blue. The orange light flared again just as Robby's tractor passed over it. Robby held his breath; nothing unusual happened.

Robby lost track of time. It seemed like only minutes had elapsed, but it must have been longer when Christine spoke again. "I don't think I can go any farther. The hill is too steep."

Robby slowed his tractor. He was quickly approaching the rear of Pete's sled.

They came to a stop on the plateau of ice.

"Everyone meet up front," Robby said. "Be careful."

He reached for the door handle and nearly leapt from the tractor when the hand grabbed his arm. It was Brynn.

"Don't leave me," he whispered.

"We have to go," Robby said. "You come with me."

"I don't want to go out there," Brynn said.

"Then I'm leaving you," he said. "Come on."

Brynn let Robby pull him from behind the seat. He covered his eyes and wouldn't look through the back window at the squirming bodies pressed against the glass. Robby left the engine running. Over the low idle he heard their wet hands squeaking against the window.

Brad jogged up beside their tractor when they jumped down past the tracks. Robby slipped on the ice, but Brynn caught his arm and helped him find his balance. They joined Brad and soon met Nate, who was running back to meet Brynn. When he reached them, Nate swept Brynn into a hug and then pulled him by the hand up to meet the others.

Robby raised his arm to shield his eyes as he came around Christine's crooked tractor and joined the group who were looking at the glowing ball in the distance. Robby understood why Christine stopped, and was glad she did. Just in front of her tractor, the ice began to slope down, and it looked weaker. Its surface was a spider web of holes and cracks. In the center of the giant ice crater, sat the top half of a giant ball of light. Its scale was impossible to judge because there was nothing else near to gauge its size against, but Robby guessed it must be at least a quarter mile in diameter.

Christine was right—it was beautiful, and cold, and you could look directly at it. In fact, Robby felt compelled to look directly at it. He began to lower his arm. To his side, Christine was reaching out towards the ball.

"Dad?" she said.

Robby turned away. He grabbed the jacket nearest to him and tugged. It turned out to be Pete's arm.

"Don't look at it," he said.

"What? Why?" asked Pete. He looked at Robby and blinked hard several times. "God, it's like that thing burned my eyes. It's all I can see."

"We have to let them loose," Robby said, pointing towards the sled.

Under the tight straps the dead were a flopping, wiggling pile, struggling to get free.

Pete rubbed his eyes while Robby reached out for more of the group. He tugged on Romie's sleeve and grabbed Lisa by the hand. They turned away from the burning ball reluctantly and listened to Robby's commands. Pete moved towards the first sled, and Romie followed behind, but Lisa couldn't mask her fear. She didn't want to go near the pile of wriggling bodies.

"Then get the others to stop looking at the light. They're hypnotized by it," Robby said.

Pete tugged at the clasp to release the first strap. Robby ran around the front of the tractor so he could pull the strap free from the other side.

"Dad?" Christine asked again as Robby ran by her.

Robby slipped while rounding the far corner of the tractor. He landed with his bare hand on the sharp ice. It sliced a flap of skin from his palm and the pain shot up his arm. When he reached the straps, he saw the first two were loose. Robby tugged on one, pulling it hand-over-hand over the top of the pile. Blood flowed from his hand, down into the sleeve of his parka. Before he could move to the second strap, bodies toppled from sides of the pile, bringing the tarp with them. Robby scrambled backwards, away from the trailer, looking over his shoulder to be sure he didn't slip down the side of the slippery ice embankment.

The first corpse to land, a bald man dressed in a pinstripe suit, flailed its arms and spun towards Robby.

Robby tripped and landed on his butt on the cold ice. The corpse pushed to its feet and spun towards the glowing ball of light. Robby watched it out of the corner of his eye to make sure it wasn't coming for him. A cascade of bodies followed quickly on the heels of the bald man. The second strap freed itself and the tarp folded down under the weight of falling corpses. They landed on the ice and clawed over each other to begin their pilgrimage to the burning light.

Robby sprung to his feet and moved down to the third and fourth straps. This time he managed to move farther away before the bodies started falling. He glanced under the sled and saw a similar avalanche of corpses falling on the other side. Romie and Pete were working their way towards the back of the sled, freeing the straps. All the tarps fell on Robby's side of the sled, and the corpses couldn't gain traction on the slippery plastic surface. With the last tarp, Robby pulled it out of the way just after he pulled the straps, so the bodies would land on the ice.

Romie came around the rear of the sled.

"You need help over here? Pete's all set with the straps," Romie said.

"Yes, but I'm worried about the others," Robby said. "Did Lisa get them?"

"I thought she was with you," Romie said. "You're bleeding, you know."

"I know," Robby said. "Can you pull the tarps out of the way? I want to go check on the others."

"Sure," Romie said. She moved towards the side of the sled. She called back over her shoulder. "Get a glove on your hand."

"Yeah, right," Robby said under his breath as he ran towards the other side of the sled. He tried to stop, but wound up sliding right into a pair of elderly corpses who popped out from behind Lisa's tractor just as Robby came around the corner. He fell backwards as he hit them. He took their legs out and they landed right on top of him. The dead woman's smiling, eyeless face was just inches from Robby as he tried to push and kick his way from under her. She wore nothing but a nightgown, and the male corpse was dressed in green coveralls. Robby could smell her old lady perfume mixed with urine and sweat, which combined to smell like rancid chicken soup.

He pushed his way free in time for a barefoot corpse to step on his bleeding hand. Robby pulled his hand back and tore the flap of skin even more. He clutched his hand to his chest and regained his feet to skitter away from the migrating corpses. Looking back he saw the procession coming from the loose pile on Brynn's trailer.

When Robby arrived at the front of the line, he couldn't find his group. Shielding his eyes from the light, Robby looked down the slope of the ice. The light's cold glow beckoned to him to lower his hands, but Robby held them up, focusing on the throbbing of the gash on his right hand to keep him focused on reality. Silhouetted by the bright light, he couldn't make out individuals, just a group of people marching down the icy slope. One figure was running up the ice, crunching through the cracked surface.

"Robby," the figure called. It was Brad.

"Where are the others?" Robby asked.

"I don't know," Brad said. "Down there, I guess. It makes you slip down into your memories. It's like the rock monster. You just get consumed by the past."

"We have to get them before they get to the light," Robby said.

"We can't," Brad said. "One look and you're trapped."

"Just look straight down then," Robby said. He pulled his hood up over his hat and used it to shield his eyes. Then, he looked down and followed the line of broken ice, shattered like glass, left by the marching feet of his friends. He moved as fast as he dared, not wanting to fall again on his lacerated hand or bruised backside. He heard Brad tromping behind him. Robby recognized Lisa's purple boots and reached out for the back of her jacket. He yanked her back and yelled her name.

"They're all here," Lisa said. She slapped at Robby's hand and tried to push away from him.

"Lisa, look away," Robby yelled. "Turn around." He grabbed her waist and tried to spin her around, but she was determined to keep moving towards the light.

"No," Lisa said. "They're all here. Everyone. I belong here."

"It's not your time yet," Robby said. He reached up and wrapped a hand over her eyes. As soon as she couldn't see the light, she became docile. Robby turned her and pointed her up the hill towards the tractor. He spoke directly into her ear. "Don't turn around. Don't look at the light. Just get back to the tractors and don't look back."

"Okay, Robby," she said. "I understand."

Brad moved farther down the hill to catch up with Nate and Brynn. They were holding hands and walking towards the light. Brad took off his jacket, threw it over Nate's head, and forced Brynn to turn around. Nate understood immediately. He picked up Brynn, clutched him to his chest and turned around.

Robby ran down the hill calling Christine's name. She didn't answer and her footprints were jumbled with those of dozens of corpses.

"Christine?" Robby called. "Where are you?"

Brad caught up with Robby and they shuffled along together, looking straight down and hoping to bump into the final member of their party. When Robby stopped and turned back uphill, Brad stopped as well.

"If I get entranced, knock this out of my hand," Robby said. He reached into his jacket pocket and pulled out the Volvo visor mirror. He aimed it over his shoulder so he could scan for

Christine.

"Robby? Are you still with me?" Brad asked.

"Yes," Robby said. "The reflection isn't affecting me."

"Do you see her?" Brad asked.

"No, not yet," Robby said. "Wait, I think that's her. I'm not sure."

"Let me see," Brad said. He reached for the mirror, but Robby wouldn't relinquish it. He tilted it so Brad could see and Brad looked over Robby's shoulder to get a better look.

"Yes, that's her," Brad said. "See the blood stain on her sleeve?"

"Okay," Robby said. He walked backwards, holding the mirror and using it to navigate towards Christine. When they got close enough, he and Brad spun, grabbing Christine by the shoulders and wrestling her away from her march.

"Let go!" she screamed.

"No Christine," Brad said. "You're hypnotized by the light. You can't look at it, or you'll walk right into it."

"Maybe I want to walk into it. Did you consider that?" asked Christine.

"What you're seeing isn't real," Brad said. "It's some kind of trick."

"There's no trick," Christine said. "Everyone I've ever cared about is in the light."

"Even so, it's not your time," Brad said.

"Says who? You? Why shouldn't it be my time?" asked Christine.

"Go up the hill and we can talk about it," Brad said.

"We're not going to let you go," Robby said.

"It's not your decision," Christine said.

"I know," Robby said. "Please?"

Behind them, down in the crater where the ball of light met the ice, a sound rang out accompanied by a flash of bright blue light. Robby couldn't decide if it sounded more like thunder, or a giant piece of paper tearing. Either way, the sound seemed to be inside his head—he felt it more than he heard it. The flash of light threw their shadows up the icy slope and reflected off a million edges of broken ice crystals.

Robby jerked the mirror back up in time to see the next flash. It erupted when one of the eyeless, lumbering corpses entered the ball of light. The corpse raised its hands with its last step and was absorbed by the ball of light. Christine clutched her hands to her ears in a fruitless attempt to muffle the sound.

Two more dead entered the light and the sound sent a double shot of pain through Robby's head. The corpses weren't deterred; they kept marching in a shuffling column towards the flashing ball of light.

Robby and Brad grabbed Christine by her arms and hauled her uphill, away from the light. They veered away from the corpses, which seemed surefooted despite their lack of eyes. Christine didn't struggle, but she twisted her head around and tried to watch the light recede as Robby and Brad dragged her up the hill. She sobbed and wailed until they reached the top, and then silent tears still leaked down her face.

The sound of corpses entering the ball of light erupted so often that it became like a constant hum instead of individual explosions.

"Everyone was in the light," Christine said to Robby. "Everyone I ever cared about."

"They'll always be there," Robby said.

Robby and Brad escorted Christine to the others who formed a small knot away from the tractors, and sleds, and throngs of dead. Pete and Romie approached and Robby ran forward to warn them to shield their eyes.

"Is that all of them?" Brad asked.

Pete answered. "There are a few dozen more still coming from the last sled. They were caught in the straps, but they got free."

"What's that smell?" asked Romie.

A sour wind from the south brought the smell of decomposition. The group faced south, looked away from the ball of light, and tried to place the source of the odor.

"It almost smells like rich soil," Brad said. "You know how it smells when you first turn it over in the spring?"

"Where's Brynn?" asked Nate. His voice rang of panic

immediately; this was no idle question.

"Brynn?" Robby called. Glancing around the group, he was careful to not look back at the ball of light.

The wind picked up and carried Robby's voice down towards the light.

Robby pulled out his mirror again.

"Oh shit," Robby said as he picked out the form of a young person sprinting and ducking between the shuffling corpses. Brynn was already halfway down the hill to the ball of light. Robby looked straight down and ran. He stretched his young legs out as far as they'd go as he ran down the ice, trying to catch Brynn before he got to the light. Before Robby saw him, he heard Brynn giggling. His voice sounded out of place as it bubbled up between crashes of thunder.

"Brynn!" Robby yelled. "Stop!"

He both heard and sensed others from his group running behind him. Nate ran by. Robby looked up to see Nate sprinting for Brynn with his arms outstretched. Robby couldn't watch Nate's progress without looking at the ball of light, so he put his head down and tried to run even faster.

"Brynn, I'm coming," Nate yelled up ahead. "Wait for me."

"Try not to look at the light, Nate," Robby yelled at the ground. "Just focus on Brynn." His voice was swallowed by tearing thunder from the ball.

Robby could tell he was getting closer to the light because his shadow was shortening underneath him. The sound crashing through him felt like it could split his skull. Feet and legs appeared in front of Robby, and he recognized Nate's boots and green pants. Robby reached for the man's hand and pulled. The thunderous sound of corpses being absorbed into the light died away and a peaceful silence settled around him.

"Nate," Robby whispered. "Did you catch up with Brynn?"

"Yes, Robby," Nate said. "He right here."

"Great," Robby said, still looking down at his feet and holding Nate's hand. "Back away from the light and let's get back to the others."

"No, Robby," Nate said. "We're *all* here. Look around you."

Robby shook his head. Cold glare from the massive ball of light glared off his cheeks and reflected off the snaps and zipper of his jacket. If he looked up at all, he knew he'd catch sight of the light and then perhaps become entranced, like the others. Instead, Robby looked to his sides, where he was surprised to find people all around him. They weren't all exploded-eye corpses, either. A man on his left wore a brown suit and white shirt. He stared up towards the light with tears streaming from his intact eyes. At his feet a toddler, wearing just a diaper and a shirt, giggled around a pacifier as it looked up towards the light. Just behind them, a dirty woman, completely naked held her hand up towards the light as if she could grip it in her fist. As Robby watched she brought her hand down to her face, like she was trying to taste the light.

Robby tugged on Nate's hand and tried to pull him backwards. Nate wouldn't budge. In fact, Nate tightened his grip and started to pull Robby forward. The grip stung Robby's lacerated hand.

"What are you doing? Let me go," Robby yelled.

"Come on, Robby," Nate said. "We're home."

Robby dug in his heels, squeezed his eyes shut, and tugged on his hand, trying to pull it from Nate's. The man locked an iron grip on his hand. Pain flared from Robby's palm as blood began to ooze from his recent wound. Finally, his hand popped free and Robby fell sprawling to his back, with his arm up to shield his eyes from the light. He flipped over and pushed to his feet, fighting against a thick stream of people, who walked towards the light.

He saw one or two corpses with missing eyes, grinning as they trudged ahead, but mostly Robby saw normal-looking men and women of all ages, locked in shuffling trances. They walked shoulder-to-shoulder, and Robby squeezed between them to make his retreat. He burst through a line of tall men, dressed in identical gray pants and white shirts, and finally got a glimpse of the magnitude of the mass of people trudging towards the light. The landscape sloped upwards from the light and people shuffled towards him as far as he could see. He spun as far as he dared to the left and right, and saw the same thing in every direction— endless people. Their faces wore broad smiles; their eyes sparkled with the light from the ball of light that drew them. Nobody spoke or made any noise. The only break in the silence was the gentle shuffle of feet.

What he didn't see was equally amazing—no snow; no road of ice; no tractor perched at the top of a hill. His adventure in central Maine transformed somehow into this climb through an endless crowd of people. Up ahead, perhaps fifty paces from Robby, a hand shot up and waved.

Robby's jaw fell open as the shout carried through the thick air.

"Robby!"

It was his father's voice calling and his father's hand waving. Robby shut his eyes fast, but before he did he saw that his father was flanked by his mother on one side and grandmother on the other. They all smiled at him with the same blank look.

"No, no, no," Robby said as he shook his head. Tears leaked out of his squeezed-shut eyes. He both waited to hear his father's voice again and prayed it wouldn't come. Robby reached out and pulled himself through the crowd, pushing through the shifting flow of people. They didn't care. Their rapture took all their attention away from Robby plowing the wrong way through their migration.

"No, no, no, no," Robby repeated again and again as his hands turned to fists and he blindly smashed through wave after wave of people. When he ran out of people to pull against, Robby kept running with his eyes shut, now yelling, "No!"

Another earsplitting crash of thunder from behind him drove him to his knees. Robby clutched his ears, his eyes still shut, and collapsed to the ground. He curled up in a ball as two more explosions burst through his head.

"Robby? Robby?" a voice asked.

Robby shook his head and some part of him registered the cold surface pressed against his face.

"Let's go, Robby. We should get moving," the voice said.

It took Robby a second to recognized Brad's voice. He opened his eyes slowly, not quite willing to trust his ears.

Brad was holding out his mirror.

"You dropped this," Brad said. "The ball of light looks like it's collapsing. We should go."

Robby took the mirror and held it up. It took a second to orient himself, and then another to understand what he was seeing. Only a couple of eyeless people still marched towards the light, and they had farther to go than their predecessors. The ball shrank down and developed continents of splotchy brown spots, which swam over its surface. Another peal of thunder rolled across the ice and blue light flashed as an eyeless corpse merged with the light. Robby saw the ball expand a tiny amount and then contract as it absorbed the body. The massive throng of smiling, migrating people was gone, replaced again with the cold icy road.

Robby let Brad help him to his feet and they jogged up the slope towards the tractors.

✪ ✪ ✪ ✪ ✪

At the top of the hill they found Pete, Romie, and Lisa at the back of the second sled. They had one snowmobile on the ice and were wrestling a second down from a trailer.

"Robby!" Lisa shouted. She grabbed Robby up into a big hug. "We didn't think you were going to come back out."

"Come back out of what?" Robby asked.

"We need to pull down a third snowmobile," Pete said. "We shouldn't ride three on one of these."

"It's okay, Pete," Romie said. "We've made it this long. What's makes you think we don't have time to pull another snowmobile."

"Who knows how much time we've got?" asked Pete. "We're rolling the dice, is all I'm saying. After all this, we're just standing around?"

"Then get moving," Romie said. "I'll finish unhooking this one. You and Brad get down to the next one."

Brad and Pete took off down the ice and doubled their pace when they heard the next blast from down the hill. The sound crashed louder, and rumbled longer, than the earlier explosions. Lisa straddled a snowmobile and motioned for Robby to get on behind her. Romie fired up the other one and drove it down the ramp to the ice. Together, they caught up with Pete and Brad and helped them unstrap the third snowmobile. Soon, without any gear except what Pete lashed to the snowmobiles before they left Portland, the five people streaked away on their snowmobiles.

Robby rode behind Lisa. He gripped her around the waist, and looked back over his shoulder for the first few miles. He tucked his gloveless hand in a fold of her jacket. The glow from the ball of light was barely visible against the clouds now. Somewhere on the other side of the clouds the sun rose. Robby thought he saw a couple more blue flashes radiating from under the ice, but it was hard to tell if it was real or just an illusion created by his over-tired eyes.

Soon, Robby rested his head against Lisa's shoulder and hoped she wasn't as tired as he was. It had been a long night of fighting for their lives and driving. It would be so easy now to just drift off to sleep and lose control of the snowmobile. Robby thought he should offer to switch positions with Lisa and take over the driving for a while, but before he could will himself to tap her on the shoulder, he nodded off.

✪ ✪ ✪ ✪ ✪

"Where are we?" Robby asked.

"Welcome back to the Dead Ferret," Brad said. "You've been here before. In fact, this is where I first met you, remember?"

"Vaguely," Robby said. He sat up on the couch and glanced around the dim living room. His boots, glove, hat, and jacket had been removed, but he was still dressed. Someone had draped a warm wool blanket over him and in the corner a kerosene stove radiated heat. "We're here because of Buster and Glen?"

"Yes," Brad said. "We figured it might not be safe over at the apartments. We don't know if there are friends of those guys still wandering around."

"Where's Christine?" Robby asked. "She wasn't with us on the snowmobiles."

Brad looked down at the floor. He was sitting in the chair over by the big window. "She went in right after you. With all the confusion, I guess we forgot to hold her back. As soon as nobody was looking, she went."

"That's too bad," Robby said.

"She was troubled," Brad said.

"Where are the others?" Robby asked.

"They're getting some food together," Brad said. "I didn't leave much to eat here."

"You'd think they'd be tired," Robby said.

"They were. We all were. We left the snowmobiles out on the highway and Pete carried you over here. Then we slept most of the day. We ate what was left of the food and slept the night through. You never woke up through any of it. You're finishing up about a twenty-four hour nap."

"Really?" Robby asked. "That's hard to believe. I'm still so tired."

Brad smiled and stood up. He dug in a box and brought Robby a bottle of water and a couple granola bars.

"So what was in there?" Brad asked.

"What? In the ball of light?" Robby asked.

Brad nodded.

Robby chewed a mouth full of granola bar and washed it down before answering. "Was I really in there? I never thought I actually went in."

"Nobody saw you go in," Brad said. "I was still coming down the hill and I was looking at the ice when I found your mirror. I picked it up and scanned all around and I didn't see you anywhere. That's when I saw Christine go in. She mingled with a bunch of the dead people and slipped right by me. I sat there for a long time waiting to see what would happen. Pete and the others went up to get the snowmobiles ready because we all thought it was all over. Then, right before the last of the eyeless people went in, you came out, yelling 'No, no, no.' So what were you yelling at?"

Robby shut his eyes and remembered his time in the big crowd of people.

When he spoke again, his voice was lower and sadder than Brad had ever heard it. "I was yelling at my dad. He was calling me to join him, to join my whole family, but I'm not ready to go yet. To answer your question—everyone was in there. I think everyone who ever lived and died."

"How is that possible?" Brad asked, his voice just above a whisper.

Robby shook his head.

"I understand why Christine wanted to go back," Robby said. "It's lonely to stay out here, knowing they're all inside. But it's what I have to do. We owe it to them to do what we can."

"So you think that's where people go when they die?" Brad asked. "They get absorbed into some alien creature?"

Robby shook his head and thought for a while before answering. "No. People don't get absorbed, but maybe that thing comes from where we all go."

"So it's a portal or something?" Brad asked.

"Or something," Robby said.

The door burst open and hadn't finished its swing before Pete started talking.

"Well it's a good thing we didn't go back to the apartments," Pete said. "Hey! Robby's awake."

Pete, Romie, and Lisa came through the door, each carrying plastic bags, full of boxes and cans.

"You guys have to see this," Pete said. He dropped his bags on the floor and beckoned Brad and Robby over to the door. Robby shook off his blankets and shuffled on stiff legs past Pete and out onto the porch. He shivered at the crisp air and followed Pete's pointing finger to the northern sky.

"Wow," Brad said, joining Robby on the porch. "I almost forgot what sky looked like."

To the north, a big hole had opened in the clouds and for the first time in months they could see clear blue sky.

"It's been getting bigger all morning," Pete said. "I think we'll have clear skies by the end of the day."

Lisa appeared in the threshold.

"You're going to catch your death out here," Lisa said. "At least put some shoes on."

"We'll just be a second," Robby said. The porch was covered and wide enough for a swing, but all the furniture had been removed for the winter. Robby put his hand on the railing and lowered himself to the cold brick steps. He sat on the second step and leaned back to look up at the sky. Brad brushed the dusting of snow from his side of the steps and then sat next to Robby. Behind them, Pete and Lisa went back inside and closed the door.

Brad glanced over at Robby. The young man looked wind-burned and tired.

"So the dead rose and walked through a portal to the afterlife. What crazy things we've seen. Do you think it worked? Do you think bringing all the dead bodies up to the light worked?" Brad asked.

"I don't know," Robby said. "I guess it depends on what we were trying to do."

"I thought the point was to drive that thing off the planet," Brad said. "I thought we would poison it and it would go away."

"Yeah," Robby said. "I guess I expected..." Robby squinted as the sun peeked out from behind a scraggly blanket of clouds. He stared at the sun even as it left blue-yellow trails across his retinas. Tears welled up and spilled from the corners of his squinted eyes.

"Come on," Brad said. He tapped Robby on the shoulder. "Let's go in and see what they brought back to eat."

"You go," Robby said. "I'll be there in a second."

"Okay," Brad said. He stood slowly and followed Robby's eyes back up to the patch of blue sky. He shielded his eyes from the sun and looked at the edge of the clouds. They were definitely receding —the clouds moved back like they were evaporating away from the patch of blue, rather than blowing away. Brad went inside and closed the door behind him.

Robby sat on the porch and stared at the sky.

He sat motionless until his shivering legs and icy feet drove him inside.

They each drove their own snowmobile, although they could have easily fit on two. Robby and Pete rode side by side in the lead and were followed at a reasonable distance by Lisa and Brad. Each sled carried an extra gas can and bag of gear strapped to the back. Lisa insisted on the safety precautions. She'd grown cautious in the weeks since their last trip north. She would say, "No sense in surviving the apocalypse just to die of food poisoning," or, "... just to die of pneumonia." The others humored her and each drove their own snowmobile, capable of enduring hundreds of miles and a week of camping with all the supplies she'd packed.

Pete held up a gloved hand and waved to the others before he slowed down. They had travelled about halfway along the tracks north to where they'd seen the ball of light. The sun burned bright in a flawless blue sky above them.

"I think it's melting," Pete said, pointing west towards the hills. The perfect white blanket of snow was dirtied off in the distance by the shapes of bare treetops poking through at the crest of a hill.

The group had monitored the snowpack carefully back in Portland. Although the sun was out and it seemed warmer outside, the snow hadn't receded or melted at all from the roads.

"Seems like it's a little softer, too," Brad said. He was stomping his left foot into the grainy snow to the side of packed tracks from the tractors they'd driven through weeks before.

"We'd do best to space ourselves out a bit, in case it gets unstable up ahead. You guys give me about a twenty second lead before you follow. You'll have enough time to stop if I break through," Pete said. "I'll trail a line." He rifled through the bag Lisa packed and came up with a long rope meant for rock climbers. Pete looped it around his shoulders and produced a harness before he tossed the slack into the snow.

"Now don't run over my line, or I'm gonna wind up on my ass," Pete said. When he spun his throttle and left the group behind, his bundle of rope flopped and danced behind him, playing itself out. Robby accelerated too, following the line and staying careful to give it enough distance so he wouldn't accidentally run over the rope.

The snow became mushier, the farther north they traveled. The runners of the snowmobiles sank deeper, and the machines became harder to turn and seemed to slog through the sugary snow. Robby heard the engine of his machine labor and sputter as he managed his speed to stay in sight of Pete's trailing rope.

The group saw the still shapes of the tractors and sleds resting on the ice. The wind had caught a blue tarp and wrapped it around the cab of the second tractor.

Robby saw the depression in the ice when Pete's snowmobile disappeared over the edge and descended out of sight. He stopped short of the edge, next to a tractor, where the end of Pete's rope had stopped moving. Scrambling from his machine, Robby leaped and grabbed for the end of the rope. The rope pulled through his gloved grip.

Brad and Lisa pulled up at the same time as Robby scrambled after the end of the rope.

"Help me," Robby yelled back to Lisa. "I think Pete's is going into the light."

Robby's second lunge brought his hands around the end of the slithering rope. He rose to his knees and pulled, but the rope jerked him forward until his elbows landed in the snow and ice. Lisa grabbed Robby's ankles and Brad ran around the young man to get his own hands on the rope.

Brad and Robby looped their hands around the rope and Lisa clutched Robby's legs to anchor him on the wet snow.

When the rope went slack, Brad fell backwards and landed in the snow next to Robby's outstretched arms. They pulled at the line, feeling very little resistance, and accumulated a pile of rope behind them.

Pete crested the hill, coming towards them at a jog.

"What are you doing?" Pete yelled. "You about tugged me off my feet."

Lisa, Brad, and Robby stood up and brushed wet snow from their clothes.

"We didn't want you to walk into the light," Robby said.

Pete approached the others while untying the rope harness.

"What light?" he asked, smiling.

"It's gone?" Brad asked.

"Go look," Pete said. "There's nothing down there but a bare patch of mud. I was going to look at it when you guys pulled me back."

Brad strode off towards the bowl without another word.

"Be careful," Lisa called after him.

Pete finished untying himself and began to loop the rope around his arm—coiling it to stow in his bag.

"Go look," Pete said again.

"When Brad comes back," Robby said.

"Yes," Lisa said. "One at a time."

The each took a turn, trudging through the snow and slush, down the icy slope to the mud where the giant ball of light had sat. Robby found a plastic comb, and brought it back up the hill like a piece of litter he meant to throw away. When Pete went back over the edge, he came back on his snowmobile, pulling it alongside the others and killing the engine.

"I think we did it," Pete said. "I think it's completely gone, and it looks like the snow is starting to melt around here."

"Is it safe?" asked Lisa. "We're basically standing on a big slab of ice which may be melting from underneath."

"I don't think there's imminent danger, but I wouldn't want to camp out or anything," Pete said.

Without discussing the matter, the four walked to the edge and took one last look down into the crater formed in the ice and snow. Lisa said "Oh!" and pulled out a camera to take a picture for Romie.

"I think my house used to be right around here," Brad said. He spun and surveyed, but the landmarks were still buried under the snow and ice. They turned and walked back to their snowmobiles. The ride south passed quickly under their treads.

They walked the last couple of miles back to the house, finding some of the crunchy snow finally melting in the sun. Back at the house, Romie had moved some folding chairs out to the porch and she sat in the light of the setting sun reading a book. She closed the book on her finger as the others climbed the stairs to join her on the porch.

"Good trip?" Romie asked.

"Great trip," Pete said. "Light's gone. Snow is melting." He beamed his approval.

"I've got good news for you guys, too," Romie said. She stood and leaned over the railing, pointing at a small patch of snow in the shadow of an evergreen bush. The group gathered at the railing and followed her pointing finger. Robby gasped and Pete clapped his hands when they saw what she saw: tiny paw-prints tracked through the melting snow.

"What are they from?" Brad asked.

"Looks like a cat," Pete said. "Did you see it?"

"Nope," Romie said. "But they weren't there this morning. I'm sure of it."

"That's the first sign of life since, well since Thanksgiving," Pete said.

"Aside from us," Lisa said.

Pete nodded.

"Shhh!" Brad said. "Look!" He directed their gaze upwards, to the leafless branches of a maple tree in the yard.

They were looking for a cat, so it took a second for the sight to register.

"Bird!" Robby said. "I see it."

They all saw it when he pointed.

The bird, a fat chickadee, perched at the end of a thin branch and twisted its head rapidly, back and forth.

Lisa brought her hands to her mouth. Pete laughed out loud.

"You think the cat was after the bird?" asked Romie. She giggled and then covered her mouth, too.

The chickadee turned towards the group, eyeing them as if it understood. It emitted a single cheep, and then fluttered from the branch. The bird only flew a couple of feet.

Just after taking off from its perch, the little bird jerked backwards and then disappeared.

The group heard a tiny pop, and watched a single feather seesaw its way to the ground.

As the sun set on Portland, everything was quiet. In the yards, the melting snow was absorbed into the faded winter grass. In the streets, the puddles sent off runners to follow the curbs into the storm drains. With only a dusting of snow in town, Portland's winter was dry, and the spring plants would suffer. But spring was still weeks away from this quiet sunset.

Up a gentle slope from Back Cove, past a large grocery store, a house looked east with the sun at its back. The patches of unmelted snow were crisscrossed with footprints, and furniture sat on the covered porch. From the outside, no movement could be seen. In the basement, next to the washing machine and dryer, and beside the furnace, five people huddled.

Romie broke the silence. "What the hell do we do now?"

"What happened to that bird?" Pete asked.

"I think it was vaporized," Robby said. "Like all the people on Thanksgiving. I think it was snatched."

"If you ask me, someone shot it," Lisa said.

"Nope," Brad said. "There was no gunshot. I heard a little pop, but that bird just jerked back and disappeared. I didn't see any of the people get snatched on Thanksgiving, but I'm confident that's what happened. We may have driven off that ball of light, but some of the goblins it brought along are still active."

"But we saw the cat's paw prints. And that's the first bird we've seen in months. Things have to be getting better," Romie said.

"Perhaps getting there, but we're not out of the woods yet," Pete said. "We still don't know why we were spared and everyone else disappeared or got their eyes popped out. I think we need to head south."

"We could go to upstate New York, and catch up with Luke's group," Lisa said.

Robby, their young leader, examined the face of each person.

"Do we all agree?" Robby asked.

They all nodded.

Ike Hamill
Topsham, Maine
January, 2013

## ABOUT EXTINCT

THANK YOU for reading *Extinct*. I wrote this book over the course of a year after having the ideas knock around in my head for several years prior. I wanted to write about a world in flux. I wanted to portray a complex series of events that covered a slice of time. This book doesn't review the drama that preceded the vines, and it doesn't explain what happened to the survivors after they defeated the ball of light.

Many readers have enjoyed *Extinct*, and many have expressed a need to know what happens next.

I'm happy to announce that a year after Extinct went on sale, the sequel finally arrived. *Instinct* is available in print and Kindle. If you enjoyed *Extinct*, but feel you'd like closure to the story, please look for *Instinct* on Amazon, or send me an email (ikehamill@gmail.com). Meanwhile, if you enjoyed *Extinct,* I hope you'll take a second to leave a review on Amazon. Sign up for my mailing list at www.ikehamill.com for a free copy of my next book.

Read on for a sample of *Instinct*.

Thanks for reading!
-Ike

### *Instinct*

## CHAPTER ONE

## New Hampshire

"YOU READY?" PETE ASKED. His voice was just a whisper.

Brad held up a finger. He pushed aside the curtain and looked across the yard. There was just enough starlight for him to see the minivan parked at the curb. He was more concerned with the concrete walkway that led from the front door to the sidewalk.

Brad turned and pointed to his eyes. He then motioned for Pete.

Pete crawled over to the window and looked. When he drew close, Brad could smell the fear on Pete. It was the same scent he smelled on himself whenever he took off his jacket.

"That was there," Pete whispered, motioning out the window. "It's runoff."

"Don't step on it. Just in case," Brad said. The last three words brought back a memory of his grandfather.

Pete moved back around to the boy's feet and Brad took the shoulders. They exchanged a glance and lifted. The boy wasn't heavy, but when they moved through doors or had to make a dash across a lawn, it was easier for two people to carry him. Pete backed up to the door and held the boy's ankles with one hand while he opened it.

After looking back and forth, Pete moved. They barely slowed for the steps down to the walk. The only time Pete hesitated was when he reached the thin stream of water that ran across the concrete walk. It was a thin dark streak in the starlight. He took a giant step over, moved a little, and then waited for Brad to do the same. The door of the minivan slid open as they arrived. Pete and Brad handed the boy through to the hands that came out from the darkness and then climbed in behind him.

Brad slid the door closed most of the way. He waited for Romie to start the wheels turning before he latched it.

"I need light," Romie said.

"Keep moving," Pete said. "I'm on it."

He ducked down under her legs before he turned on his little flashlight.

Brad helped Lisa lift the boy into place so she could snap a seatbelt over him. Lisa put her hands on his young cheeks and lifted his head up. She looked into his blank eyes and held his head for a second, like she was trying to balance it on his neck. After she was satisfied that it would stay up, she let go and moved into her own seat. Brad sat in the third row.

"Got it," Pete said. When he popped the fuse back into the socket, the headlights came on.

"That's better," Romie said.

✪ ✪ ✪ ✪ ✪

Brad looked out his window at the passing houses. They were all dark. Some of the front doors were open, inviting him into their blackness. He tried to imagine someone asleep in one of the houses. It was impossible. It felt like these houses had been empty forever, and would always be empty. They had a derelict, abandoned look, like empty skulls. There was no life inside.

They rarely talked when they traveled. Romie would slow whenever she saw a streak of liquid across the pavement. Pete would either motion for her to drive through, or signal that they should find another way around. They made terrible progress. Sometimes they would have to backtrack a mile or two just to find another path. Pete always navigated, and he always found another route when their road was blocked by the killer liquid, but sometimes the diversion would add hours to the trip.

Brad tried to sleep. It was impossible. Every time his eyes drifted shut, an alarm would go off in his brain. He felt like he was falling and he would shoot his legs out to catch himself. His eyes would fly back open and his body would pulse with electricity.

"Stop kicking my seat," Lisa whispered.

"Sorry," Brad said.

When the horizon started to glow orange, Pete directed them uphill. It always felt safest at the higher elevations. They had to get in a building before the liquid started to move again. It moved more in the daylight.

Romie pulled up in front of a tall three-story house. Brick stairs were cut into the hill. The door that led out the side porch was wide open.

Lisa unbuckled the boy.

"I got him," Brad said.

"Are you sure?"

Brad nodded.

Pete, Romie, and Lisa went around back for the bags and Brad pulled on the boy's armpits as he backed out of the van. He crouched on the curb and pulled the boy closer until his waist was on Brad's shoulder. He pulled at the side of the van to stand up with the load.

Brad was panting by the time he got to the top of the stairs. Lisa came out of the house after dropping off their bags. She helped Brad carry the boy into the house. They laid him out on a day bed in the den.

Lisa pulled a bottle of eyedrops from her pocket and squeezed two drops into each of the boy's eyes. She closed his lids and pulled a blanket over him.

"He needs a bath," Lisa said.

Brad nodded. "We all do, I think."

"Good point," she said. She walked out and left him there. Brad sat down in the chair behind the desk. He didn't mean to fall asleep. He was looking through the window at the brightening sky when he drifted off.

✪ ✪ ✪ ✪ ✪

"You want some soup?"

Brad opened his eyes to bright sun. His eyes went first to the boy, who was in the same spot where they'd left him. He blinked and saw Lisa standing in the doorway. She was holding out a steaming bowl.

"We should get him on the toilet," Brad said.

"He can wait a few minutes," Lisa said. "He's not squirming yet."

Brad nodded. He stood and propped himself up on the desk until his legs would support him. They were nearly numb from the chair. He took the soup and thanked Lisa.

"What day is it?" Brad asked. He lifted a spoon. It was the vegetable soup with the little letters in it. His mouth already anticipated the salty taste.

"Six," she said.

"I can't do it," Brad said.

"It will be tough," Lisa said. She looked over to the boy. She walked alongside his daybed and laid a hand on his forehead. She pulled back the blankets to expose his upper body before she left.

✪ ✪ ✪ ✪ ✪

The kitchen table was covered with Pete's maps.

There was no reason to keep their voices down, but Brad couldn't help it.

"I know we said one more week," Brad said. "I can't do it."

"I feel the same way," Pete said, "but we have to. Robby would be the first person to say it."

"It's the same as Ted," Romie said. "It's the same as with you."

"No," Brad said. He shook his head. "It's not the same. He's right in there, and he's still alive. If we put food in his mouth, he swallows. If we sit him on the toilet, he goes."

"Take a closer look at him, Brad," Romie said. "Even if he woke up, I doubt he'd be able to walk. He's wasting away."

"You carried him up the stairs on your shoulder. Do you think you'd have been able to do that two weeks ago?" Pete asked.

"Maybe I'm getting stronger," Brad said.

They sat in silence for a minute. Lisa stood and went back to the cabinets. She sorted through the contents again, looking for anything else they should take with them.

"I'll stay here with him. This place is up on a hill. I don't see any damp pavement around. When Robby wakes up, we'll come track you down," Brad said.

"How do you think you're going to find us?" Pete asked.

"Forget about Robby waking up," Romie said. "Who's going to stop you if you try to walk out into the daylight? You think just because we've traveled a few miles, those things aren't around to snatch you up into the air? How long ago was it that Pete tried to walk away? Three days ago?"

"Four," Lisa said.

"Just because nobody has tried to walk off in four days, you think it's safe?" Romie asked.

Brad waited to see if anyone else would try to convince him. He gave his final argument. "I saw Robby do this before. Granted, it was only for a few minutes, but I saw this exact behavior. Judy called it his 'deep cycles'. When Robby is considering a really complex problem, he sometimes disappears into himself. The good news is that when he wakes up, he has the solution to the problem. Don't you want to know what the solution is?"

Nobody answered. Brad tried to look in their eyes, but they all looked away.

Pete was looking down at his maps when he answered. "I guess I'm not confident that our current problems have solutions, Brad."

✪ ✪ ✪ ✪ ✪

When they began to pack up the van, Brad pulled Robby's body from the bed. He lifted him to his shoulder and maneuvered through the door. His hamstrings ached from the morning's exertion, but he had to admit that the others were right—Robby was only a fraction of his former weight. He would chew and swallow when food was presented, but his body burned right through the energy. Brad could feel the heat radiating off of the boy's head. His brain was like a furnace inside there.

Romie slid open the door when Brad came across the walk.

"I thought you were staying," Romie said.

"He has until tomorrow," Brad said. "I'll wait and see the next place."

Lisa was driving. She waited for Brad to buckle Robby in before she pulled away from the curb.

With each mile west, they found more hills. As long as Pete could keep them out of the valleys, they seemed to find less killer liquid that they had to avoid.

Brad decided to break the silence. "Pete, you need to tell me how you can see the difference between normal water and the killer stuff," Brad said.

"It's not hard," Pete said. "The killer stuff looks alive. It pulses. It has a heartbeat."

Thirty minutes passed before Pete was able to show him an example. Brad moved forward and squatted between the front seats. Pete pointed through the windshield at a dark streak across the road. At first, Brad thought Pete was making it up. There was a hill on the right side of the road, and it looked like rain or snowmelt had run down the hill to cross the road. Lisa turned and looked behind them. She was nervous to back the vehicle away from the dark patch of asphalt, but Pete told her to stay put.

"We'll go if it comes at us, but Brad needs to be able to see this," Pete said.

"I'm more worried that we'll get boxed in," Lisa said.

Pete ignored her. "There! Do you see it? It's easy with the headlights."

Brad shook his head. He didn't see anything unusual about the dark spot at all. It just looked like a dark patch of road where water was flowing. There could be a thousand reasons why it was there—spring runoff and blocked drainage was the most likely suspect.

He narrowed his eyes and let the world blur. There was something there. It was really subtle, but there was something there.

"Do you see it?" Pete asked.

"I don't know," Brad said. "Maybe. I guess I need to see regular water now, so I can be sure."

Lisa backed away. Brad went back to his seat.

Brad was trying to keep himself awake when he saw Pete motion for Lisa to stop again.

"What about this one?" Pete asked.

Brad moved forward again. He did the same trick. He let his eyes blur and waited. He couldn't see anything. "I don't know. I don't see anything. I think the other one had a shimmer to it. I don't see it with this one."

"Neither do I," Pete said. He motioned for Lisa to pull forward. They'd all grown accustomed to taking Pete's word for it. He had a perfect track record for spotting the killer liquid. This time, he didn't sound completely confident. Lisa's knuckles went white on the steering wheel as they crossed through the puddle.

Nothing happened.

"See?" Pete asked.

"I think so," Brad said.

"You just have to be extra careful about wishful thinking," Pete said.

"What do you mean?"

Pete leaned over with a folded map. He triggered his headlamp and Brad blinked until his eyes came into focus on what Pete pointed to.

"You see this bridge?" Pete asked. "We would have to go all the way up here if there wasn't a way to get to this bridge. And we're on the only road that goes down into this part of the valley. So that line of water we just crossed was pretty important."

"Why?"

"Because if it hadn't been crossable there, we'd have to go all the way up here to get around," Pete said.

"Oh, I see," Brad said. "You really didn't want to have to

sidetrack like that."

"It would have taken hours," Pete said. "So I have to be extra careful. Maybe It thought I saw something, but I just hoped I didn't. You'd do best to err on the side of caution."

"Got it," Brad said.

They were rolling down into a small town. Out here, a lot of the towns were just collections of buildings that surrounded a convenient place to put a mill on the river. Brad had seen a dozen of them—they all looked the same. The road widened with slanted parking spots on each side. They passed under a dark traffic signal.

Lisa slowed at the train tracks. Where the rails cut through the road surface, it was difficult to tell if the dark area was just a shadow, or maybe a thin line of water. Pete examined it through the windshield and declared it safe. They pushed on towards the bridge.

Pete turned around in his seat. "I don't want to get too comfy, but it almost seems like there's pattern to that killer liquid. I'm going to start marking it on the map. It might be a regular grid."

Brad looked out the side window. The river was running fast and high. All the snow melting in the northern part of the state was finding its way down to the ocean. The dam near the brick mill was overrun. The bridge sat high enough over the water that it seemed like it should be safe.

"Guys?" Lisa asked.

Pete turned around.

"Does that strike you as odd?" Lisa asked. She was pointing off to the side. She stopped the van about a third of the way across the bridge.

"What?" Pete asked. He peered into the darkness.

Lisa turned the wheel and gave the van some gas. The headlights swept to the right until they lit up the bridge's railing.

"I don't see anything," Brad said.

"Those cans," Lisa said. She pointed again.

It still took Brad a few seconds to see it. Where the railing met the bridge surface, there was a grate to let rain wash down into the river below. Clustered there, Brad saw four or five soda cans. They would have rolled away except the uneven surface of the grate held them in place.

"Wrappers, too," Pete said.

Pinned into crevices around the cans, Brad saw candy wrappers.

"Litter?" Brad asked. "I don't know..."

He was cut off by a sound from behind him. Brad was still kneeling just behind the front seats of the minivan and he spun on his feet. The sound was coming from Robby's mouth, which hung open. Romie was sitting behind him. She leaned forward.

"What the hell?" Pete asked.

Robby's moan coalesced into a word. "Noooooo," Robby said.

"Robby? Can you hear me?" Brad asked. He reached out and touched the boy's hand.

Robby's eyes were still dead. They stared forward, focused on nothing at all. "Back up," Robby said. His lips barely moved.

"What?" Pete asked.

The world fell away from Brad. He braced himself on the seats as he dropped. With a bang, the van came to stop and he crashed into the floor.

He spun to see what was happening.

Lisa pushed the shift lever into reverse and gunned the engine. She wasn't looking backwards. Her eyes were locked straight ahead at the bridge that was tearing itself apart in front of them. A crack split through the center of the bridge, separating them from the other bank. The half they were on had fallen several feet.

The structure of the bridge groaned. Brad realized that it sounded just like Robby's moan.

With a thunk, the world dropped another half of a foot. The van's tires squealed on the pavement. It couldn't get traction on the sloped pavement. Just as they began to creep backwards, the bridge dropped again and the tires lost the ground they had gained.

Pete pushed open his door and twisted in his seat to poke his head out.

"We have to get out!" Pete yelled over the noise.

Lisa turned the wheel and the tires caught. They jerked

backwards and Brad fell to his ass. He grabbed for Robby's seatbelt and used it to pull himself upwards. The boy's mouth was still open and his eyes stared at nothing. The van hit something behind them and Brad fell into Robby. He grabbed Robby's seatbelt buckle and tried to release the belt.

Lisa revved the engine even higher. The tires screamed and ground at something. She thrashed against the wheel, like she could force the van to move.

"Come on," Pete said. "We have to get out."

Brad reached for the van door and pulled up on the latch. The door was heavy and he was trying to push it uphill. He got his shoulder into it and raised it a couple of feet. He reached for Robby and pulled at the boy's shirt. Even in his unconscious state, Robby was bracing his legs against falling. He resisted Brad's pull.

"Help me," Brad said to Romie. She was working at her own seatbelt.

"I can't get it undone," Romie said.

Brad heard the rushing water as Pete's door fell all the way open. He heard the engine wind down as Lisa gave up and threw it into park. When she took her foot off the brake, the van slumped forward. The door crunched into Brad's shoulder. By tugging on Robby's arm, he managed to pull him to the side a bit. Robby slid towards Brad.

Pete rolled the door open and Brad pulled Robby around.

Through the window he saw Lisa tugging at the other sliding door. She couldn't open it.

The bridge dropped again with the sound of tortured metal.

Brad pulled Robby from the van and nearly tumbled backwards down the slope of the bridge span. He held Robby with one arm and caught himself on the passenger's door that Pete had left open. He heard the muffled crunch of glass as Lisa used a tool to smash through the van's window.

"Robby!" Brad yelled. "I know you're in there. You have to help me if you want to live."

His voice was almost lost in the sound of the rushing water below.

Pete was holding the sliding door open and reaching his other hand out to help Brad climb the slope of the bridge.

With a loud "tock" the van dropped away a few inches. Brad crashed backwards into the passenger's door again. Pete couldn't help and hold the door open at the same time. He let the door slide shut and reached for Brad's hand.

They locked arms and pulled. Brad got Robby going up the slope as the van made the "tock" noise again. Brad understood what was happening—the mechanism that was supposed to stop the van from rolling when in park was giving way. The weight on Brad's arm decreased. Robby was moving on his own.

Linked together, the three climbed.

The van slipped again and Pete fell to his knees. He began to slide towards the widening gap behind them. The bridge surface began to vibrate as the rushing water tugged at the collapsing structure. Brad took the lead and pulled at both Robby and Pete. They climbed as the bridge wilted beneath them. Pete got back to his feet and let go of Brad's arm. They threw themselves forward to grab at the crack that opened where the bridge met the bank.

Behind them, the van picked up speed and skidded down into the water. Brad couldn't look back. He knew that if he lost concentration on pulling himself forward, he would be the next to slip back into the water.

He dragged Robby forward until the boy's hands found the crack. With both arms unburdened, Brad was able to climb the steep surface. He reached forward and his hand couldn't get enough friction on the horizontal road. He tried to dig his fingernails into the asphalt. Beside him, he sensed that Robby and Pete were doing little more than hanging on.

An arm shot out of the darkness and grabbed his hand.

Brad looked up to see Romie.

They climbed up onto the road and crawled away from the edge. Lisa helped Robby, and Romie gave a hand to Brad and Pete. When they got to safety, they all collapsed to the pavement. When a piece of the bridge groaned and tore away, Brad scrambled back another couple of feet.

"Flood damage?" Romie asked.

"Maybe," Pete said.

"Maybe not," Lisa said.

"Why do you say that?" Brad asked.

"There were cans and soda wrappers," Lisa said. "It looked to me that someone had waited up there for a while. Maybe they were standing guard while someone sabotaged the bridge."

"Why would someone do that?" Brad asked.

"Maybe the killer liquid, and fire monsters, and snatchers aren't the only things to be afraid of around here," Pete said.

"How did you get out?" Brad asked, turning to Romie.

Lisa held up something in the darkness. Brad didn't have to see it to understand. Lisa had given them all the same tool. It was something she had found in a convenience store. One end had a plastic cap protecting a sharp point for smashing car windows. The other end had a recessed blade you could use for cutting through a seatbelt.

"How did he get out?" Romie asked. She pointed to Robby.

The boy still had the same empty look on his face. He was staring straight forward and sitting next to Brad.

Brad reached out and shook the boy's shoulder. He didn't respond.

"I don't know," Brad said. "But he definitely moved on his own when his life was threatened."

"Speaking of which," Pete said. "We can't stay here. It's too dangerous to be outdoors like this."

They began to push to their feet.

"I need more maps. We have to get all new gear. All our traveling food was in there," Pete said.

Lisa put her hand on his elbow and Pete trailed off. She was staring off into the night.

"What?" Pete whispered. His voice was carried away by the sound of the river.

"I saw something," Lisa said. She pointed up the street.

All Brad could see was the dark traffic signal. It was bobbing and swaying in the wind. The buildings were dark. The windows were black rectangles cut into the sides. On the left, the big windows looked like they belonged to a general store. On the right, Brad saw a place he imagined had sold appliances or furniture. There were one or two cars parked in the spaces. Brad wondered how far up the hill they'd have to walk to find another suitable vehicle. It wouldn't be comfortable to pack all five of them into one of the little cars he saw. Plus, they would need to find a set of keys.

"Where?" Pete asked.

"Up there," Lisa said. "On the left. Second floor, fourth window down."

The windows above the stores could have belonged to offices or maybe even apartments for the owners. Brad counted out the windows, but he didn't see anything there.

"What did you see?" Pete asked.

"I don't know," she said. "It might have been a candle, or a flashlight."

"Maybe it was just a shooting star reflecting off the glass," Pete said.

She didn't say anything. Brad saw her head shaking in the dark.

"Let's go find a car," Pete said. He started to walk.

Brad turned to Robby, who was still sitting on the pavement. He reached down under the boy's shoulders to lift him. At Brad's touch, Robby rose on his own. Brad found that he could just tug on Robby's arm and the boy would walk. Brad kept his eyes on the window as they walked by the building.

Look for *Instinct* on sale now at Amazon!

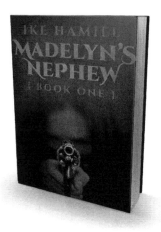

## Madelyn's Nephew

After the sun turned, Madelyn fled north to escape the riots and the encroaching glaciers. As long as the world was ending, she wanted to live her final days in the one place she had always been happy—her grandmother's cabin. She survived the Roamers, the scavengers, and the wildlife, but she can't escape her fear of dying alone.

She left behind this note:
"Gather my bones, if you find them. If a bear hasn't dragged them off, or a wolf cracked them for my marrow. My skull goes on the wall with the others. Any other remains can be planted near Sacrifice Rock. That's where my grandfather is buried, and where I dug up the skull of my beloved grandmother.
Her sweet eyes were still wise and kind, even when I only imagined them from their hollow sockets. She taught us so many things—how to hunt, trap, and fish. She should have taught me how to live alone. I never learned the trick of scaring away the ghosts. They won't shut up and leave me in peace. I guess it's time to join them."

—Madelyn

## Inhabited

They were looking for an adventure—a night of harmless fun. Miguel
has a map. Kristin's friend has the equipment. The mine leads to the
cave, and the cave is where they'll find their fortune.

But down in the darkness, something waits.

It needs them.

The caves hold a secret. They're Inhabited.

## The Claiming

It wasn't her fault.

It wasn't Lizzy's fault that she saw the cloaked people out in the yard. It wasn't her fault that she was drawn by the moonlight to watch them as they advanced on the house. And it definitely wasn't her fault when people began to die. Lizzy didn't want the strange dreams where she saw how they were killed. Even her sister was starting to suspect her.

It wasn't fair because it wasn't her fault.

Lizzy was claimed.

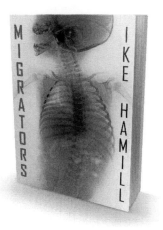

## Migrators

Do not speak of them. Your words leave a scent. They will come.
Somewhere in the middle of Maine, one of the world's darkest secrets
has been called to the surface. Alan and Liz just wanted a better life for
themselves and their son. They decided to move to the country to rescue
the home of Liz's grandfather, so it would stay in the family. Now, they
find themselves directly in the path of a dangerous ritual. No one can
help them. Nothing can stop the danger they face. To save themselves
and their home, they have to learn the secrets of the MIGRATORS.

33468181R00212

Printed in Great Britain
by Amazon